Nathaniel Grey
Obsidian Cr

The Phoenix Sa
Book 2

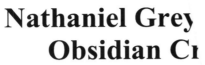

FARRELL KEELING

C000137304

Nathaniel Grey and the Obsidian Crown
Text Copyright © 2019
Farrell Keeling

Cover art by Liza Nazarova (print edition)

All rights reserved. This work may not be reproduced or transmitted in whole or in part in any form or by any means, electronic, mechanical, photocopying, recording or otherwise, without the prior permission from the author.

ISBN: 9781097136490 (print edition)

This novel is entirely a work of fiction. The names, characters, and incidents portrayed in it are the work of the author's imagination. Any resemblance to actual persons, living or dead, events or localities is entirely coincidental.

Many decades ago, one boy's struggle against a vile creature of the Foglands is falling into legend.

Yet, old records were poured over, and the priests of the City of Light had finally unearthed their champion: Horizon's Warder of Shadow, Wielder of the Flames of the First, King-in-Waiting of the Broken City, and Fierslaken's heir.

The Phoenix had risen.

Chapter 1

The cave entrance was quiet, all except for the crackle of the Cloaks' torches. The two men, peering through their jet-black masks into the distance beyond the cave, watching silently for any sign of trouble. Within moments they found it.

A silhouette formed on the ground before them, perplexingly without an owner to cast it. Then, suddenly, this silhouette began to rise – or rather, coalesce – wisps of shadow merging as they floated upwards, as if pulled from the earth itself. Tendrils flicked out and stabbed at the open air, as the black mist emerged from the ground. What appeared to be a head raised itself from the central mass. It was poorly defined at first, as if someone had pulled a black veil over a doll's face. Then a torso and arms, the body writhing and rolling over itself, congealing as it formed into a solid state. One leg lurched forward, dragging the rest of the body with it.

The Cloaks relaxed the grip on their daggers, as the figure, now corporeal, stepped into the flickering light cast by their torches.

'Crow,' they said, stepping aside in unison to allow him entry into the cave. Red-trimmed robes whipped about the man's legs as he strode past the Cloaks, without a word of acknowledgement.

The Cloaks followed, at a safe distance.

Even though he was long since used to the caves, Crow still found himself shivering involuntarily every time he crossed the threshold. Although tempered by their cage, his masters' powers remained a frightful prospect, as Crow had experienced first-hand.

Nothing grew in the dank soil outside the cave and nothing that lived dared approach it. Inside, it was worse. Every step taken towards the centre of the cave system, where all the trails converged, seemed to draw all the warmth from your flesh.

The wind swirled around him, crying out a warning, as if feebly attempting to snatch him back from the cold clutches of the cave. But the gusts retreated quickly, as soon as he'd turned the first corner. Even the flames that crackled from the Cloaks' torches appeared to angle back towards the cave entrance, as if desperate to flee with the wind.

But most disconcerting of all, were the voices. A multitude of whispers and hisses followed his every step, as formless shadows darted across the illuminated cave walls.

Crow stopped in front of what appeared to be a dead end in the cave. This *dead end*, however, was a most curious thing, for three shapes, distinguishable from the muddy brown of the cave, jutted out from the rock. Two of them looked resigned to their fate, but the one in the middle had been caught in motion, hands outstretched before it, as if seeking to throttle an unseen foe.

Crow took a few steps further, until he was but an inch away from the middle figure's contorted hands and the whispers fell suddenly silent. Expectant. The crackle of the torches and nervous intakes of breath from the Cloaks were the only sounds to be heard, as Crow slowly descended onto one knee. His outstretched hands curled open, as if to receive an offering.

Flames sprouted from his open palms, but these were only a deathly imitation of fire. The flames were black as shadow and exuded no warmth. If anything, his hand was made colder for them. Unlike the desperate flickering of the torches, the black flames in Crow's hand undulated and billowed, like dense smoke from a chimney stack.

'What does this one seek?' the walls suddenly hissed.

'An audience with my masters,' Crow replied.

'What does this one offer?'

'A gift of shadow,' said Crow, raising his hands aloft, 'that was gifted unto me.'

The shadows along the walls paused for a moment, as if to scrutinise this offering, then one by one they trickled down the walls. Slinking and writhing across the soil, like dark snakes they approached.

He made no attempt to resist, as the shadows slithered up the hem of his robes. But his back contorted and he groaned softly, as they explored the exposed flesh of his arms. Circling the black flames in his palms for a moment, they then withdrew – seemingly satisfied with what they found – and departed back to the walls.

'The masters would speak,' the shadows announced.

'The Crow would listen.' Crow bowed his head, extinguishing the black flames with a clench of his fists.

The cave slowly darkened as the torch flames behind Crow were dimmed. No matter how hard the flames fought and flickered in protest at the shadows, they were gradually suppressed until they barely rose above the brim of the torch cups. Naught could be seen of the figures before Crow except for the tips of fingers clawing out of the darkness.

'You have returned, Crow,' a husky voice rasped. *'What news do you bring?'*

'Greetings, my lords, I wished to report the progress of my mission,' Crow said.

'The Szar is willing?' the voice sounded almost surprised.

'After some discussion, yes. The Regal's hate for Lycans is rivalled by none, my masters. All that stands in the way is the Emperor.'

'Yes, this Tolken is quite the nuisance,' a guttural voice from the other corner spoke. *'You are certain the Szar will not fail?'*

'For the good of his people? It is without question.'

'And yet you seem disappointed, Crow,' a silky voice washed over him. Its dulcet tones were smooth, like the flat of a blade, but with a sharp edge never too far away.

'Not at all, my masters,' Crow said, adding hesitantly, 'but why wait? The Phoenix is gone. The kings of mankind, gone. The old banners that swept the sky have fallen, even as we speak, Räne – Fog take it – crumbles to dust. Who is there to stand against the Reckoning?'

The voices were silent for a short while. Long enough for the Cloaks to begin twitching anxiously and for Crow to wonder if he had asked the wrong question.

'Horizon teeters on the edge of chaos, Crow. But before we are free to save it, it must embrace the beginnings of its end,' the silky voice said, although its tone suggested that Crow was wandering dangerously close to its edge.

'And what of Grey?'

'If all goes to plan, he won't be a concern for much longer,' the guttural voice said, *'proceed with your task, Crow. Everything rests on the Obsidian Crown.'*

'As you wish, my masters,' Crow bowed his head further.

'From darkness comes new beginnings,' the three voices sang in a horrid cacophony that shook the foundations of the cave, causing small chunks of rock to dislodge from the ceiling.

With that, light flooded back, illuminating the cave, as the shadows that cupped the torches withdrew and resumed their unsettling chorus of whispers.

'From darkness comes new beginnings,' Crow echoed faintly.

Chapter 2

A low groan escaped from Nathaniel's lips. He feebly attempted to raise a hand, to shield his eyes from the light that had unceremoniously tore into the room.

'And good morning to you as well,' a voice rang out distantly.

Whistling away, far too merrily for the time of day, a slightly younger Regal with short blonde hair that was slicked back like his brother's red, yanked back the other curtain.

'So! How are we feeling today?' Solas inquired with a broad, deeply dimpled, grin, snatching up a chair by Nathaniel's bedside.

Nathaniel could only find the strength to groan his discontent, burying himself even deeper into his pillow.

'Athrana's grace. That well?'

'Three,' Nathaniel mumbled contritely into the pillow.

'I'm sorry?'

'Three... I only had... three drinks.'

'I wouldn't be so sure. Fortunately, however, I do remember last night, so perhaps I could paint you a more accurate picture?'

'Please don't,' Nathaniel begged.

'You see, you got the number right, but you were awfully far off on the quantity.'

'Oh, Gods.'

'Because after a couple of tankards of Gamrial's finest, we stumbled into our old friend, Pegs.'

'Oh no.'

'Who happened to have just arrived in the day with a fresh supply of wine.'

'Please stop.'

'Now, not only did your eye wander to one of the good dwarf's barrels, but you, in your infinite wisdom, thought it would be a great idea to challenge him - *A dwarf*, I might remind you - to a drinking contest.'

Nathaniel was pretty sure already that he didn't want to hear how this particular story would end.

'And?' he breathed.

'Oh, Pegs finished his barrel long before you did,' Solas's glee was palpable. 'Although, you had lost consciousness about halfway through.'

Solas roared with laughter, as he watched the horror dawn on his brother's face.

'Then... how did I get back here?' Nathaniel murmured, glancing about the room for some evidence of his return. A pale tunic, blemished with wine, lay tossed on the floor beside his bed along with a shoe on its side. The other curiously appeared to be missing.

'Don't worry, I just about managed to drag you back,' Solas smiled, jumping out of the chair. 'Although, not a moment sooner before the city got a chance to witness you wail out '*A Fine Maid's Awaiting*.' He winked wickedly at his brother, vanishing through the open doorway, before the hairbrush had even left Nathaniel's hand.

'Aespora toray,' Nathaniel cursed under his breath.

Once he had reluctantly prised himself from his bed, Nathaniel pulled on some fresh clothes and stumbled down the freezing steps outside his room, only to find his father at the door. The man on the other side was someone he'd not seen before.

He was dressed in all black with hooded robes trimmed with red. Under the hood, a sharp chin poked out. The man's gauntness was accentuated by a small amount of facial hair cropped to a fine point, which gave his jaw a dagger-like shape.

'What you're asking of me is treasonous,' Nathaniel heard his father whisper back wearily. 'I need time to think about it.'

'Time is in short supply, Grey,' the man spoke in clipped tones. 'You have until the wedding to decide where you – and your family's – loyalties lie.'

The silence that followed was palpable. Nathaniel wondered if the two had resorted to an even lower volume and edged further down the stairs to investigate.

He thought he saw the man's head turn slightly in his direction upon the first creak of wood, but if he had been noticed, no other indication was given.

'Until tomorrow,' the man said briskly.

Nathaniel's father only nodded in reply, then closed the door, as soon as the red hem of the man's robes had whipped out of sight. He muttered something incoherently under his breath, freezing when he turned and caught sight of his son crouching on the stairs above.

'I can come back later,' Nathaniel said guiltily.

At first his father gave him a look that suggested he was due a scolding, but he merely sighed and shook his head.

'No need,' he motioned for Nathaniel to come down the stairs.

'Who was that?' Nathaniel inquired.

'An old friend,' his father replied curtly, failing to hide a grimace. 'All recovered this morning? I hear you had an active evening.'

Gods, Nathaniel thought, *had Solas told him everything?*

'Never better,' Nathaniel lied, trying hard to ignore his stomach's garbled protests.

'Really? Well, in that case then, you won't mind giving your brother a hand down at the markets? There's a few things that need doing before the wedding, nothing too strenuous I'm sure for that heavy head of yours.'

Nathaniel groaned. It was *his* wedding, couldn't his brother handle it?

'Yes, father,' Nathaniel said, slumping forward. Truth be told, he was more worried about going back into the city after the celebrations the night before.

'Try not to get into too much trouble now, alright?' Nathaniel's father ushered the young Regal to the door. 'We wouldn't want your bride to be too embarrassed when you meet her, now would we?'

*

As Nathaniel perused the line of stalls, he was finding it difficult to remove the man with the red-trimmed robes from his mind. Who was he? And if he was an 'old friend,' why had he never met him before?

What you're asking of me is treasonous.

No matter how many times Nathaniel turned the words over in his head he could glean no further meaning from them.

What did the man want from his father that was so horrible it could be considered treasonous?

'So, who do you reckon Father has set you up with?'

Nathaniel snapped out of his thoughts and gave his brother a bewildered look. 'Sorry, what?'

'I said, what poor soul do you reckon is going to be stuck with you for eternity?' Solas smirked.

'Oh, shut up,' Nathaniel laughed, punching his brother playfully across the shoulder. 'You're just jealous.'

Solas snorted, 'please, at least I can talk to girls.'

To demonstrate, he paused by one of the stalls to offer a few honeyed words and a wink to one of the vendors. The girl made a show of rolling her eyes, but a wry smile and a faint blossom of red on her cheeks gave her away, once her attention had reverted back to her wares.

'See?' Solas swept his hand grandly before them, 'effortless.'

'And how much did you tip her?'

'My sheer charm is payment enough.'

'Of course it is.'

They paused by another stall, so Solas could buy some items on their father's list. Despite his brother's best efforts, the storekeeper insisted upon taking them through all his other wares; in particular the more expensive alternatives to their intended purchases. Nathaniel's eyes began to wander.

Their city was truly a marvel.

Sunlight shone in between the two mountain peaks that guarded the city, making the snow that dusted them glisten. Beyond the concentric circles of market stalls lay a long, paved stone road that rose into the third mountain, bisecting increasingly affluent and ornate buildings. The tiered plateaus rising into the mountain, on which the houses and taverns were built, forming a spiral staircase to the main gates of the palace.

The Regal palace, the centrepiece of their grand city, with all its high-rising spires and dome-topped towers, looked incredibly fragile against the mountain face. Indeed, the sight of the palace barely clinging on to the rock made Nathaniel feel somewhat uneasy. He wondered how anyone ever managed to get any sleep inside.

At that moment, a strange nagging feeling brought Nathaniel's attention back to the markets. His brow furrowed as he caught sight of someone familiar. A man, covered from head to toe in black hooded robes that trailed past his feet and blossomed around him, stood in front of the stall that he and Solas had passed but a moment ago.

Wasn't this the man that his father had been talking to at their house?

He made to move toward the man but paused. What would he say? Would the man even answer his questions about his father?

As if aware of the torrent of thoughts aimed in his direction, the robed figure turned away from the stall and looked straight at him. Although, it was impossible to tell for sure where his eyes wandered, given that his head was swallowed completely from sight by his low, drooping hood.

However, that was not even nearly the strangest thing about the man. It was the scythe; similar to that used by farmers to harvest their crops, except the blade was far longer, and the handle was bleached white, like bone. While that in itself was peculiar, it was more that people didn't seem to notice it.

This was not the man he'd seen before.

Nathaniel's hand crept to his rapier. It was forbidden to unsheathe your weapon in the markets, let alone anywhere within the mountain's glare. Yet here, as clear as day, stood the man with a brandished scythe, untroubled by the market guards.

The girl at the stall dropped an array of trinkets on the table before her. Nathaniel felt himself tense, as he waited for her to notice the tall scythe-wielder ahead of her.

She eventually took her eyes off her wares and, for a brief moment, looked straight at the man in the robes. She didn't even flinch. In fact, she didn't seem to register the man's presence at all, let alone his gleaming scythe.

Was he missing something? Was this just normal now? Surely someone else was seeing this?

The pair stood there for what seemed like a while, gazes – he thought – locked, then the man raised his arm and waved toward him.

Nathaniel's eyes widened when a bony hand – literally, it appeared to be just bone and nothing else – slid out of a cavernous sleeve.

He grabbed his brother's shoulder and spun him around, but when he looked back, the man had gone.

Chapter 3

Regal weddings were highly extravagant affairs. From every corner of the hall Nathaniel was subjected to a barrage of sensory assaults. From the guests' colourful array of formal dress to the platters of fine cuisine, beautifully presented on the long dining table that spanned the hall's length.

Nathaniel stood with Solas by the doors, greeting newcomers and exchanging hushed words with each other between arrivals. He needed the distraction. The thought of the skeletal man was difficult to shake from his mind.

Nathaniel couldn't help but wonder if he was going mad. Apparently, no one else had seen the tall cloaked figure, or an unsheathed scythe.

'You're thinking about it again, aren't you?' Solas said out of the corner of his mouth. 'About that *skeleton*,' he said, rolling his eyes.

'I'm telling you, Solas, I know what I saw,' Nathaniel insisted.

'It's the hangover talking, brother, to draw a weapon in the markets–'

'–is treasonous, I know, so why didn't anyone stop him?'

Solas sighed and bowed as a pair of women, dressed flamboyantly in bright green, passed them into the hall.

'How much longer do we have to keep doing this for?' Solas groaned once the latest guests were out of earshot, tugging uncomfortably at the collar of his white tunic.

'Until everyone is inside, little brother,' Nathaniel whispered back, shaking the hand of another Regal noble and returning his toothy grin with a smile of his own.

Solas snorted in response, 'well, it seems we'll be here forever then.' He grimaced, as he strained to adjust his waistcoat.

'I give up,' Solas announced solemnly. 'The stupid wedding has beaten me.'

Nathaniel was about to reply but his words fell short, as his eyes caught a flash of gold. Flanked by a Royal Guard bearing the black and gold of the Royal House, and another man, cursed with deeply ridged scars that ran diagonally across his face, came the Emperor.

Despite the simplicity of his gown, he cut a magnificent, almost God-like, figure, draped in the shimmering gold of his station. The Obsidian Crown, a delicate piece formed of black leaves, was balanced atop the Emperor's head, so perfectly it appeared to almost float above his hair, like a halo.

Emperor Tolken passed the threshold of the hall and paused before the two boys.

'Ismäera preserve thee, Nathaniel Grey.' The Emperor inclined his head.

Embarrassingly, Nathaniel found himself caught between the same greeting and an awkward half-bow. Fortunately, the Emperor did not seem to mind. To his right, Solas was equally awed, although the object of his wonder appeared to be the scowling, scarred man beside the Emperor.

'Ismäera preserve all, my Emp– I mean your Grace.'

Nathaniel found himself stumbling over his words and felt himself blush but tried to make it look like he was unaware of it. The Emperor chuckled, but indicated his mirth was in no sense aimed at Nathaniel's expense, as he gently gripped the boy's hands, the sheer warmth exuding from him easing Nathaniel's concerns.

'Please,' he smiled, 'just Jael.' The Emperor's eyes were dark but as every bit intense as the sharp blue of his scarred bodyguard. However, where the bodyguard's wide eyes seemed to scour the hall like a hawk for prey, the Emperor's eyes were more gently curious.

The scarred man rolled his eyes and scoffed.

'Have my words upset you, Draeden?' the Emperor inquired of his scarred companion.

The name sounded distinctly familiar. Indeed, given the man's outspokenness, it was clear that Draeden was more than just a mere bodyguard.

'You lower yourself in bandying your name around as freely as you do,' he said.

'I see no issue in 'bandying' myself to the people.'

'You could do better than a *Grey*.'

'What do you mean by th–,' Nathaniel interjected, earning him a swift elbow from his brother.

Draeden narrowed his eyes at Nathaniel. They cut so sharply into his own, Nathaniel began to wonder how anyone ever dared look at him. 'You would do well to guard your tongue as well as your brother does, *boy*,' he said, then turned back to the Emperor, 'and what of your concessions to the sheep-herder?'

Tolken's smile, whilst perhaps slightly thinner, remained almost as firm as his patience. 'The Samaii Chief's name is

Emir,' he said, 'and if you do not feel comfortable acknowledging him so, then his title will more than suffice.'

Draeden's cursory glance past the two boys toward the throng of guests and the grimace that followed, suggested that he found the idea of talking to another person – let alone the Samaii Chief – distinctly unbearable.

'He is a guest of the Regal people, Draeden,' Emperor Tolken said, more sternly this time, 'and I expect you to be at least tolerable.'

'Perhaps that would be agreeable, your Grace, if your tolerance stopped with the Scorched,' Draeden replied bitterly, before whipping his arms out from under his cloak and storming off. 'I sincerely hope for your sake you treat your bride with more respect, *boy,*' he hissed, as he passed Nathaniel.

Tolken watched him leave and shook his head sadly. 'You must forgive Draeden for his… mood,' he told the brothers. 'He only wants what is best for the Empire.'

He offered them both another smile and indicated that he would go and greet the other guests.

Nathaniel garbled something that was a cross between 'your Grace' and 'Jael,' whilst Solas remained captivated by the scarred Draeden, who had marched towards their father.

Whilst slightly perturbed by the man's treatment of him, Nathaniel found his mind occupied with other matters… in particular, the attendance of the Scorched. There had been rumours that a few tribe's members had travelled over to Horizon, but nothing concrete, until now. Perhaps he had seen them already, no… a silly thought, they would surely have stood out from the other Regals. Then again, he had never seen a Scorched man or woman before.

So many questions ran through his head. Did they look as fearsome and rough at the edges as the stories suggested? Would they arrive on the backs of wild horses, swords cleaving the air as their untamed beasts reared before them.

'I can't believe it, do you know who that was?' Solas murmured beside him.

'What did he mean by *"tolerance stopping with the Scorched?"'* Nathaniel said absently.

'I can't believe the Szar came!'

'The Szar?'

'Draeden Kusk. The Szar. The one the Emperor was arguing with.'

Nathaniel was about to point out that the Szar had disrespected the Emperor but thought better of it, 'I thought I'd seen him before...'

'He's a war hero,' Solas looked at him incredulously. 'They say he's killed thousands of Lycans.'

'Looks like one of them nearly returned the favour,' Nathaniel noted darkly.

'Apparently, he got the scars during the last rebellion,' Solas continued unperturbed. Solas stood on his tiptoes for a moment, to check if anyone was coming up the steps. 'And' he whispered, grinning maliciously, 'I heard that he's still got its hand.'

Nathaniel had never seen such admiration from his brother before and found it almost amusing how unfazed he was by the Emperor's appearance.

Nathaniel looked past Solas at the scarred Szar, as he engaged in conversation with his father beside one of the Emperor's banners, supported by poles lining the walls. Even from across the hall, the deeply trenched scars glared vividly out at him. He shivered as his mind pictured a severed hand framed atop a desk. Surely no one would be so morbid as to keep a hand as a war trophy. However, studying the Szar's grim demeanour, he was starting to think that he just might.

'Master Grey?'

Nathaniel tore himself away from the Szar, disturbing thoughts still swirling in his mind, and turned his attentions to the servant who had appeared before him.

'Which one?' Solas smirked.

'Master Nathaniel Grey, sir,' the servant replied apologetically.

Solas clutched his chest as if wounded.

'Forever the bridesmaid,' he said, in mock disappointment.

The man laughed nervously and produced a folded slither of paper from his breast pocket, offering it to the older sibling. Nathaniel thanked him, and opened the message, which was short and read simply:

"Meet outside, in the Orchid Gardens."

The note bore no signature, let alone any indication of who it had come from, and when Nathaniel looked up he found that the servant had disappeared out of sight.

'Whose it from?' Solas inquired, slyly peering over his shoulder.

Nathaniel shrugged, showing his brother the slip of paper. Solas' eyes flickered over the note once and his face broke into a wide grin.

'What is it?' Nathaniel said.

'Oh, nothing,' he replied, his grin broadening further.

'You know who it is,' Nathaniel said, narrowing his eyes at Solas.

'A hunch, nothing more,' Solas held up his hands defensively, 'you'd better get going.'

Nathaniel glanced back at his father, who still remained by the Szar's side.

'Don't worry about father,' Solas said, 'if he asks, I'll tell him you were occupied with one of the nobles or something.'

'You're sure you'll be fine on your own?'

Solas nodded, somewhat reluctantly, and ushered him away from the steps, 'go on, quickly, before father catches you.'

Solas must have caught sight of more guests arriving, for Nathaniel heard him groan audibly as he edged away.

He kept his head down, forcing himself to avoid looking in his father's direction, darting out of the hall through the open archway without trouble.

He found himself in a long corridor, well-lit, with sconces either side illuminating the black and gold carpets that trailed off into the distance. There were several heavy wooden doors on either side, thankfully all closed. Nathaniel was expecting his father to leap out at any moment, scolding him for abandoning his post. With that in mind, he made every effort to step quickly and quietly until he had rounded the bend at the end.

The note he had received felt heavy somehow inside the breast pocket of his waistcoat, and he found himself plucking it out once again. No matter how many times his eyes danced over the words, he could glean no further meaning from them. But Solas - he seemed to have known exactly who it was from. But how? Had he recognised the handwriting? There wasn't exactly much to assess... but perhaps.... Nathaniel drew the note under his nose. No, not even a scent, and, as he passed into yet another corridor, he became abruptly aware that he had absolutely no idea where he was going.

He had thought that he vaguely remembered where the Orchid Gardens lay, but apparently the memory was fainter than he had realised. There was certainly nothing around him to suggest he was even going in the right direction.

Just as he was about to retrace his steps, however, Nathaniel caught sight of something darting across an adjoining corridor. A flash of green. Perhaps the hem of a dress?

'Hello,' he called across the hallway.

Nathaniel stood there for a while waiting, but no one stepped out to greet him. Had he imagined the green dress too?

'Psst!' a hand beckoned to him from around the corner.

Glancing back to see if anyone else was around, Nathaniel half-walked, half-ran to the end of the corridor, in time to see the back of a green dress whip out of sight once more.

Breathing a sigh of relief, he gave chase. He realised quickly, as he was led across what felt like miles of winding hallways, that he would have had no hope of finding the Gardens without his mysterious guide. Each sharp turn presented a new passageway, seemingly the same as the previous one. Left, left, right, left, right… Nathaniel began to wonder if he would find his way back to the great hall.

Another sharp turn was taken, and Nathaniel had to steady himself, nearly tripping and tumbling down a sudden decline of stone steps that spiralled into one of the palace's turrets. He peered down into the gloom, his eyes picking up no sign of movement given the dim light cast from the few torches bracketed on the brick walls.

'This way,' a voice echoed up towards him.

They must have been getting close, Nathaniel thought, as he raced down the turret, taking two steps at a time in his eagerness to catch up with the girl. Indeed, sweet aroma of vanilla, had begun to permeate the air, the further down he went.

And sure enough, when he finally reached the bottom of the turret, he found himself on a large balcony, facing the bowl of land between the three mountains, stretching from the market to the outlying farms.

The balcony itself was lit by braziers, surrounding a greenhouse that sparkled under the moonlight. Orchids of midnight blue, scarlet and violet swayed before his eyes as he stepped inside and, at the centre of it all, the girl.

She cut a resplendent figure in a green dress that flowed loosely over her frame, covering all but her shoulders and forearms, and just allowing for the tips of her slippers to poke out from under the hem. The skirt had multiple layers, each fold lined with tiny sequins that glittered subtly in the night.

She held up her hand suddenly and Nathaniel stopped dead in his tracks, 'that's close enough,' she said.

'Right, sorry,' he replied, 'I probably shouldn't even be looking at you, let alone standing here… bad luck and all.'

'Well, it's too late now isn't it?' she said.

'Yes, I think… probably… you look….' Nathaniel hesitated, fumbling for words, '…nice.'

She placed her hands on her hips and cocked her head to one side, 'just nice?'

'I… don't know, this is all quite strange.'

'To be talking to a girl?'

'I've talked to girls before,' Nathaniel replied indignantly, suddenly reminded of the similar conversation he'd had earlier with his brother. 'I think it may be the veil, would you mind?' he motioned for her to pull the veil back over her head.

She leaned forward slightly and held her hands together, 'you know, I'd love to, but… I'd hate to ruin the surprise.'

'I'm sure I could live without it,' Nathaniel grinned.

'I'm sure you could,' the girl giggled.

'You look… beautiful,' the words finally fell out of Nathaniel's mouth, clearing the sudden pressure he felt on his chest.

'Thanks,' she said, rolling the material round her fingers, 'it's a bit much, but… I suppose it is a wedding, after all.'

'It is indeed,' Nathaniel said, his eyes wandering over the girl's veil, seeking any possible chink in the material that could give him some idea of who his future wife was. He was left disappointed. The veil, while fine in appearance, was so frustratingly opaque, it was difficult to see even an outline of the girl's face. Indeed, it puzzled him how she could manage to see out of it.

She giggled as Nathaniel squinted before her and held out an arm. 'Would you escort me back?' she asked, twirling her fingers at him.

'I would be honoured,' he smiled, 'but what if we are caught?'

'There's no harm in simply walking up the turret together, is there?' she said, shaking her arm insistently.

The thought of Nathaniel's father storming into the greenhouse crossed his mind, and he cringed at the prospect of a public scolding, especially in front of his bride-to-be. *No*, he told himself, *don't be ridiculous*. His father would still be with the Szar or the countless other guests that littered the Great Hall, and his brother was unlikely to reveal where he'd gone.

Pushing his worries aside, Nathaniel went to link arms with the girl. Even this close to her he could still only wonder as to her appearance.

'Come on,' she sighed, tugging him along with her beyond the orchids.

It was a silly thing, his curiosity, for it would not be long before he witnessed his bride unveiled at the altar. He pictured his father beaming with pride and the Emperor clapping, as brightly coloured confetti criss-crossed the Great Hall. Onlookers, made up of nobles and commoners, filling the palace, right down past the marble stairs, clapping and cheering.

However, his day dreaming was interrupted abruptly. They were not alone.

'Who's that?' his bride whispered.

A boy, surely no more than ten or eleven years of age lay in wait as they emerged from the greenhouse, blocking the entrance to the turret. He stared at them intently, as he sharpened a sword that looked far too heavy for him to hold, going rhythmically back and forth across the curve of the blade.

As they approached tentatively, the boy jumped to his feet. Whetstone and sword still in hand, his eyes widened, brimming with excitement.

Chapter 4

The boy was not a Regal, that much was clear. His dark skin and braided hair marked him as an inhabitant of lands beyond Horizon's shores. The boy had to be one of the Scorched, a nomad of the Scorched Isles.

What struck Nathaniel most, was the sheer height of the boy when he rose. He had to have been at least five years his junior, but already he stood about half a foot taller.

'Grey!' the boy bowed before them, harsh accent belying his seemingly good nature. 'It would be an honour to challenge you.'

'Errrrr,' Nathaniel began. 'What do you m-'

The boy dropped the whetstone on the ground beside him, as he considered Nathaniel.

'Hmm. It would probably not be appropriate to be bloodied before the wedding.'

Bloodied? What did the boy intend? Nathaniel glanced at the sword and then back at the Scorched child. *Surely not?*

'Shall we say till first garment rip?' the boy suggested, tilted his head inquisitively.

'Well, now just a wait a momen-'

'May the Sun grant you her favour.'

The boy cracked the tip of his sword twice against the floor, startling both Nathaniel and his future bride, then charged with his arms aloft.

Nathaniel's eyes widened, and he pushed the girl aside, before throwing himself under the boy's arm at the last possible

30

second, avoiding the blade by a hair's breadth, as it arced above him.

Ozin's Throne! He's actually mad!

A mischievous grin that would have made Solas jealous played across the boy's face.

'Ha! That was *really* close!' he said, 'next time, not so lucky?'

The Scorched boy spun the sword in his hand, watching Nathaniel intently, perhaps waiting for him to move.

Does he really want me to fight him? Nathaniel thought.

'I don't want to hurt you,' Nathaniel splayed his palms out in front of him.

'Hurt me?' the boy folded his brows together confusedly. 'You do me honour, Grey,' the boy said, pointing his sword at Nathaniel.

Nathaniel's eyes crossed to the girl, who remained where she had fallen a few paces away.

What am I supposed to do?

He didn't really want to fight the boy, but the idea of looking like a coward in front of his bride wasn't exactly appealing either.

'Enough!'

The voice cascaded down the turret, its force almost bowling Nathaniel over where he stood. He swiftly snatched his wandering hand away from the rapier at his hip and felt compelled to drop his head too, as if observing one of the Elders. Such was the authority in the stranger's voice that it had kneeled the Scorched boy before him.

The man who stepped lightly down was no Elder but yet another of the Scorched. If Nathaniel had thought the boy was abnormally tall however, he was to be humbled by the giant that approached them. Bending to avoid hitting his head on the crest of the turret entrance, a Scorched man, with braids swinging about his thighs, approached the three.

His clothes, like the boy's, were most curious. A tan shawl, of some sort, was wrapped tightly over his shoulders, exposing muscular forearms and midriff. The sarong, loose and falling just above his sandal, was also of the same colour. In fact, the only colour present in the man's dress could be found from the assortment of beads that hung around his neck and over his braids, gently clacking together as he walked.

Heavy-set, as well as towering, with thick cords of muscle stretching across his entire body like a suit of armour, the Scorched man cut a most imposing figure. And yet, he carried himself with such grace that defied his sheer density. Like a lion, he advanced towards them, silent but for his clacking beads.

His eyes swept the balcony, passing over both Nathaniel and his bride before falling on the Scorched boy, whose grin had instantly dissipated.

'Would you leave a sister in the sand?' he said, his voice so deep the words sent tremors across Nathaniel's skin.

The boy delicately dropped his sword and then stooped to offer his outstretched hand to Nathaniel's bride. She brushed herself off, gave the boy a fleeting glance, which Nathaniel imagined was something akin to a glare, and wrapped her arm around Nathaniel's.

The man remained silent, as he folded his arms, but there was something in the way he looked at the boy kneeling before him that suggested no words were needed.

'It was just a challenge, father,' the boy muttered sheepishly.

'Sun above, Naseri! You can't fight the boy on his wedding day whilst in his wedding garb!' The Scorched man shook his head incredulously.

'But he is yet to be oiled!'

The man's chest heaved with a short bark of laughter, more boom than bark.

'My child! Our feet no longer grace the sand, things are different here!'

'But-'

The Scorched man raised a hand that could have swallowed Nathaniel's face whole.

'Not another word! Now, our hosts have requested our presence for the feast, so make your peace with our friends.'

'I beg your forgiveness,' Naseri clenched a fist to his breast and bowed to them both, still looking utterly perplexed.

'I should go also,' the girl said. Nathaniel felt his chest deflate as she unravelled herself from him.

He felt suddenly torn as he watched her gather up her skirts and follow the Scorched boy up the stairs. With a strangled wince, which he hoped hadn't come out as pathetically as he feared, Nathaniel caught her hand just as she began her ascent.

'I don't even know your name,' he said lamely.

33

'Soon,' she promised, and he could have sworn she smiled under the veil. Then with a squeeze of his hand, blooming his chest briefly once more, she was gone.

Soon.

The word rolled around inside his mind, provoking fanciful thoughts of what was to come. Nathaniel could see himself lifting her veil in front of a hundred onlookers. Yet, her face, no matter how hard he tried to picture it, was a blurry haze of changing facial characteristics. First, she was blonde, then dark haired, blue eyed, then green. A kiss exchanged would send raptures of applause across the hall, and confetti would dance above heads, buoyed by the cries of adulation.

'Soon,' Nathaniel whispered longingly.

The tall Scorched man's beads clacked as he drew in beside Nathaniel.

'You know, Regal, in my land, the bride and groom before their Joining would be held together in total darkness in a windowless hut for a week. You would be allowed only water to stay alive and each other's company to keep you warm.'

Nathaniel looked at the man and was startled to find him without a grin, or any sign he was joking.

'I am Emir,' the man said, mimicking the clenched fist bow of his son. 'Please forgive my son, I fear his brashness is due to the lack of his brother's presence,' he shook his head, but there seemed to be a hint of pride in his smile.

'Nathaniel,' Nathaniel replied, making an awkward attempt at imitating the man's bow, 'is your other son alright?'

The man shook his head.

'Not here, Regal.'

There was no malice towards Nathaniel in the dark look that crossed the man's face, but it was clear that the topic was a dangerous one to broach.

'So, you're the Samaii Chief?' Nathaniel said, hurriedly trying to move the conversation elsewhere.

'I am indeed. You don't seem fond of my people's marriage rituals?'

'N-no!' Nathaniel began to bluster, 'Not at all! I–'

'Calm yourself, Regal,' the man chuckled. 'I would agree they are somewhat… strange… for those not familiar with our ways.'

'Errrr… a little,' Nathaniel admitted with a blush. He was anxious to get to know his bride, but the idea of spending a full week alone in a hut with anyone, let alone a girl, filled him with unease.

The man's laughter shook Nathaniel where he stood. 'I share your concerns, Grey! But think of it this way: once the week has come to pass, you would have forged an unbreakable bond with your promised one. You would know her soul before you know her face.'

Or be sick to the teeth of each other before the first night is out, Nathaniel thought grimly.

Chapter 5

The smell of orchids clung faintly to his nostrils, even by the time Nathaniel had returned to the Great Hall, which had become considerably busier in the last hour. The throng of nobles and fellow guests, from all over Horizon, had since doubled. A steady stream of servants flowed from the kitchens bringing cutlery and jugs of wine to the table.

Food had been carefully arranged in floral shapes. A coruscating kaleidoscope of colours, competing with the elegant extravagance of the guests' formal dress, as they flocked slowly to the table.

Nathaniel was, however, searching the seas of visitors for a flash of green. Though, wherever he looked, he could not find the girl in the green dress.

He was suddenly very eager for this feast to be over and done with.

'Is that... your Emperor?'

Naseri's sudden appearance by his side almost caused Nathaniel to jump. He followed the boy's gaze. The Emperor, quickly distinguishable by the shimmer of his golden gown, was engaged in conversation with a couple of human nobles. They looked incredibly pale, as if they'd never been out in the sun before. They were also rather stiff of neck, looking down upon the Emperor past their noses. Although, that may have had more to do with the ridiculous looking ruffs that encircled their necks.

Féynians, Nathaniel wagered, noticing the frilly umbrella that the noblewoman held closed by her side. It looked so fragile, he wondered how it managed to withstand a light breeze, let alone the constant rainfall that plagued the land.

'Yes, it is,' Nathaniel replied to Naseri, watching closely as the Emperor gripped the man's hands and accepted a curtsy from the noblewoman, which was remarkably graceful despite the bulky nature of her dress.

Nathaniel wasn't sure why, but something felt... wrong. Perhaps it had been his father's face - stone-set - or even the sneer he could have sworn the Szar cast at the Emperor's back, as they followed him to the archway Nathaniel had passed under earlier. The Szar had been in a bad mood, Tolken had said, nothing more. And yet, the discomfort that gnawed at him just wouldn't go away.

'I need to go,' Nathaniel said suddenly, adding a rushed 'sorry', as he sprang away from the boy. Naseri looked once again confounded as to what he could have possibly done to cause offence.

Unsure what forces drove him, Nathaniel gave chase just as his father's head disappeared around the corner.

It's probably nothing, he thought.

It was tradition for the Emperor to take leave before the feast began and give thanks to Athrana for a bountiful harvest, but what were the other two doing? Perhaps they had simply gone to pray with Tolken? Or it was just coincidence that they had gone in the same direction.

Approaching the archway in a crouched position, Nathaniel took a careful peek around the corner. The Emperor had gone, so too had the Szar and his father.

They can't have just vanished, Nathaniel thought, they had to be in one of the rooms. He passed from door to door, pressing his ear against the cold oak but coming back each time with nothing. Maybe they had gone to another prayer room?

But just then, a loud crash, like that of a handful of metal platters being dropped, alerted him to the third door he had passed. His hand on his rapier, Nathaniel launched himself at the door, barrelling it open with his shoulder.

This was indeed the prayer room. Candles lay in dozens of little alcoves across the walls providing a faint light from the walkway to the statuette of Athrana, hands cupped out before her, like a beggar asking for change. Behind her, the moonlight cast ethereal patterns over the statue through a beautiful, multi-coloured stain glass window that made up the back of the room.

Nathaniel's father, the Szar, and the Emperor and his bodyguard were all here too. However, the manner in which he found them left much to be desired.

'Wh-what's going on?'

After gently closing the door behind Nathaniel, his father gripped him by the shoulders and shook him. 'What are you doing here?' he stared at Nathaniel with wild eyes, 'go back to the feast, and put that away!'

Nathaniel hadn't even registered that his rapier had left its scabbard. His attentions were focused entirely on the surreal scene laid out before him.

Beyond the bloodied, crumpled form of the Emperor's bodyguard, Tolken was on his knees, hands grappling at his assailant, who held him in a chokehold. A dagger lay flat under his chin and the Obsidian Crown had fallen on its side, in between him and his late bodyguard.

Blue eyes, as cold as ice, regarded Nathaniel.

'I'm going to assume, for your sake, *boy*, that you have inherited some of your father's intelligence,' the Szar growled, digging the tip of the blade deeper into the Emperor's exposed flesh.

'Sheathe your blade and hold your tongue.'

'Let the child leave, he has no part in this,' Tolken gurgled through bloody lips.

'Silence traitor!' Draeden hissed down at his captive, causing the Emperor to groan as he tightened his grip across Tolken's throat. 'What did I say, boy?' the Szar turned back to Nathaniel.

'Do as the Szar commands, Nathaniel, please,' his father said, eyes pleading with the floor, as if hoping it would swallow him up.

The rapier twitched by Nathaniel's side, as he looked between his father and the Szar in utter disbelief at what he was witnessing.

'What... what is this?' he demanded of his father, 'what is this?'

'This is for the future of our Empire,' the Szar said. 'Here we cut out that last dreaded weakness.'

'What is he talking about? Father? Father!'

'Did you honestly think our dear Jael's bleeding heart would stop with the Scorched, boy?' the Szar continued, amidst Nathaniel's father's committed display of silence. 'Oh no! Our beloved Emperor conspires with the animals!'

Nathaniel felt his breath catch in his throat. 'What do you mean?'

'The time has come… for peace,' the Emperor wheezed. 'The Lycans need not be our enemies–'

'They are beasts! Do you forget already what they did to Councillor Raël? They have no dignity! They are unworthy of anything but servitude, and they even failed at that!'

'Please, Draeden, let my son leave,' Nathaniel's father begged.

'No,' the Szar pointed the dagger, still tinged with the Emperor's blood, at Nathaniel. 'The boy stays. It's high time he decided where his loyalties lie.'

'Draeden…'

'Quiet, Laevan!' the Szar snapped at his father. 'Well, boy?' Kusk stared at Nathaniel with those cruel, blue eyes.

Loyalty.

What Nathaniel saw before him was so far removed from that concept, it beggared belief.

Had the Szar forgotten the pledge he made? The pledge every Regal made to those who bore the Obsidian Crown.

Nathaniel made a step forward.

Till my blood dries up, I give it freely for the people–

'What are you doing, boy?' The Szar watched Nathaniel advance towards him, rapier in hand, with wide eyes.

–till my body decays, I give it freely for the Empire–

–till my heart gives out, I give it freely for the Emperor.

'Stop right where you are!'

'I serve the Emperor,' Nathaniel said quietly, hand trembling as he raised his rapier, 'now release hi–'

40

Crack!

Nathaniel's knees began to buckle. Stars flickering before his eyes, as he collapsed to his knees.

Rolling on his back, he fleetingly saw his father looking down upon him, as his vision darkened, like a spilled pot of ink oozing across a blank page.

'I'm sorry, my son,' he thought he heard his father say, just as the last speck of light was blotted out.

Chapter 6

Nathaniel awoke, taking several sharp gasps of breath. The air tasted heavy and stale, like ale left too long in the sun. To make matters worse, it was pitch black... wherever he was. Drips of water, echoing in the quiet, were all that permeated the dark, terrible silence.

Where was he? And how had he gotten here?

He then became abundantly aware of a throbbing sensation on the back of his head and ran a hand through his hair. Dried blood, cracking between his fingertips, brought a grimace to his face.

As he withdrew his hand, the memories came flooding back painfully. The Emperor, kneeling on the floor... a dagger held to his throat... the sneer of the Szar... the sadness in his father's eyes as he blacked out.

But why?

Memories of the day fluttered by in their morsels, images flashing before his eyes like sparks, words whispered from the darkest corners of his mind.

One seemed to stand out from the rest, refusing to be shoved back into the depths of his consciousness.

A doorway and two men. His father and the man with the red-trimmed robes.

What you're asking of me is treasonous, his father had said.

You have until the wedding to decide where you – and your family's – loyalties lie, the other had replied.

Nathaniel slapped a hand to his forehead.

Of course.

In their own house, his father had been discussing the murder of the Emperor and he'd been too blind to see it.

But, why was he here? Alive? He was a witness to the whole thing, he was–

Nathaniel gasped with realisation.

Tolken's death would bring an outcry. Doubtless, even if the blame had been pinned on the Emperor's bodyguard, there would have been long investigations and countless interrogations. But if the Szar could produce a live suspect...

A quiet anger took hold of Nathaniel, and he clenched his fists so hard he thought the knuckles would pop off. Then they fell limply by his side.

He had fought and he had lost. But why? Even with his father standing beside the Szar, it had felt right to take a stand. Yet it was he sitting in the cold, while the Szar, and his father, slept snuggly.

NO! he thought resolutely, *I will not waste away here!* He had to escape, he had to tell everyone. Surely people would believe him! Why would he want to kill the Emperor? And on his own wedding day no less!

He tried to jump to his feet but was snatched back to the uneven cobbles, just as soon before he could manage to put his weight on one leg.

Groaning as he pushed himself back against the wall, Nathaniel ran a hand across an arm, cursing softly when it brushed against metal.

He'd been chained to the wall, like an animal.

43

The only way it could have been more humiliating would have been if they fitted him with the old chain-suits that had once been used for Lycans.

Steel clacked about the stone as he kicked his legs out in frustration. For how long was the Szar intent on keeping him down here?

The sound of a heavy door screeching brought Nathaniel back from contemplating his fate. As it was prised open, he brought himself up to his knees, with the loud grunts of the man pushing it echoing all the way down to his cell.

Footsteps followed the grunts. Amber drops of light illuminating parts of the staircase that led down to the barred pit in which Nathaniel was chained. The drops spread slowly, collecting together in pools as the footsteps came ever closer. As its bearer descended the steps, this flame, although so small in its lantern, seemed, to Nathaniel's ill-adjusted eyes, to be almost blinding.

'Who comes?' Nathaniel queried of the lantern-bearer from behind an outstretched hand.

The cloaked figure, face hidden in shadow, sighed and walked on past his cell, his fine black cloak trailing as a stool was dragged back across. With another sigh, although this time tinged with disgust, the figure perched atop the stool, placing the lantern carefully beside his boots.

The boots looked expensive, not to mention the black tunic that adorned his visitor. Was the city already in mourning? How long had he been in here?

'Did you do it?' the man asked bluntly.

Nathaniel squinted past his hand but found that little other than the man's attire was apparent to him. The lantern's light stretched only as far as the bottom of his chin.

'Who are you?' Nathaniel said.

'Did you do it?' the question came again somewhat more impatiently, his visitor's knuckles cracking as his fists clenched together. This time, the voice sounded distinctly familiar to Nathaniel.

'Solas?' Nathaniel tilted his head up towards the shadowed face.

The stool creaked as his brother leaned forward, staring down at Nathaniel. The lantern finally illuminating his features. His eyes looked dark around the rims, like he hadn't slept for weeks, and his dimples, once proud accompaniments to an infectious grin, were the only impressions of his usual self that remained.

'Did. You. Do it?' Solas hissed.

'What? Kill the Emperor? Are you mad? Ozin's Throne, Solas, of course I didn't!'

Solas' features appeared to soften with his words and he leant back into the darkness, nervously playing with his hands.

'Draeden – the Szar – says you killed him. Slaughtered him and his bodyguard in cold blood. The people are calling you... 'Kinslayer.' No one saw it coming-'

'Solas, I–'

'–and father. Well father hasn't been the same since the wedding. Not since what he saw, since–'

Nathaniel pulled himself up towards the bars of his cell, as close as the chains would allow, and peered up towards his brother.

'Solas, please,' he pleaded.

'–you... you attacked him,' Solas choked.

Nathaniel felt the blood drain from his face and his grip on the iron bars falter.

Attack their father? This could not be. These were the Szar's words, they had to be! His father would not, could not, do this.

'Solas,' Nathaniel insisted, 'I didn't kill the Emperor. You know I would never attack father! It was the Szar!'

Nathaniel heard Solas' breath catch in his throat, and he leant forward in his stool, the light from the lantern catching his mirthless face once more.

He stared down at his hands, pondering on his brother's words for a moment. However, just as Nathaniel thought he'd finally got through to him, Solas shook his head sadly and looked down at Nathaniel with impossibly cold eyes.

'Father said you would try to blame Draeden,' he said quietly, as if this was final confirmation of Nathaniel's guilt.

Then with a cry the stool he was sat on was sent spinning across the floor, as he snatched up the lantern and cast himself away.

'Solas!'

'Fog take you, Nathaniel! Murdering the Emperor wasn't enough for you was it?' Solas shouted back as he climbed the stairs, 'you would have killed father, wouldn't you? And the Szar too!'

'You can't believe that! Solas! Solas!'

Solas' hurried footsteps paused above Nathaniel, his ragged breaths filling the cells. When he spoke, each quietly spoken word was articulated with such venom, they cut into Nathaniel, shocking him into a momentary silence.

'If you ask for mercy, brother, maybe the elders will petition for your exile. But I think the Szar, rightly, has his mind set on the Stone for you.'

'It wasn't me!' Nathaniel cried up to the pools of light, which were quickly evaporating. 'Please! You have to believe me! Solas! The Szar has betrayed us all! Solas! SOLAS!'

Not another word was returned. All Nathaniel heard was the slamming of the door, plunging him back into darkness.

Chapter 7

The Lycans considered Old Fire-Eyes quite the enigma.

Some said he'd been a journeyman, seeing all the world had to offer on foot. Others thought he'd been driven here, to the Lycans, running from some dark purpose. Some, in hushed tones, in the darkest corners of Sanctuary, spun tales of murder and Majik.

Nonetheless, he was liked well enough by most, although there were those still bitter over his rise to the top.

But he had been somewhat subdued of late.

He seemed rarely present in conversation. Not exactly cold, but his usual warmth was rarely seen nowadays.

Samir was pretty sure it had all started with the Regal.

What was her name?

Ahh, it would come back to him.

During the past year he had spent as Old Fire-Eyes' aide, he had seen the young Regal regularly. Young. The thought made him chuckle. Youth, he had learned quickly, was a luxury long enjoyed by Regals - notably so, compared to Lycans, and even more dramatically so, compared to the short lives of humans.

A Regal could live through a thousand years, before you'd even realise they had passed adolescence. For all Samir knew, she could easily be that old.

He had been uncomfortable at first, escorting her to Old Fire-Eyes' chambers. Whilst he was not nearly old enough to remember the Lycans' bondage under the Regals, he had heard stories about their difficult past. Indeed, at first, this *shared history* had seemed to make a monster of the Regal, accentuating the cruelty of her sharp eyes and harshly prominent cheekbones.

But she was different.

She seemed kind. And perhaps it had just been for Old Fire-Eyes' sake, but his brothers and sisters seemed to accept her. Well... almost everyone.

To begin with, Old Fire-Eyes had been equally kind.

But that had all changed a few months ago.

One night, Samir, and half of Sanctuary, he imagined, had suddenly awoken to a pitched argument a short distance away from the dormitory.

Raised voices could be heard coming from Old Fire-Eyes' chambers and Samir was pretty sure he'd heard something breaking against one of the walls inside. Though, even the most curious of his brothers and sisters hadn't dared venture close to it.

'I don't care!' the Regal shouted, as she whipped open the door, so fiercely Samir was surprised it didn't break off its hinges.

She was clearly in some distress. Her blue eyes awash with tears, she brushed past with a hard shoulder that almost knocked the nearest Lycan off his feet, despite the woman's slim frame.

'Oh, get out of my way, would you!' she snapped, without looking up at Samir.

Her long blonde hair then whipped out of sight down a corner, leaving the gathered group with something far more terrifying.

The door behind Samir, now wide open, exposed the room's remaining inhabitant, a thunderous expression burning across his lined face.

That, alone, was enough to send most running back to their dormitories.

Old Fire-Eyes merely spun and walked back to his desk, placing his shaking hands on its surface, claws digging into the wood.

'Leave me,' Samir heard him growl, just loud enough for him to hear.

Even months later, Samir hesitated on the threshold, clutching the letter with a Regal seal in his hands.

Taking a deep breath, he whispered, in a higher-pitch than he expected, 'you have a message, sir.'

Samir edged backwards, away from the door, as if it were liable to suddenly burst into flames.

He briefly considered just slotting the letter under the door. The thought of experiencing Old Fire-Eyes' fury alone was a most terrifying thought.

'What is it?' came the response a moment later.

'A letter, brother.'

'Come in, then.'

Sun above... too late now, Samir thought.

Tentatively, he edged through the door. To his relief, he found that the furniture appeared to be largely in order, with no fresh dents or scratches across the walls.

Old Fire-Eyes crossed the room and sat in his armchair, as he did most often nowadays, staring at the flames dancing in the fireplace in front of him.

There was something grand about him still, even in his morose state. A sheer presence that extended beyond his leadership of the Brotherhood and beyond Samir's imagination. What glories and atrocities have been witnessed by those intense, grey, amber-rimmed eyes that so captivated everyone?

Old Fire-Eyes had seen things. Knew things few others did. And the gravity of those experiences loomed over those who locked eyes with him.

'You have something for me, Samir?'

With a start, Samir suddenly realised he'd just been staring at his leader for the last minute or so.

Thankful Old Fire-Eyes hadn't appeared to notice his blushes, with a nervous cough, he placed the letter on the arm of the chair.

As Old Fire-Eyes took the letter and examined the seal, Samir eyed, with trepidation, an old, but deep set of scratches that stretched across the wall behind the desk. By the Sun, he hoped it wasn't bad news.

'Did Fael say anything when he gave you this?' Old Fire-Eyes queried.

'Just that it was important that it got to you as quickly as possible, Brother,' Samir said. He then added hesitantly, 'although, maybe I judged him incorrectly, but Fael seemed on edge.'

Old Fire-Eyes seemed to consider this for a moment, as he span the envelope about in his hands, before splitting the seal neatly with an extended claw.

After pouring over the contents, he dropped the letter against his thigh and murmured bitterly under his breath, something that sounded like 'Kusk.'

'Brother?' Samir said apprehensively.

Thorne folded the parchment methodically until it was no larger than his palm and tucked it into the breast pocket of his waistcoat. 'Little wonder Fael was ill at ease,' he sighed heavily. 'The Emperor is dead.'

Samir let out a sharp breath. 'What?' he said. 'How?'

'It matters little now, Samir, pretend I never told you. News will spread in time, of course, but until then... I need to make certain preparations.'

'Of-of course,' Samir began to bow but, after a sidelong glance from Old Fire-Eyes, he quickly collected himself. No bowing, he remembered.

A flicker of a smile, all too rare these days, crossed Fire-Eyes' face, disappearing as quickly as it had come.

'Oh, and Samir,' Old Fire-Eyes called, halting him in his tracks, as the young Lycan was retreating out of the room.

'Yes, Brother?'

'Do ask Brother Marcus if he would be so kind as to prepare for another newcomer. Tell him it will be most... irregular.'

Nodding in affirmation, more than was necessary, Samir realised, he launched himself through the door, before he could cause himself any further embarrassment.

*

As soon as the door was closed, Old Fire-Eyes rose from his seat, flicked open the letter again and tipped the contents into his open hand.

A dozen petals of varying size and colour nestled against his palm, a gentle, but distinct fragrance mixing pleasantly with the warmth of the flames before him. Old Fire-Eyes brought his hands to his face and breathed deeply, allowing himself to drift to a better place, a better time, with…

'Sunflowers and orchids?' a voice called.

Closing his fist behind his back, like a child attempting to hide a stolen bounty of sweets from his mother, Old Fire-Eyes span on the spot and stared, wide-eyed at the dark corner of the room. 'How long have you been hiding back there?' he demanded.

'Long enough,' came the reply.

Old Fire-Eyes narrowed his eyes and tilted and his head, sniffing the air but to no avail. Not even the vaguest hint. How could she never have a scent?

'Ozin's Throne,' he said, shaking his fists before him, 'don't keep skulking there!'

From the dark corner of his chambers, behind one of his bookcases, a woman emerged. As softly as a Hunter, she padded past Old Fire-Eyes, long maroon dress trailing the floor behind her.

An open book that lay on his desk, its pages yellow and wrinkled with age, apparently caught her eye. He watched her incredulously, as she ran a polished nail across the length of a page, which bore a faded drawing of a banner, and inside a sword smothered with flame.

She recited the words on the page beside it as her hand traced the blade.

'Till dusk doth come, slumber we must

At the stroke of midnight, the lost embers return

Bearing the flames of the First, the heir's lead we trust

With fang and claw, beckons darkness to dust'

'Still taking a great interest in Fierslaken's Kingsguard?' the woman removed her hand from the book and turned to lean on the desk. 'How long have you slaved over those two pages?'

'It's good to see you too,' the old Lycan grumbled. 'Still breaking and entering I see.'

'Darling, I'm hardly breaking in, if the front door's left open,' she retorted with a grin.

He snorted derisively and joined the seer by his desk. He lifted the lid from a small metallic pot beside the book and carefully dropped the petals inside, but the seer caught Thorne's hand as the lid hovered above.

He looked down at her, staring at the opaque veil. Still to this day it bothered him that he could never see her eyes.

'The Hunter thinks you're making a mistake,' she said.

Old Fire-Eyes grimaced, she had an remarkably firm grip, despite her size. 'He thinks a lot of things,' he said, 'but then often fails to take his own advice.'

The seer smiled wryly, a somewhat shaky smile that belied her usual composure, releasing Old Fire-Eyes's hand so he could close the pot once more. 'For what it's worth, darling, I think you're making a mistake too.'

'I assume, after all this time, this is not a social call?' he asked brusquely, brushing his hands free of pollen.

'The letter,' the seer said simply.

'Of course.'

'Troublingly, it would appear that the shadows are stirring quicker than expected,' the seer said.

'Yes... troubling for us all,' Thorne agreed, 'so it does have something to do with Tolken's death?'

The seer shrugged, then looped her arm around his. 'Perhaps nothing... or everything,' she said mysteriously. 'I will say this, however. The timing cannot be coincidental.'

'When we're finally on the verge of peace? It can only be Kusk,' Thorne growled. 'But why? Why now? He may despise Lycans but surely he would never consider serving the Necromancers?'

'Perhaps. Perhaps not. But could he not be nudged towards a desired goal?'

'What do you know?' he asked quietly, turning to face the seer.

'Hm?'

'Zakariyanna. What do you know?'

The seer sighed. 'You know I can say no more. I am bound by–'

'–rules that cannot be broken,' he grimaced, 'you're not the first to use those words.'

'Nor will I be the last,' Zakariyanna smiled sadly and padded softly towards the open door.

Pausing briefly, she turned to face the old Lycan, considering him for a moment.

'Do take care, dearest, but remember… you cannot run from your destiny forever.'

As she glided through the doorway, he thought he heard her whisper '…and neither can your bloodline.'

Chapter 8

Nathaniel's breath caught in his chest.

Something had rustled in the opposite corner of his cell. Rats were his first thought, but the sound suggested something larger.

'Hello?' he called out to the darkness.

A sudden scrabbling against the floor caused Nathaniel's heart to race once more. Whatever it was that had made the noise before now appeared to be coming straight at him, and it was certainly no rat.

'Athrana's grace,' Nathaniel muttered, as he tugged against his metal bonds in vain. 'I'm not dying here! Not in this damned cell!'

The scrabbling stopped.

'NOW, WHO SAID ANYTHING ABOUT DYING?' a deep, rasping voice asked.

Boomed was perhaps the better word, indeed the stranger's words seemed to rattle Nathaniel's bones. So much so, he feared they would suddenly snap, if he uttered another syllable.

Nathaniel squinted into the darkness but couldn't make out anything of his own body, let alone his cellmate. Such was the sheer blackness that hung over them.

'You've been here this whole time?' Nathaniel said.

HMM. THAT'S AN INTRIGUIGING QUESTION,' the other said thoughtfully. 'WELL... TECHNICALLY, I'M ALWAYS HERE... OR THERE. BUT THAT'S BESIDE THE POINT.'

'What do you mean?' Nathaniel frowned. 'Who are you?'

'WELL, I SUPPOSE WE HAVE *MET* – IN A WAY – BEFORE,' the voice boomed contemplatively. 'WHY NOT?'

There was a sound like a heavy tablecloth being pulled from a stone table, then light suddenly bloomed back into Nathaniel's cell.

'Ozin's beard!' Nathaniel recoiled and sprang back against the wall.

The thing that sat across from him was no man. For a start, it didn't seem to have any skin and just stared at him through hollow eye sockets, with flames dancing in the recesses.

Nathaniel stared in disbelief.

How could this – this thing – see? Indeed, how could it have a conversation with him without ears or, seemingly, a tongue?

The skeleton caught him glancing around his skull. 'YEP, I HAVE A SKULL FOR A HEAD,' he said, mimicking the circular motion Nathaniel was making with his head. 'AND, I'M AFRAID TO SAY, THE REST OF ME ISN'T A HUGE IMPROVEMENT ON THAT EITHER.'

'You're – you're a skeleton!' Nathaniel said.

'SURPRISE!' the skeleton cackled, splaying his hands out beside his skull and waving them rapidly to-and-fro.

At a complete loss for words, Nathaniel could do little else but stare at the abomination that sat before him. Could his short stint in the cells have already fractured his grip on reality? Surely not? But how else could he explain what was happening? This couldn't be real... it couldn't.

'WELL, I MUST SAY, YOU'RE TAKING THIS RATHER BETTER THAN YOUR GRANDFATHER DID, THE FIRST TIME WE CROSSED PATHS... OOF! WHOA BOY,' the skeleton chuckled. 'ALTHOUGH,' the skeleton absently scratched at its chin, 'NOW THAT I THINK ABOUT IT, I REALLY OUGHT TO PAY HIM A VISIT SOMETIME TOO.'

'I'm sure he'd appreciate that,' Nathaniel just managed to murmur sarcastically, 'but he's dead.'

'THORNE GREY? OH NO, NO, NO, BOY. HE'S VERY MUCH ALIVE AND WELL. THE WHOLE BURNING ALIVE SCHEBANG DIDN'T EXACTLY PAN OUT.'

'The whole what?'

'YOU KNOW?' the skeleton said, miming a large explosion.

Nathaniel stared back at the skeleton in puzzlement.

HMM. I HAVE BEEN TOLD I OVERSHARE.' The skeleton fingered some of the crater like dents atop its skull, 'I THINK I'M BEGINNING TO SEE WHY...'

Nathaniel shook his head. 'This cannot be real...'

'IF I MAY INTERJECT?' the skeleton said, raising its hand, 'WOULD THIS BE A BAD TIME FOR INTRODUCTIONS?'

Nathaniel, who had been staring at his feet and shaking his head in pure disbelief, looked up at the skeleton. 'No, please, go right ahead. It's not like this can get any stranger.'

'I'M DEATH.'

'De-?' Nathaniel stuttered.

'YES, YES. DEATH,' the skeleton said, nodding happily.

'THE GRIM REAPER,' he added, making speech marks with his bony fingers. 'THAT ONE.'

Nathaniel stared back, wide eyed. Realising his mouth was agape, he closed it.

'NOW,' Death said, holding out three fingers. 'YOU HAVE A GRAND TOTAL OF THREE POSSIBLE ALTERNATIVES AVAILABLE TO YOU…'

Then his voice trailed off and he closed his hand, bones crackling. 'ACTUALLY, NEVER MIND. I DON'T RECALL THOSE BEING OF MUCH HELP TO YOUR GRANDFATHER EITHER,' he said, scratching his chin.

'What, in Ozin's name, do you want from me?'

'WANT? BY MICTLANTECADES, IT'S TOO EARLY FOR COLLECTION! DEPENDING ON HOW THESE NEXT FEW HOURS GO…'

'Collection? What? Do you mean–'

Nathaniel's eyes widened in horror and he slowly began to press himself into his corner of the cell.

The sudden, barking laugh that escaped Death's jaws did little to help Nathaniel's galloping sense of terror, as he pulled hi knees up to his chest.

'ONE SECOND!' Death said, waving at Nathaniel apologetically, shaking his head and clutching his ribs with his other hand. 'THE LOOK ON YOUR FACE!'

'You mean you're not going to–'

'–COLLECT YOU? OH NO, I JUST SHOW UP WHEN – SHALL WE SAY – *CERTAIN* PEOPLE MAY BE ABOUT TO MAKE AN UNFORTUNATE ERROR OF JUDGEMENT. TAKE THIS GUY FOR EXAMPLE.'

Death pulled out a large, battered piece of parchment from his robes, which, unless Nathaniel was imagining that too, glowed in Death's bony hands.

'LETS SEE… LET'S SEE… AHA! EXHIBIT A: NIALL RIORDAN, DROWNED IN HIS OWN BATHTUB. TALK ABOUT KILLER NAPS,' Death chortled, then paused to look up from his parchment. 'WHAT? TOO CREAM CHEESE? SOMETHING MORE CAVIAR PERHAPS? HOW ABOUT… THIS ONE: MAX ROUNDSTONE. OH DEAR, THIS IS A GOOD ONE. ON A DARE – DRUNKENLY, I SHOULD ADD – HE AGREED TO CLIMB THE SORCERORS' SPIRE,' Death snickered. 'TERRIBLE DECISION.'

'Erm.'

'YOU WOULDN'T BELIEVE HOW FAR THIS GUY GOT. I'M NOT ASHAMED TO SAY I LOST A BET,' Death ceded with a bobble of his skull, as he rolled up the parchment and tucked it back into his robes.

'Death… If this is actually real, and you're actually real… what did you mean about my Grandfather? My Grandparents have been dead for a long time, my father told me.'

Death's jaw clamped close with such a crack Nathaniel half-expected a tooth or two to come flying out. But instead, he just sat there quietly, burning eye sockets boring into his, purring within the gloom of the cell.

'WELL... THIS WILL COME AS QUITE THE SHOCK THEN,' Death said quietly, looking upwards.

'What do you mea–'

Before the question could fully leave Nathaniel's lips, a deafening scraping sound above brought his attention back to the stairs beside him. Lighter feet pierced the moonlight that was cast down to his cell.

'Solas?' Nathaniel called hopefully.

'Not quite,' came the reply.

The woman that descended the stairs was beautiful. Long blonde hair fell sleekly past her shoulders to the small of her back. She was clothed to travel, with dark leggings and knee length riding boots.

Nathaniel felt a lump rising in his throat. Was it already time for the Stone?

The woman brought the lantern up beside her face as she peered down at the chained Regal before her. The blue of her eyes bore down upon him with such intensity Nathaniel was reminded of the Szar's sharp gaze. Yet, what edge they may have once had, appeared now dulled; though she did well to hide it.

'So you're the one that has the city all abuzz,' she murmured, 'Nathaniel Grey, the Kinslayer–'

'I'm no Kinslayer!' Nathaniel snapped, wincing as the shackles tugged against his limbs.

He thought he saw the woman's mouth beginning to twitch into a smile, but her face quickly composed itself back into the steady mask she wore upon arrival.

'I hope not,' she replied, reaching behind her belt. Something clicked, and her hand returned with a heavy looking set of keys. 'Otherwise, I'm making an awful lot of effort to break out a murderer.'

Breaking out? Had he heard that right? Nathaniel eyed the keys dangling beside the bars with suspicion.

Draeden – the Szar – says you killed him. Slaughtered him and his bodyguard in cold blood.

Nathaniel shook his head violently. 'I can't leave,' he told the woman, 'I can't.'

'Then how else do you propose to remedy this situation?' she replied calmly.

'I-I have to set things right, clear my name!'

'Do you think you'll be allowed to do that?'

'The Elders will hear my case, they have to!'

'Will they now? Should you even be given that chance, it will make for an interesting case when your own father speaks out against you.'

'My father wouldn't–'

'–wouldn't he?'

Father said you would try to blame Draeden.

His brother's words still stung him now.

'They... they have to believe me,' he whispered, the all too brief conviction he had felt was quickly slipping away.

I think the Szar has his mind set on the Stone for you.

The sound of something clattering by Nathaniel's feet caused the Regal to jolt where he sat.

'Are you going to free yourself, child, or keep me waiting till they catch us both?'

He stared at the keys for a moment, then, without a second thought, snatched them off the floor and set his hands to work.

The shackles were difficult to release, being almost welded together with rust but fortunately came apart after a few earnest attempts, almost threatening to snap the key halfway through.

When Nathaniel looked up, the door was already open and the woman halfway up the stairs, beckoning him to follow.

'Who are you?' he called after her, the cramp in his legs making it difficult to keep up the pace she was setting.

'You can call me Illumina,' she replied, just before slipping past the door.

'But–'

Nathaniel's voice faltered as soon as the fresh air hit him.

His breath turned to fog where he stood and though the breeze that whistled along the street was gentle, it bit through his soiled tunic like a knife through parchment.

But he didn't mind.

He was more aware, at that moment, of the large shape looming above him against the mountain, casting the two Regals into a darker shade of dusk. In the distance he could just make out the flames of braziers, flickering against the midnight sky. It had not been that long ago since he himself had stood atop one of the balconies of the Emperor's Palace, looking forward to seeing his bride unveiled...

The snarl that left his lips had nothing to do with the cold.

'Shall we proceed or do you wish to freeze to death instead?' Illumina hissed from the darkness.

You could leave her. Find the Szar and make him pay.

'With what weapon? And past all the palace guards?' he muttered to himself.

The loss of the rapier's weight by his side felt heavy, a sort of tangible lack of presence, like a finger stripped of its ring.

Nathaniel forced himself to tear his eyes away from the palace and hurried up the narrow path beside the Regal woman.

Outside, he was no less uneasy than he had been in his cell. In fact, he was struggling to decide whether he preferred his damp confinement to the silhouette set by the castle-like walls that suffocated the street.

'You still haven't told me why you're helping me,' he said.

'One would think you would be grateful for your freedom,' Illumina replied, taking a turn up a flight of stairs that seemed to materialise out of nowhere.

She wove them through numerous streets and staircases, some even thinner than the last. There were a few diverging paths that Illumina paused to ponder over, but otherwise she seemed to know her way around the maze they found themselves in, virtually instinctively. Had he somehow escaped himself, Nathaniel knew he would have been horribly lost on his own.

He watched the woman ahead of him cautiously. *Who are you?* He thought to himself.

65

The woman carried an air of certainty about her, like that of the higher-borns Nathaniel had greeted at his wedding. She was of one of the great Houses of the Regal Empire, he was certain, or at least was once.

But by Athrana's grace, why then would she be helping him?

He tried scrutinising her clothing for clues, as he followed her up another set of stairs that, this time, were winding up in a tight circle. However, there was little else beyond the grey pallor of her skin that discerned her as a Regal.

Perhaps she is a commoner? No, it couldn't be. If the Szar had his way, word of his 'deeds' would have spread like wildfire over the Black Mountains by now.

Still, although it left his question largely unanswered, there were other things that appeared more pertinent.

'I've not seen a single guard,' Nathaniel realised, 'where are they?'

'There are none,' Illumina replied, her level tone suggesting she was displeased with their pace, 'at least, none for a while.'

'How can that be?' Nathaniel scoffed, 'especially for what I di– what they think I did.'

Gods, even I'm starting to believe I did it.

'You've not been down to the cells before have you?' Illumina remarked with a wry chuckle.

Nathaniel hesitated a moment before offering a reply, 'have you?' he asked carefully.

'As a prisoner you mean?'

A nervous laugh escaped Nathaniel's lips, 'ermmm…'

'No, I have not.'

Relief washed over Nathaniel, as they took yet another turn up a path, which appeared to angle up against the mountain side. Perhaps he had imagined it, but he thought he could make out lights in the distance.

Their route moulded itself into steps once more and still no guards halted their escape.

This felt easy, too easy.

'There should be guards,' Nathaniel insisted, 'these cells are right under the palace!'

Illumina remained silent this time, although at every corner they came to, one of her hands would suddenly snap to the daggers at her belt. It appeared that she too had become troubled by their completely unopposed escape.

No guards for a while she had told Nathaniel. Did that mean they were supposed to have bumped into a few by now?

'We're almost there,' Illumina said, pointing out a white gate ahead and, beyond it, a dozen or so lights flickering in the distance.

They were so close.

BANG!

The gate was suddenly blown off its hinges, bouncing not once but twice before its crumpled form skidded to a halt before them.

Nathaniel was not quite sure what he had thought he'd seen, or even whether he should believe it. However, it seemed as if a gigantic shadowy fist had crashed against the metal.

Dogs barked in the distance and little lights flickered on around them, as a man climbed through the now open gateway. Red trimmed robes flapped about his boots as he strode determinedly towards the two of them. Nathaniel gasped in recognition.

Illumina jumped ahead of Nathaniel, dagger bared.

'You're blocking my way, human,' Illumina growled.

Still the man in the red-trimmed robes advanced.

The dagger flew from Illumina's outstretched hand, but as the blade spun towards its mark, a shadowy mist sprung from the man's hand and the dagger dropped lamely to the ground.

'That racket will have attracted half the city guards,' the man said. 'Give the boy to me and you'll still have time to escape, Regal.'

'That's not going to happen.'

Just as Illumina reached for another of her daggers, a wave of shadow crashed into her side, lifting the Regal off her feet before she could even begin to retaliate. Even the cry that escaped her lips was short-lived, as her body collided against the wall with a CRACK that made Nathaniel cringe.

She didn't get up afterwards.

'Illumina!'

More shadows came, this time coiling around Nathaniel's arms and legs, pinning him where he stood. The more he struggled, the more the shadows bit into his skin. He could barely move his head to get a better look at Illumina where she lay.

Gods, she's not moving...

'What have you done?' he yelled at his approaching assailant.

'The woman will live, Regal,' the man replied dryly.

'You! This is all your fault!' Nathaniel yelled at the man, 'I heard what you told my father! I know this was your plan! And you weren't even there when they did it!

There was something about the man's look that made Nathaniel cold to his core. Unimaginable horrors cried out in silence, veiled by silent lips, but squirming against his eyes as they fought to be free of the cage the man had conjured for them.

'Is that so?' the man said, 'you could have easily avoided witnessing the death of your Emperor. You could have been wedded before your people even found Tolken's body. Yet, your interference has ultimately proved a masterstroke of a fate.'

'What in Ozin's name are you talking about?'

The sound of raised voices attracted the man's attention back to the crumpled gate behind him.

'It appears fate would not have us tarry,' the man muttered under his breath.

He grasped Nathaniel's shoulders firmly.

'Say farewell to your home, Nathaniel Grey.'

'What? Wait–'

A film of black began to fall over Nathaniel's eyes, obscuring his sight, just as the first guardsman began to step over the remains of the white gate. He raised a lance and Nathaniel thought he heard something shouted at them, but the guard's voice was dulled, the words elongating and twisting out of shape.

The ground beneath Nathaniel shook and then caved in, and the Regal was falling.

If he screamed, he could not hear it.

He could feel nothing.

See nothing.

The darkness swallowed him whole.

Chapter 9

It took a moment for Nathaniel to fully register the fact he was still alive, as he was busy being violently sick. By the time his stomach had emptied enough for him to raise his own head, the man with the red-trimmed robes was already sinking into the shadows encircling his legs.

'Hey!' Nathaniel cried, lunging towards his kidnapper, tripping and tumbling over himself. By the time his side had smacked into the ground, the man was already gone.

Nathaniel howled and smacked his fist into the ground.

That man... he too had played a part in the Emperor's murder. It was he who had pushed his father into it all.

Yet here he was, alive.

Nathaniel swallowed hard upon recalling the crunching sound Illumina's body had made as she was tossed against the wall. He hoped the man hadn't been lying when he'd said she was alive.

But why was he here, especially when the Szar wanted him sentenced to the Stone? Nathaniel glanced around his surroundings, wondering wherever *here* actually was...

At first the paving blocks underneath, so similar to those in Obsidia, had made Nathaniel question whether he'd even left home. Nonetheless, as his eyes turned skyward, that thought was quickly banished.

A circular courtyard framed by red-leafed oaks, rustling in the wind like a ruffled paper bag, surrounded him. To his back lay a paved path large enough for two carts to wheel through side by side.

There was a fountain that stood in the midst of it all, seemingly large enough to wade in. A stone figure had been erected in the middle, brought to one knee by some unseen great weight across its shoulders. Its palms were upturned above, as if to support this load, water arcing from within each hand either side back into the bowl of the fountain.

But this feature was made to be dwarfed by the behemoth lying in wait just beyond it.

With its round base spanning the entire courtyard and pointed tip, the tower had the appearance of a giant stake piercing the clouds above.

'–not listening to me. I did it!'

Ozin's beard! Nathaniel thought desperately, *not now!*

'Bore off,' came the other voice, closer than the last. 'I've seen you struggle to light a candle. There's no way you've mastered air.'

'I'm telling you, I think I've got it! Look!' the first voice insisted excitedly.

The footsteps stopped.

'Go on then,' the second voice sighed.

Nathaniel peeked over the top of the bush he had hid behind and saw two boys, humans, around his age, dressed in midnight robes split at the front from the waist down. Golden sparks burst across a shoulder of their garbs.

Were these the Warlocks his father had once told him about?

He looked past the Warlocks toward the towering structure behind them.

The Spire.

Dalmarra.

He was in Dalmarra?

No. He couldn't be.

Surely it was impossible to have covered such a distance in a matter of seconds.

One of the boys, greasy hair drawn back against his scalp, had his arms outstretched towards the other, his long blonde hair strapped into a pony-tail.

'Well?' the boy with the pony-tail said, looking highly unimpressed with his friend's efforts.

'You didn't feel that?' the first boy frowned.

'If it's boredom you mean, then yes, I feel it,' the second boy replied mirthlessly.

The vein on the first boy's temple stood pronounced, as he thrust his arms forth once more, throbbing with his apparent exertions.

'There!' he said proudly, arms collapsing by his sides, 'did you feel it? You must have this time.'

'Felt what?' the other boy replied impatiently.

'Your hair! I moved it,' the first proclaimed with a beam.

'That's just the breeze,' the second said, patting at his pony-tail all the same, as if to check it was still attached to his head.

'No, I'm telli–'

'Remind me exactly what it was that you *moved* in your room?'

The boy with the greasy hair mumbled something out of earshot into his feet.

'A quill? You moved a quill,' the boy with the ponytail said incredulously, 'and you're sure it didn't happen to just fall off your desk?'

As the other boy began to bluster, Nathaniel slowly crept out from the bush and edged away to the paved path.

Once the foliage around the path had fully concealed him from the Warlocks, Nathaniel broke into a run, not caring for stealth any longer.

The path meandered and curved so wildly, it was impossible to tell if anyone had pursued him. Indeed, the two Warlocks' voices had long since been drowned out.

WHAM!

One moment Nathaniel was running, the next he was sprawled on the paving blocks nursing his head after it had collided with what felt like a brick wall.

Bronze armour plates creaked as the 'brick wall' turned.

It was unlike anything Nathaniel had ever seen. Blue bolts of lightning crackled across the soldier's heavy armour, as if the very suit was alive with Majik. Another stood in wait just beyond them both, close to a giant set of gates that were fit to guard a city. They dwarfed even these 'lightning soldiers.'

Lances, tipped with spear-heads the size of Nathaniel's thigh, were grasped in one hand. Neither made a move or gesture after, or even said a word. They just stood there, staring silently through their closed visors.

'Ummmm,' Nathaniel said.

Still they stared.

'I just need to leave.'

KACHING!

Both lances were snapped up in the air, angled towards their prey like spears.

'I'm not here to cause trouble,' Nathaniel said, raising his hands and backing away. 'I was kidnapped!'

The soldiers paid no heed to his pleas and advanced steadily towards him.

'Why won't you listen to me? I haven't done anything wron–'

BOOM!

An explosion at the gate blew both its doors wide open and sent the closest lightning soldier flying into foliage. The second whirled around, armoured knee and lance slapping against the paved stone in an effort to keep upright. Meanwhile, Nathaniel stumbled and fell onto his side with a wince.

All at once, the city suddenly roared with life. Once gleeful bawls, carried distantly in the wind, cascaded into a clamour of shrieks and cries, coming from every possible direction. The tip of the Spire, jutting out over the edge of the oaks beside Nathaniel, lit up like a bonfire in the night sky.

Dazed, the Regal frowned at the haze of smoke and dust billowing out from the wreckage of steel and cracked paving blocks.

'NATHANIEL GREY!'

The shout seemed to come from the smoke itself, but then a large shape emerged from the fog, carrying a sword of giant proportions across broad shoulders.

Whilst not quite as tall as the lightning soldiers, he made up for the difference in mass, his skin writhing as it fought to keep the sheer amount of muscle in check. He used his free hand to brush the dust off his black sleeveless overcoat, as he looked toward the kneeling lightning soldier with gleeful eyes.

Silver eyes.

His face split into a grin when he found the Regal beyond it.

'Nathaniel?' he called to him.

Nathaniel nodded hesitantly, hoping that the sword wasn't for him.

'Today's your lucky day, little Regal,' the Hunter hefted the sword over his head as he spoke, the effort seeming somewhat minimal.

I'm not little, Nathaniel bristled at the words.

He followed the man's glance toward the run of trees on the right of Nathaniel where the second lightning soldier was quietly picking itself up from the floor.

'What are you waiting for, Nath? We don't have all day!'

Nath? Now I'm being called Nath?

The first lightning soldier was slowly cutting the space between itself and the lone Hunter.

The absence of Nathaniel's rapier had never felt so heavy.

'Regal!'

Shaking himself out of his stupor, Nathaniel bounded forward, narrowly avoiding the second lightning soldier's lance. The spear tip striking his shadow where it lingered on the paving block.

The other paid him no heed, fortunately more interested in its armed quarry. The two combatants held their blades in line with each other's, while their feet danced a slow caper back to what remained of the gate.

'What now?' Nathaniel gasped upon reaching the Hunter.

'There'll be someone waiting for you outside,' the Hunter instructed him.

The lightning soldier's lance had almost reached the tip of the Hunter's broadsword.

'You're not coming?' Nathaniel gave the man a shocked look.

'Not a chance!' the Hunter grinned back, as if Nathaniel were really the mad one for missing this opportunity. 'Now go!'

The Hunter's hand, brick-like in density, shoved the Regal away, just as the lance shot forward.

The sound of steel on steel echoed behind Nathaniel, as he burst through the film of dust, almost drowned out by the Hunter's raucous laughter.

'Mad,' Nathaniel shook his head. 'He's actually mad.'

The laughter that escaped from his lips felt both soothing and perverse. In one day, he'd escaped the Stone, had somehow landed in Dalmarra and bumped into a Hunter. Surely things couldn't get any stranger?

'Mr. Grey?'

Apparently, *things* could.

Nathaniel briefly glimpsed a pair of hands flash in front of him, before a hood was draped over his head.

'Mmmmm! 'Geroff!' Nathaniel cried out, his voice muffled through the cloth.

Whoever had a hold of Nathaniel was strong. Strong enough that he had both the Regal's wrists pinned behind his back with one hand as he shepherded Nathaniel blindly forward.

"Ou'll 'egret this!' Nathaniel exclaimed. Adding "robably,' wondering how many times

Nathaniel groaned as his shin caught something hard, then he was lifted and shoved roughly onto a seat.

"Emme go!'

A door slammed shut beside Nathaniel as the hood was lifted from his head.

'Nathaniel Grey… at last,' a voice spoke. Its owner bathed in shadow.

Chapter 10

A man draped in dark robes sat before him. The lower half of his face was the only part of his body visible – besides his pale hands – with his lips curled into a cold, hangman's smile.

There was something disquieting by how at ease he seemed within the darkness of the carriage. Indeed, it were as if the dark moulded itself around him, like a throne for a king.

'Forgive the rough welcome,' the man waved a pale hand casually, as if discussing the weather. It was clear that the statement was not a request.

'That man... the Hunter,' Nathaniel looked for a window, but found the carriage to be lacking in such concessions to light. The man opposite him remained perfectly poised as he fumbled around.

'Boulder will have the situation under control–'

'–you call that under control?' Nathaniel's eyes widened, 'blowing up the Spire's gates and fighting those-those things! Are you trying to start a war? Who in Athrana's name do you think you ar–'

A sharp chill running down the length of the Regal's spine silenced him suddenly.

Nathaniel could not see the man's eyes, yet he had felt such a piercing gaze that had all but frozen his insides.

'Who are you?' Nathaniel whispered.

'You interest me, Regal, so I will indulge you. I am called the Shadow,' the man replied. His answer did not bring Nathaniel any warmth. 'Normally I would have preferred a more...

subtle extraction, but I needed a guarantee that you would be brought to me unharmed and unspoilt by Warlock hands–'

'–you mean kidnapping more like!' Nathaniel yelled, finding his voice once more. 'First, I've been thrown in a dungeon cell, then some man controlling shadows whisks me off here! And now, I've you to thank, do I?'

The Shadow's seemingly impenetrable composure faltered, if but for a moment.

'Say that again,' he said softly.

'What?' Nathaniel replied.

'About the man who wields shadows!' the Shadow's voice did not rise, yet it seemed to carry more force all of the sudden, crushing Nathaniel against his seat.

Nathaniel swallowed. 'It's as I said... he held shadows in his hands... he hurt Illu -- the woman I was with.'

The Shadow leaned forward, folding his hands together, 'what did he look like?'

'He... he had a pointy beard, dark robes,' Nathaniel recalled. 'They were red at the bottom.'

The Shadow calmly leaned back into his poised position, as if he'd never left it in the first place.

'Crow,' he said.

'Crow?' Nathaniel frowned.

'This man you speak of, Nathaniel. His name is Crow,' the Shadow replied, 'a dangerous man by all accounts... and of great interest to me too.'

'Why would a man like *that* interest you? Who exactly are you?'

'Why do you think you interest me, Nathaniel?' the Shadow smiled wryly.

'What do you mean by that?' Nathaniel blinked at the question.

The carriage door swung open abruptly and light flooded the inside.

Before Nathaniel could begin to ask where they had arrived he was dragged out of the carriage, the hood swiftly restored over his head.

'Where are 'ou 'aking me?' Nathaniel growled.

'This is for your own good, Regal,' the man said.

Nathaniel was stopped dead in his tracks, as what felt like rope was being tied around his waist, binding his arms to his sides.

''Et me 'o!' Nathaniel demanded.

'As you wish, Regal.'

The ground beneath Nathaniel vanished after he was shoved forwards, the roar of the air drowning out his cries as he fell.

There was a snap, like a whip against stone, that shook every bone in his body, and then he was still.

Nathaniel fought against the urge to be sick as he swung helplessly to-and-fro.

Gods… Am I… dead?

Shouts seemingly coming from all directions appeared to suggest otherwise.

''Elp!' Nathaniel cried, squirming where he hung.

Something cut cleanly through the rope, bringing Nathaniel crashing painfully into solid ground.

'Who's this guy?' a voice muttered amidst Nathaniel's groans.

'Fancy pants ain't from these parts, that's for sure,' another guffawed.

'Wait... I've seen the likes of these before,' heavy handed fingers probed the material of his tunic. 'Spitting hell,' the first voice breathed, 'it's a blasted Regal!'

'Fael?'

'It can't be. He must be halfway back to the Black Mountains already.'

'What about Old Fire-Fyes' woman?'

'You bonehead!' a third chipped in. 'You never seen a woman before? Why don't we remove this first, eh?'

The hood was jerked off Nathaniel's head in one head scalping tug, bringing him face-to-face with a boy kneeling before him. The boy looked around his age, with curly brown locks tickling the top of his brow. He had a sharp jaw, well pronounced by high cheekbones and gaunt cheeks. Though, the boy was built like an ox, with broad shoulders framing a shirtless, soot covered torso. The two other boys standing either side of him, thickset arms crossed like thugs, looked even larger and stared down at their quarry with something akin to grimaces.

The boy in front of him frowned.

'You're not Fael,' he said.

'Sorry to disappoint,' the words slipped from Nathaniel's lips quicker than he could catch them.

The boy snatched a handful of his tunic, dragging Nathaniel up close. 'Who in the blazes are *you* then?' lips baring as he snarled to reveal a set of unusually large incisors poking out underneath. Abnormally so, in fact.

Nathaniel took a sizeable intake of breath as soon as the realisation struck him.

Lycans. Three of them.

Nathaniel felt his hand twitch beside his belt and had to remind himself once again of the fact he was completely unarmed.

Athrana's grace, what are they going to do with me?

One of the boys either side suggested throwing Nathaniel 'out the mines.'

He was in the mines?

'You blazing stone-head, don't be stupid!' the boy who had a hold of him growled back, pushing Nathaniel roughly to the ground. 'We're taking him back to Sanctuary, come on.'

The two thuggish-looking boys exchanged a dim look with each other.

'Now!' the third boy commanded, chucking the hood carelessly behind him, 'and cover his damn eyes!'

Chapter 11

Half-carried, half-dragged, Nathaniel was ushered uphill, tripping regularly on the haphazardly uneven surface of the mine. The air was so stale that Nathaniel found himself almost suffocating underneath the hood.

''Ere are 'ou 'aking me,' Nathaniel spoke, attempting to sound braver than he felt under the circumstances.

'Quit your whining, Regal,' the boy in charge said.

'What are 'ou going to do 'ith me?' Nathaniel said.

The boy gave a sinister chuckle in reply.

Nathaniel felt his stomach drop.

On some turns, new voices greeted them, and others expressed curiosity toward the Lycans' prisoner.

'Off to eat poor Fael, again?' someone chuckled.

Athrana's grace… please, please, please, don't let these beasts eat me! Nathaniel thought desperately.

'Not today,' came the response. 'We've got a *special* guest for 'ol fire-eyes.'

''et me 'o!' Nathaniel cried out.

'Would you keep it down!' the boy growled at him.

'Hope you've got a good reason for the hood, Brother, I doubt fire-eyes will see the funny side of this a third time.'

'Oh, believe me, he'll see my side, this time.'

Soon after, the ground began to even out. Their steps echoing as they traipsed along.

'Almost there, grey-skin,' the boy said, all too eagerly.

Aespora toray… where were these animals dragging him? And who in the name of Ozin was this Old Fire-Eyes character?

Their footsteps came to a halt. A brief pause, swiftly followed with a sharp rap of knuckles on wood.

Silence.

A chair was pushed back in the other room.

'The door is open,' someone called from the other side.

The two boys hoisted Nathaniel off his feet once more past the threshold before lumping him back down, only to be pulled ahead by a third set of hands.

'Sorry to disturb you, Brother,' the boy began.

'Is this how we treat our guests now, Gabriel?' the voice was stern and yet exasperated. 'Don't you think Fael has been frightened out of his wits with your pranks one time too many?'

Nathaniel felt the boy's hand dig uncomfortably into his shoulder.

'Sorry, Brother, but *this one* isn't Fael.'

'I beg your pardon?'

'He isn't Fael,' the boy repeated. 'We have an intruder.'

Another unceremonious tug of the hood and Nathaniel was left blinking rapidly at the sudden change in light.

A moment of silence elapsed, broken by a soft chuckle.

'This is no intruder, Gabriel,' said the stern voice. It seemed to be coming from the blur in front of him, slowly sharpening into focus.

85

The man's mid-length ginger hair – despite his own obvious attempts to tame it with wax – flew wildly back over his head. His nose looked like it had been broken a long time ago and hadn't quite reset, and he had a darkly intense pair of grey eyes, each rimmed with a line of amber. They appeared to flicker and flare, like flames, the longer Nathaniel stared into them.

This must have been the man the Lycans referred to as 'Old Fire-Eyes.'

'Nathaniel, I presume?'

He nodded hesitantly.

'You know him, Brother?' Gabriel said, his hand loosening on the Regal's shoulder.

'*Of* him. Gabriel, oh yes,' the man said. 'In much the same way he knows *of* me.

'This is Nathaniel Grey. My grandson.'

Nathaniel's jaw dropped and Gabriel's hand slipped off Nathaniel's shoulder entirely.

'I didn't know, Brother.'

'Well I must confess I wasn't expecting him quite so early,' the man raised an eyebrow inquisitively at Nathaniel. 'You may leave us Gabriel, I'm sure you're all tired from working the mines.'

Gabriel nodded his thanks, parting, Nathaniel noticed, with a scowl. The two boys beside him gave Nathaniel curious looks, shrugged and followed suit, leaving the Regal alone with the grey-eyed man.

Unlike the Lycans who had escorted him, the man before him was well dressed, wearing a clear white shirt underneath a tweed waistcoat that matched his eyes. Like the Lycans however, his feet were bare underneath his trousers.

'My apologies,' the man said. 'Gabriel can be a bit brusque at the best of times, but the boy means well. But I anticipate you have questions?'

'You said I was your grandson,' Nathaniel stuttered, staring at the old Lycan.

'Yes, I believe I did.'

'But my grandparents are dead.'

'Not for a long time I'd hope.'

'You're a Lycan.'

'I'm beginning to think that your father left out a lot of the key details.'

'This is a lot to take in.'

'Then perhaps you should have a seat.'

The man held out a hand towards the cosy looking armchair off to his side, which sat facing the lit fireplace.

'Please,' the man said.

Nathaniel looked at the armchair suspiciously. It all seemed too comfortable here. He wondered how long it would be until he was back in a cell pleading his innocence.

'It won't bite,' the man added, with a wry smile.

Nathaniel shot him a dark look and approached the chair tentatively. After thoroughly inspecting the cushions, he

87

slowly lowered himself into the seat and let out a soft groan. It took a great deal of restraint to not just doze off then and there.

He had so many questions to ask.

The man pulled up a wooden chair beside him. Only the patches of silver hair amongst the red above his ears belied the Lycan's apparent youth.

'I am Thorne Grey,' the man introduced himself.

My Grandfather is a Lycan, Nathaniel thought with a shiver, *I'm related to Lycans.*

'So, I understand you've had quite the interesting few days?' Thorne said.

Nathaniel shot him a sour look.

'I wouldn't call them *interesting*,' Nathaniel replied bitterly.

'Hm, perhaps not, although I must ask–' Thorne showed a moment of hesitation, '–how is your grandmother?'

'My grandmother?' Nathaniel frowned, 'my grandmother is–'

'–very much alive' Thorne interrupted, 'I'd hope so anyway. She was the one who rescued you from your cell I'd wager. A woman by the name of Illumina?'

Nathaniel shifted uncomfortably in his chair. The memory of the woman's body being swatted away like a fly by shadows was difficult to forget.

And you just left her there.

Nathaniel told Thorne everything. How he'd been rescued from his cell after the Szar's betrayal, how they'd come to meet the man in the red-trimmed robes – a man who could wield shadows.

Thorne urged Nathaniel on with his story but scratched against his stubble even more vigorously after he'd learned of Illumina's fate.

'She's tougher than anyone realises,' Thorne insisted. Though he did look rather concerned.

He then told Thorne of his arrival at the Spire, his encounter with the large, bald Hunter with the massive sword, and the meeting with a man who called himself The Shadow. Thorne went rigid in his chair. The amber in his eyes flickered dangerously.

'That's impossible,' he murmured. Whether it was to either himself or in reply was unclear.

Nathaniel could not help but fidget with his hands. Trying as best as he could to avoid wallowing in the silence that had crept upon them. Thorne's eyes appeared glazed, staring off into some great unseen distance, lips moving, as if trying to piece together a word.

'Thorne? What am I going to do?' Nathaniel said. 'Athrana's grace, I shouldn't even be here!' he looked down at his soiled wedding garb in dismay. 'And mixing with bloody Lycans at that! But the Szar wants me dead and I– Gods! You probably don't even believe me.'

Thorne rose abruptly from his chair and placed his hands atop the fireplace sill, bending his neck down toward the flames. Next to his eyes, the fire seemed almost cold.

'I believe you,' Thorne spoke finally. 'But I'm afraid there is precious little else you can do. In fact, as inconvenient as you may find Dalmarra, you could not be anywhere safer–'

'–I couldn't be anywhere safer?' Nathaniel said in disbelief, 'I was made a prisoner in my home! And now I'm supposed to believe I'll be safer here? With *Lycans*?'

Thorne chuckled.

'I admit it could be slightly out of your comfort zone, Nathaniel, but–'

'–slightly?' Nathaniel rose from his chair. 'Are you mad? Look at me!'

'How you look is inconsequential,' Thorne said.

'I'm not staying,' Nathaniel insisted. 'I can't!'

'Then what else will you do, hm? Go back and seek vengeance against the Szar, with the full might of the Regal Armada at his beck and call? No? Then perhaps you'd prefer to seek your fortunes elsewhere? But with what coin, I'd ask?'

There was a sizeable purse of silvers Nathaniel knew he'd left back in his room in Obsidia. He did not have to have to pat down his tunic however, to know how little he had on him.

'I'll... I'll find something,' Nathaniel said determinedly, as he strode to the door.

'Perhaps... I've heard the Old Grit is in dire need of mop-boys,' Thorne remarked mildly. 'But to what end? I imagine you'd survive, for now, but do you honestly believe that the Szar would not come looking for you eventually? What then?'

'Then I'll go elsewhere! Far away! He'll never find me!'

'Unless you plan to board an expedition across the Southern Seas, I doubt that,' Thorne countered, 'and I think you and I both know that's not a life for you.'

'You don't know me!' Nathaniel snapped. 'I didn't ask to be here!'

'No, you didn't. But if you stay, you'll have somewhere safe for now. A place for you to gather your thoughts and prepare your next move perhaps?'

'Did you not just see the look I got from that other Lycan?' Nathanial pointed at the door. 'They'd kill me the first chance they get!'

'Gabriel is many things, but a murderer, he is not,' Thorne laughed. 'He is simply suspicious of your intentions.'

'Then what exactly is this place?' Nathaniel said, 'I'm supposed to believe you're just miners? I'm sure it must go down a treat with the humans.'

'There are no humans in this mine, just Lycans,' Thorne said. 'And it's so much more than just a mine.'

'Is that so?' Nathaniel narrowed his eyes.

'I'll tell you what, Nathaniel. I'll make a deal with you: you can leave whenever you want but, if you choose to stay, I will do everything in my power to help you clear your name.'

'And how would you go about that?'

'For that, I will need time but the offer stands.'

Nathaniel supposed there was some truth in Thorne's words... but still, to trust a Lycan – even if it was his Grandfather – was a dangerous gamble in itself.

'I'm... not sure.'

'Give it a day, at least,' Thorne said.

A day with Lycans... How did I get in this mess? Nathaniel thought.

'I suppose I could,' Nathaniel agreed grudgingly.

'Thank you,' Thorne said. 'Brother Marcus should be outside already to show you around. I think Sanctuary may surprise you.'

Nathaniel turned as he grasped the door's handle.

'A day,' he said.

'That's all I ask,' Thorne replied.

*

The moment the door had closed behind the Regal, Thorne turned back to the table behind him.

'Hear all that, Vigil?' Thorne spoke into the room.

A rod, concealed under a pile of paper, flashed green.

'I was present,' Vigil's voice entered his mind.

'The Shadow... alive?' Thorne shook his head in disbelief, 'surely it can't be.'

'A pretender then, perhaps?' Vigil suggested, *'the Shadow's connections and resources are a considerable temptation. Maybe one of his followers has taken up the mantle.'*

'Perhaps,' Thorne mulled the thought over. It brought him no more ease. 'But why now? The timing of it is rather peculiar.'

'Indeed,' the rod hummed green in agreement, *'the Regal Emperor murdered and a man who can bend shadows to his will?'*

'You don't think that–'

'–I think you know exactly what that means, Thorne.'

Thorne looked back at the table.

'It may soon be time to come out of hiding, old friend,' Thorne said.

The rod fell silent with that remark.

Thorne sighed and dropped heavily into his chair, his body suddenly weary.

'Precarious times,' Thorne murmured.

The small pot-full of petals he kept on the table was calling to him.

'Not now,' Thorne thought, 'not now.'

He closed his eyes but there she was watching him. Every feature so defined, so tangible he could almost touch her.

'Thorne,' she called to him.

Chapter 12

'Brother Marcus' was already outside waiting for Nathaniel, as he stepped out of his Grandfather's office.

Grandfather...

It felt so strange to say, regardless of what he was. His Grandfather was alive, his grandparents were alive.

'Nathaniel, I presume?' the man greeted him.

With his easy smile and wavy brown hair caressing his forehead, Brother Marcus seemed a kindly man. Enough so that he almost made Nathaniel forget where he was.

'Brother Marcus?' Nathaniel inquired, wondering if he looked half as tense as he felt.

'That would be me,' Marcus smiled and motioned for Nathaniel to follow him. 'Welcome to Sanctuary.'

'Why is it named so?' Nathaniel frowned.

They took a right turn, into one of the narrow corridors. It all appeared to have been carved out of bedrock, with the walls and ceiling looking as jagged as the floor had felt down in the mines.

'Well... I'm sure you've had your suspicions,' Marcus replied.

'So, it's a hideout... for Lycans?' Nathaniel enquired.

'Not so much a hideout, as a safe space for us to grow and learn.'

'Learn? Learn what?'

Marcus pointed out the archways as they went along, three abreast, all leading into a room filled with desks and stools.

94

'A classroom?' Nathaniel said.

'You didn't think we spent *all* our time fighting each other to the death in mud-pits, did you?' Marcus chuckled.

'So, it's a school?' Nathaniel blushed, eager to move the conversation elsewhere.

'Of a sort, yes,' Marcus said.

More classrooms were dotted about Sanctuary. However, the most interesting of all lay down one long, dark corridor.

A set of double oak doors, with vines inscribed upon their frames – curiously like those found on the Obsidian Throne, Nathaniel noted – blocked their path.

'What's this?' Nathaniel inquired.

'Something I hope will convince you to stay,' Marcus smiled wryly, before pushing open the doors.

The room was like nothing else in Sanctuary.

The slate floor ended here, to be replaced by a soft, red carpet spanning the entire space. The room was roughly circular in shape, with four tiers of bookcases. Each tier connected by spiral staircases, and slatted walkways with rich mahogany bannisters ascending up to the chandeliers. It seemed it would have better belonged in the Emperor's palace.

Only the Lycans, bare footed, as they perused the thousands of leatherbacks at their disposal, reminded Nathaniel of where he was.

'This library,' Nathaniel whispered, 'its… incredible.'

'Our late leader, MakVarn, built this,' Marcus said proudly. 'Thorne took it upon himself to expand upon his work and– what are you doing?'

Marcus whipped out an arm just as Nathaniel attempted to cross the threshold.

'But–' Nathaniel frowned.

'You are more than welcome to spend your time here,' Marcus said. 'As soon as you have showered… and changed,' the Lycan looked pointedly at Nathaniel's dirty tunic.

*

Managing to prise Nathaniel away from the library, Brother Marcus led the Regal back the way they came to Thorne's office.

Three corridors branched off here. The one they took, led to a room almost as large as the library, which housed what must have been a couple of hundred wooden bunkbeds. However, unlike regular bunkbeds – two beds, stacked vertically – these towering structures went up to six layers, with ladders that zigzagged their way up each structure. *Pity the Lycan that's prone to sleepwalking*, Nathaniel thought.

Personal belongings – a few books, a couple lyres lying in the low-hanging hammocks, and wooden boards for dice or chess – were scattered about, hanging from hooks or draped over the edges of beds and ladder rungs.

A number of Lycans were huddled together in the middle of the room, tossing a ball in the air to each other.

'I'm afraid the bunk-beds have been taken,' Marcus told a perplexed Nathaniel. 'But I think you'll find the hammocks just as comfortable once you get the lay of them.'

Nathaniel squinted into the gloom. In the far corner of the room, ragged-looking hammocks were hanging, three in a row, off poles that looked like they could nearly support the weight of the material. Nathaniel looked on in horror.

'That's where I'm sleeping?'

'Oh yes,' Marcus replied. 'We have a few other dormitories dotted about, but this is where most of the older children stay.'

He instantly thought of Gabe and shuddered. Nathaniel hoped the Lycan boy and his cronies wouldn't be there. Brother Marcus secured a pile of clothes – but no footwear – and a towel for Nathaniel from the washroom.

Opposite the dormitory, was the food hall. A room even larger than the dormitory with a cavernous ceiling, housing a number of bench-tables spanning the length of the hall. Plates and bowls were dotted about the tables, stacked in piles, cutlery poking out over the ceramic edge.

'Well I believe this is where we part ways,' Marcus said, stopping outside the archway that marked the end of the corridor. 'This is for you,' Marcus handed Nathaniel a folded piece of paper, 'and the washrooms are behind you.'

Nathaniel thought he saw Brother Marcus wink before he departed.

This is all so strange.

With a frown, Nathaniel peeled open the paper. It looked like Brother Marcus had given him a timetable of sorts.

Monday.

Mines 10:00 – 11:30

A History of Horizon 2:00 – 3:00

Weapons Wielding 4:00 – 5:00

Literature and Herbalism classes was also dotted about the timetable on Wednesday through till Friday. However, at a glance, Nathaniel determined that the general structure of the days remained much the same.

'I didn't say I was staying!' Nathaniel called after Marcus but the Lycan had already disappeared.

There was just the one washroom, which lay beyond another archway. It was a large rectangular room with white-tiles, some ridged with moss at the fringes, covering the floor. Shower taps were housed atop the wood panelling, which separated the room almost cleanly in half.

Worst of all, however – the room was still in use.

A girl, with her back turned, folded a towel around her body, humming a tune that sounded distinctly similar to *A Fine Maid's Awaiting*.

No wonder Brother Marcus had left with a wink.

That bloody fool dumped me in the girls' shower room!

Half-expecting to see a gaggle of Lycans outside the showers, giggling at his plight, Nathaniel caught himself in between leaving the room and issuing an awkward cough.

Threading her hands through her damp, auburn hair, she turned. Bright green eyes, playfully curious, flickered over him.

Her lips were full, her cheeks plump, but didn't lack definition. However, her smile was something truly to behold. Like her eyes, it seemed to toy with you, yet Nathaniel could not decide if the crookedness of her white teeth made her prettier.

Why does it matter? You are promised to another! Nathaniel reminded himself furiously. He must have made some strange utterance, for the girl chuckled lightly.

'Lose something, Regal?' she remarked with a raised eyebrow.

'What? No!' Nathaniel snapped out of his delirium, blustering heavily, as he strained to find anywhere else to rest his eyes, other than on her. 'Athrana's grace! I wasn't– I mean– I was just–'

'Sneaking a look?'

'Gah! Gods alive! No! I just – I've come to the wrong shower room.' He could already feel heat spreading across his face like wildfire.

'Not at all, this is the only one,' she said, before he could dash away.

The only one? Nathaniel frowned. Had he heard that right?

As the girl closed the distance between them, Nathaniel became aware that his legs weren't responding the way they should.

'I suppose you're Nathaniel then?' The girl said. 'Gabe wouldn't shut up earlier about the "pretty boy grey-skin".'

She was so close now he could see the dozens of freckles, spotted over the bridge of her nose and the tops of her cheeks.

'I suppose I am,' Nathaniel replied stiffly, conscious of the fact that he was already pressed as far against the wall as possible. 'And you are?'

'You can call me Brey, Regal,' she said, raising an eyebrow, as he edged away from her. 'Never seen a girl before?' she added slyly.

Would she prefer if I stared? Nathaniel thought incredulously, wondering what he'd done exactly to earn this treatment.

He muttered a strangled 'thanks' and strode past Brey into the shower room.

Although he couldn't be sure, Nathaniel thought he saw the girl grinning out of the corner of his eye, just before he ducked behind the wood panelling. Thankfully, no one else had been there to witness his blunder. Waiting until long after the girl's footsteps had faded away entirely, he lobbed his towel over the wooden separator and began to unclothe with shaking hands.

The men and women shower together? He shook his head. No. The girl had to be playing some trick on him. Or maybe it was that other Lycan, Gabe's bright idea.

Tentatively, he examined one of the levers that jutted out from the damp, ridged wood panelling, which made up the floor. Satisfied that it hadn't been somehow rigged against him, he gave the lever several tugs and then placed a hand under the tap that ran above him, feeling his whole body contort.

The water was even colder than he had been warned but he suspected that the Lycans were far more used to it than he. With a reluctant grimace, Nathaniel gritted his teeth and immersed himself underneath, biting down on his tongue to fight back the cry that rose against his throat. As the cold shock began to wear off, he slowly rose his rigid arms to wash

100

himself, pushing aside the strangely erratic thoughts about the girl running amok in his mind.

But she was attractive, a sly voice purred in his head, *sneaked quite the peek didn't you–*

'No!' Nathaniel hissed to himself, 'I am promised to another.'

Promised indeed. I'm sure she'll be waiting with open arms – provided she doesn't mind the smell of these Lycans – oh! Or the minor fact that you murdered their Emperor.

'I am no Kinslayer,' Nathaniel whispered, sinking into a crouch. 'I am no Kinslayer.'

Chapter 13

Nathaniel had slept terribly.

No amount of preparation could have readied him for what it would be like to share a room, large as it may have been, with dozens of others. Dozens of Lycans.

Not to mention the fact that the girl, Brey, had been more difficult to shake from Nathaniel's mind than he'd have liked.

They shower together… they sleep in the same room like dogs huddled together in an alleyway…

Though, the fact that the girl's half of the dormitory was walled off had brought some measure of relief. However, a thousand different thoughts pulled him to-and-fro as he left the dormitory, exiting into the corridor outside. *You should have said this, you should have done that… Why are you even thinking about this…? You shouldn't have gone there at all.* The last thought spoke over the others. It seemed to carry his father's voice, in all its weariness.

Damn him! Nathaniel thought, *he left me to die! He backed the Szar over his own flesh and blood! But damn him, wh–*

Mid-thought, Nathaniel collided headfirst with a tower of books, which sent him sprawling against the floor, books showering all around.

'Sorry,' a deep voice spoke. 'I didn't see you there.'

Nathaniel looked up from his seat on the floor and gave a start.

A Scorched boy, about his age Nathaniel thought, and almost as tall as the Samaii Chief he'd met back at the Emperor's Palace, towered over him. He had a handsome, wide-jawed faced, with dark, hooded eyes. Unlike the Samaii Chief, however, the boy's thick mass of braids were tied together with a knot behind his back. One arm was outstretched towards Nathaniel, whilst the other balanced what remained of the books that hadn't been knocked from his hands.

'I know you, Regal, your name is–' the boy scrunched up his face, '–Nathaniel?'

'Uh, yeah,' Nathaniel grasped the boy's hand and allowed himself to be pulled up. The boy didn't seem to register the weight at all. 'Does anyone not know me here?'

The boy blushed.

'I may have heard a few others speak of you,' he admitted. 'Gabriel keeps talking of how he wants to–'

A hand slapped against the Scorched boy's back before he could complete his sentence. A couple more books toppled from his grasp.

The Lycan that had dragged Nathaniel to Thorne's office the day before, Gabe, had appeared from round the corridor. The same two thuggish Lycans flexed their arms behind him menacingly.

'Alright, Sammy?' Gabe grinned.

'Samir,' the Scorched boy corrected him, straining to keep hold of the remaining books.

'So, you're still here then, Regal?' Gabe glowered at Nathaniel.

'For now,' Nathaniel said, returning the dirty look the Lycan had sent his way. 'At least until the wet dog smell puts me off.'

'What's that, grey-skin?' Gabe growled, taking a step closer.

103

Sat on his haunches, Samir looked torn between picking up the rest of his books and watching the development in front of him.

'Uhhh,' Samir began tentatively. 'Maybe we can just forget about this and go to class—'

The boy's words fell on deaf ears.

'You heard what I said, *dog*,' Nathaniel retorted.

Gabe's mouth wrapped itself into a snarl, the Lycan raising himself to his full height, which still fell just short of Nathaniel's.

A few Lycans, attracted by the commotion, had begun to gather around them expectantly.

'Not this again,' a voice rang tiredly across the length of corridor.

The crowd parted instantaneously as two girls stepped through. The first was quietly pretty. Though with her stiff upper lip; cropped dark hair, falling neatly either side of her chin; and her stoic pose, she had done her level best to suppress any aspect that was likely to appeal to the fancies of another. Considering, brown eyes were set upon a narrow face, too pale to be anything but Féynian. Nathaniel had the impression that the girl's eyes were judging all that fell under her gaze.

The second girl Nathaniel recognised immediately. Brey's knowing smile made him feel uneasy, as if it had been he in the shower the day before and her the spy.

But I wasn't spying! Nathaniel thought.

Annoyingly, whatever way his thoughts made his face turn seemed to amuse the girl all the more.

They stopped next to Samir.

The Féynian girl, arched her brows at Nathaniel and shook her head disapprovingly at Gabe.

'Boys,' Nathaniel thought he heard after the soft *tsk* she made under her breath.

'Yes boys, do leave *some* of the action for us in the practice room,' Brey smirked beside her. 'Hey, Samir,' she smiled sweetly at the Scorched boy, who muttered a quick 'hello' before hiding amongst the books.

Brey had her hair in two separate braids, which fell over the front of her shoulders. One of which she twirled in her hands, a playful smile touching her lips, as her green eyes crossed Nathaniel's grey.

The towel – although still disturbingly fresh in Nathaniel's memory – had been replaced by a black chemise, which both the girls wore. The garb was divided in two, like riding skirts, and tied at the waist with a cord that fed into the material itself. Brey's one however, sat closer to her thighs than Kaira's.

Stare at your feet if you can't control your eyes, fool!

Gabe had looked as if he were about to hit him but withdrew his hand, as quickly as if it were his own mother scolding him. The Lycan also appeared suddenly concerned with how he stood.

'Kaira,' Gabe said, puffing up his chest. 'Brey,' he added with a curt nod to the green-eyed girl.

105

'Awhhh, Gabriellll!' Brey puckered her lips with feigned sadness. 'Still sore about that little spar we had?'

Going a shade of crimson Nathaniel thought highly funny, Gabe ignored Brey and kept his attention focused squarely on the girl beside her. 'Got Weapons Wielding today?' he inquired.

'I might,' Kaira replied impassively, her eyes betraying not even the slightest hint of anything. 'Why?'

There was a saying about Féynians that had reached even the highest peaks of Obsidia – *loose with their money, but with their words they tiptoed across a razor's edge, as slim as a whisker.*

'Oh... no reason,' Gabe said innocently as he scratched at the muscle of his tensed arm. 'Just thought you wouldn't want to miss the action.'

'And what made you think that?' Kaira replied.

'Well...'

Gabe not so subtly tensed his other arm, encouraging a derisive snort from Brey. Kaira's lips, on the other hand, didn't budge an inch.

'Is that it?'

'You keep me waiting, Kaira – someone else will have to fall into my arms.'

'I'm willing to take that risk.'

'You know where to find me when you change your mind, Kaira,' Gabe said. 'See you in the practice room, *Regal,*' Gabe growled quietly to Nathaniel. His shoulder smacked into

Nathaniel so hard that he almost found himself back on the floor with Samir's books.

'Aespora toray,' Nathaniel cursed him as he passed.

'I wouldn't waste your worry on him, Regal,' Kaira spoke loudly. 'He's all bluff and bluster half the time, I wonder how anyone can stand to listen to him.'

Nathaniel doubted the Lycan would simply let the matter go.

Just one day, Nathaniel thought to reassure himself. He could survive in the viper's nest for that long. Athrana knows what compelled him to stay for even that amount of time.

Reluctantly, he followed the Lycans to the three-arched classroom he'd passed with Brother Marcus the day before. The Scorched boy known as Samir walked beside him, somehow managing to cradle all the books in his arms, whilst burying his nose between an open page.

Nathaniel thought some of the looks he'd received from Gabe and the other Lycans had been unpleasant enough. However, by the time the hour had passed, he realised they didn't come close to Skew's murderous stare.

Skew was awfully thin and lanky, compared to his more physically imposing brethren. With black, beady eyes, almost as hollow as his sunken cheeks, which were grizzled with stubble. Long, bedraggled grey locks curtained his face, which seemed to be permanently affixed with a frown, as if the top of his lips had been smeared with dung.

When Nathaniel had dared ask if Skew had a book he could borrow for the lesson, the Lycan's nose travelled so far up his face it was wonder how it didn't just fly off.

Most disturbing of all however, was how Skew would grasp the stump of his severed right hand so tightly whenever he caught sight of the Regal.

As if it were my fault, Nathaniel thought.

Indeed, if there were any doubt that the Lycan didn't like him, Skew quickly dispelled it at the first available opportunity.

'The Regals first made landfall in the Scorched Isles almost nine hundred years ago but proceeded to lose half their ships to the Isles rocky shores,' Skew said. He placed a particular emphasis on *'Regals'* as he spoke.

Gabe and his friends seemed to be acutely aware of this and had to stifle their laughter between their hands.

Athrana's grace, Nathaniel thought. *Is this entire lesson going to be aimed against me?*

'Regal!' Skew turned on Nathaniel suddenly, snapping the book he was holding against the table. 'How many of the Scorched were slaughtered by the Regal Armada in the Desert of Amran?'

Putting aside the fact he couldn't quite recall what his tutor had told him about the Slaughter of Amran, did Skew really expect Nathaniel to know *exactly* how many had died?

'Extract your nose from the book, boy!' Skew cried. 'I asked you a question!'

Nathaniel could feel the Scorched boy's eyes upon him.

'I don't know,' Nathaniel said quietly.

'I'm sorry, Regal?' Skew said.

'I said, I don't know,' Nathaniel repeated himself.

'Fifteen hundred, Regal. Fifteen. Hundred. Including women and children,' Skew rapped the open page of the book with his remaining hand.

Nathaniel was silent.

Skew took it as a challenge.

'Maybe we'll have better luck this time, eh?'

Skew mercilessly flicked through the pages of the book, ripping some of the pages in the process. 'Hmm… let's see… ah yes. How many Scorched men and women did the Regals bring back to Obsidia in chains?'

And how many slaves were bought and sold by the Free Cities, Lycan?

It was not that Nathaniel hadn't been taught about the atrocities his kind had committed in the past. Tolken had certainly made sure it was included in Regal education during his rule, but to be ridiculed for it now, for something which had occurred long before even his father had been bor–

'I said no looking at the book, Regal!'

'I don't know,' Nathaniel said through gritted teeth.

Skew's lip curled.

'Pity,' Skew sneered. 'How quick we are to forget our sins, aren't we, Grey?'

Whispers brewed in the room.

Those who hadn't already had their fill of Nathaniel rose from their seats to get a better look.

'Grey?'

'Like, Thorne Grey?'

'That's Old Fire-Eyes' grandson?'

'I did tell you.'

Nathaniel paid no heed, he was concentrating hard on biting back a retort as he stared into the endless pits of Skew's eyes. Nine hundred years hardly seemed 'quick,' even by Regal standards.

The rest of the lesson was much of the same, no matter how little attention anyone else paid. Although Skew did seem to tire of his efforts towards the end, grudgingly titling him 'Grey' or 'boy' instead of the usual – '*Regal.*'

Nathaniel was the first to rise from his seat the moment the lesson concluded.

Samir had turned to face him, thumbing his lips thoughtfully.

'Rega– Nathaniel–'

Nathaniel didn't stick around long enough hear what the Scorched boy was about to say. All he could think about was escaping the classroom, before Skew could trap him within another of his unfair questions. Although, that didn't stop Nathaniel from feeling slightly guilty for ignoring Samir.

Ozin's Throne! Why do you care? He may be Scorched but he's still a damned Lycan like the rest of them!

Frustratingly, the guilt refused to dissipate.

Nathaniel shook his head and focused his attention on the passageway before him. He had an hour to spend. Most of the Lycans would return to the dormitory, so he quickly ruled that out as an option.

110

He supposed he could just try and find a way out but how far would he get through the mines? How long before he attracted suspicion?

No, he would play Thorne's little game and then he was gone.

But where could he go for the time being?

The idea of wandering past hundreds of Lycans, with all their ogling didn't appeal either – it seemed like there was only one real option.

Chapter 14

The library doors beckoned Nathaniel toward them, whispering grand promises of what lay inside. It was a temptation he simply could not resist and one, now that he was clean, that Brother Marcus couldn't deny him.

He followed a few Lycans inside. A couple gave him a frown as they went the opposite way.

'Another Regal?'

'Wasn't that Fael?'

'I dunno... he wasn't ginger, was he?'

The voices drifted off behind him.

Fortunately, most of the Lycans here were more focused on the books, lying on their laps or on the tables that were set up in rows of three in the middle of the floor. Cushions were dotted about close to the curve of bookcases, which towered over all else.

Either side of where the first bookcases began, two staircases spiralled up to the second floor, and then the third and fourth. The library was even larger than he could have imagined, with more rooms extending off from the other floors.

Still, there were too many Lycans for his comfort. Some of them were beginning to notice him now, elbowing others who still had their heads down and pointing in his direction.

He finally found a space on the fourth floor, an alcove hidden away in between two bookshelves with a couple of chairs and a table in between them. Only one of them was occupied.

'Ahhh, Nathaniel,' the woman beamed underneath her veil. Her smile was her only feature that availed itself to him, other than her nails, polished to a gleam. The maroon dress she wore – simple in design, and yet, beautiful – fell over her feet and, along with the veil, covered almost her entire body. 'I was beginning to think you would never come!'

She placed the book she held gently on the table before her and rose, flicking a long braid of dark hair behind her shoulders. There was something mystifying, and terrifying all the same, about the woman that Nathaniel couldn't quite place his finger on.

'How do you know my – never mind – everyone seems to know my name here,' Nathaniel said irritably. 'Who are you? You don't seem–'

'–to be a Lycan?' she suggested.

Nathaniel laughed nervously. If she wasn't a Lycan, what was she? And what was she doing here, waiting for him?

Waiting for you? Where did you get that idea from?

'You just seem different,' Nathaniel shook the thought away. 'Not in a bad way,' he added hurriedly.

The woman's smile had not faltered once but it was what he could not see that troubled him most.

Like with the Shadow, Nathaniel was certain he would have known if the woman had been staring at him a distance away with his back turned to her. No… it was more than that. Having her looking at him wasn't merely unsettling, it was both glorifying and embarrassing. He felt naked to the core, as if flesh and bone were not a barrier to her hidden gaze. On a whim she could have reached into him and seized his soul, whispering to Nathaniel his sweetest dreams and most solemn secrets.

113

'You seem troubled, Nathaniel,' the woman noted. 'Are you alright?'

'I… Yes…I'm fine,' Nathaniel said.

No, I'm bloody well not! Who are you?

'Well, I best be off, I think Thorne would worry, if he caught sight of me again,' the woman laughed softly.

He probably couldn't stand you looking at him for too long either, Nathaniel mused.

'Wait, you know Thorne?'

The woman paused in between the bookcases.

'Oh yes,' she said. 'Ever since he wore the Sparks and had those *dreadful* pantaloons.'

It was hard to picture Thorne in billowing breeches, he burst out laughing at the thought. The woman chuckled with him.

Hang on…

'Did you say he wore Sparks?' Nathaniel inquired

'Oh yes, didn't you know?' the woman said. 'Thorne used to be a Warlock.'

Nathaniel coughed in surprise.

'Well it was a pleasure meeting you Nathaniel,' she smiled, her maroon dress floating past the corner of the bookcase.

For how long he stood there stunned he could not say for sure. Thorne Grey, his Grandfather, a Warlock and a Lycan? And who had that women been who knew so much about him? Things just kept getting stranger.

He turned away and noticed that the book the woman had been reading sat half-open on the table-top.

'Hey! Uhh, my lady,' that seemed fitting. 'You left your–'

The 'lady' had, of course, long since left the alcove and, by the time he'd rushed back to the balcony overlooking the library's core, he could not spot her amongst the Lycans below.

Nathaniel was on the topmost floor, and it was hardly busy, so he surely would have noticed someone so colourfully dressed making her way down the spiralled steps. He waited for a moment then checked the other alcoves one by one. They too were empty, and he doubted she would have moved to another below.

The book remained when Nathaniel returned. It was a hefty tome, leather-bound with yellow, parchment like pages that crinkled to the touch.

Curious, he turned it aside.

Lifting the Veil – the Beginner's Guide to Majik, it read, *by Arcturius Pax.*

A book on Majik… Actual Majik.

Suddenly, realising the nature of what he was holding, Nathaniel snatched his hand away. As if the book was liable to set him on fire, with a mere touch.

What had that woman been doing with a book on Majik?

An errant thought suddenly struck him as he stumbled back towards the gap in the bookcases – Thorne had been able to wield Majik.

Nathaniel whipped his head back to the book on the table.

If Thorne had been able to use Majik... could his father? Could he?

Tentatively, he returned to the table and sat down slowly in the chair the woman had previously occupied. He'd seen her with the book open, so it couldn't possibly be harmful, yet he still felt reluctant to put his hand upon it.

What's the worst that could happen, it's just a book! Nathaniel tried telling himself. Still, Majik had a sneaky way of surprising you. Even more gently than the book had been handled by its previous owner, Nathaniel turned to the opening page. The first few lines twisted knots in his stomach.

Majik is not for the faint of heart. It is fire and brimstone, rain and storm. It shackles you to its whim as much as it frees your imagination. Know this apprentice: you are NEVER in control, for Majik is a force beyond controlling.

Nathaniel should have dropped the book then and there, and have been done with it, yet he was captivated.

You may only hope to appease Majik, manipulate it to your will but disrespect it, and it will sap your very existence until you are little else than a gibbering husk of flesh.

He flicked on a few pages.

A number of diagrams covered the two pages before him, some bearing strange symbols. One image in particular caught his attention – a rough sketch of a hand, a lone flame writhing between contorted fingers.

Conceiving fire – see page 44, it read underneath.

116

Licking his lips nervously, Nathaniel laid back in his seat and began brushing through the pages at speed.

Chapter 15

Click. Click.

Click. Click.

Click. Click. Nothing.

Nathaniel was disappointed to find that, rather than teaching him how to loose a torrent of flames from his palms, he would have to start small, very small. It was probably for the best, given he was already struggling with the first exercise, and everything around him – on closer inspection – was probably highly inflammable.

Click. Click.

Click. Click.

Click. Click.

No matter how hard he concentrated on clicking his fingers, the spark simply refused to emerge. There must have been something he was missing, something he'd misread or misunderstood from the book. Nathaniel just hoped no one would find where he'd hidden it in the alcove.

The Weapons Wielding room, or the 'blood pit,' as Brother Garrett had jokingly – he hoped – introduced it, was already packed with Lycans, lining the tapestry covered walls. They stood in huddles of four and five, bragging to anyone who'd listen about their past bouts. All, invariably, seemed to involve a great number of broken bones and bloodied noses.

All fell silent when Brother Garrett appeared, or rather, as Nathaniel observed, stumbled in. His eyes had a dazed look to them, as if the Lycan wasn't entirely sure where he was. His shirt, half-untucked, and made of white linen - an interesting choice given the man seemed to attract filth - was admirably clean despite the rest of him.

Yet, his mere presence commanded respect, a different kind of respect to that which had been paid to Skew. As his eyes scanned the room, Lycans sought to meet them rather than avert their gaze. Backs became straighter and chests puffed out, much to Garrett's satisfaction.

'So!' he said, his voice was gruff, almost hoarse, as if the man spent half his time shouting out orders to disobedient soldiers. He staggered to the other end of the room, supporting himself against the tapestry that was draped across it.

'So!' his eyes scoured each individual, pausing momentarily by Nathaniel.

'Fael?' he leaned forward, catching himself on the tapestry before he could tumble over, nearly taking the whole thing down with him.

Too late, Nathaniel noticed that no one else around him found this quite as amusing as he did. Not even Gabe, who gave him a look like he'd just stripped naked and done cartwheels across the floor.

'Something funny, Fael?' Garrett barked at him.

Who in Athrana's grace was this Fael?

Nathaniel shook his head briskly.

'Brother Garrett,' a boy with blonde hair and red cheeks cleared his throat.

'Yes, yes, what, Iden?'

'Fael left. He's Nathaniel Grey,' the boy squeaked.

119

Garrett stared at Nathaniel blankly then the realisation dawned upon his face.

'Another Grey!' he belched.

Nathaniel was unsure whether the man meant thought that was a good or a bad thing. At the very least it was an improvement on Skew.

'I also have a *very* special guest for you all today,' Brother Garrett nodded past his students.

Nathaniel spun around and jumped, several of the Lycans audibly gasping.

The 'guest' clung to the shadows in the corner furthest behind them, black sleeveless overcoat and long raven hair camouflaging him within the darkness. Were it not for his gleaming silver eyes, Nathaniel could have passed the spot a hundred times without noticing the man.

'Is that-'

'Ozin's beard!'

'Did you see his eyes?'

'That's a blazing Hunter!'

'What's he doing here?'

There was something different about seeing a Hunter quietly observing them all, sword draped against his back. Nathaniel hadn't really had the time to properly take in the bald Hunter who had gate-crashed the Spire. Yet here stood another, silver eyes, as sharp and sinister as a cat's, appraising the gaping Lycans coolly.

They hunted demons, yet some claimed they were demons themselves. A strange twist of fate turning them against their former brothers and sisters – Fogspawn of the Foglands. Many a tale there was of the Hunters of Horizon and so very few of them that ended well.

Before he realised it, Nathaniel had become trapped within the Hunter's gaze and quickly peeled himself away with a shudder. It had been as if the Hunter's eyes were a giant magnifying glass, closely inspecting any weakness he could exploit. Even Garrett seemed a little nervous. His eyes snapping regularly back to the Hunter's dark corner, as he paced the room, as if to make sure he was still exactly where the Lycan could see him.

'Since for some of you this will be your first time, we're going to make sure that you all understand how to handle a sword,' Brother Garrett barked at them all.

The Lycan threw out his arm to the baskets leaning against the wall behind him where wooden hilts could be seen jutting out over their brims.

'Well? What are you waiting for lads? A written invitation? Get!'

A great deal of pushing and shoving took place as soon as Brother Garrett had clapped his hands, the Lycans swarming towards the baskets. Nathaniel heard Gabe boast about how he was going to impress the Hunter. Some made similar promises, but most were just downright scared of the man with silver eyes.

Nathaniel gave up trying to push in through the crowd and sat back in wait. The Scorched boy stood beside him, chewing his lip thoughtfully, whilst staring blankly ahead. He'd not spoken to Samir since running out of Skew's History class and he'd actively ignored him since then.

Say something to him!

What could he say? The fact that Samir was a Lycan hardly made matters any easier.

'REGAL!' Garrett made Nathaniel jump.

The Lycan marched towards him, keeping remarkably upright despite his violent swaying. His eyes were set into a squint, as they ran Nathaniel closely up and down, like he was inspecting a sword for notches to re-sharpen. He gave a satisfied grunt at his legs and a 'hm' at his arms.

'Sabre?'

Nathaniel blinked.

'Do you use a sabre, boy?' Garrett growled.

'Uhh, no,' Nathaniel said, 'a rapier.'

The man ran a grubby hand through his beard. It was difficult to tell where the grime started and stopped. His arms looked as if some attempt had been made to cleanse them and then he'd got bored halfway through his forearms. His beard, perhaps hiding another colour underneath, was singed black from coal. The only part of his body that appeared completely untouched by dirt was the top of his bald head.

'I thought it might have been one of the two,' the man nodded absently to himself. Nathaniel almost flinched as he leant in suddenly with a quizzical expression, 'I thought you preferred lances?'

'Our guardsmen do,' Nathaniel said.

122

'Hm, hm,' he grumbled in acknowledgement, 'and why haven't you got a sword? Think you'd do just as well against these lot with your fists?'

'No!' Nathaniel resisted the strong urge to shout back 'sir!' and salute.

'Well that raised nose of yours says something else, lad,' Garrett snorted. 'You'd best guard it well before someone buries it in the dirt.' Garrett went off with a chortle.

Nathaniel still wasn't sure whether the Lycan was joking or not but moved quickly to grab what remained from the baskets, lest the Lycan roared at him again. There were no rapiers to be found, nor any weapon made from steel. There were shortswords, the wooden blade no bigger than his forearm, and a lone longsword, the top of the hilt meeting his hip.

Wooden swords. What were they – children?

Nathaniel picked up the longsword, weighing it in his palm. It would have to do.

'Get into a pair Regal, you're holding us up!' Garrett growled at him.

Gabe and Nathaniel instantly caught eyes and each made to move towards the other. The former, however, was hauled away by Garrett to demonstrate footwork to the class before he could reach Nathaniel, Samir stepping out to block the Regal's path.

'That would be unwise,' Samir's deep voice advised. He hadn't looked up once from the latest book he was immersed in.

'For me? Or him?' Nathaniel pointed at Gabe with his shortsword.

Samir didn't have an answer for that.

'Well... I guess we'd better...' Nathaniel raised his sword, somewhat reluctantly given how tall the Scorched boy was.

Fortunately for Nathaniel, Samir seemed far less interested in their bout than he had been in the book he had previously heldin his hands. Parrying the Regal's blows half-heartedly. When Nathaniel disarmed him, Samir didn't look particularly surprised, if anything, quietly pleased that his hands were rid of the sword.

'You fight well, Nathaniel,' Samir said kindly.

Nathaniel felt another pang of guilt watching Samir stoop for his sword.

After a few more bouts with Samir, with Nathaniel taking it significantly easier on the Scorched boy, Garrett called 'SWITCH!'

The Lycans lowered their wooden swords and shuffled about the room instinctively. Samir found one of Gabe's cronies, who seemed just as apprehensive about the boy's height, as Nathaniel had been, and Nathaniel found Brey.

'Uhhhh,' Nathaniel said.

'Don't tell me you've never fought a girl before?' she raised an eyebrow mockingly.

'No! I mean... I wouldn't! Not that I – uhhh...' Nathaniel said skittishly.

He wasn't just annoyed that the girl's words were entirely true – in his tutored sessions, he'd only ever fought boys, after all, the guards only recruited men. In fact, as far as Nathaniel knew, the only women who took the sword in the Regal Armada were the infamous 'Sisters of the Dagger,' and Emperors' daughters. Not it wasn't just that, which got on his nerves. Brey seemed to be able to twist his tongue in such a way that made even basic speech laborious.

THWACK!

'OW!' Nathaniel rubbed the part of his arm Brey's sword had struck and gave the girl a dirty look.

'Clumsy me,' she smiled innocently.

THWACK!

Nathanial barely had time to knock the second blow away from his other arm.

'Better learn quickly how to hit me, Regal,' Brey said, advancing towards him.

He dodged a few of her efforts but, having to parry the rest, was slowly forcing him back to a wall.

The effort of protecting himself without accidentally harming the girl was proving tremendously difficult. Although, she kept encouraging him to do the opposite.

'SWITCH!'

Nathaniel blew a sigh of relief and lowered his sword.

THWACK!

'GAH!' Nathaniel cried, clutching his right arm. 'He said "switch!"'

'And I told you to try and hit me,' Brey sauntered away, grinning slyly at him over her shoulder.

125

Nathaniel shook both his arms out, trying his best to ignore the throbbing soreness the girl had left him with.

'Regal,' a familiar voice growled.

Gabe held his sword extended toward him.

Now Gabe, he didn't mind hitting.

Nathaniel leaped past Gabe's outstretched arm, the Lycan stumbling back to avoid the thrust of Nathaniel's sword.

They moved back to the middle of the room, before Gabe began to hold his own. His technique was sound, if a little sloppy, but what the Lycan lacked in speed, he more than made up for in the strength of his blows.

The bout seemed to last for ages. One would push the other back, then the other would dodge a blow and gain back the ground they'd lost. Some of the other Lycans had left their own bouts to watch the fight. Even the Hunter had unfurled his arms.

Nathaniel's sword glanced off Gabe's and the two jumped back. Circling one another. Gabe had already thrown off his sweat-drenched shirt and Nathaniel was tempted to follow suit with his own.

The two flew towards each other again, swords striking quickly but neither managing to find a way through the other's defences. Nathaniel wondered whether they were more likely to chip their swords till they snapped.

'So... you can hold... a sword... at least,' Nathaniel said grudgingly, through heavy breaths.

'The sword... isn't... everything... grey-skin,' Gabe's breathing was equally laboured.

'What... would you... know... dog?'

Gabe side-stepped past Nathaniel's tired lunge and threw his fist out.

CRACK!

Nathaniel was suddenly on his back, lights dancing around his eyes, a familiar metallic taste on his tongue.

Someone, he couldn't quite make out who, was squatting down beside him.

'Sorry, Regal. I heard you talking about rapiers with Brother Garrett. You're more predictable than you think.'

Nathaniel tried muttering something coarse in return but it was taking all the effort he had just to keep his eyes open. An eye open. Then... neither.

*

Voices spoke distantly around Nathaniel, fading in and out of hearing. Occasionally he would catch a word or two, '...broken arm... touch of salve... damn Garrett ...'

His body ached but he could just about adjust himself where he lay.

Am I still in the practice room?

Nathaniel tried to open his eyes.

Only one would cooperate and his vision was fuzzy at best. Suddenly alarmed he moved a hand to his head only for it to be gently steered away.

'Ah good, you're awake! No, I wouldn't advise doing that. I've put some salve on that eye of yours and it won't heal as quick with you poking around it! Really, you must stop touching it, child! Can you hear me?'

The sight in his left eye was beginning to clear up.

He was lying down on white linen sheets in a steel framed bed. Most of the other beds were empty around him, bar the one directly opposite Nathaniel, where a blonde boy with rosy cheeks sat nursing his bandaged arm. The boy who had named him to Brother Garrett.

Iden… was it?

'Nathaniel, can you hear me?' a severe looking woman waved her forefinger about in front of him.

Nathaniel nodded.

Sister Mire, she called herself, wore a long white dress with sleeves closely cuffed to her wrists. Her hair, completely greyed, was tied together in a large bun behind her head. No matter how tightly she pursed her lips together as she fussed over Nathaniel, the woman couldn't hide the kindness in her smile-lined eyes.

Nathaniel hated to admit it to himself but this Lycan made him feel oddly at ease.

'I believe I had you down for Herbalism on the Wednesday Nathaniel, although, I must admit, I had hoped I wouldn't see you so soon,' the woman tutted at him.

It wasn't his fault that Gabe had decided to knock him unconscious. The stupid brute.

128

'I understand you received quite the Lycan welcome,' Sister Mire said, dipping her fingers into a silver pot lying on the table beside him. An awful smelling white paste, which reeked of eggs and sour milk, came out of it.

'If you call being punched a welcome,' Nathaniel said bitterly, eyeing the paste on the woman's fingers with a degree of apprehension.

'Now hold still,' the woman cupped Nathaniel's chin in her hands as she angled her pasted fingers towards his black eye.

Nathaniel whimpered softly as the paste was rubbed onto his swollen eyelid. He should have batted the Lycan's hand away but he was rather fearful of what Mire might do, if he acted upon the inclination.

Athrana's grace, it smells terrible!

'Do you remember Samir coming to visit you?' the nurse inquired.

'The Scorched boy?' Nathaniel said.

The woman made a sharp *tsk* through her pursed lips and gave him a look that brought a rush of heat to his cheeks.

'I think he'd prefer, Samir, but yes, the *Scorched boy*,' the woman said. 'He didn't do much else than read but at least he was less of a nuisance than that girl.'

Nathaniel felt his whole face go as red as the boy on the bed in front of him.

'A– a girl?' Nathaniel asked tightly. *Brey?*

'Oh yes, quite a pretty little thing,' the woman said. 'If not a tad infuriating,' Mire added, with a dismayed shake of the head.

129

Definitely Brey.

'She kept trying to poke you awake. I had half a mind to drag her out by her pigtails and give her a reason to stay the night, would it not give me more trouble to deal with.'

Mire snapped her head suddenly, mid tirade, to the arch leading out of the hospital wing and fell silent.

'Well it seems you're very popular, Regal,' she said tightly, 'I could send him away if you're not up to it?'

Him? Gabe? Whoever it was, the woman seemed eager for him to be gone.

'No, that's fine,' Nathaniel eased himself up against the frame of the bed, slowly under the woman's watchful eyes.

She nodded tartly to whoever stood outside.

'I won't be far, if you should have need of me,' she promised, before whisking off to the blonde boy's bedside.

A strong part of Nathaniel hoped it was Gabe, so he could teach the Lycan a lesson. His one working eye and aching muscles, however, protested at the thought.

Nonetheless, the man who walked toward him was certainly no Lycan.

Where Mire's slippers cracked against the Medical Wing's flagstones, his boots made barely a whisper. Not even the man's overcoat rustled, every movement was clean and controlled. A green pendant, which Nathaniel hadn't noticed before, glowed above his chest. Silver eyes, that had seen more blood spilt than Nathaniel hoped to ever see, glistened.

'Greetings Nathaniel,' the Hunter said.

The man had a heart-shaped face lined with dark stubble. He was handsome, perhaps he would have been too pretty were it not for the puckered scar cleaving his face diagonally in two. Raven locks fell in a shower above his bare chest, exposed between the opening of his overcoat, revealing a chilling litany of scars, bruises and burns.

His voice was gentler than Nathaniel expected, though not enough to ease him from the bed frame his back was plastered to. He may have been smaller than the bald Hunter who had rescued him at the Spire but there was little doubt about which of the two frightened him more.

'When Sist–' Nathaniel checked his words, so close he had been to speaking like one of the Lycans. '–Mire, spoke of a visitor, I did not expect to see... you.'

'And few wish to,' the Hunter replied crisply.

Nathaniel wished the Hunter would take the seat beside him, it was awfully uncomfortable having the man leering over him.

'I understand you agreed with Thorne to stay a day, to think things through?' the man said.

And look where that day has got me already.

'That's true,' Nathaniel said, shifting about in his bed. But how much had Thorne told him?

'Have you decided whether you're ready to face your kind?'

Nathaniel grimaced. Apparently, he'd been told everything.

'If I keep running, maybe I won't have to,' Nathaniel said.

'Kusk isn't one to leave loose ends,' the Hunter said.

131

What business is it of yours, Hunter? Nathaniel thought. He would have asked Mire to throw the silver-eyed man out, had he been anyone else but a quietly terrifying demon killer.

Nathaniel looked the man in the eyes, determined not to flinch away. The eyes were definitely the worst part. The Hunter could have been thinking of a dozen dastardly things and Nathaniel wouldn't have had half an idea until a sword had been buried in his chest.

'Why are you here? Did you come all this way just to tell me how doomed I am?'

A strangled gasp left Nathaniel's lips for the dagger, which had suddenly materialised into the Hunter's gloved hand. So quick it had appeared that Nathaniel wasn't quite sure where it had come from.

The Hunter planted it next to the pot of horrible smelling paste on the table beside Nathaniel as casually as if he were slipping a note. It had a wide guard and had clearly been well looked after, although some of the scratches on the blade's surface were beyond the help of any polish.

'I came to offer you something on top of what you've already been promised,' the Hunter's silver eyes bored into his own. Were they challenging him?

Nathaniel's eyes flickered back and forth between the dagger and Sister Mire, who somehow remained completely oblivious of it.

'What's that for?' Nathaniel said hesitantly.

'You fought well against the Lycan but there was truth in what the boy said. He told you there was more to a fight than the sword itself. There's more to it than that – more even than the hands and body that wield it, more than the breath in your chest and the blood pounding in your ears. It's more than a touch, more than a feeling, and even more then. I can help you realise that. Whatever you decide to afterwards, will be entirely on your shoulders but at least you may survive just a little longer.'

'You want... to train me?'

'If you wish to find me, Regal, I'll be in the practice room,' the Hunter announced, straightening his overcoat. 'Keep the dagger. Or at least hide it.'

The Hunter padded away, as silently as he'd entered.

Nathaniel's eye leapt to the dagger he'd left behind. What was he to do?

He snatched the dagger and stowed it underneath his blanket, just as Sister Mire turned, subsequently jumping in total startlement to find Nathaniel's bed bereft of his silver-eyed visitor.

Her eyes darted to the Regal worriedly.

Nathaniel clutched the dagger close to his heart and offered a weak smile.

Chapter 16

Illumina remembered her home well. So, naturally, it alarmed her that she failed to recognise the dark little chamber in which she found herself hanging, like a hunk of salted meat that had been left to dry.

Got to get out.

She wrestled against the chains, biting her tongue as the shackles dug further into the broken skin of her wrists.

No use.

She thrashed about suddenly against her bonds, screaming silently into the ceiling.

At least Nathaniel was in the wind, if the not-so hushed talk between the guardsmen outside her cell was to be believed.

Still, she wished more than a thrashing upon the man with the pointed beard, who had tossed her aside with little more than a glance and a flutter of his fingers. Shadow wielder indeed. He would see how well his shadows protected him from a knife between the ribs, and even worse, if Nathaniel had been harmed...

A latch was lifted on the chamber's door. With a grating noise, as wood scraped on stone, it opened.

Flanked by two Royal Guardsmen in black and gold, Draeden Kusk marched into her chamber. With a few curt words, his personal guard bowed and departed, closing the heavy oak door behind them. Pacing the length of the chamber, Kusk watched her silently, squinting his blue eyes at her, as if trying to gauge the reality of what they saw.

'It's been a long time, Illumina,' he said finally.

'Likewise, little brother,' Illumina replied tersely.

She rattled her shackles.

'Care to release me?'

A ghost of a smile flickered across her brother's face, before it was surreptitiously quashed.

'I see you managed to not only slip into the city undetected, but also free our Emperor's murderer right under our very noses,' Kusk said, pacing the length of the room. Each prolonged step made the room appear larger than it was.

'I suppose I should be glad that you have brought the frailty of our outer defences to my attention.'

'Did the fact that you killed Jael come to your attention also?' Illumina retorted.

'Our little murderer has sought refuge with the Lycans, to make matters worse,' Kusk continued undeterred, his grimace deepening.

'No Royal Guardsmen in here, Draeden, why don't you just admit what you did.'

The Szar turned. His cold, blue eyes boring into hers.

'Whatever I have done, I did it for the good of the Empire,' he said coldly.

The knife withdrawn from his belt looked all the more crueller in his hands. It seemed keen to bite into flesh, still drunk off the aftertaste of blood that had washed its wielder's hands over the years.

'Don't do this, brother,' Illumina pleaded, as Kusk slowly crossed the space between them.

'I do this for the Empire… my sister.'

There was a hint of sadness in Kusk's eyes, betraying the conviction in his voice. 'Make it easier for yourself and tell me where the Lycans hide,' he pleaded with her.

'Draeden… please.'

Kusk's head fell against his chest briefly as he sighed.

'Forgive me, Illumina.'

Illumina's eyes widened as the blade dug greedily into her side, engorging itself on her blood.

A cry came deep from the very depths of her stomach, scratching and grating against the doors of the room. Hairs stood on end, as it reached the guardsmen, and hands lowered to the familiarity of their swords. Calloused fingers tightening against their grips.

Chapter 17

In the deafening silence, Nathaniel's blood pounded an unsteady drumbeat in his ears. He tightened his grip on the dagger in one hand and held the wooden longsword across his body.

Lunging to the left, the wooden sword narrowly striking nothing but air.

Then a dagger cut an arc behind Nathaniel's shoulder.

The blade was left unappeased.

A sharp clicking noise, like metal on stone, penetrated the drumming of his ears.

Nathaniel spun around, sword raised.

A cry of triumph quickly tapered off into a startled 'gah!' as he tripped, then tumbled, onto the practice room's floor.

'Pick up the weapons, Regal,' the Hunter – Zaine – instructed him, for the umpteenth time.

'Was that you?' Nathaniel said, certain he couldn't have 'tripped' again.

'Your hands are still empty,' the Hunter ignored the question.

Muttering in annoyance to himself, Nathaniel patted the ground around him hands grasping the wooden handle first but coming up short of the dagger.

Where has the damn thing gone?

'You get to take that blindfold off when you land a hit on me,' Zaine said.

Nathaniel withdrew his hand with a scowl.

'What is the use is this? I can't even see what I'm fighting.'

Nathaniel jumped as something smacked against his boot.

'Again!' Zaine said sharply.

Nathaniel picked up the dagger carefully and held it out before him. He wasn't sure how much more he could take of this ridiculous fumbling in the dark. He had half a mind to just throw the dagger blindly at the Hunter and hope for the best.

'When, Gods forbid it, will I ever have to fight blind?'

'Over here,' Zaine said, somewhere behind him.

CRACK

The dagger clattered off the wall harmlessly.

'Why are you forcing me to do this, Hunter?'

'I force you to do nothing other than what we had agreed upon,' Zaine replied.

'But how am I learning to better my wielding of a sword? I will not fight the Szar with my eyes closed,' Nathaniel said.

'Blind or no, the Szar would dispatch you just as easily,' Zaine said flatly, 'watch your footing!'

Something knocked against Nathaniel's thigh, almost upending him once again.

Nathaniel uttered an exasperated growl, yet another blind swipe returned fruitless.

'You are impatient, Regal,' Zaine said. 'If you wish a fight be done quickly, you may as well hand your opponent your own sword than allow them to sully their blade.'

Nathaniel almost wished someone would strike him down where he stood.

'Blindfold suits you, Regal,' a familiar voice sniggered.

Nathaniel ripped off the cloth around his eyes, blushing furiously at the curly haired boy, grinning as he leant against the archway.

'What do *you* want?' Nathaniel said.

'I was going to apologise for the black eye but I – woahh… where did you get that from?' Gabe pointed at the dagger Nathaniel clutched in his hand.

'What's it to you?' Nathaniel said.

The Hunter was already standing between them before Nathaniel had taken as much as a step towards Gabe.

'You're welcome to watch us train, Lycan, but if you insist on playing the fool, I will ask you to leave,' Zaine said.

Nathaniel was about to protest. However, the idea of Gabe being dragged out by the scruff of his neck was a possibility too good to give up.

Gabe stepped up to the Hunter, staring resolutely into his silver eyes. 'They say you Hunters are the fiercest fighters in Horizon,' he whispered.

'So *they* say,' Zaine replied blandly.

'Skew says you're a demon.'

Zaine's face remained expressionless but Nathaniel thought he saw the Hunter's hands tighten, ever so slightly, on the hilt of his practice sword.

Nonchalantly, Gabe stepped over to the baskets beyond Zaine and pulled out two short-swords. He twirled them in his hands as he faced the Hunter.

'Let's see what you're made of, Hunter,' Gabe said.

Nathaniel barked out a laugh. 'You're not serious are you?' he asked incredulously.

Gabe smirked in reply.

'Eager to fight demons are we, Lycan?' Zaine remarked with a raised eyebrow.

'Hoping for a slight challenge, for once,' Gabe replied, sending a pointed look Nathaniel's way.

'If that is your wish,' Zaine said, although there appeared to be a subtle warning hidden in his words. 'Nathaniel, would you mind?'

Nathaniel shook his head, eager to see what would happen.

Gabe frowned, as the Hunter leant his sword against the wall, and he waved his own pair at him questioningly.

'No need, Lycan,' Zaine said simply.

It was not a boast.

When it became clear that the Hunter would not be the first to approach, Gabe lunged toward his opponent, swords swinging.

As soon as the blades fell, Zaine was already long gone, sidestepping out the way as calmly as one on a midday stroll. The Hunter may as well have been carrying a basket of fruit.

'Lucky,' Gabe merely shrugged and flung himself into another charge.

Again, the Hunter dropped a shoulder and spun out of the way. No matter how tight the space or how narrowly Gabe's blades appeared to flash by, Zaine somehow always found room effortlessly.

The large Lycan boy seemed delighted at first, laughing off each failed attempt, before quickly launching another. But, as beads of sweat began to form across his brow and each breath became more laboured, Gabe's enthusiasm began to wear. The assaults became gradually more frantic, more desperate. Nathaniel winced as he saw the Lycan leave his chest increasingly open with each heavy-handed swing.

Suddenly, Zaine disappeared behind him. The Hunter's long coat and raven hair swirled so fast, he appeared to move, not as a man, but a mass of shadows.

'Wha–' Gabe looked at his hand in surprise, as the first sword clattered against the back wall.

The large Lycan turned and swung blindly at the space the Hunter had formerly occupied. By the time his arm had completed its arc, both his hands were empty.

'What in the blazes?' Gabe opened and clenched his fists, as if to make sure his swords hadn't suddenly turned invisible.

'You take risks, Lycan, I respect that,' Zaine spoke. 'But one too many could easily get you killed.'

The Hunter stood against the wall, his arms crossed loosely under his chest. Gabe made a start when he saw his swords stashed between the Hunter's legs. His jaw swinging, as he looked between Zaine and his hands.

No matter how many times he witnessed the Hunter's capabilities, Nathaniel still found himself shaking his head in disbelief. Where Gabe's chest heaved and glistened with sweat, it was as if Zaine had been observing from the wall all along. There was not even a hair out of place to mark his exertions.

'That's impossible!' Gabe said, thrusting a finger in the Hunter's direction. 'You must have cheated.'

The Hunter's brow raised in what looked like a rare show of amusement.

'We could go again, if you feel so strongly about the matter?' Zaine suggested.

Gabe's eyes danced between the Hunter and the swords he'd been relinquished of, as he considered the offer.

'Bah! I don't have time for this!' the Lycan growled finally, spinning on his heels to storm out the practice room.

Chapter 18

The Hunter's training regimen was brutal.

Two sessions, once in the morning before classes and once in the evening before bed. Often times, it was a struggle to just to limp out of the room once they'd finished, let alone drag his sore body to the showers. However, the Hunter treated every session as if it were his first. There was always a problem to be fixed, a chink to be smoothed, and praise was rarely given, if ever.

Any spare time that Nathaniel could grasp, he spent exclusively in the library, poring over the text in *Lifting the Veil*, until his eyes felt heavy.

He sat, curled up, in one of the alcove's plush armchairs, his hand outstretched before his eyes.

Picture a door in your mind, between this world and the plane of power. The door is but a fraction ajar and a draft tickles the tip of your nose.

Click.

Grasp the breeze of change, mortal. But gently, for you do not yet realise what you hold, squirming in your grasp.

Click.

The breeze will tempt you. Open the door, it will whisper. Resist you must! For to open that door is to embrace the eye of the storm. A deathly miasma to darken your soul.

143

Click. Click. Click.

Once temptation is mastered, draw on the breeze, apprentice. Fuel the desires of your mind.

Click. Click. Click. Click. Click.

Nathaniel's fingers felt raw.

'Athrana's grace!' Nathaniel cried frustratedly. 'This stupid book makes no sense!'

As he was about to hurl the book against the wall, a gentle cough caught Nathaniel by surprise.

Turning towards to the gap in the bookcases that made the alcove's entrance, he found Samir squeezing his wide shoulders through. Guiltily, Nathaniel dropped the book back on the table. Despite Samir's gentle demeanour, he felt strangely uneasy about what he might do if Nathaniel damaged a book in front of him.

'I am not aware of this Regal ritual,' Samir tilted his head curiously at the book in front of Nathaniel.

'It's not a Regal ritual,' Nathaniel said irritably. 'What are you doing here?'

'I thought perhaps you would like some company?' the boy proffered the pile of books cradled in his thick arms, all new, Nathaniel suspected.

Nathaniel shrugged indifferently and returned to his book. 'Do as you wish.'

The boy smiled and took up the seat opposite Nathaniel, arranging his books in neat piles before him.

'Grasp the breeze of change… grasp the breeze… grasp the breeze…' he muttered to himself, over and over. *How can I grasp what I can't see?* He snorted. *Zaine would love this book*, he thought derisively.

Nathaniel held out his hand and closed his eyes.

He pictured a door. Ornate, with inscriptions in the wood, and a solid brass door knob.

The door knob twisted slowly. Then, with a tired groan, the door opened.

A wave of emotions struck Nathaniel. A feeling of such completeness filled him from head to toe.

He waggled his fingers before him, chuckling at the tingling sensation that tickled his fingertips.

Gods alive, I feel… incredible.

The door creaked open a fraction more. Whatever lay behind it was still shadowed from Nathaniel's eyes.

Perhaps if I can open it just a little more…

The breeze will tempt you.

The door melted away abruptly as Nathaniel's eyes flew open.

Nathaniel's sudden disconnection from the source left such a feeling of loss, he almost collapsed where he sat. The warmth flooding from his fingertips, leaving him cold at the core.

'Regal!'

Nathaniel looked down from his outstretched hands in horror.

Books were scattered in a spiral around the room but it was the table that caught his attention. Flames crawled greedily across its surface, licking away at the wood.

'Athrana's grace!' Nathaniel jumped up, almost stumbling backwards over his own chair.

'What did you do?' Samir bellowed.

'I don't know!' Nathaniel yelled back.

The fire was showing no signs of stopping as it spread to the table's legs, creeping ever closer to the red carpet.

Nathaniel began clicking furiously at the table but, no matter how hard he pictured the open door in his mind, the feeling would not return.

Samir had taken one of the cushions from his chair and began beating the flames against the table from a distance. Soon after, the pillow too was abandoned to the fire.

'Get help!' Nathaniel shouted.

'What?' Samir said.

'I said–'

The flames suddenly extinguished before their very eyes, as if a bathtub of water had been emptied atop it. Smoke fizzled up in corkscrews away from the charred table-top.

Nathaniel looked at his hands confusedly. As far as he was aware he had not touched the source, could he have done it by accident?

'Which of the two of you did this?' a voice said coldly.

Nathaniel looked up from his hands and felt his stomach drop.

Eyes burning more fiercely than the fire he'd caused, Thorne Grey filled the gap between the bookcases, his hands shaking.

Nathaniel glanced at Samir, who sat frozen in a crouch, with a book under his arm and a hand placed on another.

The boys held their silence, neither of them daring to breathe.

'Who. Did. This?' Thorne demanded, each word grating on the boys' senses.

Nathaniel raised his hand meekly, refusing to meet his Grandfather's eyes, for fear they might set him alight.

'My office,' Thorne said. 'Both of you. Now.'

*

'How long have you been practicing *this*?' Thorne pointed at the book he'd taken from the now severely burnt table. It inexplicably appeared to have been untouched by the flames. 'How long?'

'Just now,' Nathaniel lied.

Thorne's eyes narrowed.

'Maybe a few days…' Nathaniel said quietly.

'A few days?' Thorne echoed him incredulously.

As much as he tried to convince himself otherwise, Nathaniel couldn't help but feel nervous, as he looked into the fiery amber of his Grandfather's eyes. Samir must have felt the same, as he kept his eyes fixed on his knees, as he shifted about and tugged at a handful of his braids. Either that or, perhaps, he was simply uncomfortable without a book to hand.

147

Thorne alternated between dry washing his hands and looking furiously in Nathaniel's direction, as he paced the length of the office.

'I really don't see what the problem is–' Nathaniel began.

'YOU DON'T SEE THE PROBLEM?'

The amber in Thorne's eyes threatened to erupt.

'But I–'

'YOU SET THE DAMN TABLE ON FIRE!'

'I only–'

'YOU READ A FEW CHAPTERS AND THOUGHT YOU COULD WIELD MAJIK? YOU COULD HAVE TURNED THE LIBRARY TO ASHES!'

'Thorne, I–'

'WORSE! YOU COULD HAVE HARMED YOURSELF! OR SAMIR!' Thorne waved his arm toward the Scorched boy, who looked even more uncomfortable at being mentioned. 'THIS IS WHY THEY SHACKLE WARLOCKS IN THE DAMN SPIRE! YOU COULD HAVE– YOU–'

Thorne inhaled deeply and began knuckling his forehead. When he spoke again, it was far more measured, though his voice still shook.

'Was it just Samir that saw you?' Thorne inquired softly.

'Yes,' Nathaniel replied.

Samir nodded.

'No one else knows?'

'No one. I swear!'

148

'Did anyone teach you beforehand? Or offer to?'

'No!'

'So, no one gave you the book? You just… found it?'

The woman in the maroon dress flashed briefly to mind. Nathaniel wasn't sure if it had been her book.

'No,' Nathaniel said, finally.

She technically hadn't given him the book. *But she hadn't made any effort to get it back either.*

Thorne's eyes narrowed, as he considered Nathaniel's words for a moment. Methodically tapping his fingers against the book's cover. Nathaniel had no idea what amount of bravery compelled him to speak but the words seemed determined to tumble from his mouth.

'Teach me,' Nathaniel said. His tongue may have been willing but his lips resisted against the attempt, foolish or not.

'What?' Thorne lifted his head from his hand.

'Teach me,' he insisted. 'I know you were a Warlock,' Nathaniel stupidly added.

Thorne's face told Nathaniel he had made a mistake. Probably of epic proportions, as it flashed from horror, through confusion, and on to intense fury.

'Who–' Thorne's voice had taken on a deathly calm, which somehow managed to be even more terrifying than when it was raised. '–told–' the book trembled in Thorne's grasp. '–you–' both Nathaniel and Samir edged back. '–tha–'

A sudden knock at the door caught Thorne mid-sentence.

Brother Marcus burst through before Thorne could even ask who had knocked.

'Brother... I am in the middle of somethi–' Thorne paused, raising his eyebrows at the brown-haired man before him, whose face was half-drenched in blood from a gash above his right eye.

'Marcus...Who has done this to you? I thought you and Garrett had settled your differences?'

Another time Marcus may have laughed, yet here he actually looked very concerned.

'This was not Garrett's doing Brother. We have a problem – it concerns the boy too,' he nodded at Nathaniel. He seemed oddly relieved that Nathaniel was there.

Thorne frowned and gave Nathaniel a searching look.

What must he think I've done now? Nathaniel thought exasperatedly. He watched the blood trickling onto Marcus' chin and felt a pang of guilt. *What have I done now?*

'What's happened, Marcus? If not Garrett, who did this to you?'

'Never mind that. You need to come with me, Brother, both of you. I've locked her in my office.'

'We have an intruder?' Thorne asked, eyes wide.

'She?' Nathaniel said, 'who's she?'

'No time to explain, just follow me.'

Marcus burst out of the room, the door swinging behind him.

'We'll finish this discussion later,' Thorne growled back at both boys. He was already out the door as soon as the last word had left his lips.

Nathaniel and Samir shared a look, each pushing back the lumps rising against their throats, and followed Thorne out of the door.

Chapter 19

Thorne strode on ahead, with the two boys half-jogging to keep up. His hands were balled into tight fists as he whispered furiously to Brother Marcus.

"She," Marcus had said. Why had he not spoken her name? Had she been the one to give him that cut? And why was it important that he came?

The Lycans they passed on the way seemed amazed to see Thorne outside of his office. Nonetheless, they quickly scrambled out of his way the moment they caught sight of his eyes.

He's still angry about the damn book, Nathaniel thought. *But why? He couldn't be that mad over a burnt table?*

'Has he ever been that angry before?' he whispered to Samir.

The Scorched boy appeared to think on Nathaniel's question, before going suddenly pale.

Great.

They stopped outside a door not too far from Sister Mire's hospital wing.

'She's in here?' Thorne nodded at the door.

'Yes, Brother,' Marcus said, 'the girl insisted on seeing Nathaniel when she awoke. At least, that is who I imagined she was referring to...' he said, taking a swift glance in Nathaniel's direction.

'What do you mean?' Nathaniel frowned.

Thorne shot Nathaniel a swift look, forcing him to avert his eyes.

'You have her bound?' Thorne said.

'And relieved of all her weapons. Believe me I checked. Thoroughly,' Brother Marcus said earnestly. The cut above his eye was still bleeding profusely.

Thorne thumbed his lip as he considered this then turned to Nathaniel. 'I need you to go in,' he said.

'Me?' Nathaniel said. He'd imagined Thorne would be the one to go in. Or at least all of them together.

'Yes. If Marcus has her as well restrained as he says, you'll be entirely safe.'

Nathaniel raised his brows.

And if he hasn't?

'Thorne, are you sure about this?' Marcus said cautiously. 'The girl's a complete unknown.'

'I trust you've contained the situation, Marcus. But, right now, we need information. Who she is, why she came here, and, importantly,' he said, turning to Nathaniel, with a concerned expression, 'why she was expecting to find you.'

Marcus nodded along but appeared no less uncomfortable with the idea.

'Will you go in?' Thorne asked Nathaniel. His tone suggesting the matter wasn't entirely up for debate. He glanced at Samir who, as subtly as he could, shook his head warningly.

Ozin's Throne! What will I find inside? Nathaniel turned to Thorne, took a deep breath, and nodded.

Samir let out an almost inaudible groan.

153

Nathaniel placed his hand against the door and pushed it slightly ajar. Just wide enough for him to squeeze through.

'You'll be safe, Nathaniel,' Brother Marcus reassured him. Though, the Lycan didn't seem overly convinced.

Nathaniel took a deep breath, then slipped inside.

Brother Marcus' office was smaller than Thorne's and, in truth, far messier. The room smelled of ink, parchment… and something Nathaniel couldn't quite place but hoped was dead. Papers and books were stacked in unstable towers – so high, they grazed the ceiling, almost forming an archway of their own – on either side of Marcus' desk. A few pages had been nailed to the few spaces on the walls that were visible behind the books. Some containing beautifully hand-drawn portraits and sketches, and others wild, almost indecipherable scribbles.

A lone candle, amidst piles of paper, illuminated Marcus' desk. The piles clearly separated hastily to make space for it. While the flickering light the candle emitted seemed to barely brighten the area around it, Nathaniel was immediately aware of the pair of startlingly blue eyes that were fixed on him. Keen as daggers, under thick brows that made her eyes seem all the more sharp.

A scowl darkened her features.

Although she hadn't been kept in solitude for long, Nathaniel got the impression that his arrival had only made matters worse. She had been bound tightly to the chair with rope. Uncomfortably so, if the twist of her lips was anything to go by. Like Brey, her blonde hair was plaited but in one long braid, which fell below the desk and out of sight. Unlike Brey, however, her face was tightly drawn, there was no playful smile for him.

154

'Kinslayer,' the Regal hissed.

Nathaniel felt himself wince.

So, she knew of the Emperor's death and what the Szar had likely told everyone of him. Yet he didn't recognise her in the slightest.

'Who are you?' Nathaniel said.

'You don't know?' the girl seemed surprised by that.

'I assume it was you who gave Brother Marcus that cut?'

'*Brother Marcus*,' she grimaced. 'Gods, you're already speaking like those animals.'

Nathaniel felt his cheeks go red. He hadn't even realised what he'd said.

'What's your name?' Nathaniel said hurriedly.

'An interrogation from the Kinslayer... lovely,' the girl rolled her eyes.

Nathaniel frowned. Had the girl not asked for him like Marcus had said? *What do you want from me?*

'This isn't an interrogation,' Nathaniel protested.

'Then unbind me,' she said.

Nathaniel began to move towards the desk but found himself hesitating. The girl may have been unarmed but it seemed highly unwise an idea to free her.

'No?' her lip curled, 'I thought not.'

'Broth– the Lycans... they want to know why you would come here. How did you even find this place?' Nathaniel looked at the Regal questioningly.

155

'I didn't.'

'Then how did you get in here?'

'I followed one of your precious Lycans, Kinslayer.'

'Inside Sanctuary?'

'Is that what they call this hovel?'

Nathaniel took a deep breath. The girl's short replies were beginning to get on his nerves.

'Did it feel good?' the girl asked.

'What?'

'Did you feel good when you murdered the Emperor?'

Not this again. The memory of his brother's accusations were still horribly fresh in his mind. He could almost picture Solas before him, eyes cold and accusing.

'I didn't kill Tolken,' Nathaniel said quietly.

'I suppose you didn't try and kill your father either,' she said coldly.

'I DIDN'T KILL ANYONE!'

Nathaniel didn't realised he had crossed the room, until his fists had smacked against Marcus' desk. The girl flinched, as if she had been slapped.

'I didn't kill anyone,' he said, more measuredly this time.

She leaned forward.

'I don't believe you,' she whispered.

Nathanial swallowed hard, his hands trembling as he gripped the desk. He was not quite sure how, but the girl's words managed to be more scathing than his brother's. He turned his back on the Regal and went to the door.

'Enjoy your freedom while it lasts, Kinslayer,' the girl said gloatingly. 'If I can find you, so can anyone else.'

He took one last glance back at the girl, as he closed the door behind him, feeling a shiver trickle down the length of his spine. The girl's eyes may as well have been two searing hot balls of flame, for the way she glowered at him. Nathaniel was surprised they didn't burn right through the door. While the Lycans were wary of him, and it was clear some disliked him, none of them came close to the level of contempt he had felt, when he'd looked into his fellow Regal's eyes.

She didn't just dislike him.

She hated him.

The Lycans were waiting for him outside. At least Marcus and, now, Mire were. Samir and Thorne, however, were nowhere to be seen.

'Are you alright? What did she say?' Brother Marcus asked. The Lycan looked unhappy about the cloth that was held tightly to his head by Sister Mire.

'She just said she followed you,' Nathaniel said. He couldn't tell them about her accusations.

'Is she still tied?'

'She's tied?' Mire screeched. Marcus uttered a sharp gasp from the extra pressure applied to his wound.

'We don't know how dangerous she is—'

'You've got a girl, no older than fifteen years, tied up like some monster?' Mire said shrilly.

157

'She was armed,' Marcus said weakly.

Mire looked on the verge of inflicting an even more serious wound upon the Lycan, until Nathaniel intervened.

'Where's Thorne?' Nathaniel inquired.

'Oh... he went back to his office,' Brother Marcus said, actively avoiding meeting Mire's reproachful look. 'I don't think he wants to be disturbed, but he left you this.'

Marcus passed Nathaniel a sheet of paper, which had been folded in half. The note had been quickly written and the ink looked blotchy, as if the letters been hammered into the page dot by dot.

NATHANIEL,

I'VE GONE BACK TO MY OFFICE. I KNOW I SAID WE'D SPEAK OF THE EARLIER MATTER BUT WITH THE CURRENT SITUATION AT HAND, I NEED SOME TIME TO MYSELF – TO THINK.

DO NOT ATTEMPT TO PRACTICE MAJIK INSIDE SANCTUARY AGAIN.

I WILL KNOW IF YOU TRY.

THORNE

What did he mean, "I will know"?

All the same, he felt reluctant to test the matter.

'If no one else will help this girl then I will!' Mire marched past them both, into Marcus' office.

Marcus attempted to warn her again only to have the door slammed in his face. Clutching the now damp cloth, Marcus stared at the door perplexedly.

'Will she be alright?' Nathaniel said quietly.

'The girl? Or Sister Mire?' Marcus raised an eyebrow.

Chapter 20

It was almost impossible to focus on where he was going, without his mind wandering to the blonde Regal lurking nearby.

She thinks I did it. She thinks I killed him.

He switched corridors, almost bumping into a Lycan in the process.

She just wouldn't listen. And the look she'd given him...

'Hey, Nathaniel,' a voice sang sweetly.

Athrana's grace... not now...

Brey sauntered over beside him, twirling a pigtail with her hand, frowning at the sullen twist to his face.

'Gods, who spat in your tea?' she giggled.

Brey seemed to miss the exasperated look he sent her way.

'Going to practice with the Hunter?' she asked.

'Why do you care?' Nathaniel snapped.

Brey grabbed Nathaniel's arm suddenly, her eyebrows pinching together as she frowned concernedly.

'What's wrong?' she said.

'Nothing,' Nathaniel snatched his arm back from the girl, 'leave me alone.'

A hurt look crossed Brey's green eyes and, when Nathaniel turned the second corner, she had disappeared altogether from his side. Guilt instantly wracked his stomach and he clenched his fists, not sure exactly why he was angry. At least Zaine's training would offer a distraction.

160

Wait.

Someone was making a lot of noise in the practice room. Was Zaine practicing on his own?

He peered round the corner and felt a growl rise from his stomach. Standing in the middle of the room, blindfolded as the Hunter danced from one spot to the other around him, was Gabe.

The boy was swinging his two swords wildly around him. A sheen of sweat coating his bare torso. Zaine caught Gabe with a whip of his practice sword, which took the Lycan's legs right out from under him. The Lycan was roaring with laughter, in between large gulps for air.

'Ozin's beard... we HAVE to do that again!' the Lycan jumped back to his feet and tore off his blindfold. 'Oh, it's you,' he blinked at Nathaniel.

Nathaniel gave the Hunter a sour look.

What is going on here?

'Same time tomorrow?' Gabe looked back at Zaine.

'If you can deign to be on time for once,' the Hunter replied.

'I'll get you next time, Hunter,' Gabe promised with a waggled finger, dropping his swords by the wall on his way out. 'Later, Regal,' he winked at Nathaniel.

Zaine shook his head after the Lycan.

'At least one of you are on time,' Zaine sighed, plucking Nathaniel's practice sword from the basket behind him.

'You're training the Lycan now?' Nathaniel blurted out.

'So it would appear,' Zaine said casually.

161

Nathaniel raised his arms as he thought of something to say but with the words were lacking, let his hands slap lamely against his side.

'You're upset?' the Hunter ran a hand across the practice sword. Gloved fingers drumming against the wooden blade.

'I'm not upset!' Nathaniel said indignantly, staring fixedly at the practice blade. 'I just... What?' he said in exasperation, when he looked up to notice the upturned corner of Zaine's mouth.

The Hunter never smiled.

'Gabe can be arrogant but holds no more animosity against your kind than Thorne does, and–' he held up a hand as Nathaniel began to protest, '–you disservice yourself in pushing away *any* who extend a hand in friendship.'

Nathaniel shook his head and turned on his boot heels. *No one understood.*

'Where are you going, Regal?'

'Somewhere else,' Nathaniel said curtly.

'Don't isolate yourself, Nathaniel,' the Hunter's voice followed him as he walked away, 'or there will be no one to catch you when you fall.'

'Fog take you, Hunter,' Nathaniel growled to himself, when he was certain Zaine was too far away to hear him.

Not bothering with a detour to the freezing showers, Nathaniel headed straight to the dormitory.

His feet stretching some distance over the edge, Samir lay in the bottommost hammock. The Scorched boy was, unsurprisingly, leafing through a leather-bound book, periodically dipping a quill into the inkpot resting on his chest to make notes. He wasn't even aware of Nathaniel, until the Regal was halfway up the ladder beside him.

'Nathaniel!' Samir's voice seemed to make the ladder ripple. The boy carefully planted the ink pot on the floor before waving the open pages of his book at him. 'You must read this, it's fascinating! There is quite a bit of material missing–!'

Nathaniel sighed and squeezed the bridge of his nose.

Could he not have just a moment of peace?

'–but I think this is an excerpt from the Shadow War! I can't believe the library had this–'

'Samir! Stop! Just stop!' Nathaniel said exasperatedly.

Samir faltered mid ramble.

'Oh,' he said, drawing the book back to his hammock.

Nathaniel tried closing his eyes, to ignore the uncomfortable squirming building inside his stomach. However, all he could see were Brey, Gabe, and Samir's faces, each eying him contemptuously.

Don't isolate yourself, Zaine's words rang back and forth in his mind.

Damn you, Hunter!

'Hey, Regal!'

Athrana's grace… what now?

Nathaniel rolled his head over to where the shout had originated from. In the middle of the dormitory, surrounded by his fellow Lycans, Gabe stood atop a table holding a poster up beside him for all to see.

163

'I didn't realise you were blazing famous!' Gabe pointed at the poster with a broad grin slapped across his face.

Nathaniel felt his jaw drop.

'Oh my,' Samir's deep voice rumbled beneath him.

In black and white, framed with bold lettering, the poster bore his likeness. Most of the Lycans didn't seem to share Gabe's awe and those who were closest to Nathaniel found a sudden urge to distance themselves from him. Even Samir, who easily towered over them all, shuffled uncomfortably underneath.

Heart pounding, Nathaniel jumped out of his hammock, boots almost tripping on the ladder's rungs as he raced down.

'Where did you get that?' he demanded of Gabe. The Lycan made no objection when Nathaniel snatched the poster out of his hands.

It read, "WANTED! FOR THE MURDER OF EMPEROR JAEL TOLKEN. CAPTURED ALIVE. 50,000 GOLD PIECES. BY ROYAL DECREE."

Nathaniel gulped as he stared down at himself. His hair was slicked back against his head, as it had been before he'd left Obsidia. But his face was set into a cruel mask – eyes wide and lips sneering.

'Did you do it?' Gabe asked, whistling when Nathaniel was not forthcoming with an answer. 'Blaze me, Regal. You really did, didn't you?'

The poster crinkled in Nathaniel's trembling hands. He wanted to lash out at something, anything but his muscles were so taut he couldn't even move.

This was the Szar's work. It had to be.

164

'Did you do it or not?' Gabe asked impatiently. 'Hey, Regal! Regal!'

Gabe's voice dimmed as Nathaniel stormed away.

How had the poster found its way to the Lycan Sanctuary? Did the Szar know he was here? Were there Regal spies lying in the shadows, biding their time until the right moment came to strike?

His feet picked up into a trot as he left the dormitory. Then, before he realised it, he was sprinting through the corridor, not giving a backward glance to the Lycans he smacked shoulders with on the way.

When he finally came across the door to Thorne's office, without bothering to knock, Nathaniel burst straight in. Thorne, Marcus, Garrett, Skew, Mire and the Regal girl all turned to look at him.

Thorne appeared to have calmed somewhat from their encounter, although his eyes still carried an edge. Marcus, the cut above his right eye now stitched together, was doing his utmost still to avoid Mire's glare, whilst Garrett picked at his teeth with a thumb Skew's eyes narrowed and he pursed his lips at Nathaniel's appearance. Behind Mire, the blonde Regal watched Nathaniel coolly, as he shook with barely restrained rage.

'Nathaniel...' Thorne began.

'You!' Nathaniel pointed the rolled-up poster at the girl, 'this is your doing!'

The girl raised an eyebrow at him but remained otherwise silent.

'Where did you find that?' Marcus looked at the poster with wide eyes.

'Gabe had it! Now everything thinks I did it!' Nathaniel said.

There was more than a hint of smugness in the curl of the girl's lip.

Brother Garrett's harsh bark of laughter made the entire room jump. 'Pickpocketed by a child!' Garrett chuckled.

'Marcus?' Thorne said.

'Vaera had it on her person when I caught her following me in the city markets,' Brother Marcus cleared his throat.

Vaera? The name didn't mean anything to Nathaniel but it seemed strange nonetheless, for it didn't suit the girl. From the way the Regal grimaced at the mention of her name, it looked like she felt the same way.

'The Regal had what?' Skew screeched, 'give me that, boy!' Skew lunged toward Nathaniel, snatching the poster out of his hands. The Lycan's beady eyes bulged as he stared down at Nathaniel's likeness.

'So,' Skew glowered at Thorne, 'you've allowed more than one Regal in, who's a threat to our people–' Skew's hand shot to Marcus's stitched cut.

'The girl merely wanted to question Marcus, she did not expect to be cornered in some alley like a sewer rat!' Mire's voice rose in contention with Skew's.

'– but we've been harbouring–' Skew extended a bony finger towards Nathaniel.

'Skew…' Garrett grunted warningly.

'–this! This…' Skew's eyes flickered back to the poster, '…this Kinslayer!'

Thorne's fist cracking against the desk cut the Lycan short.

The fiery amber in Thorne's eyes had been stoked once more. Though he spoke measuredly, the words shot out of his mouth, as if they were afraid of his lips.

'I'm not going to decide anything until I find out more,' Thorne said quietly.

'Isn't it obvious?' Garrett growled past his thumb, 'the girl came here, hunting the boy,' he nodded at Nathaniel.

Nathaniel felt his stomach lurch. He looked at Vaera for confirmation, but the girl was suddenly avoiding his gaze.

'Well?' Thorne looked at the girl questioningly.

She rolled on the balls of her feet uncomfortably under the heat of Thorne's eyes but she would not answer.

'What if I told you that you've been led to believe a lie, Vaera, that this was all the Szar's plan to gain power?' Thorne said.

'Draeden Kusk?' the girl snorted, 'the man's a war dog. Sure, he despises Lycans, but he has no desire to hold the Obsidian Crown for long.'

'And why does he hold it at all?' Nathaniel rounded on the girl, 'what happened to the Emperor's daughter?'

'She is indisposed,' the girl replied tightly, 'the Empress-in-waiting grieves with her mother.'

The accusation was clear in the harsh tone of Vaera's words. Still, Nathaniel's stomach squirmed. He should have been there for her.

'And how would you know that?' Nathaniel snapped. 'How do you know the Szar hasn't decided to kill her too?'

The girl gave a bitter laugh.

'By Athrana's grace, Kinslayer,' Vaera said, 'your tongue lies so freely it's a wonder how it doesn't just slip out of your mouth.'

'I'm not lying!' Nathaniel shouted.

'ENOUGH!' Thorne's fist smacked the table a second time, its legs wobbling threateningly to the point of collapse. 'The fate of our two peoples rest on the deliverance of the truth. Vaera, I convened with your Emperor by letter to seek an alliance between Regals and Lycans. Tolken agreed in principle but the man foolishly shared our discussions with the Szar. You freely admit Kusk hates Lycans, so is it too far a stretch to suggest he'd–'

'Kill the Emperor?' Vaera's jaw dropped, 'yes! It is! Kusk had his disagreements but he was Tolken's loyal servant!'

Which made it all the more easy for him to slit the Emperor's throat, Nathaniel thought darkly. *But how could anyone ever believe Tolken's Szar had done it?*

'Ask yourself this: if he despises Lycans so much, why was he so quick to demand Nathaniel suffer the Stone? This, after allegedly murdering the Emperor – a Lycan sympathiser.'

'Perhaps Kusk held duty above personal belief,' Vaera folded her arms with a scowl.

Nathaniel scoffed.

Duty… Hadn't that been what had gotten him this awful mess to begin with? Duty to his people, to the Emperor. *Till my*

168

heart gives out, I give it freely for the Emperor. How different things would have been if he'd simply emulated the Szar's brand of 'duty.'

'Where does the motivation lie for Nathaniel to murder the Emperor?' Thorne said, 'a Regal, having just killed a Lycan sympathiser, immediately seeks refuge with the Lycans?'

Vaera's brow furrowed.

'The Szar, on the other hand,' Thorne continued, 'had every motivation. And, now, as Emperor, he can enforce his beliefs on us all. Unless, we can stop it.'

'What are you suggesting?' Vaera inquired.

Thorne drummed his fingers thoughtfully against the desk. 'I think it's time for Nathaniel to return to Obsidia. I think it's time your Elders heard the truth, before the Szar can muster their support, and send an army to march on Dalmarra.'

'This is insane!' Skew's voice burst out like air from a popped balloon. 'These two know where we are, Thorne! What's to stop either of them...' Skew's eyes latched onto Nathaniel in particular, '...from giving us all up?'

'Hate to agree with Skew,' Garrett shivered with reluctance, 'but he's got a point, Brother.'

'A drunk's approval is hardly worth much,' Mire gave Garrett a withering glance.

'Military logic,' Garrett shrugged.

'Marcus?' Thorne turned to the brown-haired man.

'I think Nathaniel is trustworthy,' he said slowly. 'The girl... I'm not convinced,' he added with a hesitant glance at Mire.

169

For once, the Herbalism teacher did not seem to object to his statement.

'I have no reason or wish to betray you, at least not most of you,' Vaera gave a pointed look at Nathaniel.

Thorne thought on this a moment and accepted the girl's words with a nod.

Garrett shook his head and Skew howled.

'You're letting them go? Back into the arms of that madman!' Skew cried. If his eyes bulged any more, Nathaniel was certain they would burst. 'Have you learnt nothing in the last fifty years?'

Thorne fixed the greying Lycan with a cold stare. 'I have learnt that peace is always preferable, wherever you can find it. You of all people should know that, Skew.'

Skew's lips quivered, as he drew his remaining hand protectively over the stump of his right arm. For the moment, the Lycan was silent.

'You surely wouldn't send them alone?' Sister Mire said.

'Rest assured they won't be,' Thorne said.

Mire seemed relieved at that.

'They'll have the best protection in Horizon.'

'You don't mean…' Mire brought a hand to her mouth.

'I'm afraid so.'

Everyone but Thorne jumped at the voice that rose from the darkened corner of Thorne's office.

Bright silver eyes watched them from the shadows.

'Have you been there all this bloody time, Hunter?' Garrett grumbled.

'Long enough,' Zaine replied, his voice so gentle it beggared belief. 'It has been quite some time since I climbed the Black Mountains.' The Hunter unfurled himself from the darkness and padded beside Nathaniel. 'I'm sure Dez wouldn't mind holding down the fort a little while longer.'

Vaera looked at the Hunter curiously. Did he frighten her too?

'Once more into the breach, my friend,' Thorne said gravely.

*

With Mire, Garrett, Skew, and Marcus ensuring the corridors were clear of Lycans, Thorne accompanied Zaine and the two Regals to the Mines. The floor angled down into a torch-lit tunnel. A door, which looked like it had been carved from the very rock around it, stood at the end.

Thorne pulled open the door, immediately releasing an icily cold draft of air. This would have frozen Nathaniel to his core, had he not been wearing the fur cloak his Grandfather had given him. Even so, he grimaced as the frigid wind streamed past his face, causing his eyes and nose to run.

It hadn't been the only gift.

Before they'd left Thorne's office, the Hunter had thrust a rag-bound package against his chest without so much as a word. Inside, a sword of a finer steel than he had ever laid hands on, had glinted up at him. Glimmering, as if fresh from the forge. It was slightly shorter than the ruby-encrusted longsword the

171

Hunter carried in the scabbard at his back, but no less impressive. Nathaniel adjusted the thick, leather belt that carried the sword across his tunic, with a slight groan. Its weight would take some getting used to.

'I don't think we can trust her,' Nathaniel said in a low whisper to Zaine, nodding at Vaera's back.

The Hunter's face may as well have been fashioned from stone, in how it remained so impassively steady.

'Whether we can or cannot, it makes little difference,' the Hunter said matter-of-factly. 'Thorne will not force Vaera to stay in Sanctuary against her will and you could not expect to go far within Obsidia. Certainly not without an arrow through your chest, were you to attempt the journey without her.'

Nathaniel rolled his eyes. The thought of how far they had to travel, with this troublesome girl, left a bitter taste in his mouth.

Past the entrance to the mine, Nathaniel found himself in a large, gloomy cavern. The dark punctuated by a dim column of moonlight in the centre, streaming in through a manhole-sized fissure in the rock above, about a hundred feet or so from where they stood. *That must have been where the Shadow's men dropped me*, Nathaniel realised.

A number of tunnels veered off in various directions from the cavern. To the left, to the right. Some appearing to head up towards to the surface. Some diving downwards, deeper into the earth.

Much to Nathaniel's chagrin, Thorne led them towards one of the deeper tunnels.

'Dead ends,' Zaine said simply, when Nathaniel pointed at the rising tunnels.

A few pickaxes and wheelbarrows, layered with coal dust, lay inside the tunnel. Some of the axes had been left buried in the wall, with Nathaniel coming close on several occasions to walking straight into a wooden shaft, as they stumbled through the gloom.

They came into another cavern at the tunnel's end, with Thorne taking a turn into yet another tunnel, this time rising upwards. Yet Nathaniel was to be left disappointed when it levelled out, long before it would have led to the surface. More tunnels followed, with Thorne seemingly picking and choosing which way they went at random.

I wouldn't have had a chance, if I'd tried to escape.

Once they'd travelled through what felt like several miles of tunnels, they came to an abrupt stop by one of the wheelbarrows that was leaning up against the mine's wall. The wheelbarrow was covered by a large rag, which, when removed, revealed a pitch-black crawl space carved into the wall.

'You want us to crawl through that,' Vaera looked between the bulky clothes she bore and the narrow tunnel in horror.

'It'll be a bit of a squeeze but you'll be out of it momentarily,' Thorne reassured her.

With a nod from Thorne, Zaine herded a reluctant Vaera into the tunnel, relieving her of the travel pack. The girl's groans echoed back to them, as the Hunter followed her in.

Nathaniel and his Grandfather remained, scratching their plumes of red hair awkwardly as they waited for the other to

173

speak. It was strange. He'd only known Thorne for a few weeks but he felt reluctant to leave him.

'I–' Nathaniel began, before his jaw snapped quickly shut once more, thinking better of it.

'It's going to be tough,' Thorne said, 'but if I could do it, I know you can.'

'You've been to Obsidia?' Nathaniel frowned at his Grandfather.

'Oh no,' Thorne gave a wry chuckle, 'let's just say I… had a similar journey when I was your age.'

Thorne suddenly grasped his shoulder and looked at Nathaniel very seriously. 'Promise me you won't use Majik,' he said, his voice dropping so low Nathaniel had to lean in to catch the words.

'I–'

'Please,' Thorne pleaded with him, 'you don't realise the dangers.'

'What do you mean?' Nathaniel asked.

Thorne licked his lips nervously as he spoke. 'There's a reason the Spire chains the power of Warlocks,' he explained. 'To use Majik, even when chained, is to wrestle a mountain. Unchained… the mountain could collapse upon you.'

The thought of not embracing that euphoric feeling he'd first experienced in the library, filled Nathaniel with a strange sense of dread.

'Then come with me,' Nathaniel said, 'you could teach me how to control it!'

Thorne shook his head sadly, 'I can't leave Sanctuary, just please, promise me.'

'Very well, I promise,' Nathaniel agreed reluctantly.

Thorne seemed relieved. He released Nathaniel's shoulder and nodded towards the tunnel. 'You don't want to keep Zaine waiting, now,' he said with a wink.

Thorne frowned, as he watched his grandson disappear through the tunnel, dwelling on a nagging thought. *Once the door is opened...*

Chapter 21

Nathaniel did not consider himself to be especially claustrophobic but the crawl space beyond the wheelbarrow had been a testing experience. His muscles had seized up sporadically, as he wriggled through and his throat felt tight, as if he were sucking air from a straw. The fact that he had to push his roll bag along in front of himself as he squeezed through, hardly helped matters either. When the roll bag finally disappeared out of the tunnel and a gloved hand reached down toward him, it was a massive relief.

After the mines and tunnels of the Lycan Sanctuary, the pale moonlight bouncing off Dalmarra's towering walls seemed almost too bright for his eyes. Nathaniel blinked when that same gloved hand held out his belongings to him.

The other Regal, Vaera, was a few paces away, brushing off coal dust from her clothing. She glowered as soon as she noticed Nathaniel watching her, and he hastily turned his attentions elsewhere. A cloaked man stood beyond Zaine and Vaera, clutching the reins of three horses: two mares and a rather restless stallion, which Zaine had gone over to comfort.

Outside of Dalmarra's walls, acres of green fields seemed to stretch endlessly in all directions. To the West, a rather ominously dense forest, double the breadth of the city, swallowed whatever moonlight dared stray too close to its edge. It made Nathaniel uncomfortable just to look at it.

'Be thankful, Regal, that your home does not lie in the Silent Forests' path,' Zaine made Nathaniel jump, appearing so suddenly by his side.

'Have you-?' Nathaniel said, nodding in its direction.

'I have.' Zaine stared at the forest for a few seconds, through narrowed eyes. 'It was an... *interesting* experience.'

It is just a forest, Nathaniel thought, frowning. Yet the longer he stared at it, the more the discomfort within him grew, like rot from the roots. He shivered despite his cloak.

'We're going to put some distance between us and Dalmarra, before setting up camp,' Zaine announced. 'Pick one of the mares, you two.'

*

After several hours, Zaine brought their horses to a halt outside a small clearing of wide-coned trees and bushes. Nathaniel dismounted and led his white nosed, chestnut mare – Bela – around the half circle of trees and into the clearing. It was an effort to walk normally, given how long it had been since he'd last been in the saddle. If Zaine noticed, he kept quiet, whilst Vaera, perhaps not as subtly as she thought, gave him a sidelong look that bordered on a sneer.

They tied the horses to the trees behind them, before setting up the campsite. The Hunter, quietly amazed – at least that was the meaning he took from the twitch of Zaine's eyebrows – at Nathaniel's inability to light a fire, had shown him how to do so. As soon as the wood began to smoke, the Hunter disappeared into the trees surrounding their camp in search of food, leaving Nathaniel alone with Vaera.

The Regal girl had drawn a menacing dagger from her belt, the moment the Hunter had melted into the shadows. Nathaniel's hand twitched towards the pommel of his sword but he resisted the urge to bare steel.

Vaera's attention was largely fixed on the blade in her hands, as she set about sharpening the dagger's edge. However, it was intermittently broken by a dark glare at Nathaniel, from across the fire. Garrett had been certain she'd come to kill him. While Vaera hadn't as much confirmed this, her silence was hardly contributing to Nathaniel's comfort, sitting alone with her. Certainly not whilst she had a dagger to hand. He found himself wondering whether he could parry a knife mid-flight as he watched her balance the blade's handle on her palm. It seemed like something the Hunter would manage with ease, but him...? Never mind that, what was to stop her from sticking it in his back as he slept? The Hunter had to sleep at some point.

'Are you deaf, Kinslayer?'

Nathaniel gave a start, almost drawing his blade by accident.

'What?' Nathaniel blinked at Vaera.

The girl fingered the dagger in her lap, her blue eyes looking at him contemptuously.

'What exactly do you plan to do, when we reach Obsidia?' she asked.

'So, you're talking to me again?' Nathaniel replied exasperatedly.

The girl whipped her neck back arrogantly. 'I am only curious as to how you will convince the Elders of your *story*.'

The emphasis she put on *story* made it somewhat clear that she still believed his account to be fictional.

'If you still think I'm lying, what are you even doing here?' Nathaniel demanded.

Vaera sniffed and returned to sharpening her dagger.

For the life of him, Nathaniel could not understand why the girl hadn't left already …or attacked him. If she truly believed he had killed Tolken, by rights, he should already be dead.

'I see you haven't killed each other yet.'

Nathaniel nearly tripped over his feet, as he tried to scramble up, whilst fumbling for his sword at the same time.

Zaine stood in between two trees, with a deer casually slung over his shoulder. Vaera's dagger was embedded in the tree, mere inches away from Zaine's ear. Vaera's arm was frozen in place before her, the blood completely drained from her face.

Zaine dropped the deer by the fire and proffered the girl's dagger back to her.

'You have good reflexes,' he told her calmly, as if he hadn't been two inches from death, placing the blade back in the palm of her hand. 'Take a care that they don't rule over you.'

Wide-eyed, Vaera squeaked an apology and quickly returned the dagger to her belt. The Hunter knelt on the ground and pulled out his knife.

'You can put that away now,' he said. Nathaniel hadn't even realised he'd drawn his sword.

The knife in Zaine's hand paused above the deer's belly. He had become as still as a statue. His silver eyes didn't even blink.

'Zaine?' Nathaniel whispered.

179

'On second thoughts, arm yourselves,' he said quietly.

The ruby hilt had materialised in the Hunter's gloved hand, not making even the tiniest sound as it was drawn from the scabbard at his back.

Alert, Nathaniel spun his head around the camp, looking for whatever foe Zaine had sensed through the surrounding foliage. Beside the fire, only grasshoppers disturbed the fragile silence of the night.

Vaera had a dagger in each hand this time, though she held them hesitantly before her. Given the frown that creased her brow, it seemed she too could not discern what trouble the Hunter had unearthed.

Remembering the blindfold practice Zaine had subjected him to, Nathaniel began to wonder if this wasn't a continuation of the Hunter's bizarre training practices.

'Out where I can see you, slowly,' Zaine's voice cracked like a whip.

Whatever he could see, whoever they were, Nathaniel hoped for their sake they'd do what the Hunter said.

A hand, then an arm, then two, rose slowly out of the thicket of tall shrubs that formed the back of their camp. His curly hair tousled and littered with tiny green leaves, Gabe gave them all an uneasy grin.

Nathaniel groaned as he lowered his sword.

'Nice to see you too, Regal,' Gabe winked at him, 'and you, my lady.' The Lycan bowed graciously with his arms aloft, a cocky half-smile upturning his lips, as he looked at the blonde Regal over Nathaniel's shoulder. Her raised daggers, however, made it clear she had no intention of returning his flirtatious manner.

'And the rest of you?' Zaine said.

'Who says I didn't come alone?' Gabe shrugged. 'Can I put my arms down now? I'm starting to ache.'

'So you won't object to me making sure?' Zaine said, pointing at the bushes with his sword.

Gabe licked his lips uncertainly.

'Wait!'

Another pair of hands rose from the bushes and another, paler than the first, soon after that.

Brey's vibrant green eyes looked upon them all innocently and Kaira's brown had retained their naturally cool edge. Nathaniel's stomach knitted itself into knots, when Brey looked at him. The crooked, playful smile had taken leave for a tight-lipped stare. The look Kaira gave him seemed to be edged with steel as well, though what he could have possibly done to spite the Féynian was a mystery to him. Nathaniel was relieved when Zaine resumed his line of questioning.

'How did you find us?' Zaine interrogated them. 'The trees shield the campfire and I've made multiple sweeps behind us. I find it hard to believe any of you three would know what signs to look out for.'

'Maybe we got lucky?' Gabe grinned smugly.

Nathaniel scoffed. It seemed highly unlikely that anyone could just stumble upon the Hunter, unless it had been his design all along.

'For the love of Ozin, Gabe, just tell the Hunter already,' Kaira rolled her eyes.

'You had to spoil it didn't you?' Gabe shook his head at the pale girl.

'So, a random accident then?' Nathaniel said sarcastically.

'Not quite…'

The three Lycans turned back to the thicket of bushes behind them.

One of the bushes emitted a deep sigh, then bristled as a large shape rose into the night.

'Samir?' Nathaniel called out to him.

Heaving a large sack over his shoulder, which Nathaniel would have been surprised to find contained anything other than books, the tall Scorched boy reluctantly joined his fellow Lycans.

'Hello,' Samir spoke down to his feet.

'You tracked me, Samir?' Zaine inquired. With the Hunter's face looking as impenetrable as stone, it was unclear whether he was, impressed, curious, or furious.

The boy mumbled something in the affirmative.

'Samir was brilliant!' Brey said loudly.

'I mean, I might have found you in the end…' Gabe grumbled.

'I had heard the Scorched were practiced trackers,' Zaine said. 'But as far as I'm aware, you've been in Sanctuary for years.'

'We cut our teeth on the desert sands, soon after we learn how to stand on two feet,' Samir said defiantly. Perhaps it was Nathaniel's imagination, but Samir seemed to suddenly stand taller, prouder. He pushed out his chest in front of them in a kingly manner, as he spoke. Nathaniel could almost feel the heat of the Scorched sun blistering his skin, the warm air drying out his throat.

'A child of the Sun who cannot find his way across the endless dune sea, is a child who will not survive into manhood,' Samir said, as if reciting from one of his books. All at once the grandeur slipped away as he finished and the humble boy, who hid behind books, stood before them once more.

'Why do I recognise you, Lycan?' Vaera broke the silence. The Regal had taken to her feet, a vague look of recognition crossing her eyes as she squinted past the fire at Kaira.

'Why do I feel the same, Regal?' Kaira raised an eyebrow daringly.

The two girls held a stalemate of a stare, both appearing to hold cards close to their chest that could harm the other.

'Must be my mistake,' Vaera muttered after a moment.

'Perhaps,' Kaira agreed.

They looked away, deciding to pocket their cards for another occasion.

'Did any of you decide to tell Thorne before you left?' Zaine asked.

'Do you think fire-eyes would have let us go if we had?' Gabe said.

'I think 'fire-eyes' would have your hides, had he the merest inkling,' Zaine had taken a deathly tone of voice, as he advanced towards Gabe.

The Lycan maintained a brave face to his credit, though his eyes kept flickering to the Hunter's unsheathed sword.

'No, Brother Grey doesn't know,' Kaira stepped out ahead of Gabe. 'But we wanted to come and you cannot afford the time to take us back... and, I might add, we're certainly not leaving.'

She crossed her arms and stared at the Hunter, as if in challenge.

Gabe gave the dark-haired girl an urgent look, as if to say: *I hope you've got more to persuade him with than that!*

Her eyes remained fixed on Zaine's, who was as expressionless as ever. It felt longer, though Zaine decided upon a course of action in seconds.

'As you wish,' Zaine said, turning his back on the newcomers. 'But remember, my priority lies with the Regals,' he added warningly before returning to the deer.

Nathaniel thought he should have been angry at the Hunter but, in truth, he felt strangely relieved to see the Lycans... even Gabe. The Lycans themselves looked surprised that the Hunter hadn't sent them packing, back the way came.

'How in the blazes did you do that?' Gabe said, staring at Kaira in astonishment.

'You men are all the same,' Kaira replied matter-of-factly, in an almost bored tone, as if she were used to having her way. 'All bravado and bluster, until reason renders you speechless.'

All the same, with the Hunter nearby, she had kept her voice down to almost a whisper.

'Reason, my-,' Gabe snorted under his breath.

Brey made a sharp 'hm!' as she passed Nathaniel, holding her nose up all the way over to Vaera's side of the fire.

Great, just what I need, two girls wanting to stick a knife in my back!

He jumped when he turned to find the other Lycan girl, Kaira, standing right in front of him, with her arms crossed under her breasts. She bore the same expression as she had with the Hunter. Yet, the girl may as well have been snarling, for all the ill will Nathaniel felt coming his way.

'I'm going to make this clear once and only once, Regal.'

'Make what clear?' Nathaniel said, acutely aware that he was slowly edging back to the fire.

'I don't believe you killed your Emperor,' she said.

'I–wait. You don't?' Nathaniel looked at the girl in surprise.

Then why do I feel like you're still angry with me, Lycan?

'No. I don't think you'd have the stomach for it,' Kaira said plainly.

Nathaniel frowned. The girl had a strange way of reassuring him.

'Well, if you don't think I did it–'

'What I have to say, concerns Brey,' the girl continued to shepherd him toward the flames.

Ah.

'What about her?' Nathaniel swallowed hard. He was beginning to feel the heat of the campfire on his back.

'I heard you were quite rude to her back in Sanctuary,' she said.

Had he been? He seemed too busy stumbling over his words when Brey was around to have time to be rude.

'If you decide to upset her once more, I won't hesitate in doing the Szar's dirty work for him.'

He hadn't mentioned the Szar and the girl hadn't been at the meeting in Thorne's office… how did she know?

'Have we reached an understanding?' Kaira inquired. The look she gave Nathaniel suggested that his input on the matter was a mere formality.

'I–yes!' he said, glancing back at the leaping embers that were now dangerously close.

'Good,' the girl replied, as she went to join Brey and Vaera.

Vaera moodily stoked the fire with a stick. While she did not openly object to the Lycans' company, she certainly didn't appear enthused about the prospect of sharing a journey with four of them.

Kaira may have said all she needed to, but Nathaniel got the impression the other two girls had unfinished business with him. One at a time, and sometimes simultaneously without either girl realising, Brey and Vaera would shoot a cold look in his direction. It was a wonder how they didn't snuff out the fire. What a situation he found himself in. If the Szar didn't kill him, either Vaera or Brey probably would for him.

Chuckling away, with Samir, already buried in one of his books, in tow, Gabe gave Nathaniel such a fierce clap on the back, he was almost sent sprawling into the campfire.

'Whatever she told you to do, ginge, I'd just do it,' Gabe advised him.

'It's Nathaniel,' he replied irritably.

'Whatever you say, Regal,' Gabe shrugged.

The Lycan dropped himself heavily onto the grass and put his feet up to the fire. Samir looked up from his book to give Nathaniel a reassuring smile.

'Women are… strange,' he murmured, blushing into his book a moment later after realising he had spoken his thoughts aloud.

Nathaniel could not find it in himself to disagree.

Chapter 22

Tap. Tap.

Vaera sat bolt upright, staring out at the dark expanse, past her outstretched legs. Waiting.

Must have imagined it, she thought.

Her hackles remained raised and unconvinced. With a soft shrug, the Regal nestled herself back into the bump of grass she'd made her bed and closed her eyes.

Tap. Tap.

Vaera sat upright again, looking all around herself but could see nothing in the immediate vicinity. *A small animal perhaps? Or a larger one*, she thought darkly.

'I swear to Athrana, Lycan, if that was you I'll–' she whispered, as she crawled to Gabe. Though he was very clearly - and very noisily - asleep. Indeed, it was a wonder that the low rumble of his snoring, like waves smacking against a cliff face, didn't disturb the local wildlife, let alone their small camp.

But *someone* had poked her as she slept, Vaera was sure of it. Yet everyone appeared deeply submerged in their dreams. At least, she assumed the Hunter was. It was impossible to tell from where he was positioned, facing away from the dwindling campfire.

No, she couldn't have imagined it, certainly not twice. One of them had to have been playing her for a fool. As Vaera was considering whether to give one of the Lycans an unpleasant awakening, some movement by one of the knolls, at the edge of visual range in the dark, caught her attention. Squinting through the pitch black, she could see a woman sat observing them all. Or just her.

Perhaps she is from a nearby village, Vaera thought.

Vaera waved her arms but the woman remained unresponsive.

Is she lost?

The woman suddenly rose, turned on her heels, and began marching back over the knoll.

Does she want me to follow?

She glanced back at their camp, debating whether to wake one of the others. As soon as Vaera had turned, however, that strange feeling of being poked in the back of her neck resurfaced, and she looked back to find the knoll occupied once more.

The woman raised her hand and beckoned her to follow, before disappearing once more. Deciding it was probably not worth disturbing any of her companions, the Regal hurried over to the knoll.

'I'm coming, I'm coming,' Vaera muttered.

The woman stood in front of a pair of forked trees that marked an entrance, of sorts, to a circle of oaks, forming a grove. An amber glow, seemingly emitted from within the grove, haloed the woman, illuminating her and her strange clothing for a brief moment.

Vaera thought that the maroon dress and matching veil she wore were beautiful and shapely, but entirely unsuited for travelling any distance. From her garb she could have been a noble's wife, but what was she doing out in the wilderness, so far from any city?

189

'Who are you?' Vaera asked the woman, 'are you lost?'

The smile she got in return took her breath away. Even though she could see so little of her, Vaera thought instantly that she must be beautiful.

'As lost as any other, darling,' she beamed, 'hoping to find answers... and questions.'

Vaera frowned at the woman's strange response.

'So, you're not lost?'

'Me? Not quite. But I wonder if you've not been led astray?'

There was something... different about the woman. Her face remained hidden behind her veil, yet, Vaera had the uncomfortable feeling of one who was being, not only watched, but stripped bare for all to see.

'What do you mean? Have you been following us?'

The woman smiled again, laying her hand out toward the grove. The lights continued to flash within, but it was unclear from where... or from what.

'There is nothing here that will harm you,' she said reassuringly, noticing Vaera's hesitance.

As terrible an idea as it felt, Vaera found herself trusting the woman's words, and with a deep breath, she stepped inside. Lilies formed a white carpet across the grove's floor, but it was what lay just under the leafy ceiling that grasped the Regal's attention. Hundreds of fireflies pirouetted over their heads at such a speed that they left impressions of their movement in blurs of light, like shooting stars.

'Tell me, have you decided whether you're going to kill him yet?'

Vaera's breath caught in her throat.

'I don't know what you're talking about,' she said quietly, 'who are you?'

It suddenly became important for Vaera to feel the weight of a blade in her hand. However, her fingers were stiff against the handle at her waist, as if it were encased in stone.

What does she know?

'You can call me Zakariyanna,' the woman inclined her head and continued. 'So, darling, is he aware of your potentially fatal intentions?'

'My intentions – whatever they be – are of no concern to you,' Vaera said coldly. 'And why are you following us? Who even are you?'

Zakariyanna brought her hands together and smiled. It was perhaps the sweetest smile Vaera had ever seen, but she was determined nonetheless to keep a hold of her dagger. The woman crouched down and took a seat in the middle of the bed of lilies, indicating the space in front of her for the Regal to join her.

'You have nothing to be afraid of, darling,' she said soothingly.

There was something really strange about this woman, Vaera thought. But, at the same time, she felt oddly drawn toward her. It was as if all that separated the two of them were a series of strings, held taut between.

She planted herself on the floor, the flower bed forming a soft seat underneath. Her eyes followed Zakariyanna's hands, as they caressed the petals in front of her. Sweeping across, to-and-fro, in a hypnotic fashion.

191

'You are most curious, Regal,' the woman remarked, her attention not leaving the flowers. Not that it would have made any difference; even as close as Vaera was to her, she could barely make out the tip of her nose from behind her veil, let alone her eyes.

Perhaps she has none, Vaera thought grimly. *Why else would she hide them?*

'And what makes you think that?' Vaera replied hesitantly.

What does she know?

'There are several in your party that will ride the chariots of change across this fragile land. And yet it is you, at this moment, holding the reins.'

The lilies, over which Zakariyanna's hand flew, suddenly changed. In their place, stood tall orchids, vibrantly purple before Vaera's widening eyes.

'How did you—'

'It is you who shall decide whether the reins are placed in another's hands. Whether another summer will go by unhindered.'

Zakariyanna plucked one of the orchids from the ground and held it away from her. The petals seemed to pulse in tune with the fireflies, as if one.

'Or whether we fade into oblivion.'

Zakariyanna's words brought a lasting sense of dread, knotting itself deep in the pit of Vaera's stomach. The flower the woman held wilted, shrivelled and turned black, before drooping against the back of Zakariyanna's hand. Ashes fell in the space between them and then the orchid was gone.

'I don't understand,' Vaera murmured, 'what reins… what are you talking about?'

Zakariyanna's smile now seemed cold - almost frightening - and made Vaera faintly aware of the strings that tugged at her once more. She let the woman grasp her hands and lift them up high enough for Vaera to see what was now held between her trembling fingers.

A crown of black leaves glinted up at the Regal.

The Obsidian Crown felt heavy despite its delicate appearance, almost too heavy for a head, Vaera thought. She twisted it around her hands, dazzled as it cast sparks of light across the grove.

Without warning, she felt her fingertips become damp. Vaera initially thought she had been so engrossed in the crown that she had failed to notice that it was raining, but it was not so. The maroon dress that covered Zakariyanna remained as dry as her own clothes. Frowning, Vaera drew back a hand and shrieked, as blood ran from her fingers.

She dropped the crown, as if it were a hot iron, which dissipated into the air like a mirage, and scrambled to her feet.

'You did this,' Vaera murmured, shuddering. She gave Zakariyanna a mournful look, 'you did this,' she murmured once more.

'Darling–' the woman began to say, but the Regal was already sprinting away, as if to escape her own shadow.

Tears stung Vaera's eyes as she tore out of the grove, although she wasn't quite sure why. All she should could think about was that damned crown… and all that blood… so much blood.

Why would she show me that? Why?

She looked over her shoulder to see if the woman had followed her out and, in that split second, collided with something solid, knocking her off her feet. She wondered at first if she'd hit some kind of wall. A stupid thought, given they were far from any kind of settlement. Indeed, the man that stood over her was no such obstacle.

She gaped at it... him... whatever it was, that towered over her. Two amber eyes, within a shiny golden face, gleamed down upon the ground in which Vaera lay.

'FORGIVE ME, CHILD,' the golden man smiled, extending a hand toward her. She settled on 'man,' for that was indeed what he resembled.

Vaera allowed the man to lift her back up to her feet, her thanks mumbled into obscurity as she stared at what stood before her in utter amazement.

'WHY DO YOU RUN?' he inquired. His voice was settled, virtually morose in its lack of expression. She felt suddenly calm in his presence.

'I–'

The sound of leaves crunching behind them attracted Vaera's attention. She uttered a strangled cry upon spinning round to find Zakariyanna stalking towards them. The sweet smile was gone and instead her mouth formed a hard line underneath the veil.

'Stay away from me, witch!' Vaera cried. 'You hear me? Leave me alone!'

'AH, SISTER,' the golden man greeted Zakariyanna with a sad shake of the head, 'MEDDLING IN DREAMS NOW?'

'Brother,' Zakariyanna replied, 'I thought that was your forte?'

The golden man looked back at Vaera, who quivered behind him, staring down at something unseen on her hands, and muttering over and over again to herself.

'So much blood… so much blood…'

The golden man sighed.

'IT APPEARS YOU HAVE UPSET THE REGAL. WHAT DID YOU SHOW HER?'

'Merely, a choice she must make,' Zakariyanna said.

'YOU THOUGHT IT WISE?'

'I thought it necessary.'

'SO WE MUST HOPE.'

The golden man planted a hand gently on Vaera's shoulder. 'THIS IS JUST A DREAM, REGAL,' he said reassuringly.

'Just… just a dream?' Vaera said hopefully.

'YES,' the golden man smiled and placed a fingertip against her forehead, 'SLEEEEP.'

*

Vaera gasped sharply, as she rose to her knees. She spun her head to-and-fro and found herself, to her relief, once again surrounded by her fellow companions.

Just a dream. Yet it had felt so real…

A hundred lights had blinked all around her, like sparks snapping off a grindstone. Then she'd held something in her hands...

Vaera felt her breath catch in her throat.

She slowly angled her neck down toward her lap, sighing with relief upon finding her hands bare and dry. But there had still been that strange woman, who had known so much about her... and that... man. Had he been made of gold?

She gave herself a shake and twisted to the other side.

It was just a dream.

Yet, something still irked Vaera. An inescapable feeling scratching at the base of her skull.

Out of the corner of her eye, Vaera could make out a group of trees that formed a grove.

Just a dream.

She turned over once more. Still, the trees lurked in the back of her mind.

But was it really?

Her cloak flew aside, as Vaera pushed herself to her feet.

No harm in having a look.

The Lycans snored on around her, oblivious, Nathaniel muttered something incoherently in his sleep, and Zaine remained motionless where he sat. How he ever managed to get a wink of sleep sat up like that was beyond her, it was as bizarre as seeing a horse asleep on its legs.

Just as Vaera thought she had made a clean escape, however, an all too familiar voice stopped her dead in her tracks.

'It is unwise to explore alone at this hour, young Regal.'

Zaine's back remained still, but she was certain it had been his voice.

'Have you been awake this whole time?' Vaera hissed.

The Hunter was already on his feet, as though he had been so for hours. With his long raven locks and black overcoat underneath the dark, bruised sky, he may as well have been a walking shadow.

'Can't sleep?' he asked.

'Bad dreams,' she replied hesitantly, 'what's your excuse, Hunter?'

His hand leaned against the pommel by his waist, as he looked down upon her bemusedly. 'Someone has to keep you all alive, don't they?'

'I suppose...' Vaera murmured her assent. She could feel the grove scratching at her neck all the while but resisted the urge to look back. 'Well... goodnight.'

She began to trudge away but Zaine had appeared by her shoulder the second she'd turned back.

'Do you have to follow me? What about the others? Don't they have to be kept alive?'

Zaine merely smiled and tossed something over his shoulder. A sharp growl emitted from their campsite a moment later, dark oaths spilling into the night.

'They'll be fine for now, I think,' Zaine said.

Gabe would not be happy in the morning; the thought brought a smirk to Vaera's face.

197

The two forked trees, bending towards each other to almost form an arch, looked all too familiar, as was the light that trickled from within. Zaine kept a firm grip on his sword, as they passed in-between them, not offering an explanation for his sudden edginess. Vaera thought she could see his eyes shifting rapidly side to side, scraping every last detail from every dislodged piece of bark to the last twisted blade of grass.

The fireflies they found inside she remembered. Every detail, as she glanced around, serving only to further Vaera's discomfort and draw the gnawing sensation deeper into her stomach.

'Something wrong?' the Hunter asked, watching the Regal closely as she bent down in the middle of the grove.

'Oh no…' Zaine thought he heard her mutter in despair, as she cradled something atop her lap.

'Is everything alright, Vaera?' Zaine said, 'you're shaking.'

The Hunter went over to touch the Regal's trembling shoulder, but she just as quickly slapped his hand away. His eyes moved down to the patch of lilies upon which the Regal sat, and the orchid, made all the more brilliantly violet, held in her pale clenched fist.

'Vaera,' Zaine began.

Vaera seemed to be holding back tears, as she roughly pushed past the Hunter and stormed out with the orchid still in hand. Zaine remained briefly where he stood, then kneeled down by the lilies, his gloved hand caressing the spot where she had uprooted the lone orchid.

'Something… amiss,' he murmured to himself.

Frowning, he shook his head solemnly and departed into the night.

Chapter 23

Vaera had been in a dark mood since they'd left the camp in the morning. When Samir dared ask if she was alright, he had been met with only a bleary-eyed scowl that sent him scurrying back to the safety of his books.

Certain he would be met with something sharper than a look, Nathaniel made an attempt – rather foolishly, in hindsight – of his own, as they were saddling the horses.

'What?' Vaera had muttered bluntly, as he edged tentatively towards her back.

'I... uhhh... is everything alright?' Nathaniel inquired, instantly regretting his course of action. It was an effort not to stare at the daggers stashed in Vaera's belt.

He steeled himself against the lash of her tongue, only to be left utterly perplexed by the Regal's tired sigh.

'I have been... troubled... of late,' Vaera turned to face him.

Nathaniel frowned, waiting for the bitter mutter of 'Kinslayer' under the girl's breath. It was not forthcoming.

'Why are you staring at me like that?' Vaera snapped suddenly.

Nathaniel shook himself, and held out his hands placatingly.

'I'm sorry, I just wanted to see if you were-'

'I don't want to talk about it,' the Regal said, returning to her bags.

Nathaniel thought to press his fellow Regal further, but fortunately found the sense enough to leave before he could make matters worse.

At least she didn't call me Kinslayer.

It probably meant nothing. She was tired, and she had still been less than pleasant. But still. It was an improvement.

With Nathaniel and Samir, and Gabe and Kaira seated on the mares, Vaera and Brey took up the back of Zaine's tall stallion. The Hunter insisted they went at barely much more than a canter, so as not to strain the horses further.

Having lived in Obsidia all his life, Nathaniel found it both surprising and maddening that there was so little in the way of civilisation, once they had left Dalmarra. Rolling hills, dotted with trees, dominated the landscape. Unworked green pastures would give way to the occasional field of golden wheat that tickled their boots as they rode, or fade into brushes of wildflowers.

Brey had caught a few in her hand as they ploughed through, which she weaved into a circlet. Gabe presented Kaira one of the flowers with a flourish that left the short-haired Lycan rolling her eyes. She made as if to throw the wildflower over her shoulder but hid it away the moment Gabe's eyes turned back to the path ahead. Even Vaera plucked up a smile, as she drifted a hand through the flowers.

Once in a while, a horse would gallop past them, presumably taking its rider back to Dalmarra. The riders casting curious looks their way. Zaine always had his hood up, long before Nathaniel's ears caught the steady drum of hoofbeats.

When the light began to dwindle, the Hunter decided it was time to set up camp once more. Nathaniel reckoned they couldn't have travelled more than ten miles that day. Though given how laboured Bela's breath seemed, as they pulled to a stop by a river-ditch, she may as well have galloped all the

201

way to the Black Mountains. Nathaniel patted Bela's mane a little guiltily, as she guzzled water.

'We need more horses!' Nathaniel had whispered urgently to Zaine after he'd dismounted from the stallion. Hearing Bela's ragged breath, he stopped himself before he could add, *or I'll be a thousand years gone before we make it to Obsidia!*

'You see any cities nearby, Regal?' the Hunter waved his hand around the green expanse that stretched around them in every direction. 'Féy would be too far a detour. We'll have to wait for one of the villages, or a farm. There surely will be one of the two nearby.'

The Lycans avoided Zaine's pointed gaze, lowering their eyes to the reins in their hands. The Hunter could hardly send them away, but it would be their fault if Nathaniel didn't make it to Obsidia in time.

If the horses make it that far, Nathaniel thought with a rueful shake of the head. He shuddered to think what they'd do if they couldn't find another horse to spread the burden. A slow canter to the Black Mountains would take weeks.

However, true to Zaine's estimation, they came across a plume of smoke in the horizon, which couldn't have belonged to a particularly large settlement. Sure enough, the hills gave way to brown ploughed fields and a large barn lined with haystacks. A man in slacks led a couple oxen with a plough towards the far corner of his land. He pulled the beasts to a sharp halt when he heard the incoming hoofbeats and waved his arms towards them. Nathaniel wasn't quite sure if it was an invitation to come closer or an attempt to ward them off. Zaine seemed to take it as the first. The farmer had a pitchfork ready in his hands to greet them once Nathaniel and the others had made it round to the farmhouse. The way his hands kneaded the shaft, it looked like only the smallest provocation would encourage him to wield it against them.

'Ho there!' the farmer greeted them uncertainly. He was as grey and grizzled as Skew, but his eyes held far more warmth in them. All the same, he held his pitchfork tightly in his hands as if he expected trouble. 'What can I do ye' for?' His eyes seemed to rest a moment longer on Nathaniel and Vaera in particular. He kept snapping his head to the brick house with its smoking chimney, which lay a few paces to his left.

'Horses, if you have them to spare,' Zaine replied plainly. 'We have too far to travel with only these three.'

'I might,' the man chewed his lip thoughtfully. 'If you have the coin.'

'That won't be a problem,' Zaine patted his stallion's saddlebags.

'And might I ask who's buying?'

'I'm not sure you would like to know,' Zaine said doubtfully.

The farmer angled the pitchfork against his body. 'I don't sell horses to just anybody that come here, what have ye' to hide man?'

Zaine sighed and then slowly lowered his hood.

The farmer blinked at Zaine's silver eyes.

'A Hunter,' he said breathlessly; the man's knuckles were white against his pitchfork.

'If you're willing to part with them, I'd be happy to compensate you generously,' Zaine continued on as if he didn't notice the man quivering where he stood. He retrieved a bulging pouch from the saddlebags of his dark stallion and threw it to the farmer.

The man just about caught the purse before it smacked against his gaping jaw. He poked it open and licked his lips at the contents.

'I do have the horses to spare...' the man mumbled to himself, '...and Tab do badger me about the markets...'

He pocketed the pouch after a moment's consideration, then threw an arm over his head for the group to follow him into the barn.

'Quickly now wit'ye', quickly now,' he ushered them in, grumbling something about how his wife would beat him with a saucepan if she caught him with them.

The barn had been sectioned in half, with one side filled with pens for the chickens and goats, and more haystacks, and the other half as a makeshift stable for the seven horses. One of the mares poked her muzzle over the gates and shook her mane, as the farmer approached with the group in tow.

'Easy now, easy now,' he said, smoothing the mare's mane. 'Usually I'd take a couple to Dalmarra for the markets every now n' then, once their grown n' all,' he told them. 'Sell well when the crops don't.'

'Your wife isn't keen on guests?' Zaine inquired.

'Not on *certain* guests,' the farmer said, wincing at the thought.

'Yet you'd deal with a Hunter?' Kaira arched an eyebrow inquisitively.

'I'm not fool enough to think yer' all the same,' the farmer insisted hurriedly. 'But yer' being here, Hunter, it ain't good news.'

The man shook his head as he patted the horse's muzzle.

'Then we will be swiftly on our way,' Zaine replied. 'We seek a roof further on before nightfall.'

The Lycans and Regals shared a relieved look. Even a rotten pallet in some dark cellar would be a welcome reprieve from the elements.

The man fingered his lips, observing the darkening clouds gathering outside the barn with some unease.

'There be a town – Greymound I think – but a couple miles on,' he said, using his pitchfork to point out the hills rising beyond his crops. 'But the folk there... aren't the most welcoming.'

'What do you mean by that?' Vaera asked.

The farmer snorted.

'Let me put it this way, Regal, when ye' get there, I think ye' should just let one of the humans do the talking,' he nodded towards the Lycans.

'They're not– ow!' Vaera glared at Kaira whilst rubbing the sore part of her arm where the Lycan had elbowed her.

'Thank you for the warning,' Zaine interjected.

The man nodded, wrinkled eyes looking suspiciously between the two girls.

205

'I'd offer ye' a roof here, Hunter, to all of ye,' the farmer said with a wave of his hand, sounding like he meant it. 'But my wife... she been terribly jumpy, what wit'the Regals n' all.'

'Regals?' Nathaniel blinked.

'My people were here?' Vaera sounded even more surprised.

'A group of 'em, they came looking fer a boy – one of their own,' the man screwed up his face in remembrance. 'Something 'bout him being *someone of import*', they wanted to know if we'd seen him.'

Nathaniel stifled a gasp and edged a step back, pulling the hood of his cloak tighter around his face. He felt the Lycans' eyes on him but refused to meet them.

'How very strange,' Zaine remarked.

'Oh yea,' bad news they were, I tell ye' now,' the farmer shivered suddenly at the memory. 'Chilled my old bones, Hunter.'

'Why's that?' Gabe asked, his eyes darting up from the pommel of his sword.

'They just... came out of nowhere.' The farmer drummed his fingers nervously against the shaft of his pitchfork. 'They asked their questions, I answered, then I swear I just turned my back fer a second n' – Poof! Thought it might'a been ghosts, had the wife not seen them either.'

'These Regals... they were soldiers?' Zaine inquired.

'They weren't armoured if that be what ye' mean, and I don't remember seeing any blade or bow. They were just dressed like ordinary townsfolk, 'cept, they weren't ordinary.'

The farmer glanced back outside the barn, as if he expected one of the Regals to jump out the wall as they spoke.

'How do you mean?'

The farmer leant past his pitchfork, and said in a bare whisper, 'women.'

'They were women?'

'Every last one of 'em.'

Vaera and Nathaniel shared an uncomfortable look. These Regals sounded awfully familiar…

'You are absolutely sure of that?'

'As sure as I see ye' stand before me, Hunter.'

'Then I suppose we'd best keep an eye out.'

'And fer the boy,' the farmer said. 'I don't know what they what they want wit'im, but I could see it in their eyes… 'aint nothing good, Hunter, 'aint nothing good.'

The man shook his head grimly, lumbering past the group to the barn's entrance to point out a strip of mud running adjacent to the edge of the ploughed fields. 'Follow this here path. Should take ye' to the hills, n' then Greymound be no farther.'

Perhaps it was owing to the farmer's need to be rid of them as soon as possible, rather than his generosity that he insisted the Lycans take whichever of the horses they desired.

'What's so strange about them being women?' Brey had huffed, as soon as the farmer was out of earshot. She seemed to take the farmer's words as a personal affront. 'Men always seem to find something strange in a woman who isn't utterly feeble,' Vaera sniffed.

207

'What stories would they have left to tell, if a woman had the audacity to be capable of defending herself?' Kaira added. The three girls gave Nathaniel, and the two other boys pointed looks, as if they'd made comments to the contrary.

Samir frowned, apparently not quite sure what was going on. Gabe, on the other hand, seemed to be on the verge of a retort, before shaking his head and fiddling needlessly with the saddle of his gelding. Without voicing any accusations, the women seemed to have mastered the knack of making the others feel guilty for things they weren't personally responsible for.

'Nathaniel…'

Zaine was leaning beside Bela's saddlebags beckoning him to come closer.

Nathaniel hoped nothing was wrong with his horse.

'What is it?' he asked, 'is Bela okay?'

'The horse is fine, Regal, I was wondering what *this…*' the Hunter pulled a metallic rod from behind his back, '…was doing in your possession?'

The rod was a strange thing. Runes of various shapes and sizes had been carved into the metal like the veins of a leaf. He had thought it a knife at first glance given how it spanned the length of the Hunter's forearm, curving to a sharp point, like a fang.

'I've… never seen that before,' Nathaniel said, looking perplexed.

'Strange…' the Hunter muttered.

'Strange? Why?' Nathaniel asked.

208

'It belongs to Thorne,' Zaine said, holding the rod away from him, as if he were considering throwing the thing away. 'Well… it stayed with him at any rate.'

It stayed with him?

Zaine talked about the rod as if it were a living thing with legs.

The Hunter's brow knitted against his forehead. For a moment, Nathaniel thought Zaine was going accuse him of lying but he merely placed the rod back in Bela's saddlebags, without further comment. Nathaniel stared at the saddlebags in stunned silence for a moment, before chasing Zaine to his black stallion.

'What is that?' Nathaniel demanded. The Hunter's face was as impassive as stone, though his brow remained wrinkled still as he stepped into the stirrups.

'What is it?' Nathaniel asked.

The Hunter did not answer. Was there a measure of concern in those silver eyes?

'How did it end up in my saddlebags? Did Thorne put it there?'

'Get back on your horse, Regal, we've a long way to go,' Zaine said, busying himself with the reins.

'Athrana's grace, Hunter! Why won't you tell me what it is? Are you afraid of it?'

Nathaniel instantly regretted his last sentence. There was not a single crack in the Hunter's granite-like face, as he stared ahead unblinkingly toward the darkening horizon.

'The rod has a mind of its own,' was all the Hunter told him. He dug in his spurs and urged the black stallion ahead at a trot.

Nathaniel clambered onto Bela's back and gathered the reins. *It has a mind of its own. What on earth had the Hunter meant by that?*

'Well...' he cleared his throat. 'I guess we better get going.'

One of the girls muttered something quietly behind Nathaniel, encouraging a subsequent derisive snort.

'Did they *have* to come?' he hissed back to Gabe.

The curly-haired boy shrugged as if to say, *just try and stop them.*

Chapter 24

Darkness had almost fully descended upon Nathaniel's party by the time they had reached Greymound. A mile out from the farm, they'd had to navigate through undulating hills, before the terrain flattened out into a litter of ploughed fields that stretched as far as the eye could see. Dots of amber winked across the numerous slate and tile buildings inside the settlement, multiplying as the horses drew closer to Greymound's log walls.

Boots, hooves, and cart wheels had ground the earth around Greymound's perimeter into a dusty ring. Corkscrews of dust were kicked up behind Nathaniel, as Bela followed the Hunter's black stallion through the village's archway.

A handful of street peddlers pulled their wares in carts and barrows under cover, as bulging black clouds converged overhead. They all turned to face the newcomers, their expressions souring when they caught sight of Nathaniel and Vaera. The farmer had warned them that Greymound wouldn't be particularly friendly but Nathaniel was still surprised by the open hostility.

He drew his hood as low over his eyes as it would allow. With a backwards glance, he noticed that Vaera had done the same.

If that wasn't strange enough, the villagers actually gasped when Samir rode past. Indeed, those peddlers who hadn't yet found refuge, began to speed up their efforts.

'A Scorched! Here!' Nathaniel heard one of the villagers exclaim to another.

Nathaniel found himself gaping in open-mouthed horror at some of the other, less savoury, comments about Samir that reached his ears. Commendably though, Samir rode on, staring straight ahead, appearing not to notice the personal nature of the insults. Nathaniel couldn't understand what was wrong with these people. Humans and Dwarves came and went each year in Obsidia, without issue. And, under Tolken's reign, while the Scorched were less common, they were viewed more with curiosity than dislike. The people of Greymound however, looked a minor provocation away from hanging them all from the nearest tree.

'People fear what they are not used to,' Zaine said, glancing at the expression on Nathaniel's face.

'What have they to fear from us more than any other traveller?' Nathaniel said.

'Imagine if a handful of armed Lycans strolled through your people's farms one day. What would be the first reaction of your people, I wonder?'

Nathaniel blinked.

'That's different,' he protested.

'Is it?' Zaine said. 'Regals are no more used to Lycans, as a people deserving of rights and dignity, than these people are to the Scorched.'

They took a turn into a street lined with dwellings, where wide eyed children still played in the dust.

'The relationship between Lycans and Regals is completely different,' Nathaniel insisted. 'We've a shared history, these people, they... they just–'

'If you would allow Lycans to walk among your people, Regal, in time you would come to accept them,' Zaine said.

'That won't happen,' Nathaniel scoffed. 'The Szar certainly won't allow that to happen.'

'Tolken believed it could,' the Hunter countered. 'Had you shared the Szar's worldly views, you wouldn't be here now.'

Nathaniel had no retort for that.

Zaine tugged his reins back and stopped his horse in the middle of the street. A wide building, at least twice as tall as any other nearby, had caught the Hunter's attention. A sign, shaped in the silhouette of a rearing horse, swung gently in the breeze above the words, THE PRANCER. A faint buzz, emanating from behind the door, became more apparent the closer they got to the inn. As they dismounted, the door was flung open, spilling soft music out into the street. The man that burst out with it lurched towards them, his arms swinging by his knees, looking particularly worse for wear.

''scusemewouldya,' the man's words rolled into each other. He gave the Scorched boy a strange look, as he barged past. Vaera looked horrified as she watched the man take a tumble onto the street, before picking himself up and staggering away.

'Looks like you after your first ale, Gabe,' Brey giggled behind her hand.

A stab of annoyance daggered Nathaniel's stomach, though not for Brey's laugh. In fact, he wasn't quite sure what it was for. He avoided Kaira's inquisitive eyes, as he restrained a grimace.

'Perhaps, we should keep going to the next town?' Samir enquired, discretely.

'Under *that*?' Gabe stuck a thumb up at the dark, swollen clouds overhead. They looked fit to burst, at any given moment.

'I'm not sleeping outside again,' Vaera said firmly, folding her arms against her body and shivering despite the relative warmth.

'This will do for tonight,' Zaine said. No one contested the matter, after the Hunter had spoken.

A wiry boy, who had been leaning against the tavern's front, stepped forward hesitantly, offering to stable their horses. After a moment's consideration, in which the boy tugged uncomfortably at his collar, the Hunter agreed and gave him a silver coin. Nathaniel suddenly thought of the inscribed rod, which had mysteriously appeared in his saddlebags, and pulled it out before him. He was certain his grandfather had put it there for a reason. But why? Surely Thorne would have told him its purpose rather than leave him with this strange puzzle. Even though it currently seemed of little use, he felt oddly drawn to it.

With a shrug, he tucked the rod inside his belt. If Thorne thought it important enough to keep, then perhaps, in time, he too would divulge its secrets.

Vaera audibly gagged, as they crossed the threshold, and looked as if she were about to mount a series of complaints. However, perhaps remembering her previous statement, she pursed her lips tightly. Not that Nathaniel disagreed with her. The smell of ale and sweat hung so heavily inside the tavern, you could practically taste it. Gamrial's rose-scented bar in Obsidia seemed a lifetime ago.

It was particularly quiet tonight. A handful of the tavern's patrons dotted the long benches that lined the middle of the tavern and most of the tables buried in the shadows were unoccupied.

A few of the inn's patrons swayed dangerously to the sombre tune of a lyre. The bard looked as if he sincerely regretted ever coming across Greymound. For the most part though, people sat quietly at their tables, bathed in candlelight, exchanging hushed words or blowing plumes of smoke from their pipes.

They must have cut a strange bunch; two Regals, four Lycans, and a Hunter, hidden within the shadows of his hood. Indeed, many raised their heads from their tankards to observe the newcomers with apparent discomfort.

'I'm not sure about this,' Nathaniel heard Samir murmur beside him.

'Are you mad?' Gabe said, hungrily eyeing the platters of steak being carried about by the white-aproned serving maids.

'Well, what do you want, what do you want?' a screechy voice cut in.

The innkeeper, a bony man with long, wispy hair that was receding halfway over his head, crossed the floor to meet them. A toothy smile fought with a grimace, as if the man were unsure whether he really wanted their business. His mind quickly settled when he caught sight of the coins glimmering in the Hunter's hand.

'And how may I serve, my lord?' the innkeeper's back creaked, like a ship's hull, into a half-bow.

There was a rattle of metal, as Zaine dropped a handful of silvers into the innkeeper's outstretched hand.

'Three rooms, food, and drink,' Zaine said briskly.

'Of course, of course,' the innkeeper gave an even more ingratiating bow, though raised an eyebrow at the grey-skinned Regals, and both when turning to Samir. 'I'm sure I could find your... servant... a pallet in the attic?' he nodded towards the Scorched boy.

Gabe snorted loudly at that and the book Samir held trembled in his hands. Nathaniel found himself wondering for a moment what it would be like to experience the ire of the gentle Scorched boy. The innkeeper looked between them confusedly.

'The boy will be staying with us,' Zaine said. He palmed a coin into the man's hand, perhaps a little harder than necessary, for the innkeeper actually bit his lip to mask the pain. 'And we'll want a table to ourselves, preferably backed against a wall.'

'As my lord wishes,' the innkeeper dipped his head once more.

They were guided to one of the alcoves, cut into the walls of the tavern. Inside it, a serving maid was bending over a table, straightening a somewhat soiled cloth. The innkeeper, who had introduced himself as Marlo, sent the maid scurrying with a few hissed commands.

'Would this be suited to my lord's needs?' Marlo said, waving his hands dramatically over the table, as if it were a King's lounger and not stained with grime and spilt ale.

'This will do,' Zaine said.

The innkeeper's eyes flickered to the bags they lumped under the table, before settling on the rod attached to Nathaniel's belt.

'Will there be anything else?' Marlo inquired. His eyes had not left the rod. Nathaniel didn't like how the man was staring at it.

'Just food and drink, innkeeper,' Zaine replied.

'As you please, my lord,' the man bowed graciously. His mouth sagging back into a grimace the moment he turned away.

'I don't like him,' Samir muttered tightly, as soon as Marlo was out of earshot.

'Does the servant dare speak?' Gabe grinned slyly. He returned an innocent shrug to Kaira, after she kicked him under the table.

A moment later, the maid returned to their table with foaming tankards and a platter with an array of meats and vegetables. The sight was enough to make Nathaniel drool. Though, as soon as he had taken his first mouthful, the tavern's door creaked open. The cold air rushing in from outside pricking the hairs on the nape of his neck.

Three newcomers entered, rainwater still dripping from their hooded cloaks. Not an inch of skin was revealed, from their thigh high boots to their leather gloves. After briefly scanning the room, they strode to the table nearest to them and set themselves down, without stripping off their cloaks or even, Nathaniel noted, lowering their hoods.

Marlo was already at their table, rudely asking what they were doing in his establishment. One of the hoods tilted in his direction and a couple of coins, appearing seemingly from nowhere, rolled towards his end of the table. Marlo stared at them for a moment, suspiciously Nathaniel thought, then scurried away with the coins in hand.

'Who 'a 'ey?' Gabe spoke through a mouthful of food.

'Subtle as always,' Kaira noted.

As far as Nathaniel was aware, Zaine hadn't taken a bite from his food. His hood remaining motionless, though Nathaniel was certain his eyes had been scanning the room constantly.

'They've kept an eye on us from the moment they stepped foot inside,' he said.

'They're Regal Assassins?' Gabe said, rising to grab another look. Zaine quickly dragged him back down to his seat.

'Do you feel a need to put yourself in danger, Lycan?' Zaine scolded Gabe, who merely shrugged in response.

As casually as he could manage, Nathaniel looked around the room in a sweeping arc, as if he were merely taking in his surroundings. If the newcomers suspected his true intentions, no indication was given. Indeed, they remained as static

'I can't see their faces,' Nathaniel spoke into his drink.

'Or any weapons,' Kaira chipped in, 'they seem like the rest of these people.'

Vaera appeared to be looking shrewdly at the newcomers but did not say a word.

'Did you not listen to a word of what that farmer said?' Gabe leant past his tankard, 'that's exactly what those assassins want you to think! It could be any one of these– would you stop blazing elbowing me!'

'Stop waving your arms around like a loon, then,' Kaira hissed back.

'You're going to get us noticed!' Brey growled.

Gabe glanced between the girls, his face a curious mixture of bemusement and shock. 'Are you both seriously stupid enough to think we haven't been already?' he gestured at the crowd before them, some of whom had already shared a cold look toward their table.

'Keep your voice down, Lycan!' Zaine's voice was hard this time, spurring Gabe into silence.

The three remained in the same rigid position for much of the night. Their hands folded together before them, staring inwardly. If they talked at all, Nathaniel could not hear even the faintest murmur of their voices.

More villagers flocked into the tavern as the night went on, precipitating a change of tune from the bard. Jaunty songs bounced around the tavern, each accompanied by the crack of ceramic mugs against wooden tables. The people of Greymound were bizarre. No matter how well the bard performed, the villagers would pelt him with sprouts or whatever vegetable came to hand, roaring for their favourite songs. Each coarser than the last.

Brey had a funny glint in her eyes, as she stared sternly at Nathaniel over the rim of her tankard. The Lycan girl seemed to enjoy making him feel as awkward as possible, when she wasn't flirting with Samir or Gabe. She'd pause every now and then to give him a pointed look, as if he'd said something unpleasant to her.

Nathaniel looked to Kaira for help but the Lycan appeared more interested in the bard's rendition of *A Fine Maid's*

Awaiting. Vaera would mostly scowl in his direction, if he dared look at her. He wondered whether he preferred her open dislike of him to Brey's strange games.

Trying his best to cool the heat in his cheeks, Nathaniel looked past the throng of villagers at the cloaked three opposite them. One of the inn's patrons tried to sit with them but quickly reconsidered his decision after one of the hoods turned to face him.

'They have the look of the *Khadim,*' Samir said all the sudden.

'The what?' Nathaniel gave the Scorched Lycan a quizzical look.

'The *Khadim,*' Samir repeated simply, as if the term was common knowledge, '*they who shroud themselves.*' When one of my people are widowed, they are usually swift in finding another partner. But there are those who are not always so willing. Some choose to never remarry, for they believe it would bring dishonour to the deceased. So, they hide their bodies from the light, in order to resist the temptation of another. We call them, *Khadim.*'

'That's so sad,' Brey said.

Nathaniel thought he heard Vaera mutter something to the effect of, 'I don't know why women bother in the first place.'

'Are they kadim, Sammy?' Gabe interjected, pointing at the three opposite them.

'*Khadim,*' Gabe rolled his eyes as Samir corrected him. 'I'm not sure, I... don't think so.'

'So, they might be the assassins after all,' Gabe growled. He leant forward, as if to rise, but the slightest quiver of the

Hunter's hood caused Gabe to reluctantly slump back into his seat.

'Revealing themselves to their target seems a strange tactic, even for the Sisters of the Dagger,' Zaine said.

Nathaniel gulped. The Hunter made it sound as if he had made up his mind. Assassins for certain. He glanced at Vaera out of the corner of his eye. The Regal looked more thoughtful than worried, as she stared at the cloaked three. Tracing an index finger across her lower lip, as if she was considering something.

She avoided looking at Nathaniel for the rest of the evening.

Chapter 25

Nathaniel's footsteps seemed to echo loudly, as he walked the path to the greenhouse.

It seemed awfully familiar.

'Come on, this way,' a voice pushed him into a stride, a girl's voice, although he couldn't quite tell from where.

Words were whispered into his ear, as if the girl's chin rested against his shoulder. Nathaniel spun about, determined to find the source, but the path stood empty.

'The girl is important,' Nathaniel told himself. But who was the girl he so desperately needed to see? And why?

'In here. Closer,' the voice sang sweetly.

Something green flashed before his eyes, disappearing out of sight within the confines of the greenhouse. An odd sense of foreboding polluted Nathaniel's stomach, bile rushing up his throat, as he stepped through the doorway.

A sea of white lilies had flooded the inside of the greenhouse, rustling against his ankles. Nathaniel only had eyes for the girl, however. Her back was turned as she knelt, so all Nathaniel could see was the green of her dress and the purple shimmer from the orchids entwined around her hair. The girl's shoulders were heaving up and down, as she suppressed a sob into her chest.

'Hey,' Nathaniel said, making his voice as soothing as he could manage. 'Are you okay?'

The girl's shoulders froze mid-raise.

'You should not have come,' she said.

The voice was familiar but warped, difficult to make out.

'It's alright,' Nathaniel said reassuringly. He reached toward the girl's shoulder, but a hand snapped tightly against his wrist, holding him away from her.

'Gah!' he cried out in pain, 'Let go of me! I was just–'

Nathaniel's jaw dropped as soon as he saw the girl's face.

The orchids didn't just cover her hair, they *were* her hair. A shower of purple poured down either side of her cheeks. The purple petals, which separated her lips and eyes from the red of her face, quivered as she spoke.

'Why?' she demanded of him, shaking Nathaniel about as if he were a rag doll.

Nathaniel grimaced. For a hand formed of flowers, her grip was iron.

'Why did you do this to me?' the girl sobbed.

'Do what? I… I don't know what… you're talking about,' Nathaniel replied through gritted teeth as he fought to wrestle the girl's hand from his arm. She was going to break his wrist if she kept holding on, but she didn't seem to care.

'This is all your fault, Kinslayer!'

With a shrill cry, the girl made of flowers grabbed at his jerkin with her other hand and dragged him into the lilies.

'This–' she struck against his back once.

'Is–' she struck him twice.

'Your–' she struck him thrice.

'Fault!' and once more for good measure.

Nathaniel felt the girl's hold on him slip, as she again burst into tears. Petals pouring down her dress.

'By Athrana's grace,' Nathaniel gasped, crawling away from her. 'Who are you?'

The girl looked at him through her hands.

'Do you burn for him?' she said.

Not quite sure if he'd heard the girl right, Nathaniel frowned.

'What?'

The ground underneath Nathaniel's back fell through and suddenly he was falling through the lilies. He saw the girl lunge towards him, but her hand only clipped the tip of his boots.

Nathaniel cried out but no words emerged from his lips. The dark was swallowing him. Further and further he fell, until the greenhouse was little more than a white speck. A lone star, dotted on the horizon.

He grappled blindly towards it, like a man fighting to save himself from drowning. The star blinked out of existence and then all became black.

*

Nathaniel gasped and opened his eyes.

The room was dark but something seemed to stir within the shadows.

'Who's there?' he called.

'Foolish girl!' a sharp voice replied.

'Well… that didn't go as planned,' a second conceded.

From the corner of his room a third hummed a tune that sounded distinctly familiar.

Nathaniel grappled at his bedside table. Once his hands had closed against the candlestick, he closed his eyes and focused as best he could on the image of a lit flame.

Sorry, Thorne.

He felt the warmth of the candle against his hand and opened his eyes, jerking at who stood before him.

Their hoods lowered, three grey-skinned Regals surrounded his bed. One, with a shock of red hair that curled uncontrollably over her shoulders, stooped over to grab something from the floor.

'So, you have a Warlock in your party, Kinslayer?' she said accusingly, inquisitive eyes washing over him.

'Don't be foolish, Davina,' the eldest tutted. Her hair was almost completely white, as if the Regal had dipped the top of her head into snow. She held her hand to her lips, staring at him, or through him – he couldn't quite decide – with a pondering expression.

The third, seemingly unaware of the events transpiring around her, hummed away merrily, as if she had not a care in the world. Long, dirty blonde hair fell just above her waist and upturned eyebrows gave her eyes a dreamy quality.

Nathaniel frowned at their robes. A dark blue, which could pass for black in the shade, but a different colour to those worn by the hooded three in the tavern, he was certain. Perhaps they had merely changed their clothes?

'How else can you explain this?' the one called Davina pointed at Nathaniel. Her boot nudged something heavy onto its back. It was Samir.

Athrana's grace... had they–

The humming Regal made a strangled sort of coughing noise from the back of her throat.

'Oh, calm yourself, Kailena – the dog will live,' Davina said.

Nathaniel sighed in relief.

The humming assassin looked up at the ceiling, as if purposefully ignoring Davina's words.

'We'll probably need a Warlock for this,' Davina said, nodding towards Nathaniel's bed.

'Oh yes, why don't we just hop on a cart all the way back to Dalmarra and fetch one?' the older Regal snapped back. 'Stupid girl!'

'I said *probably*,' Nathaniel heard Davina mutter sourly under her breath.

The older Regal tapped her bottom lip thoughtfully, as her eyes scrutinised the space which separated them from Nathaniel.

'Uhhh,' Nathaniel began uncertainly, 'you realise I can hear you... right?'

Davina continued twirling the dagger she had extracted from the floor, as if she hadn't heard him. The youngest of the Regals, the humming blonde – who Nathaniel wagered was his own age – continued with her tune, whilst the oldest assassin shot him a glance that should have nailed him against the headboard.

'I wonder...' the snowy-haired assassin mused.

BANG!

A flash of silver blurred from the older Regal's outstretched hand. Nathaniel let out a startled cry as the air where the blade had struck welted into an angry green glow around him, like a translucent cocoon. The knife clattered to the floor.

The green glow faded, leaving the end of Nathaniel's bed as it had been before.

What had just happened? Had he done that? No, he couldn't have. Putting aside the fact that Thorne had asked him not to use Majik, he would have surely felt its warmth surging through him had he meant to deflect the knife.

Davina's raised eyebrow had more than a hint of smugness about it. 'I already tried that,' Davina said.

'Oh, hush girl!' the older Regal replied irritably. 'This is no ordinary shield. No Warlock these days could come up with something this powerful on their own. Why, I'd go as far as saying you'd need a – BOY! Where did you get that?' the eldest Regal pointed at the rod lying on Nathaniel's bedside table.

Although positive she couldn't get anywhere near it, Nathaniel snatched the rod from the table with a blush. He hadn't stolen it from Thorne, but who would believe that it had just appeared in his saddlebags?

'So, you can hear me then?' Nathaniel said.

227

'From whom did you pilfer that rod, boy?' the older Regal demanded, her eyes suddenly flaring.

Nathaniel felt angry for the flush in his cheeks. *Who are they – and assassins no less – to make demands of me?*

'I didn't steal it!' Nathaniel said adamantly, certain that that had been the implication. 'And I didn't kill the Emperor!' he added with a growl.

Kailena stared at Nathanial, dreamy eyes giving him a searching look. 'That's not what your father says,' she said softly.

'Why are we wasting time talking, Lucerne?' Davina caught her dagger in mid-air and rolled her eyes impatiently. 'We have a job to do,' she jabbed the dagger in Nathaniel's direction.

'You would do well to watch your tone, girl!' Lucerne said sharply. Her eyes had still not left the rod Nathaniel clutched tightly against his chest. *Why is everyone so obsessed with this useless lump of iron,* he wondered incredulously. Thinking back to the greedy look in Marlo's eyes when he'd spotted it.

Lucerne crouched beside his bed close to where the green welt in the air had appeared, narrowing her eyes. 'I don't know how you're managing this, boy but know this: nothing has ever stopped the Sisters from completing their task. Hide behind this shield for as long as you wish but you won't–'

CRASH!

The three assassins whirled round, Lucerne and Davina with daggers at the ready. The door was snapped off its hinges, as Zaine burst through into a crouch, sword held diagonally across his body.

Lucerne lowered her dagger slowly, whilst Davina kept her own raised, almost choking as she spat, 'demonspawn.'

'Zaine,' Lucerne gave the Hunter a curt nod.

'Lucerne,' Zaine said, straightening up, his face set in stone. 'Clever of you to drag me away with a Blissgiver sighting. How long must you have had to carry that old corpse around Horizon, I dread to think.'

Davina muttered something under her breath that sounded like, 'not as clever as you think, demon.'

'So,' Lucerne replied through almost pursed lips. 'What ever will we do now?'

'Leaving would be a strong start,' Zaine suggested.

'Give me the boy and it'll be an even quicker finish,' Lucerne countered.

'I'm afraid that won't be happening.'

'You think it smart making yourself another target for the Emperor?'

'His Grace and I are already at odds, this will hardly change matters.'

'And what of the rest of your kind? Will they take well to being associated with this error of judgement? And all that it entails?'

'Don't make idle threats, Lucerne. Especially not ones you can't enforce.'

'Then we are at an impasse.'

'It would seem that way.'

The older Regal thumbed her lip thoughtfully. 'Sisters!' her voice cracked suddenly like a whip. 'With me!'

'What!' Davina shrieked. 'That's it? We're just letting him go?' she shot a dirty look in Nathaniel's direction.

The red-faced look Lucerne gave the Sister suggested she was close to having her ears boxed.

'Girl... you will follow me of your own will,' she began slowly. 'Or I will drag you out by your curls. Do I make myself clear?'

'Yes... Sister,' Davina bent her head like a chided dog, as she followed the older Sister out of Nathaniel's room.

Once Kailena had also departed, Lucerne ran her hawk-like eyes between Nathaniel and Zaine. 'This isn't over,' she promised.

'I would be almost disappointed if it were,' Zaine replied dryly.

Lucerne pursed her lips so tightly, it looked like she'd swallowed a handful of lemons. After a final angry glare at Nathaniel, she turned and slipped out after her fellow Sisters.

Nathaniel jumped out of his bed and crouched beside Samir's unconscious form. 'Samir, hey, Samir!' Nathaniel patted a muscular shoulder. The boy did not stir.

What if that Sister - Davina, he remembered - had been lying? What if they'd really killed Samir? A cold feeling filled the pit of his stomach. The Sisters of the Dagger had been after him but, Lycan or no, Samir had tried to defend them both. Nathaniel swallowed hard. This was his fault.

Zaine stuck his boot against Samir's side. The Scorched boy coughed and spluttered, and his eyes finally blinked open.

'Urgh,' Samir groaned. He held a hand gingerly to the back of his head. 'What... what happened?'

'We've had visitors,' Zaine said.

'The Regal assassins? I... I woke when they came, I tried to stop them but...'

'Get dressed,' Zaine said briskly. 'We need to leave. Now.'

The Hunter stalked off without another word. Nathaniel hoped he wouldn't leave them alone for long.

'Sisters of the Dagger...' Samir's deep voice hummed towards the empty doorway.

Nathaniel could hardly believe it himself.

The Sisters of the Dagger, all three of them!

Nathaniel had listened to many a tale about the Sisters, back in Obsidia. His father even used to scare him and Solas into going to bed on time with the famous trio – 'watch out boys! The Sisters are creeping up the wall, they're creeping through your windows, they're–' That had sent them both up like a shot. Lucerne sounded vaguely familiar from the stories but the other two, Davina and Kailena, were new to him. How he was still alive, however, seemed a feat beyond luck's reach.

You tried to save me, Nathaniel gave the Scorched boy a grateful look. 'Thank you,' he told him.

The Scorched boy looked embarrassed and craned his neck around the room, as if in search of a book to hide himself behind.

231

'It is barely dawn… be reasonable,' the man said with barely restrained irritableness. Though, he held out his hand expectantly before him, eying the pouch strung around the Hunter's belt.

'I won't ask again, innkeeper.'

A few of the men sat on the benches behind Marlo, were suspiciously well armed. The table was bare of any food or tankards and the men watched keenly, as they fingered the swords at their belts.

Zaine was apparently in no mood to bargain, however, for he threw down his hood to the audible gasps of all those sitting on the tavern's benches. Those who hadn't returned to their seats bolted, after one look at Zaine's silver eyes. The innkeeper uttered a high-pitched squeak and withdrew his hand as quickly as if it had fallen in a viper pit.

'You will have our horses ready in the next five minutes,' Zaine said commandingly. He did not touch his sword, nor, indeed, did he make a single move towards the man. Though, the threat was as evident in his quiet voice, as if he'd held his ruby pommel sword to the man's quivering throat. 'Move quickly, innkeeper.'

After blinking rapidly like he'd been slapped, the innkeeper suddenly jolted into life and began barking orders at the few terrified stragglers on the benches behind him.

'So, those three we saw yesterday were the assassins after all,' Vaera said as they departed The Prancer. She had looked torn between disappointment and curiosity that Nathaniel had survived their visit utterly unscathed. His curly locks frizzy and in such disarray, almost as though he had been struck by lightning, Gabe looked half-asleep. His bed had to be upturned before he would join them.

'Five more minutes wouldn't have killed any of you,' he had grumbled. Nathaniel would have found Kaira's scolding of the Lycan highly amusing, had an attempt not just been made on his life.

With the Hunter nearby, it was possible that the Sisters wouldn't think of returning for a second attempt immediately, of course. Still, Nathaniel hardly wished to test the matter by lingering for too long.

Brey had been silent, ever since they had appeared at the three girls' room. She wore the same worried expression he'd seen in the Lycan Sanctuary, after he'd met Vaera for the first time. He cleared his throat awkwardly and made it look as if he were tightening his saddlebags on Bela. He almost wished the girl would go back to being upset with him.

Under a pale blue sky, bleeding amber, the sun wavered lazily over Greymound's dusty streets, as if it too had been roused far too early from its slumber.

'Where to now?' Nathaniel turned to Zaine once he had mounted Bela.

'Morne,' came the reply.

*

Strung in shadows, three cloaked in black watched the seven riders chase the dawn.

'Do we follow, Seeker?' one of the cloaked spoke.

The Seeker considered this for a moment.

'No,' she decided, after the last horse tail had whipped around the corner of houses. 'We will return to Is Drĕmăra.' she could not hide the bitter disappointment in her voice. She had thought – hoped, she conceded – that the child might be the one, but the boy's eyes had not borne the sign.

'What a pity, *Seeker*.' drawled the other voice, belonging to Isen. He was practically gleeful.

No doubt Isen greatly anticipated her returning bare-handed to the Sun Court. The wretch would stop at nothing to wring her out to dry and take her place. The Seeker scowled underneath her hood at the thought. She had fought off other challengers like him before, to get to where she was now and she would continue to do so until her last drawn breath.

Chapter 26

The open spaces of Greymound, where sunlight had shined freely over the dust and scrub, were gone. Shadow was in ascendancy in Morne, where buildings huddled together like rats in a storm, as if to escape the bitter breeze that blew through the narrow streets. As the daylight faded, sparks flying from the forges, that hadn't yet been boarded over, were all that stood to bar the dark that laid claim to the city.

Mud squelched underfoot, as they trudged through its streets. Nathaniel could feel Bela's hooves sink further, the longer his mare left them in the muck. He found himself wondering whether there were cobblestones below or just layers of hardened clay. Vaera was particularly vocal in expressing her disgust, much to the amusement of Brey who accompanied her.

Morne was quieter too, not quite possessing the hustle and bustle of Obsidia. Zaine had called it the 'city of smoke and whispers'. Nathaniel could understand why and it did little to distil his fears, after being nearly murdered in his bed.

Around every corner they turned, these whispers seemed to follow, giving Nathaniel the uncomfortable feeling of being watched. On one occasion, he had caught a local, garbed in a grey coat that hung to his ankles, staring at him as he passed. Another watcher, for there were many, was covered in so much soot and charcoal dust that he almost blended into the street's shadows.

Nathaniel could only return his gaze for so long and was grateful when Gabe eventually sent the man scurrying deeper into the shadows with a gruff, 'what are *you* looking at?'

'What's wrong with everyone here?' Nathaniel thought aloud, 'I thought Morne was meant to be…'

'Not quite so dreary?' Zaine suggested.

'Well… yes,' Nathaniel agreed reluctantly.

'It once was. Long ago Morne was the backbone of Horizon's war machine. Forged anything from swords to horseshoes.'

'And now?'

The Hunter regarded Nathaniel, at least he thought he did. His hood had largely turned to face the Regal. Even if he could see the man's silver eyes, Nathaniel never could tell if the Hunter was simply considering his words or scrutinising him.

'It can be… difficult to ease back into peace,' he replied measuredly.

It felt good to be away from Greymound and its untrusting eyes, yet Nathaniel couldn't ignore the sinking feeling in his stomach as he looked at his surroundings.

This was what he imagined Räne – the Broken City – would be like, a pale imitation of a once proud city. Ghosts wandering aimlessly through the fog trying to remember a time when their home stood proud. The few remaining forges of Morne even generated enough smoke to give the permanent, eerie appearance of fog. Nathaniel half-expected the Sisters of the Dagger to suddenly burst out of the smoke.

Nathaniel tucked his head deeper into his hood to guard against the misty rain that had already soaked their legs and mounts.

'How long must we stay here?' Nathaniel found himself shouting behind the Hunter.

They had arrived in Morne earlier in the day to replenish their supplies. While the thought of a warm bed and something to eat - other than the animals Zaine had hunted outside the villages they'd passed - was an enticing one, Morne scared him more than he cared to admit.

'Not for long,' Zaine said.

Truth be told, the city wasn't all that worried him. Ever since the Sisters of the Dagger had made an appearance in Greymound, Brey's attitude toward him had softened. She gave him one of her pretty crooked smiles when he twisted his head back. *Pretty?* He blushed and looked back ahead at Zaine's black stallion. *Where had that come from? Do you not remember who you're promised to?*

Well... actually, when Nathaniel thought about it, he didn't. In fact, all he had to go on was a green dress. No face, not even a name.

She usually occupied his dreams as that strange flower girl, running away from him down the corridors of the Emperor's palace. Tapestried walls with vaulted ceilings blurred around him but there was no floor, just a carpet of black and gold rippling above a dark, empty expanse.

Sometimes the carpets would lead him to the girl, before suddenly whipping out from under him, plunging Nathaniel into the black. At other times, he found himself revisiting Athrana's prayer room, where the Emperor's body lay - always in the same position - sprawled on the steps to the altar, as thick blood oozed, like oil.

Kinssssslayerrrr

A voice that seemed befitting of a serpent, would hiss accusingly from the shadows.

237

Sometimes he'd turn round to find the Szar, his long, puckered scar creasing as he sneered at Nathaniel, pointing accusingly. The black leaves of the Obsidian Crown bleeding over his forehead.

Lately though, Brey had begun to creep into his dreams.

First, it had been nothing more than a glimpse of brown braids, disappearing into an adjoining corridor. A distraction he'd shrug off, before pursuing the girl in the green dress.

Then those green eyes had appeared. She'd beckon him away and Nathaniel would find himself standing at the junction of two corridors, not certain which one to take.

Why was she in his dreams in the first place? He had not asked for this!

Vaera called Nathaniel's name loudly, snapping him out of his delirium. Her horse had overtaken Brey's and now trotted directly behind Bela.

'You seem troubled,' Vaera said.

She wasn't glaring at him for once. The change in behaviour made him oddly uncomfortable.

'Just thinking about... things,' Nathaniel replied cryptically. If he had told her of his dreams, he expected her sympathy would be particularly short-lived.

'What things?' Vaera pressed.

He thought for a moment, then said, 'I worry what I'll find when we return to Obsidia.'

'Your family?' she asked.

The memory of his brother peering through the bars of his cell with cold eyes made him inadvertently shiver. Not to mention the last memory of his father...

No. He did not – could not – want to think about it.

'I...'

I What? Speak!

'I... would rather not talk about it...' he finished lamely.

'Oh.'

Vaera's soft response and raised brows somehow made Nathaniel feel a hundred times worse than any insult she could have flung his way.

Idiot, he thought to himself. *Perhaps you would prefer her to bury a dagger in your back instead?*

She fell back behind. Nathaniel, feeling a fool, sunk back into his troubled thoughts, wishing he'd had the courage to share them.

Hammers rung against anvils in an almost orchestrated harmony. A song of steel to guide their small procession through the tight squeeze of Morne's streets. There were no dome-topped buildings here. Bricked towers, blackened by smoke, stood at irregular angles, almost seeming to lean toward each other. Overhead, fogged windows leered down at them.

Had Nathaniel been on his own, he imagined it would take him days to navigate his way out of the winding corridors that snaked around the city. Even if someone hadn't tried to murder him shortly beforehand.

Eventually, the streets broadened out into a wide cart path, a few hundred paces away from the North gate - a massive wooden construction, fitted with thick metal bars. Beyond the burgeoning crowd of cart-pulling merchants, charcoal-covered blacksmiths, and villagers, the towering gates were slowly closing inwards. The city guard, outfitted in fine armour, formed a cordon in front of the gates, keeping the surging crowd back.

One of the guards, his helmet tucked into the crook of his arm, climbed onto a stack of wooden crates to address the citizens. 'Right! Listen up you lot,' the guard hollered, somewhat pathetically, 'it's time for you lot to return to your homes!'

'We don't even live here!' one of the merchants cried.

'Where are we supposed to bleedin' go?' yelled a second.

'Alright! Alright! There are taverns nearby and the rest of you will have to sit tight until this messy business gets sorted–'

'–messy business? What bloody messy business?'

The guardsman squeezed his eyes shut, looking like he suddenly regretted bringing up the matter. 'It doesn't matter!' he waved his hand dismissively, 'all you need to know–'

'Well how 'messy' is it?' someone shouted from the back.

'Yeah!' another added his voice to the mob. 'On a scale between one of you lot fell off the wall and the Dwarves have come to conquer us all, how bad is it–'

'Hey! What did you say about Dwarves?' a third voice, like gravel, responded angrily.

'There's been a murder, okay!' the guard said exasperatedly.

'A murder?' one of the merchants repeated dimly, 'you're going to pull the city to a halt for one bleedin' murderer?'

The guardsman's helmet almost dropped from his arm, 'no we–'

'–one bleedin' murderer? What? Did they kill the bleedin' Steward?'

'The *Stewardess!*' the guardsman growled impatiently, 'is in fine fettle. And it's not just any damn murderer, we're talking about an Emperor killer–'

'–blimey!' a woman cut in, 'we have an Emperor?'

'Not our Emperor, damn you! The Regal's Emperor!' the guardsman pointed behind him at the gates.

'But–'

'ENOUGH! No one in! No one out! Stewardess' orders!'

Chapter 27

'Merchant?' said the innkeeper, frowning. His eyes flickering between Zaine's drooping hood and his ruby-hilted sword, unsure what to make of the Hunter.

The owner of The Hammer and Anvil was a miserable man, though not unkind. He introduced himself as Jarl, 'just Jarl,' and led them inside.

'Something about these lot rub me up the wrong way,' Gabe muttered darkly but stopped abruptly, when Zaine's hood had briefly flicked in his direction.

No music was played, but at least the inn's patrons weren't half as openly hostile as those they'd come across in Greymound. In fact, they weren't much of anything. Of the few that occupied the establishment's benches, only a couple lifted their noses from their tankards to acknowledge them. In much the same manner as those on the street, they stared blankly at Nathaniel and his companions, like cattle interrupted mid-grazing.

There was something very strange about the people here, who seemed to reflect the husk of their once proud city. Morne's people looked haggard, far too past the point of caring about the passage of time. Nathaniel wondered how he looked through their dulled eyes. Did a reminder of the outside world bring them hope? Or fill their mouths with the bitter taste of their once fruitful past?

Before they were even seated on the benches, serving maids had arrived and planted half-filled goblets of wine on the table. When they had heard how much coin it would cost them to stay the night, Gabe choked on his drink. Jarl merely scratched at the strip of hair that remained on his head, though some colour briefly returned to his cheeks.

Zaine however, handed over two gold coins and some silvers without complaint. 'Two gold? For *this* place?' Gabe spluttered. The innkeeper was halfway between them and the kitchens but he must have heard Gabe's indiscreet comment, for he bowed his head and hurried the rest of the distance.

'Did you always have to do that?' Kaira fixed the curly-haired boy with a less than approving look.

'Do what?' Gabe said after a long gulp.

Kaira shook her head mildly in a way that made it clear she wasn't going to spell it out for him.

'It could be worse,' Nathaniel said. At least it smelt better than The Prancer back in Greymound and the patrons here looked less likely to attempt to rob or attack them.

A flash of pink caught his eye as he searched the tavern. The woman was quick to hide it underneath the strange, long grey coat most of the Morneians seemed to wear. Even so, from their table she seemed awfully...well, clean. Every one of the people their party had seen, appeared to have some amount of grime or mud on them, presumably from their labours outside. However, this woman seemed unnaturally – for Morneians – untouched.

The hood hid all but her lips, which split into a pearly white smile, when she noticed him staring at her from the back of the tavern. Too white a smile, he thought. He returned his attentions back to the table, his cheeks burning.

'You just had to go and murder the Emperor, didn't you, ginge?' Gabe sighed, like a father scolding his child for having

243

muddied their clothes. He went to lift the goblet to his lips and frowned, presumably at the now empty contents.

'What?' Gabe held his hands up defensively against Kaira's withering look. 'He knows I'm only joking!'

Nathaniel glanced nervously at Vaera. The Regal's face had gone taut at the mention of Tolken. No doubt, she was already reminding herself of the reason she'd tried to sneak into the Lycan Sanctuary in the first place.

Great, Nathaniel thought, *just what I need right now.*

'We only just arrived,' Samir's voice rumbled from the depths of his book. 'How do they know Nathaniel's here?'

'Lucky guess?' Nathaniel suggested hopefully. He hadn't seen any other Regals, nor any posters bearing his likeness for that matter. How did the Szar know he was in Morne? And how did he hold sway with the city's officials?

'I wouldn't count on it, Regal,' Zaine said dryly. 'It seems we will have to find another way out of the city.'

'I have an idea,' Gabe said, his eyes glistened troublesomely.

'If it involves fighting the guardsmen, you can keep it to yourself,' Kaira said. Her voice carried so much authority on occasion, Nathaniel thought the girl would settle in well amongst the lords and ladies of Féy. A silly idea of course, what with her being a Lycan.

Gabe's chest deflated and he muttered something into his goblet that sounded like, 'no fun at all.'

'We can't just sit here,' Nathaniel said, slapping his goblet against the table with more force than he realised. Embarrassed, he took a quick survey of the tavern to see if he had drawn any attention. No one seemed to care, though, he thought he saw the Pink Lady's hood twitch in their direction briefly.

'If you have a better plan, Regal, then speak,' Zaine challenged him.

Nathaniel looked down at his goblet. Truth be told he didn't. But they couldn't just wait around until the Stewardess opened the gates. Eventually, Zaine's coin would surely run out or someone would discover that he was here. He wondered if the Sisters were close by, stalking the shadows, waiting. He daren't lower his hood.

Nathaniel glanced back at the benches beside him. He could have sworn that the Pink Lady was sitting closer to them than she had before. Was she listening in on their conversation?

When they were eventually escorted up to their rooms, the Pink Lady remained on the bench, even closer to its edge. Nathaniel thought he felt eyes on his back, as he followed Jarl up the stairs.

Chapter 28

The Obsidian Throne made for a highly uncomfortable seat. Draeden wondered how Jael had managed to survive it for so long, without so much as a cushion to safeguard his rear. He shifted his weight from one side to the other, as subtly as he could manage, and put his attention back on the peasant before him.

There had been a few farmers like him from Obsidia's border reaches, complaining of taxes on grain prices. Grain prices! Meanwhile, in some hovel in Dalmarra, the Lycans were nesting and plotting, and these people were more concerned about their damn levies?

Draeden dismissed the man with a raised hand and vague promises. The farmer didn't look entirely convinced but arched his back into a stiff bow, before being escorted out. How many Lycan rebellions had he put down, so people like that could sleep safely and then make their little demands of the throne?

Draeden shook his head solemnly; this wasn't for him. Jael always had a knack for this kind of thing – the trivial matters of the State. He peeled the circlet of black leaves from atop his head and rolled it about in his hands. How could a thing so delicate feel so heavy?

A reflection that was not his own shone back from the polished surface of the Obsidian Crown. Dark eyes, gently curious, staring into his pale blue.

The crown clattered noisily against the marble floor.

Within seconds, lances were raised and guardsmen rushed to his side.

'Your Grace! Are you–'

He waved them back to their posts, as he stooped to collect the crown. Blue eyes stared back at him now.

'Bring in the next petitioner!' Draeden barked.

A woman, smooth of face, despite her plume of snowy hair, appeared. She carried herself with the sheer level of certainty that only a life, long-lived as a Regal, could earn. She did not wait for the guardsmen to fully open the doors and her shoulders only narrowly avoided scraping either frame as she passed through.

'Sister Lucerne!' the Guardsmen by the door announced.

He had not necessarily expected her to be swinging a bag containing the head of the boy. However, the Sister's especially stern look didn't suggest she was bearing any news he would consider welcome.

'Sister,' the Szar greeted Lucerne with a curt nod.

'Draeden,' Lucerne replied stiffly.

Lucerne had never been one for titles. A tendency that she hadn't bucked, even after he'd taken over the Obsidian Throne.

'There were complications,' Lucerne said, bluntly, looking the Szar squarely in the eye. 'That you will want to hear in private.'

The Szar's eyes narrowed at the assassin, then flickered to the guardsmen behind her.

'Leave us,' Draeden commanded.

The Emperor's Guardsmen shared uneasy looks. The last time the Emperor had been left alone with only a guard to protect him, Tolken, and his bodyguard, had been slaughtered by a mere child.

'That was not a request,' said the Szar coldly.

One-by-one they walked the length of the throne room's narrow hall of pale columns, peering behind each for hidden assailants. Once the last guard was out, Draeden fixed his eyes on Lucerne.

'Continue.'

Lucerne took one last glance at the double doors behind her, before turning back to the Szar.

'We tracked the Kinslayer to a human village, south of Féy, and waited for the right moment to strike,' Lucerne explained. 'Once he was isolated, however, my sisters and I ran into some... unexpected difficulties.'

'As you mentioned,' Draeden replied curtly. 'Though I doubt this is the first complication the *famous*—' Lucerne's lips pursed tightly, '—Sisters of the Dagger have had to overcome. So why do you return to me empty handed?'

'The Old Ones have favoured Nathaniel Grey,' Lucerne said.

The laughter that escaped the Szar's mouth was cold and mirthless.

'You think me a fool to believe your excuses?' Draeden said.

Lucerne bristled, before quickly regaining her composure.

'Had you charged me with hunting the Kinslayer across the Southern Seas, I would not return until I had scoured every last drop of ocean for his head,' Lucerne's voice was tight as she spoke, yet tinged with defiance. 'Punish me for my failures, if you must, but do not pass the blame to my Sisters for their mentor's inability to defeat the will of an Old One.'

'You sound sincere, Sister but I find your explanation... an impossibility,' the Szar said.

'I understand the gravity of what I suggest,' Lucerne said sharply. 'But I would not ask for a private audience without evidence.'.

'Your word, and that of your fellow Sisters, is the only shred of evidence you seem to carry.'

'I have more – the Conductor – stolen from our vaults. It now lies in the hands of the Kinslayer.'

'So, another Grey wields the rod,' the Szar spoke his thoughts aloud.

'It may be nothing your Grace,' Lucerne said. 'Nonetheless, I know at least a few of the Royal Guardsmen would be old enough to remember some of the stories. If it were to spread that we were potentially hunting a Ph–'

Draeden had risen from his seat, blue eyes furious.

'He. Is. No. Phoenix,' the Szar hissed.

'I did not claim he was, your Grace,' Lucerne replied calmly. 'I merely wished to protect the throne against any harmful rumours that could have arisen.'

'Do you have *anything* else?' Draeden's voice was ice, as he settled back into the throne.

Lucerne's eyes narrowed even further at the emphasis. 'Only, that the boy claims innocence in a convincing manner.'

Was that just a statement or more of a question, assassin? Draeden pondered. Lucerne's tone had been typically unclear on the matter.

He had known Lucerne for centuries. Had broken bread with her. Had fought beside her in the deserts of the Scorched Isles and on the snow-capped peaks of the Black Mountains. Yet for all the time spent, he could still not read her. There were flashes of understanding, of course, but Lucerne was roughly the same as she'd always been. Only a rare moment of candidness would reveal how she truly felt about something.

Perhaps he ought to keep a close eye on her.

'Should my Sisters and I resume the hunt for the Kinslayer?'

The Szar gave Lucerne a searching look. *What game are you playing, Sister?*

'No,' Draeden decided. 'Let him come to us. Let him make the first mistake.'

'As you command.' Lucerne said with a sharp nod, turning sharply on her heels. 'I will inform the Guardsmen they may return to their posts.'

The Szar tapped one of the throne's arms methodically, as he watched Lucerne sweep out of the door. He only stopped, as the guardsmen began filing back in.

'So, you have greater pretensions, boy?' he whispered to himself.

Chapter 29

Rumbling like a building collapsing in on itself, Gabe snored intermittently through the night. Samir somehow managed to sleep through this unnatural racket but Nathaniel found himself wide awake in bed. He lay on his side, staring down into the dimly lit streets below his bedside window, waiting. For what, he couldn't quite say.

The almost total silence – admittedly, punctuated by Gabe's irregular growling – felt strange. The absence of hammer blows and the caterwauling of drunkards made Morne feel even more hollow.

Nathaniel glanced at the door, checking it remained just as closed as it had been the minute before. He half expected it to be blown off its hinges every time he looked away. He supposed it was a good thing that Gabe was in the room with them. Still, Nathaniel would have felt far safer with the Hunter kneeling – as that was how he apparently slept – at the foot of his bed.

A blur of movement in the corner of Nathaniel's eye brought his attention back to the window. A pink dress revealed underneath an unbuttoned grey coat. The 'Pink Lady' traipsed the muddy streets, looking this way and that. Had she just left The Hammer and Anvil now?

Nathaniel slipped out of his bed slowly, keeping an eye on the Pink Lady's movements, as he began to dress.

*

It had been some effort to open the latch of his window and slip out without waking the Lycans sleeping beside him. Though, considering Gabe's snoring, Nathaniel wondered whether he could have broken the window instead, without them noticing.

In Morne's quiet streets, the squelching of mud underfoot seemed to echo around Nathaniel. He made sure to keep his distance in his pursuit of the Pink Lady, whilst keeping track of every corner she turned.

He almost lost track of her several times and, on one occasion, had to make a guess as to where she'd gone. Nonetheless, fortune, it seemed, was on his side, as he spotted the tail of the Pink Lady's grey coat slip into an alleyway, lodged between a boarded-up smithy and a nondescript building.

The alleyway hadn't been fully claimed by the ocean of mud that appeared to be steadily drowning Morne. Cobblestones peaked through the middle, leading to a small courtyard and what appeared to be a warehouse beyond it, with a vaulted roof and broken windows. Long glass shards hung precariously from the top of the window frames like icicles. A faint light from within, reflected by the remaining glass, formed tiny amber pools on the cobblestone.

Nathaniel thought he heard the Pink Lady make a sort of disgruntled groaning noise, as she faced the warehouse door. After discarding the now soiled handkerchief she'd used to pull it open, she disappeared inside.

What was she doing in there?

Nathaniel made to follow her but found himself somewhat reticent. There was something that put him on edge and he wasn't particularly sure why. Was it the warehouse or who might be inside?

Is this a trap? Nathaniel thought suddenly. Surely not? The Pink Lady had seemed rather interested by their conversation in The Hammer and Anvil but there was nothing to say she was interested in *him*, particularly. He was being foolish. That being said, with all that light in the warehouse, what was to stop her noticing Nathaniel the moment he set foot in the alleyway?

He didn't allow himself to ponder on that question. Nathaniel padded through the alleyway and across the raised cobblestones, as quickly as he could manage, in a crouch. *Please don't go to the window. Please don't go.* He thought desperately, mouthing silent prayers to Athrana and any of the Gods who'd listen, in the vain hope his luck would hold.

He took the night's silence to be a good sign, once he'd reached the broken fragments of the warehouse window.

Then he heard the voices. Hushed tones spoken with such urgency. He craned his neck over the window's edge. The Pink Lady had stripped off her grey coat and stood, somehow taller, with her hands slapped to her hips in front of a man with red-trimmed robes.

That man needed no introduction.

Crow. Here, in Morne. That couldn't be a coincidence.

'He need not be dead, just delayed until Kusk can get the Elders' assent,' Crow's clipped voice instructed.

'And what of my city, Crow?' came a woman's voice, annoyingly high pitched, yet equally commanding. 'What of your promises?'

'The moment Kusk gets his army, consider Morne, and all its lands and steelworks, a close ally of the Regals.'

'And what about now?' she demanded shrilly. 'How much longer must I suffocate Morne, to further your goals?'

'I'd suggest you detain the Regal quickly, Stewardess,' Crow said.

The woman's dress made a whipping noise as she rounded on Crow. 'And how would I manage that? The boy's protected by a Hunter!'

So, she had recognised Nathaniel at the tavern. Or, at least, one of his travelling companions.

'Whichever way you wish. Have your guardsmen drag him out, if you must,' Crow's shoulders heaved slightly with indifference.

'Guardsmen?' the woman squeaked, 'are you mad? I don't want a battle inside my own city!'

'It's not my concern how you solve the matter, *Stewardess*,' Crow's lips curled, wrapping around the Pink Lady's title mockingly.

The Stewardess scrunched up balls of pink silk in her clenched fists. 'As you say, Crow,' she replied. Her words edged with venom.

Crow didn't notice or, more likely, didn't care. He was already submerging into a pool of shadows, before the Stewardess had finished her sentence.

The oaths she spat towards the space Crow had formerly occupied should have snuffed out the candlelight around her.

Nathaniel didn't stick around to catch the rest of her vile tirade, creeping away as quickly as he could.

Crow knew they were coming but he didn't want Nathaniel killed? Wasn't he working for the Szar? It didn't make any sense.

Nathaniel felt an itch on the back of his neck as he closed in on the alleyway and looked behind his shoulder. His stomach lurched. The Stewardess stood behind one of the cracked windows, lips curling smugly, watching his escape.

A strangled gasp escaped Nathaniel lips as he burst into a sprint. He took a tumble into the mud after smacking his shoulder against the alley's wall. Ignoring the pain, Nathaniel clawed his way back up to his feet and scrambled away. For a brief moment, he stood outside the alleyway facing the huddled masses of brick buildings, the next, he was looking up at the stars spiralling over Morne's towers, his head throbbing. Nathaniel blinked.

The stars flickered over a man's face. His grizzled chin poking out underneath iron helmet, as he looked down upon Nathaniel.

'I got 'im, Mistress!' the guardsman proclaimed. His voice was deeply guttural, like he was trying to speak through a throatful of tobacco.

Nathaniel blinked once more. A woman's face joined the guardsman's underneath the stars.

'And how, guardsman, did he get past you in the first place?' she spoke reproachfully.

The guardsman's chin went beetroot red. 'Well... I – errr... That is to say Mistress, I –'

'Oh, spare me your excuses, fool!' the woman waved her hand dismissively. 'Take the Regal to the mansion – and quickly guardsman. I'm sure my father will appreciate some company.'

Chapter 30

Nathaniel found himself standing in a bright white room. Maybe *room* wasn't the right description – *room* implied that the space had walls, corners, a defined area. The white surrounded Nathaniel completely, however. Bending around him, stretching endlessly above and beyond him. It was impossible to tell where the light started, for it seemed to come from everywhere at once.

'NATHANIEL GREY.'

A man appeared behind him. Painted gold. At least, Nathaniel thought that was far more probable than the man being actually made of gold. He held his hands together over his short sleeved white tunic. His angled eyebrows, darting towards his nose like arrows, would have given his white eyes a mischievous look had they been capable of expression. His hair looked statue-like. A darker, solid gold mass, stationary atop his brow, no matter how he moved.

'Where... who are you?' Nathaniel's voice sounded far-off, as if it had echoed back to him through a cave.

The golden man held out his hand. 'A GUIDE, ONCE FOR YOUR GRANDFATHER, AND NOW FOR YOU.'

'For my Grandfather... Thorne? What do you mean?'

The golden man smiled and draped his arm around Nathaniel's back, leading the Regal to a wooden door, embellished with a silver handle. The door stopped at the same level as their feet did, giving the white room the appearance of a floor. Yet it cast no shadow, nor seemed to be firmly attached to anything. It merely hung in the air.

'Wait!' Nathaniel said. Something scratched at the back of his mind, faint memories of a woman in pink. 'I need to go back.' There was little in those memories to go on but he felt the need nonetheless.

'THE CELLS CAN WAIT, YOUNG REGAL,' the golden man replied softly, his soothing voice turning the Pink Lady to smoke in his mind. *Why had he wanted to go in the first place?*

'AFTER YOU,' the golden man said, opening the door and tucking the key he'd used inside his robes.

The door looked strange in this realm of white. Nathaniel would have expected something more... ethereal, something sitting between existence and non-existence.

'What's through there?' Nathaniel inquired, peering through the doorway.

'SOMEWHERE... DIFFERENT.'

Darkness flooded from the inside, or perhaps they had been pulled into it, the moment Nathaniel stepped nearer. The howl of surprise that cut against his throat bore no sound. Stars tore past them at an alarming speed as Nathaniel dove headfirst towards an unseen ground. He looked over to the golden man. His arms were flayed out either side, as if diving into a pool. Perhaps he was even enjoying it, though the golden man's unchanging expression gave no indication on the matter.

257

Nathaniel wasn't sure which was more terrifying – knowing that, at the speed they were falling, the inevitable impact would kill them or not knowing when this inevitability would occur.

Nathaniel closed his eyes.

When he opened them again, the darkness had disappeared and the two of them were standing on solid ground. And quite unfamiliar ground it was too.

Nathaniel glanced around the room. The black and white tiles underneath Nathaniel's boots had been polished till they held a reflection. Most of this hard work, however, had been marred by spatters of blood, cracks, dents, and scorch marks over much of the floor.

Nathaniel looked up, just in time to see a ball of fire, spitting sparks as it hurtled towards him, and threw himself out of its way. The golden man looked entirely unfazed when it flew through his tunic, which wavered as if he were a mirage. The fireball splashed harmlessly against a marble column behind him, leaving a fresh scorch mark.

'How did you–' Nathaniel felt his jaw swinging.

'Welcome to the Sorcerers Spire and the Hall of Majik.' Hands behind his back, the golden man ambled through the carnage ahead, as if he were taking a leisurely stroll through a garden.

About a hundred blue-robed Warlocks raced about the Hall they entered, hurling fire, whipping out their opponents' legs from under them with gusts of wind, and impaling former colleagues on stakes of brick, mortar, and tiles they'd summoned from the floor. Giant statues, the height of the hall, stood overlooking the bloodbath below, with sombre, jewelled eyes.

Amidst all this confusion, two knights in golden armour lugged a heavy looking metal trunk towards them. Three more of these knights brought up the front and rear, carving out a bloody path through the Warlocks.

'PROTECT THE KINGSGUARD!' the Warlock closest to Nathaniel cried. A burst of flames set her robes on fire a second later.

Kingsguard? Nathaniel thought. There hadn't been a King in Horizon since –

'FOR FIERSLAKEN!' someone bellowed from the crowd.

The rallying call was met with a roar from half the remaining Warlocks. It was difficult to tell who fought for whom in the chaos. Given the way the Kingsguard swung blindly at any Warlock that came to close, Nathaniel wondered if they knew either.

A golden helmet flew over Nathaniel's shoulder as one of the Kingsguard was blown from the trunk. The trunk banged loudly against the tiles, loud enough for Nathaniel to hear it. Whatever was inside must have been very heavy. Almost before one side of the trunk had struck the floor, one of the remaining Kingsguard swooped in and grasped the handle, urging his comrades on with a raised gauntlet.

Someone grabbed Nathaniel's shoulder and dragged him back, just as the Kingsguard escaped through a marble archway and out of sight. It didn't register that it was the golden man, until Nathaniel found himself back where they had begun. The calm silence of the white room felt almost eerie after hearing the cries of the warring and dying.

Impassive as ever, the golden man watched Nathaniel quietly at first. Perhaps, to give the Regal a chance to process everything that had just happened.

'What did you think?' the golden man said eventually.

Nathaniel's heart still raced, as if it had been he wielding Majik in battle. Perhaps he had imagined it but he could have sworn he felt something stir inside him. It was as if the mere sight of Majik had rekindled that warm, fulfilled feeling he'd first embraced in the library of the Lycan Sanctuary.

'What did I think?' Nathaniel's words came out between breaths. 'Why were they fighting each other? Is that happening now? How did you even get us there?' The questions flew from Nathaniel's lips quicker than he could finish them. He winced – he knew it wasn't happening now. Fierslaken was an old cause – a legend even – and far too long ago to be fresh in the memories of men.

The golden man held his silent gaze long after Nathaniel had finished his barrage of questioning. Why wouldn't he answer? The image of a golden armoured Kingsguard being swatted away with Majik, like a leaf in the wind, came to mind.

'The trunk!' Nathaniel said suddenly. He looked at the golden man expectantly, 'that's what they were fighting over?'

The golden man reached for the door's silver handle. 'Not the trunk itself–'

'–but what was in it,' Nathaniel said, bracing himself for another rapid descent.

When their feet found solid ground once more though, the dark refused to relent.

'WELL... THIS IS MOST IRREGULAR,' the golden man seemed baffled, as he swung his head about the veil of black that had fallen over their surroundings.

Nathaniel felt his insides contort. If the golden man had no control over what had just happened... what did that mean for them? Were they doomed to stay in this darkness forever?

'Wait,' Nathaniel said, leaning to peer at something below their feet, 'what's that?'

The golden man followed Nathaniel's gaze to the scene blooming below them.

A man forged from fire, with black coals for eyes, treaded lightly through a carpet of white lilies beneath them. The man somehow failed to notice Nathaniel and the golden man peering down at him through the glass floor that separated them. But, Nathaniel wondered, the Warlocks hadn't been aware of them either.

A girl, in a green dress, her hair ornamented with purple orchids, was the centre of the man's attention. The girl was weeping. He approached her cautiously, as if torn between comforting her or leaving the girl to her own devices.

The girl eventually lifted her head to stare, past the man, at something hidden from Nathaniel's sight. The girl was just as unusual as the man that had approached her. Flower petals covered her skin, or were her skin, Nathaniel wasn't quite sure which. Purple petaled eyes and lips protruded from the pale scarlet.

'You should not have come,' the girl's voice was deathly cold.

Nathaniel frowned.

This all seems strangely familiar.

'It's alright,' the man made of fire spoke softly.

Petaled hand seized flaming wrist, bringing the walking inferno to his knees. The man cried out in pain, as he was shaken about like a small child.

'This is all your fault, Kinslayer!' she screamed.

Kinslayer.

The word struck Nathaniel like a hammer to porcelain.

This was familiar.

The glass creaked underneath his feet as he stumbled back.

'NATHANIEL, LOOK AWAY!' the golden man lunged toward him.

I've been here before.

Without thinking about it, Nathaniel waved his hand. A wall of fire burst from the ground, boxing him off and causing the golden man to recoil in horror.

As Nathaniel watched, the girl made of flowers had begun a flurry of blows against the man made of flames, burying him in lilies.

'NATHANIEL, LET ME THROUGH AT ONCE!' the golden man's calm demeanour had all but disappeared, as he struck his fist against the elemental divide between them. But to no avail.

Nathaniel ignored him, pressing his nose against the glass barrier.

'Who are you?' he whispered to himself.

The moment the girl had released her hold, the man made of flames began to sink into the bed of flowers. The girl was not quick enough to prevent him sliding away altogether, into the lilies' limitless depths.

'NATHANIEL!'

One by one, as the girl stared abjectly at the space the man of flames had once occupied, the petals fell. Grey skin emerged underneath, rising from her hands slowly up to the nape of her neck.

The golden man had managed to slip a hand through the barrier of flames, clawing desperately toward Nathaniel.

Her neck was almost completely free of the petals.

An arm pushed through Nathaniel's barrier. The golden man's hand only a hair's breadth away from the collar of Nathaniel's jerkin.

'Gods damn you! Show me who you are!' Nathaniel cried at the glass.

Red petals fell away to a grey chin and–

Hands seized Nathanial's arms dragging him away from the girl below.

'No! I must see her!' he yelled, 'I need to know!'

'IT IS TOO SOON,' the golden man's soothing tone had returned as he placed his hand gently over Nathaniel's eyes.

'You can't do this! You can't– You can't– You–'

Chapter 31

DING DING

'Wake up, boy!'

Nathaniel eyes peeled open.

Blurred shapes filled his vision, slowly sharpening into focus.

His eyelids felt heavy… so very heavy.

DING DING

'Don't you fall asleep on me now, boy!'

A wrinkled pair of brown eyes, sunken underneath the man's brow, stared intently at him through the metal bars between them.

Wait… bars?

'NO!'

Nathaniel slammed against his cage, darting from end to the other, and rattling each run of bars. Outside of a single torch, bracketed against the wall, the rest of the dungeon was deeply immersed in shadow. The room seemed to be almost closing in on itself, the darkness threatening to smother both light and prisoners.

Not again, he thought, remembering the dank dungeons of Obsidia.

The man in the cage beside him laughed coldly. 'You can keep doing that till your bones snap, boy but it won't get us out of here.'

Nathaniel ignored him and sprung to the door of his cell. The bars squeaked in protest but didn't budge. He threw up his hands in disgust and slumped to the floor.

Imprisoned. Again! All because he was foolish enough to follow the Pink Lady – the Stewardess, as it turned out – when he should have been sleeping safely in The Hammer and Anvil.

'Work with me, boy.'

Though tempered with desperation, the plea still came out as a command. Like a man who was used to people jumping to attention, if he so much as coughed.

'What skills do you have, Regal?'

'Uhhhhh.'

Skills? Nathaniel supposed he was good with a sword. Zaine's gruelling drills, whilst they had camped out in the wilderness, had certainly helped in that regard. No sword could get him out of this situation, however.

'You have the means within you,' a voice said.

The hackles stood upright against Nathaniel's neck.

'Who was that?' Nathaniel called out into the room, half-expecting to see a pair of silver eyes watching him from the darkness.

'Who was what?' the old man's brown furrowed.

Something metallic rolled across the floor by Nathaniel's side. Something glowing green. The rod Zaine had found in Bela's saddlebags. The rod belonging to Thorne Grey.

A wild thought crossed Nathaniel's mind, one so ridiculous it made him laugh, much to his cellmate's annoyance – *had the rod spoken?*

'Don't turn your back to me, boy!' the old man rapped his knuckles against the bars.

Nathaniel brought the rod up to his face. He hesitated a moment before whispering to it, 'was that you?'

The rod was still, then its runes flashed green. *'In a manner of speaking.'*

'I can't believe it!' Nathaniel said, barely managing to curb his excitement. 'How long have you been able to do this? Does Thorne know?'

'Your Grandfather knows better than most.'

Nathaniel had so many questions but, remembering his plight, he made an effort to calm himself and address the situation. 'You said I had the means within me, what did you mean by that?'

'Must I always spell it out for you Greys?' the voice took on a tired, condescending tone.

'Spell out what?' Nathaniel pressed the voice. 'How do I get out of here?'

The old man knocked his forehead against the bars behind Nathaniel. Moaning about how fate had spited him with a 'loony.'

Nathaniel thought he heard a yawn, but the rod was otherwise silent.

'Answer me!' Nathaniel hissed.

The rod lost its bright glow and lay cold in his hands – a useless lump of metal once more. Perhaps the old man was right. Maybe he had lost his mind after all.

The sound of a heavy lock protesting against a key forced Nathaniel's eyes away from the rod, which he hastily tucked into the side of a boot.

The woman who walked in was dressed far too splendidly to set foot in a dungeon and it showed on her face. Bereft of her pink dress, it took Nathaniel a while to realise who stood grimacing before their cells. The Pink Lady – the Stewardess of Morne, bearing the gold medallion of her station. She gave Nathaniel a suspicious look, as if she knew what lay in his boot. He did his utmost best to match her gaze and not glance down at his legs. With a sniff, she turned to the old man, still leaning against the bars, and utterly unwilling to look at her.

'Father,' she gave a curt nod.

Father?

'Daughter,' he grumbled.

'I trust you have given a warm welcome to our newest prisoner?' the Stewardess.

The man replied with a rueful shake of his head. 'Is this how you intend to torture me, Mortellia? Saddling me with lunatics till I squawk like one too? Does this amuse you?'

'This is no lunatic, father, I have caged the Kinslayer himself.'

The old man gave Nathaniel a once over and burst into a fit of laughter that had him doubled over and clutching his stomach, as if to prevent his innards from bursting out. It felt stupid but Nathaniel couldn't prevent the heat rising against his cheeks.

'By Ozin's beard!' the old man whimpered out the last dregs of good cheer with tears in his eyes. 'You mean to – Bahahaha! – you mean to tell me that this…. This infant killed the Regal Emperor?'

I didn't kill the bloody Emperor! Nathaniel wanted to scream the words at them both. Experience taught him it would be a supreme waste of effort.

'I wouldn't be so surprised, father,' the Stewardess's smile had a particularly smug curve to it. 'After all, aren't you notoriously familiar with the havoc a Grey can unleash?'

'A Grey?' the old man rose to his feet suddenly, as if stung by a wasp. 'As in *the* Greys?'

The mix of emotions that crossed the man's face, as he stared down at Nathaniel was most peculiar. Dislike was far too simple a description of what curdled in those dark eyes – a none too small portion of hate no doubt but also a grudging respect... and fear.

Having achieved the desired effect, Mortellia walked over to Nathaniel's cell. Her eyes had become frighteningly calculating. 'Now, tell me. Why should I not send a raven to his eminence, Draeden Kusk, telling him I have the Kinslayer secured in Morne?'

'Because you don't believe I did it?' Nathaniel said. It was a hopeful play, which sounded pathetic even to him.

'A pity,' the Stewardess shook her head mournfully, 'for word has already been sent to Obsidia.'

Nathaniel felt himself sliding deeper into the floor. So, she was going to serve him up on a silver platter for the Szar.

'What about Crow?' Nathaniel said, 'he's not going to be happy when he finds out you've crossed him.'

Mortellia lips curled into a wicked smile, 'it's not Crow with the army, Regal. Guards!'

Chest plates rattling, two guardsmen stumbled into the room and stood to attention.

'Take these two to my carriage and make sure to chain them first!' the Stewardess barked her orders even though the guardsmen stood right in front of her. 'If either escape... I'll have the head of the man responsible.'

The guardsmen shared a look between the visors of their helmets, bowed, and quickly retreated.

'Morne's gates open at first light!' the Stewardess roared after them.

Chapter 32

The carriage shook and trembled as it crawled over the mud and cobblestone of Morne's streets.

In the almost blacked out carriage, Nathaniel sat facing the Stewardess and her father, sandwiched between two of Morne's guardsmen. His hands and feet had been shackled together, and Mortellia had told him, in no uncertain terms, that if she heard so much as a peep, she'd have one of the guards cut out his tongue.

Her father, apparently, still couldn't decide how to feel about Nathaniel. The looks that flew his way ranged from cautious reproach to mild curiosity, as his tongue ran over cracked lips. The old man scratched at the uneven patches of salt and pepper stubble marking his jaw. Nathaniel noticed he was missing two fingers and the tips of others. Had the Stewardess done that to him? Her own father?

'Do you really think announcing your departure from the city in this way is a good idea, Mortellia?' he asked the Stewardess. 'I raised you smarter than that.'

'You also raised me to think for myself, father,' Mortellia countered. 'Besides, seeing their Stewardess, out and about, in their streets will give the people hope.'

'Right until you dash it on the rocks by leaving Morne,' the old man muttered scornfully.

'Right after opening the gates for trade to resume and merchants to go about their business once more.'

The old man turned his head back to his curtained window, muttering something under his breath. He noticed Nathaniel staring at him and turned his level look on the Regal.

'Your Grandfather cost me a great deal,' he said flatly.

Nathaniel gave a pointed look at Mortellia. Did this not qualify as a 'peep?'

The subtle nod of her head suggested quiet conversation lay in the bounds of her liking.

'Did he now?' Nathaniel replied.

'Oh yes. Almost cost me my damn life, Thorne Grey.' The old man spoke with a far-off look in his eyes, before a rueful shake of the head brought him back to the present. 'Though, I suppose it would be unfair to apportion him all the blame...'

'And who is deserving of your blame?' Nathaniel inquired.

The old man gave a derisive snort, 'it matters little, Regal.'

The carriage jerked, as it came to a sudden halt, throwing Nathaniel into one of the guardsmen's shoulder plates. Nathaniel rubbed his sore temple and sat back against the seat, scowling. The conversation that took place outside was muffled and, ultimately, short-lived. The carriage was soon rumbling on ahead again.

'You're playing a dangerous game, daughter,' the old man said.

'The game would be boring if it wasn't, father,' Mortellia replied with a smirk.

The old man shook his head, disapprovingly.

It was a strange thought to have, given his predicament, but Nathaniel felt oddly relieved. At least, he wasn't the only one who had a difficult relationship with their father.

271

The journey became a little less bumpy once the carriage had left Morne in its wake, only jolting occasionally, as it ran over stones or potholes on the road.

It couldn't have been long after that, that they came to another abrupt stop.

'What in Ozin's Throne...' Mortellia said.

'A complication, my daughter?' the old man gave the Stewardess a sidelong glance, with a smug expression on his face.

'If this is your work–' she sneered back.

'My work? What, with you having me caged like an animal?' the old man scoffed.

The Stewardess knocked sharply on the roof of the carriage. A square door in the middle of the roof slid back to reveal a nervous, moustached face. 'I–Mistress... there's a boy... he appeared out of nowhere! I had to–'

'Then, get him to move!' Mortellia hissed up at the driver.

'Right away, Mistress!' the man disappeared, as swiftly as he appeared, and the compartment was replaced.

A moment passed before the door slid back again and the moustached driver popped back into view. 'You won't believe it, Mistress – he's gone. I can't bloody see him!'

'Then what are we still doing here?' Mortellia demanded. 'Move on at once, you fool!'

'Right away, Mistre–aghhhhhhhh!'

Something blurred past overhead, taking the driver with it, and causing the horses to shriek outside. The loud and sharp crunch that ended the man's screaming sounded awfully fatal.

The Stewardess had shrunk away from the carriage door. 'What are you two gawking at? Defend me!' she gestured for the guardsmen to exit the carriage.

The guardsmen hesitated – Nathaniel could hardly blame them – gripped the pommels of their swords tightly and then burst out of the carriage. Though instinct suggested otherwise, Nathaniel leaned forward in his seat to peer through the now ajar carriage door. The guardsmen held their swords - trembling, Nathaniel thought - out before them, standing back to back against this unseen foe.

One of them approached something laying on the ground out of view from the carriage's doorway. 'Must have been some wild beast, Mistress,' the guard said. 'Broke Digby's neck clean.'

'The reins are snapped Mistress!' cried the other, 'the horses have done bolted!'

'Wild beasts don't leave their prey uneaten,' the old man murmured. All the smugness had dissipated from his voice and his face seemed to have gone a shade paler. His eyes sunken deeper within the shadows of his skull.

One of the guardsmen uttered a short cry outside, disappearing from Nathaniel's view by the time he'd looked back through the carriage doorway.

'It's back! It's bloody back!' the remaining guardsman howled. The man swung his sword in reckless arcs around him, cutting nothing but thin air.

Mortellia shoved a knife about as thick as a knitting needle against her father's ribs. 'Call it off,' the Stewardess commanded him. 'I know this is your doing.'

'You think I did this?' the old man looked aghast.

Nathaniel had never seen anything move as fast as the blur that took the last guardsman. The man didn't even have time to cry out. The seconds seemed like hours, as they sat altogether in the carriage, stunned to silence.

'You can come out now,' someone spoke gently from the outside. The man's voice sounded far too soft for someone who had just murdered a handful of guardsmen.

Mortellia's father groaned in response but didn't move. And, as far as Nathaniel was concerned, leaving the relative safety of the carriage was absolutely the last thing he wanted to do.

However, the Stewardess had other thoughts and the coolness of the blade that appeared against his throat made them clearer. 'Are you deaf, Kinslayer?' Mortellia hissed in his ear. 'Move!'

Nathaniel inched slowly out of the carriage, with the Stewardess in tow, making sure he remained conscious of the knife pressed against his neck. A boy, who looked barely a year or two older than Nathaniel, stood beside the last guardsman's corpse, looking extremely uncomfortable. Keeping the knife trained against his throat, the Stewardess shepherded Nathaniel forward.

'Uh... hello,' Nathaniel said, gulping down bile as he examined the bodies strewn about the road.

He was hunched over with his arms wrapped tightly around his stomach as his whole body shook violently. His eyes kept wandering down to the body at his feet. Every time he did so, he would immediately turn to the sky and shake his head profusely, as if scolding the Gods.

It couldn't have been him that had done all this, could it? The boy looked so ill that a stray gust of wind might bowl him over. His skin was draped so tightly over his face it was a wonder how it didn't snap under the strain of his jaw.

The boy suddenly looked up, fixing Nathaniel with a stare.

'Nathaniel Grey?' the boy asked. Just getting out Nathaniel's name seemed laborious for him.

The Stewardess turned the knife so only the point rested against his skin. 'You set this up?' she hissed into his ear.

'I've never seen him before,' Nathaniel said.

'To be fair... he hasn't,' the boy gave a not so reassuring smile.

The knife twisted, causing Nathaniel to take a sharp intake of breath and drawing a line of crimson that wetted the edge of the blade. 'Where is it?' she said sharply.

'Where... is what?' the boy frowned. He snuck another look at the dead guardsman and shut his eyes with a grimace.

'Your pet! The beast that did this!' Mortellia shrieked, gesticulating towards the bodies. 'You tell me right now, or I'll... wait... what are you doing with that, boy?'

Mortellia extended her finger towards the boy's chest and the gold medallion that hung from the chain around his neck. Now that Nathaniel thought about it, it looked distinctly like the one Mortellia wore.

'This?' the boy ran his fingers over the medallion, 'it belonged to my father.'

'You're a Steward's son, boy?' Nathaniel heard the old man call from the carriage. 'Dear oh dear, Mortellia, what have you done now?'

'Quiet!' she spat back. 'Well?' she said.

'Formerly a Steward. He's dead now.' The boy didn't sound particularly broken up about that.

The old man poked his head out of the carriage. There was an apprehensive look on his face that suggested he had an inkling of what the answer would be and it was not one he liked. 'Of which place, boy? Who was your father?'

'The City of Light,' the boy replied, staring at the old man. 'My father was-'

'Xalem.' The old man finished his sentence with a look of abject horror etched across his face. What followed sent a slow chill down Nathaniel's spine.

'The v-vampire,' the old man stuttered.

Nathaniel was looking at the boy with a new found dread. He wasn't sure what would be a worse way to go. At the Szar's hands, or the vampire's maw.

The vampire uttered a low groan, as he clutched his stomach. He really did look ill. 'Let the boy go, Stewardess.'

Please don't, Nathaniel thought, suddenly very reluctant to go ahead with this rescue.

'You can have the Regal, demon–'

Gods alive, don't goad it!

'–after the Szar is through with him.'

'Foolish girl,' the old man muttered behind Nathaniel.

'That won't work,' the vampire replied.

'Then I'm afraid we're at an imp–'

The vampire left no time for Mortellia to finish her grandstanding, moving so fast his shadow seemed to take a second to catch up to him. Plumes of dust rose from the road, as Nathaniel rolled away from the Stewardess's grasp.

When he looked up, he saw Mortellia held up by her throat and her blade buried in the carriage's lacquered frame beside her. The vampire's lips had parted all the way to his gums and he was taking in heavy breaths.

'WAIT!'

All turned to witness Zaine sprinting towards the carriage, Lycans and Vaera huffing and puffing behind him.

'Hunter,' the vampire's eyes had not left the Stewardess.

Gabe was the second to arrive at the scene. 'Woah.' His brow lifted as he took in the remains of the guardsmen littering the road.

'Put the Stewardess down, Valen. She need not die,' Zaine placated the vampire with one hand, whilst – Nathaniel noted – his other worked its way round the ruby pommel of his sword.

'Do your damn job... Hunter... and kill this beast!' Mortellia garbled out the command.

Valen gave Zaine a flat look. 'What's it to be, Hunter?'

277

Zaine paused or a moment and then fingers slipped from his sword. Valen closed his eyes and released his hold on the Stewardess. Mortellia fell on her knees, clutching her throat as she coughed and spluttered onto the dirt track.

Zaine turned to Nathaniel and clutched his shoulder. 'Are you alright?'

'I am now, thanks,' Nathaniel smiled uneasily. But how, by Athrana's grace, did you find me?'

Zaine nodded towards Valen.

'That monster,' she shrieked at Valen, slapping herself as tightly against the carriage as she could. 'You, Hunter! Kill that thing, this minute!'

'I don't answer to Stewards,' Zaine said, dismissively, barely glancing at her.

The Stewardess looked from person to person, searching for someone who'd jump to her aid. However, her eyes practically bulged when they met Kaira's, who was advancing towards her.

'YOU–'

Mortellia crumpled to the ground, almost immediately after Kaira's fist had connected with her jaw.

'What in the blazes!' Gabe gaped at the Lycan in awe.

Kaira curled a hair casually behind her ear, as though nothing awry had just happened. 'That,' she said, 'was a mercy.'

For once, Gabe held his tongue. No one else seemed willing to put their curiosity to words.

'What are we doing about... *him*?' Vaera spoke carefully, after Samir had handed Nathaniel his saddle bag. Nathaniel looked around, as it was none too clear who she was referring to. But she was looking out of the corner of her eyes at Valen.

'We're taking him with us, aren't we?' Gabe threw up his hands as if it were the obvious answer. 'He's a blazing vampire! We could take the whole Regal Armada on, with Valen leading the charge!'

The disgust on Valen's face suggested he didn't find the idea in the least bit as exciting as Gabe did.

'We're not going to war with my people,' Nathaniel cut in firmly. 'Thorne wants us to negotiate for peace. That's what we're going for.'

Peace. Would the Elders even listen to him? The words of a boy who everyone thought had murdered the Emperor. *And that's assuming I even get that far*, Nathaniel thought bitterly.

It was still a long way to the palace, with many an opportunity for a stray arrow or a blade from the shadows to silence his voice.

'I cannot go with you,' Valen shook his head vigorously, like the very idea of travelling with others repulsed him. 'I can already...' The vampire's black eyes had latched onto Nathaniel. There was hunger there.

Nathaniel touched his neck, his fingers coming back damp with the blood from Mortellia's blade.

'Valen...' the Hunter said warningly.

'I have been among you for too long,' Valen grimaced, 'consider my debt repaid, Hunter.'

279

'Let it be so,' Zaine accepted the vampire's words with a nod.

Gabe folded his thick arms in disappointment. Samir crooked his neck staring at the vampire in curiosity. The vampire performed a half bow, his words sounding like they belonged to an older man. 'Luck be with your endeavours.'

In the blink of an eye, he was gone.

'Well that was a stupid idea,' Gabe said.

'Where do we go now?' Brey asked.

'Tal'Shaelan, I presume,' Vaera suggested.

'I wouldn't do that if I were you.'

Kaira turned and jumped at finding the old man sitting on the carriage step behind her.

'Where in the blazes did you come from?' Gabe said.

'I'm the girl's father,' the old man said, nodding at the Stewardess's unconscious form.

Nathaniel heard a snapping noise and turned to find Zaine with his hand planted on his pommel, staring at the old man like a hawk.

'Ahhhh Hunter,' the old man gave Zaine a sour look. 'I see the years have treated you well.'

'Better than you I see, Baron,' Zaine replied. 'How did you manage to convince your master to spare you?'

The old man held up a hand and wiggled the stumps of his ring and middle fingers. 'I didn't. The men he appointed to kill me were imbeciles.'

'A pity,' Zaine said. Nathaniel heard the Hunter's knuckles crack against the sword grip.

'Perhaps you'd care to finish the job?' the Baron splayed out his arms, as if in an offer of embrace.

'You're not worth the time it would take to dry the blood off my sword.'

'Nonetheless, you should take my advice, Hunter… if you truly care about peace between the Lycans and Regals, that is.'

Nathaniel jumped in before Zaine had time to change his mind. 'Let's just hear what he has to say,' Nathaniel said, nodding at Zaine, who was looking unusually livid.

'My daughter has already sent word to his eminence, the Emperor of Obsidia,' the Baron said quickly. Nathaniel took it that he wasn't the only one suddenly wary of the Hunter. 'If the Szar seeks to retrieve the Kinslayer,' he inclined his head at Nathaniel, 'you'll find a rather unpleasant surprise waiting for you in Tal'Shaelan.'

'Tal'Shaelan is a free city, the Szar wouldn't dare occupy it,' Kaira said.

'He doesn't need to, to control who goes in and out.'

'Tal'Shaelan is the only way through to Obsidia,' Samir noted quietly. 'How are we supposed to get there otherwise?'

The Baron shrugged. 'Take the gamble if you wish, I personally wouldn't.'

'We don't have to,' Nathaniel suddenly realised.

'What are you talking about, ginge?' Gabe frowned.

'I know a way around… I think.'

'Then I leave it in your hands,' the Baron said. The old man pushed himself to his feet with a groan and began to limp towards the dark towers of Morne.

'What about your daughter?' Brey called after him. 'You're just going to leave her here, like this?'

'Mortellia will come to soon enough,' the Baron waved a hand dismissively without turning around. 'And I have no desire to go back to a cell when she does.'

'Let's get going,' Nathaniel said. 'We've a way to go, without horses.'

Chapter 33

'You sure you know where you're going, Regal?' Gabe grumbled.

Taking Nathaniel's advice, they had strayed from the well-beaten path beyond Morne. Heading west-ways, into an open plain of rolling hills and grassland.

'I'll find it,' Nathaniel replied defiantly, for what seemed like the hundredth time.

'Uh-huh,' Gabe said, not sounding overly convinced. 'You said that an hour ago.'

'I know where I'm bloody going,' Nathaniel muttered crossly to himself.

As time passed, however, their party grew evermore restless, which wasn't aided by the seemingly unending and repetitive green landscape. Even Nathaniel began to question himself.

'Struggling to remember the way?'

Nathaniel gave a start at Zaine's sudden appearance by his side.

How are you so damned quiet all the time, Hunter?

'No, I–I remember. I'm sure of it! I have to,' Nathaniel replied hesitantly.

Athrana's grace. I'm not even sure myself anymore.

Still, it was not like they had any real alternative other than to blindly follow him through the green tundra. It would be impossible to forge a direct path to Obsidia without bloodshed.

Nathaniel eyed the Hunter's sword from the corner of his eye.

Zaine would protect them if it came to it... he thought. But what of the others? Gabe would probably dive headfirst into the fray for the fun of it, before the first flash of steel. The other Lycans... he supposed they might too. None of them owed him their lives though, and Nathaniel would be reluctant to put them in danger, even if they offered. He looked back at Vaera, who was grimacing at some lewd story or other that Brey was telling her.

What of you?

Vaera had little reason to die for their cause either. He still wasn't quite sure why she hadn't already made a beeline for Tal'Shaelan, to warn the Regals of his coming.

And what of him? He had never drawn a sword to kill another, let alone one of his kind.

Then I really would be a Kinslayer.

Nathaniel swallowed hard.

I'm no Kinslayer. I'm no Kinslayer. I'm no Kinslayer.

'Is that... a grave?'

Brey was squinting at something off in the distance. A lump of square rock jutting out from one of the hills beyond them. It oddly reminded him of some of the older patrons in the The Prancer, back in Greymound. Like a lower jaw bereft of all but one lonesome, chipped tooth.

'That's it!' Nathaniel shouted, almost leaping in the air.

The 'gravestone' bore no name, but what appeared to be a set of directions.

'Follow the tears of Thün Moine to the eye of stone,' Samir read aloud.

'There, if your heart be firm, shall you return to the heart of stone.'

'"The tears of Thün Moine?"' Gabe's brow wrinkled. 'Is that a stream or something?'

'Not literal tears, you stone-head,' Kaira rolled her eyes.

Brey coughed loudly into her fist.

'Would this, by any chance, be what we're looking for?' she called from below the hill.

The Lycan was parting the grass around a stone tablet, about half the size of one of Samir's heavy, leather-bound books, hiding underneath the grass. 'Don't tell me – I know – I'm great,' Brey gave one of her crooked smiles.

The group had to fan out, wide at first, to find the next few tablets, before they could begin to work out the expected path. By the seventh tablet, their journey began to straighten out somewhat. The tablets took their party away from the hills and towards flatter ground, where great square-shaped trees dotted the landscape, across the sea of green.

After an hour, the Thün's tears ran abruptly dry. Retracing their steps did little to solve this dilemma but Nathaniel refused to accept that this was where the trail ended.

'Let's go back again,' Nathaniel insisted, waving away the Lycans' protests.

'We've been back to the last tablet three blazing times already,' Gabe groaned. 'Face it, ginge, this is it.'

The Baron's warning about Tal'Shaelan loomed ominous overhead for Nathaniel. Like a black cloud on the point of bursting, refusing to go away.

285

'We must have missed it,' Nathaniel said hotly. 'Let's look around.'

'Nathaniel, there's nothing else here,' Brey said gently.

'That's what I've been trying to tell him,' Gabe muttered.

Nathaniel bit back a retort so hard he tasted blood. He turned to the Hunter for help, but the man held his silence, silver eyes regarding him neutrally.

Well thanks a bunch, Zaine, Nathaniel thought bitterly.

Gabe shook his head. 'We're wasting time. We should have just gone to Tal'Shaelan and be done with it.'

'And risk a battle? Did you not hear what that man said?' Kaira challenged him.

'At least we know what we're facing and what lies on the other side!' Gabe barked. 'Instead we're here on a child's treasure hunt!'

'What would you have me do?' Nathaniel demanded.

The Lycan drew himself up. He may have been thicker-set than Nathaniel but he was still smaller.

'I would take us straight to Tal'Shaelan and be done with the delays,' Gabe said. 'Or are you scared of having to fight?'

That's it.

Nathaniel launched himself at the Lycan who uttered a startled cry, as he was dragged to the ground. The two of them barrelled across the ground growling at each other. Nathaniel heard a loud crunch, as if a hundred or so twigs had snapped underneath them, Brey shrieked, and then they were both falling into blackness.

*

The ground was softer than Nathaniel expected, though the landing no less painful for either of them. Loose bark and the thin canopy of grass that had failed to hold them was scattered across the damp pit floor. Looking over Gabe, Nathaniel thought he could make out a torch light in the distance and a... tunnel?

Groaning and clutching their backs, the two of them rose slowly. Gabe looked down at his feet when Nathaniel caught his eye. Was the Lycan blushing?

'I'm not sorry,' he grumbled.

'Neither am I,' Nathaniel replied, unable to restrain the grin that crept over his face. Soon the two of them were doubled over back in the dirt, clutching their stomachs as they howled with laughter.

'Nathaniel! Gabe! Are you two alright?' Zaine's voice boomed toward them.

'We're fine!' Nathaniel yelled back, his eyes scouring the edge of the pit and quickly finding what they were looking for. 'Climb down – here – there are vines. I think we've found the entrance!'

The Hunter was the first to slide down to join them. He clapped them both on the shoulder, 'good work.' Nathaniel thought he saw the corner of Zaine's mouth curl as he went past.

The rest followed soon after. Samir tightly clutching his bag of books to his chest like a new-born babe, Brey giggling with Kaira, and finally Vaera, a look of disgust plain to see on the Regal's face.

What lay beyond the dimly lit tunnel was nothing short of strange. Hundreds of rails darted off in different directions and angles, some meeting in the middle, like some sort of mad spider's web.

'Whoa!' Samir exclaimed, almost tripping over himself as he backed onto Gabe's toes, the Lycan uttering dark oaths whilst hopping on one foot.

The stone floor quickly fell into nothing, seemingly hovering, unsupported, over a great cavernous pit, just a few feet away from where Samir had stood. Most of the rails spun down into this great darkness below, although it was impossible to tell how far down they went, as they faded into black.

'How do we use this?' Gabe pointed at the run of rail close to the edge of the stone platform they stood upon.

'Ummm...'

Before Nathaniel could think of an answer, a distant clinking and rattling sound pierced the dull quiet.

Ratakum! Ratakum! Ratakum!

The rail closest to them tremored and shook more violently, as the source of the noise came closer.

RATAKUM! RATAKUM! RATAKUM!

Out of a dark corner, an empty mine-cart emerged. At least, it had seemed empty at first. However, as the cart neared, a helmeted head could be seen poking out over the top. The cart sped along the rails, with such speed that Nathaniel felt his stomach lurch just watching it skittle through corners. Yet somehow, its driver managed to keep the wheels from slipping away.

'HO THERE!' the driver bellowed at them, his deep gravelly voice managing to carry over the screeches of the cart, as it pulled to a stop beside them.

The Dwarf peered at them through opaque goggles, which seemed far too dusty to allow safe navigation of the rails. His hair, which was cut short at the sides, still stretched halfway down his back. Streaks of salt and pepper edged the chestnut locks, which were tied into plaits from the back of his neck down.

Now Nathaniel came to think of it, the Dwarf looked awfully familiar...

'I don't believe it... that's a blazing Dwarf!' Gabe pointed at the driver.

'Aye! And that's *Master* blazin' Dwarf to you, lad!' the Dwarf's long, drooping, brown moustache blew about as he spoke. 'Now, what in the bleedin' bedrock are you doing here?'

'Pegs?' Nathaniel said.

The Dwarf lowered the goggles carefully atop his barrel of a chest and blinked at Nathaniel with green gemstone eyes.

'By the stones of my father,' the Dwarf murmured, the mine-cart tilting dangerously towards the chasm below, as he leaned over its side. 'Nathaniel lad, is that you?'

'*Pegs?*' Nathaniel heard Samir whisper behind him, 'why is he called Pegs?'

'By the stone, lad! It is you!'

The side of the cart burst open onto the edge of the plateau, which the Dwarf then used to clamber over towards them. His wooden peg-leg made a dull *clank*, as it struck the cart door and then thudded against the stone floor. The Dwarf may have only reached the Regal's chest in height, but he snatched Nathaniel up in the air, as easily as one would a handful of pebbles.

'Why, last I saw that wee ginger head of yours, you had it so far down a barrel I thought you drowned!' the Dwarf chortled.

Nathaniel blushed, trying his best to ignore Brey's giggles behind him.

As if it's not bad enough already that half the Regal Empire knows...

'I was told Dwarves had great beards?' Samir spoke behind them, sounding somewhat disappointed at Pegs' lack thereof.

'A BEARD!' the Dwarf boomed, dropping Nathaniel roughly. 'Great Ozin's hammer, lad! How unhygienic would that be!' The Dwarf slapped his hand against his soot covered cheeks, as if completely unaware that he was covered from head to toe in dust and dirt.

'I see...' Samir replied weakly, adding with a whisper to Zaine, 'does the Dwarf joke?'

The Hunter only smiled wryly in reply.

'A HUNTER AS WELL!' the Dwarf splayed out his arms in welcome, 'what a rare occasion indeed!'

Thud Thud Thud

Pegs slapped his thickset hands over one of Zaine's. 'Welcome! Welcome!' the Dwarf grinned, before his enthusiasm inexplicably disappeared momentarily, as if suddenly afflicted with an unpleasant memory.

The Dwarf leant in and lowered his voice to a whisper, 'you haven't come fore the – ahem! – you know... the '*thing*' have you?'

'*Thing?*' Zaine's silver eyes narrowed at the question.

'BAH!' the Dwarf relinquished his hold of the Hunter, gave his chest a smart rap and began to limp back to the mine-cart. 'I forget myself! Come! Come!' the Dwarf spoke over his shoulder, before hopping onto the little seat at the front.

Nathaniel looked concernedly between Zaine and Pegs, but both seemed to be purposefully avoiding his eyes. *Things* associated with Hunters rarely meant good news for all involved.

'Well come on! You must be hungry!' Pegs waved his arms at them impatiently.

'Did he say food?' Gabe's ears perked up.

'I believe he did,' Brey grinned, wolfishly.

'I would welcome that,' Samir nodded.

'I am not getting on *that*!' Vaera shook her head firmly, eyeing the mine-cart as if it were liable to spontaneously explode.

'Suit yourself, Regal,' Gabe said, as he and Brey almost knocked Nathaniel off his feet, as the Lycans launched themselves towards the Dwarf's cart. 'It's a long climb down though.'

Nathaniel and Samir followed suit, squeezing themselves into the back behind the two other Lycans. At the front of the cart, where the Dwarf sat, a number of levers jutted out at various angles from a dashboard littered with dials and knobs.

'Last chance, Regal!' Pegs called to Vaera.

With a glance behind her, Vaera scowled and leapt aboard, wedging herself in next to Nathaniel.

The Dwarf pulled a few of the levers, pressed a few buttons, and clicked several switches. After a pause, he gave the cart a sharp rap with his fist and it sprung into life

'Hold on tight,' Pegs cackled, slamming the gear stick down between his feet.

The cart rolled into motion, gently at first, before abruptly lurching forwards, inciting surprised outbursts from the Regals.

'What are you lot complaining about?' Gabe shouted back. The Lycan had a look of pure elation on his face, holding his arms aloft as they neared a tunnel, light spilling faintly round the corner.

'Are you mad?' Nathaniel yelled in return, distinctly aware of how pale he must have looked.

'This is–'

The rest of Gabe's words were drowned out by the echo of the rails inside the tunnel.

To-and-fro, they swerved. Through wide open spaces and passages, so low, they had to duck their heads, pushing their chins into their chests.

The tunnel was punctuated with other entrances, from which the rails split off into various directions. Sometimes Pegs would point at one, mentioning the name of the mine, or Dún, as the Dwarves called it, to which it led.

'HOLD ON TO YOUR KNICKERS!' Pegs roared, as the cart rolled round another corner.

Nathaniel felt his stomach drop, the moment he looked past the Dwarf's thick brown mane. At the end of the tunnel, looming closer with every second, was oblivion. The rails bent down, at such a sharp angle, disappearing into the void, it defied all logic and reason.

'We're going to fall!' Nathaniel cried.

'Nonsense!' the Dwarf snorted.

'Where's the rest of the rail?' Brey said concernedly.

'Oh there's plenty left!'

'Master Dwarf...' Zaine said hesitantly.

'Oh don't tell me with all the beasties and Fogspawn you batter, you're scared of heights, Hunter? It's just a teeny dro–'

The mine cart fell.

Screams tore through the air, although they raced down at such a pace, Nathaniel wasn't entirely sure who they belonged to.

He must have been gripping the side of the cart for a while. Indeed, by the time he realised the cart had stopped, Pegs, Zaine, and Gabe were already out.

A stone gateway, of similar design to that they'd encountered earlier, framed by braziers either side, sat before them. Still dizzy from the excursion, Nathaniel eased himself out of the cart, gingerly. Samir looked positively green from the experience, clutching his bag of books tightly for comfort, whilst Vaera looked more tight-lipped than usual.

'That was blazing brilliant!' Gabe punched the air excitedly. 'Let's do that again!'

'NO!' Nathaniel, Samir and Vaera roared simultaneously.

'Come, come,' Pegs chortled away merrily. 'Even us Dwarves struggle with the carts sometimes. Why, my cousin Humber, of all the blighted buggers, was found dangling out of his cart on the way in last week...'

The Dwarf's voice trailed off into the distance as they passed under the stone gateway. What lay beyond was nothing short of astonishing.

It was as if a great city, of the likes of Obsidia or Dalmarra, had been buried underground and blended into the earth, rocks, and gems hidden underneath. Great domed tops sat alongside hard-edged buildings, with an earthy, almost bronze-like, shade to them. Every house they passed held a forge proudly at the fore. Every strike of hammer on anvil sounded like a ringing symphony of iron and steel. It was how Nathaniel imagined Morne once was.

Where a sky should have watched them, from above sat a shadowed, cavernous roof supported by a hundred or more columns of colossal height. Yet more rails weaved in and out of the pillars, with dozens of carts at a time – some unmanned – flying above. There was so much chaos, yet everything clicked into place like a well-oiled machine.

'Are you sure the Dwarves will grant us passage through the mines?'

Nathaniel jumped. How had the Hunter managed to double-back without him noticing?

'I don't see why not?' Nathaniel said. 'My family knows Pegs well.'

'And what if your father, or any other Regal for that matter, has shared with them news of the Emperor's death?' Zaine said.

'Um... well *he* doesn't seem to be aware of it...'

'If Morne is already aware, I do wonder how the Düns have managed to avoid the news.'

Nathaniel was not sure what to say. Had they not tried the mines, there was little else they could have done other than battle the Regals head on.

Just what the Szar would want, Nathaniel thought bitterly. *An Emperor murderer and Lycans fighting side by side.*

'Be wary,' were Zaine's parting words, before striding away.

Of what?

'Friends and guests!' Pegs punched out his arms proudly before them. 'Welcome to Dün Moine!'

Chapter 34

Pegs insisted that they break bread and ale with him as he led their party to the Lower City. They circled around one of the towering dome-topped buildings, which seemed a structural feat beyond the capabilities of beings so small.

'The Heart of Stone,' Pegs pointed at the bronze coloured building. 'The seat of the Thün. Well… it was anyway. Our high-borns are still arguing in there, about who should be the next Thün… when they're not sleeping off the night's wine.'

'What happened to the old Thün?' Nathaniel inquired.

'Dead,' the Dwarf replied with a rueful shake of his head.

'Dead?' Nathaniel repeated.

'In his sleep, stone rest his soul,' Pegs said. 'At least, that's what we've been told.'

'You suspect foul play?' Zaine pitched in.

'I don't suspect it lad, I bleedin' know it,' Pegs said gruffly. 'Lot of high-borns sniffing round that throne.'

Another stone gateway was tucked behind the Heart of Stone. Iron brackets held torches along the staircase that ran down past the gateway into a blind corner. More stairs followed, and more after that, until they must have descended at least few hundred metres. There were no earthy walls, only a square passage fitted with grey stone blocks lining the floor, ceiling, and walls. Several doors were sporadically fitted along the walls, mounted in alcoves. Though, other than their bronze handles, they seemed to blend into the rest of the wall.

Pegs stopped by one of the doors on the left of the passage and began running his hands up and down the stone. 'Bah, I know it's here somewhere... Aha!'

One of the stone blocks ground its way into the wall with a satisfying click. At first, nothing happened but then what must have been several gears, judging by the sound, began rattling behind the wall and the door slowly swung inwards to admit them entrance.

They came across another Dwarf sitting in the hallway inside, scrubbing furiously at the rug covering the floor. The Dwarf's head came up as Pegs approached, eyes flashing open. She had a rather thick brow, much like her kin but was unmistakeably feminine.

'Master Muriel!' she blinked, 'I—'

'Easy, Caster,' Pegs winced. 'The cleaning can wait. Would you see if the others would be so kind as to fetch some food and refreshment for our friends?'

'Of course, Master Muriel,' Caster said, bowing deeply. Then, giving curious looks to Nathaniel and his companions, she sprinted down the corridor shouting out calls to action.

'Muriel?' Nathaniel sniggered.

'Now you know my terrible secret,' Pegs chuckled. He grimaced suddenly, 'I've told that girl so many times to drop the "Master".'

Pegs followed Caster down the corridor and took a right into a small room, dominated by the long dining table in its centre. The table and adjoining chairs looked like they had been carved out of the room rather than placed there. The plump cushions covering the seats being the only things, other than the wall-mounted lamps, that had been added. Pegs sat in the chair at the end of the table and spread his hands out for them to join him.

'So, I believe congratulations are in order, my friend,' Pegs said.

'What do you mean?' Nathaniel frowned.

'Well, you've long since tied the knot, haven't you?' Pegs winked at him. He turned to incline his head toward Vaera. 'And this would be your lovely bride, I take it?'

'You would be very mistaken,' Vaera replied stiffly. Her eyes had gone even wider than Peg's servant, Caster, when they had first arrived and looked in danger of popping out of her head.

'Oh.' Pegs sat back against his chair and looked confusedly between the two. 'Forgive me, I thought–'

'That's alright, Pegs,' Nathaniel butted in hastily, hoping to move the conversation elsewhere, before Vaera added more detail. 'I was actually hoping you might be able to help us with something.'

The Dwarf was still looking at Vaera through narrowed eyes, as if he couldn't quite make her out.

'You remind me of someone, lass,' Pegs murmured.

Vaera met the Dwarf's inquisitive look with pursed lips.

He shrugged after a moment and switched his gaze back to Nathaniel. 'I'm sorry lad, you were saying?'

'I–'

'Master Muriel! Master Muriel!' Caster burst into the room, her cheeks aflush. 'Master Muriel! There's some–'

'Caster, for the love of stone, don't worry about the bleedin' carpets, I'll get some new ones!' Pegs growled.

'Not that,' the Dwarf shook her head furiously. 'There's someone at the door and they won't go away.'

'Impeccable timing as always,' Pegs sighed. 'Very well, tell them I'm coming.'

Pegs roused himself from his seat, splaying his hands out by his sides apologetically, and departed.

The mechanical creak of the door sounded from down the corridor. Leaning forward in his chair, Nathaniel caught a few words, from voices other than Pegs'. However, the conversation was largely out of earshot. Nathaniel quickly settled back in his seat the second he heard the door closing and occupied himself with the dirt under his nails.

When Pegs returned, a fresh goblet in hand, there was a grave look to his lined face that instantly troubled Nathaniel.

The Dwarf shuffled back into his seat and placed the goblet in front of him. He bent his head to finger his top knot before lifting the goblet to his lips. Pegs wiped his beard afterwards with the back of his arm and fixed Nathaniel with a level look.

'Nathaniel, lad, what's this I hear about you having murdered the Emperor?' Pegs asked quietly.

Nathaniel gulped. How long had he known?

'Uhhhh–'

'–before you ask, those were your folk at the door,' the Dwarf jutted his thumb behind him. 'They seemed to be under the

299

impression that I'd be harbouring this *Kinslayer* of theirs. Now–'

'I–'

'–don't get me wrong, lad. I've got a soft spot for you. Damn me, I do. But I liked what I heard about that Tolken fellow too and I don't usually like these fancy arse ponces.'

'I didn't do it, Pegs,' Nathaniel said.

He gulped, waiting for the Dwarf to contradict him with a raised eyebrow.

Pegs leant forward in his seat and gave Nathaniel a shrewd look, then shrugged. 'Alright, lad.'

That's it? Nathaniel looked at the Dwarf strangely.

'What?' the Dwarf raised the palms of his hands. 'You said you didn't do it and I believe you.'

'Then what did you say to those Regals at the door?' Kaira inquired curiously.

The Dwarf grinned slyly.

'I told them that you'd come here briefly, that I'd sent you back on your merry way to Tal'Shaelan, and that, if they were quick enough, they could catch you.'

Gabe barked out a laugh and Nathaniel smiled gratefully.

'So, I assume, what with all these accusations being levelled against you, this isn't a social call?' Pegs said.

'Afraid not, Pegs. I need a favour. Are any of the old mine tracks to Obsidia still open?'

Vaera looked dismayed. 'This is your plan?'

'You have a better idea?' Nathaniel asked her.

She glared back at him silently. *Probably angry at me for Peg's 'wife' comment,* Nathaniel surmised.

Pegs shook his head solemnly. 'Nathaniel, lad... those tracks have been closed for almost a century. We've had no need of them since the end of the Shadow War.'

Nathaniel slumped hard against the back of his seat, utterly deflated.

'So this was a giant waste of time!' Gabe pounded his fist on the table. 'We should have just gone through Tal'Shaelan while we had the chance! The bloody Szar's going to have his blazing army by the time we get there.'

Nathaniel sighed. He hadn't the strength to disagree with the Lycan.

'We had to try!' Brey said defiantly.

'Tell that to our Brothers and Sisters when the Regals reach Dalmarra!' Gabe roared.

Pegs smacked his goblet against the table and the clamour of voices settled. 'There is another way,' Pegs interjected quietly.

'What way?' Brey said first.

'Perhaps he means to smuggle us in his barrels?' Gabe snorted.

The Dwarf did not appear to see the humour in his words, given how his moustache bristled wildly, as if a fierce wind had caught it. 'Don't take me for a fool, boy,' the bushes of the Dwarf's eyebrows met in the middle, as he narrowed his eyes at Gabe.

'Perhaps we should we hear what Master Pegs has to say?' Zaine interjected loudly over Gabe who was muttering something to himself that sounded distinctly like 'giant ears.'

With a deep 'harumph,' which blew out the two sides of his drooping moustache, the Dwarf then nodded towards the Hunter appreciatively. 'Well, like I was saying' the Dwarf began, shooting Gabe a dark look, 'there is indeed another path you could take. It wouldn't get you inside Obsidia but it would get you close to the mountain walls… although, it would not be without considerable risk.'

Nathaniel leant in closer, 'we must get in, Pegs, we have to.'

The Dwarf chuckled, 'you would not be the first to underestimate it, lad.' He took a deep swig from his goblet, before adding, in a more serious tone, 'but perhaps you will be the first to come back sane… or even alive.'

A deep hush stole its way into the dining room. The cocky grin had drifted from Gabe's mouth, and everyone, but Pegs and Zaine, paled.

'What… what do you mean by that?' Brey asked quietly, the shake in her voice suggesting she did not particularly want the Dwarf to elaborate.

Pegs' eyes met Brey's for a moment, then he waved a hand dismissively at his guests. 'Bah!' the Dwarf thumped a fist against the table, 'there may only be seven of you but with a Divine Son among you, you may as well number a hundred!' The Dwarf chortled as he raised his goblet to Zaine. Though, another long sip did little to reassure Nathaniel.

'Demon trouble?' Zaine suggested, posing the question, as nonchalantly as one would inquire about the weather.

The Dwarf's goblet dropped against the table with a resounding *CLANG*, causing half their party to jump in their seats. Servants rushed in, laden with towels and wet cloths, but Pegs quickly brushed them aside. 'Lads, it be barely a spit on stone,' he said, amidst their protests, herding them back out of the dining room before returning to his seat, with a grim expression etched upon his face.

'Demons? This far from the Foglands?' Pegs chuckle had little mirth in it. 'No, it cannot be... not even with the things some of my clansmen claim to have endured.'

The Dwarf shuddered, and, with a glance at his empty goblet, signalled a servant at the door who returned with a flagon of wine, slices of bread and cheese, and a small barrel under his arm, presumably containing more ale. 'Please, my friends, eat, drink!' Pegs took the barrel, setting it in the middle of the table... after first re-filling his own goblet to the brim.

Zaine politely waved the offer of food and drink aside, as the Lycans swarmed over the wine, ale, and food. Vaera, on the other hand, merely wrinkled her nose in distaste and sat back with her arms folded tightly against her chest.

Nathaniel reached for a goblet and caught Vaera frowning at him from the corner of his eye. *What does she expect me to do? Die of thirst?* Still, he felt the odd need to bury his head into his chest as he poured himself a drink.

'Did any mention a demon, shaped like a woman, Master Dwarf?' Zaine inquired, 'with curled horns, perhaps?'

'It is as I said, Hunter,' Pegs replied, 'nothing has crawled from the Foglands in many a year, and certainly ne'er as far as Dün Moine.'

'And yet, Master Dwarf, some of your clansmen return mad.'

303

'Aye, lad. But if it were demons, none would return at all.'

Chapter 35

The tunnel that would take them close to Obsidia was an especially narrow one, much to the chagrin of the travellers. To make matters worse, there seemed to be an endless supply of ladders and shafts that had to be climbed, just to continue on the right path. But Pegs had assured them all that the tunnel would take them just inside the Black Mountains. *If they survived the journey*, Nathaniel felt the Dwarf had been reluctant to add.

Indeed, he had passed on the task of escorting them through part of the mine to another - a wide-eyed Dwarf by the name of Humber. However, their new companion did little to help the growing apprehension Nathaniel felt, as they went deeper into the mine.

'Gibberish they spoke, Hunter, but frightenin' gibberish it was,' the Dwarf spoke quickly to Zaine, as they trudged along the cart worn path.

They must have been getting closer, for the minecarts were scarce on this new trail, and the tracks cutting across the mud fewer. Zaine attempted to extract details of what the Dwarf's clansmen had said but Humber, like Pegs, would only stubbornly shake his head in reply to the Hunter's probing.

Samir had not spoken a word throughout the entire descent and, bar a couple of grumbles about preferring to ride through a hundred Regals, Gabe had remained uncharacteristically quiet also. Anywhere else, Nathaniel would have poked fun at Gabe, but here... he found he had not the courage to do so, for there was something gnawing at him too. It had been subtle at first, a general sense of foreboding that had now become so thick in the air, it harried his every breath.

Perhaps you will be the first to come back sane... or even alive.

Nathaniel shuddered suddenly, as if an icy hand had ran down the length of his spine. Little wonder that even the Dwarves were reluctant to return to this part of the mine.

'My father – back before I turned – used to be afraid of his basement,' Brey said cheerfully, startling Nathaniel from his stupor.

Buried as he was in his thoughts he had not registered Brey walking up beside him, nor her fellow Lycans falling back. Despite his feelings about the mine, there was something calming about her presence. *What is it about you, Lycan?*

'Why was your father afraid of his basement?' Nathaniel asked, shaking off the troublesome questions that plagued him, for the time being.

'One night he couldn't get any sleep, he thought he could hear... whispers, but he couldn't make out the words. It really used to bother him,' Brey giggled at the memory. 'He came to realise whatever was making the noise was coming from the basement, a sort of strange humming. My poor father thought we were being haunted! I suggested he put a lock on the door but he daren't go near it.'

'So... what was in the basement?'

Brey grinned at Nathaniel and rolled up her sleeve to reveal the assortment of circular scars littered below her right shoulder. 'Hornets,' she said, 'a lot of them.'

'Well, maybe we'll just find rats down here,' he said with vain hope.

Brey snorted at that.

'This is far as I go!' Humber suddenly announced, bringing the group to a halt.

The tunnel carried on for some distance after, but for how long was impossible to say. The wall-mounted braziers came to a sudden and abrupt halt, just a few metres beyond the Dwarf, who had led them to this point. The journey into a gradually darkening abyss was to be theirs alone.

Zaine stooped over beside Humber to inspect the ground, tracing a gloved hand over the dried mud. 'No one has crossed this part of the mine in weeks,' he said. 'And those that did... were fleeing.'

Humber nodded in assent. 'There be something lurking in our home, Hunter,' the Dwarf said, 'you might be wiser to face the Regals, head on.'

'It's not like I didn't tell them,' Gabe could be heard muttering at the back.

The Dwarf could only bring himself to make one fleeting glance at the passage beyond, before he began eyeing up his own boots. He shook his head sadly, 'as you wish.'

He pulled free a torch, previously strapped to his back, lit the head and then handed it to Zaine. 'May you return safely to stone,' slapping a fist to his heart.

Humber bowed before them and then hurtled back from whence they came, as if staying a moment longer would be enough to render him insane. Staring at that impenetrable darkness that lay in wait, Nathaniel found himself wishing he'd gone back with him.

'Takes a lot to scare a Dwarf,' Zaine said with a troubled expression.

It's not going to be just rats, Nathaniel thought grimly.

'Didn't Pegs say that they hadn't dug these tunnels?' Samir said, squinting past Zaine. His voice seemed even deeper in the mines.

'Humber confirmed as much,' Zaine said, clutching his green pendant tightly in one hand, as he stared at the path ahead. 'This place, there's something… amiss about it,' Nathaniel heard him whisper grimly.

And if they didn't build them, who – or what – did? Nathaniel could not bring himself to disagree with Zaine - something was very much wrong. And yet… whilst he was tempted as the Dwarf had been, to put as much distance between himself and what lay beyond, something was pulling him blindly toward it. Nathaniel wrapped his cloak closer around him. They had not moved another inch, and yet it felt drastically colder than it had a moment ago.

'Then it is a good thing we have a Hunter with us, isn't it?' Brey said, patting Nathaniel on the back, sensing his unease. Though, it was difficult to tell whether Zaine's presence truly comforted her either.

Nathaniel thought he caught his fellow Regal glaring at him, as he stood beside Brey. He felt a similar pang of embarrassment, as he had in Pegs' dining room.

She knows you are promised to another, he thought. *Though why would anyone wait for a 'Kinslayer'? And not just any Kinslayer, but an Emperor murdering, Lycan loving, Kinslayer.* He struggled to suppress a snarl. The Szar would pay for what he had done to him.

The silver of Zaine's eyes shone brightly at them all. And, as always, remained as unreadable and impassive as usual. If anything ever fazed the Hunter, he didn't let on. Or perhaps he simply never felt the cold touch of fear. Whichever was the case, Nathaniel was silently grateful to have someone in their party that even the darkness that lurked in these cursed mines would think twice about swallowing up. *I certainly would*, he thought, eyeing up the hefty scar that split the man's face.

'We shall see,' Zaine said, in answer to Brey. His overcoat whipped against the air, as he turned to lead them on.

Vainly attempting to put aside the guilt that nagged at him – he really wasn't sure if it was related more to his bride-to-be… or Vaera – Nathaniel continued walking beside Brey. The crackle of Zaine's torch accompanied their quickened breaths, as they traversed deeper into the endless darkness.

He heard the others behind him utter dark oaths, as they drew their own cloaks tightly around them to fight the growing cold. And it was a strange cold too. It seemed to begin deeper than the outer warmth of their flesh, cutting past bone to burrow its way deep into their very souls.

The only one who didn't appear to be affected by this unnatural phenomenon was the Hunter. Though, ironically, he had all the reason in the world to, given he was garbed in a considerably lighter manner than the rest.

'What was that?' Vaera said suddenly, bringing the group to a standing halt.

'Come on, Regal, I don't want to stay here any longer than you do,' Gabe chattered through gritted teeth.

'What did you see?' Zaine asked calmly.

Vaera began to point at something but faltered. 'I–it's probably nothing,' she said, shoulders dropping in resignation.

309

'Are you sure?' Zaine persisted, 'we can ill afford to take chances.'

'It's... I thought I saw something move across the walls... like a shadow–'

'Probably her own shadow,' Brey muttered.

'I know what I saw,' Vaera snapped.

'Maybe... we should go back?' Samir suggested.

'The Dwarf was right,' Gabe said, 'be better to go knock in some Regal heads on the frontline. No offence,' he added swiftly, as Vaera gave him a look.

'What? And be delivered to the Szar in pieces?' Nathaniel retorted.

Gabe shrugged, muttering something about preferring to go out in a blaze of glory.

'Quiet!' Zaine cut past the chatter, 'there's something not quite right here, and I need you all at your wariest, and *not* at each other's throats.' He looked sternly between Gabe and Nathaniel.

Brey gave Nathaniel a pointed look and, finding him at a loss for words, jutted her chin and stalked off. Vaera's eyes settled on Nathaniel shortly after. W*ell go on then*, her narrowed eyes seemed to tell him mockingly.

What have I done now? Nathaniel thought.

Perhaps it was his imagination but as they left the braziers further behind, the flames of Zaine's torch appeared to angle back, more towards the dimming light. First, Vaera's vision of shadows and now he was having his own paranoid imaginings!

Teeth chattering loudly together, as they continued, almost blindly, on their course, Nathaniel found himself thinking – to his own surprise – that, perhaps, Gabe's idea wasn't so bad after all.

Fancy yourself to be a bit of a hero now, do you? Nathaniel allowed himself to smile at the thought, before the grim reality set in. If it came to it, and they were forced to cut their way through to the palace, could he really kill another of his kind? The unspoken question left a bitter taste.

Well, they already think me a 'Kinslayer,' he mused.

'There it is again! Right there!'

Vaera's outstretched hand quivered, as she pointed at a portion of the wall lit by the torch.

Kaira whipped round, hands slapping her sides, 'Ozin's blood, Regal, are we going to have to stop every – Oh…'

'Nobody move,' Zaine said sharply.

No one questioned that order.

The shadows cast on the wall were not theirs, nor did they appear to belong to any living thing. They simply wormed their way around the light, dancing before their very eyes.

Nathaniel also became aware of a low buzz emanating from all around them, growing in pitch until it became intolerably grating, like a knife scratching against bone. Judging by his companions' grimaces, he was not the only one.

Gradually, some words could be made out among the fervour of whispers. But Nathaniel had to strain to hear them, for it was not just a few voices that spoke, but seemingly a thousand, unceasingly butting in front of each other. Each demanding to have their say.

'Darkness eternal... shadows three shall rise... blot out the light... drown the Gods...'

Samir held his hands clamped to the side of his head and kept his eyes tightly shut, reciting something, perhaps a prayer, quietly to himself over and over. Even Gabe looked ill at ease, keeping a white-knuckle grip on both short swords at his waist.

Was this what drove the Dwarves that Pegs had mentioned mad?

'What manner of monster are you?' Zaine called to the wall.

One by one the shadows gave way to a chilling silence, pausing on the wall beside them, as if considering Zaine's question.

'What does this one seek?' they began again. But, this time, in unison. In a terrifying chorus that shook the very walls around them.

They all stared at the wall for a moment, dumbfounded. Were the shadows really speaking? They couldn't all be imagining it.

'What does this one seek?' the shadows asked once more.

All looked to Zaine, the only one of them able to maintain some semblance of calm. Yet, he too seemed, to Nathaniel, to be uneasy at the arrival of these talking shadows. Initially, he thought it was because the Hunter did not know what was before him. However, there was something in the way Zaine narrowed his brows at the shadows that suggested recognition.

312

'We seek safe passage through these tunnels, we do not wish to disturb you,' Zaine said, all the while drumming a steady beat on the pommel of his sword.

'But disturb you have!' the voices cried.

'We only wish to pass through these tunnels, then we will disturb no longer,' Zaine replied.

The shadows considered the Hunter's plea, before letting out a low hiss. 'Only in darkness may you be judged.'

The shadows darted down the wall, and began to slither across the floor, arcing towards the party as snakes would toward their prey.

Startled, Zaine didn't even have time to take a step back before the first wave began to crawl up his greaves. The torch slipped from his hand as he fought to wrestle the shadows away.

'The three shall rise! The three shall rise! The three shall rise!'

The voices united in one deathly roar, like a steady drumbeat.

'Away with you!' Zaine growled. 'Stay back!' he cried at Nathaniel and Gabe, as the pair sought to help the Hunter.

'Not a chance!' Gabe advanced, jumping back just in time to avoid a shadowy tendril that extended from Zaine's chest.

Even more shadows collected at the floor, and some had begun to turn their attention to the rest of the group.

'What do we do?' Brey shouted over the clamour from the shadows.

'They're everywhere!' Vaera shrieked.

Nathaniel looked at Zaine. The Hunter was sweating profusely at the brow and grimaced as if he carried a great weight across his shoulders.

Abruptly, his eyes flashed open and his face settled into a mask of pure horror.

'Run... more are coming,' he said, quietly at first, inspiring little but blank stares.

'RUN!' he commanded them at the top of his lungs, 'AWAY WITH YOU!'

Nathaniel did just that.

He snatched up the torch and herded the girls ahead of him, only to find Gabe still rooted to the same spot. Samir remained beside him with his hands clamped around his ears.

'GABE!' Nathaniel yelled, 'there's nothing we can do!'

The big Lycan looked guiltily between Nathaniel and Zaine, cursed, then dragged Samir along with him.

*

Nathaniel did not know for how long they had ran but their feet had pounded the damp earth underfoot long after Zaine's cries had dissipated into the air. On a few occasions, the narrowness of the tunnel had caused one or two of their party to tumble to the ground until another managed to pull them back up.

They did not stop until they reached a large cavern. A small stream, trickling down from the cavern wall, separated the space in two. At the far end, Nathaniel could just make out two tunnels, which veered out at diverging angles. Daggers of stone were poised above them, suspended from the high ceiling, threatening to impale those below at any given moment.

Gabe collapsed to the ground first. His chest heaving as he struggled for breath. The rest soon followed.

'What were those *things*?' Kaira spoke through a shiver.

'I don't know,' Nathaniel replied. All he knew was that he couldn't bear to hear those grating whispers again.

'Zaine...' Brey said suddenly. 'They didn't... did they...'

No one wanted to finish her sentence. The unspoken thought of the Hunter's fate hung in their mouths like a bitter pill, too difficult to swallow. Gabe rose suddenly and started towards the tunnel they had run from.

'Where are you going?' Nathaniel called after him.

The Lycan swivelled on his bootheels, his brow kneaded together fiercely. 'We need to get him back.'

Nathaniel swallowed hard. What he was about to say was going to sound horrible, even to his own ears.

'What we *need* is to get to Obsidia.' He knew it was what Zaine would have wanted but it still made Nathaniel feel a little sick wanting to abandon the Hunter.

'You're going to leave him there?' Gabe thrust his arm back at the tunnel. 'For the shadows to pick him apart?'

Nathaniel stepped towards Gabe. 'We need to get to Obsidia, before the Szar's army can march to Dalmarra,' Nathaniel said.

'He wouldn't stop looking for you when you got lost in Morne!' Gabe said. 'Who do you think tracked down that vampire to rescue you?'

'I know. But we have to stop the Szar,' Nathaniel said quietly. 'To save your Brothers and Sisters.'

'I... you...' Gabe's face contorted with all the emotions crossing his features. Gabe bent his head and made a defeated sigh. 'Blaze you, Nathaniel,' he said softly.

Nathaniel removed a waterskin from his saddlebag and approached the thin stream, eager to distract himself from the guilt scratching at the base of his stomach.

'Do you reckon that's drinkable?' Nathaniel turned to his companions.

'With this place... I wouldn't even touch it,' Kaira said.

Samir crouched down beside Nathaniel, dipped two fingertips into the stream, and brought them to his lips.

'It's fine,' Samir said.

The Scorched boy left Nathaniel's side without another word and sat against the wall, clutching his bag of books close to him. His face, usually so calm, bore a somewhat hard edge that Nathaniel hadn't noticed before. He knew he hadn't asked Samir to join him on this journey - especially given he'd probably much rather be wrapped in the comfort of his books - but it made Nathaniel feel all the poorer for it, just the same.

'That Dwarf of yours left out that we'd have our choice of tunnels,' Kaira nodded toward the back of the cavern.

'Maybe none of the Dwarves had made it this far,' Nathaniel suggested.

'But which one are we supposed to take to get to Obsidia?' Brey lifted her torch ever so slightly, so its light touched the tunnel mouths more clearly. They both looked as gloomy and unwelcoming as the other.

'You know what must be done, Regal,' the rod's voice crept into Nathaniel's mind, causing him to jump.

You again, he thought back.

'What's up with you, Regal?' Gabe said.

'Nothing,' Nathaniel replied quickly.

Desperately, he reached for the voice, begging for more guidance but that appeared to be all it wished to say. Nathaniel looked over his companions and made his decision.

'I'll take Samir and Kaira down that one,' Nathaniel indicated the left tunnel.

'I'm not good enough for your little group?' Gabe growled.

'It's not that,' Nathaniel shook his head. 'I need you to make sure that Brey and Vaera get through safely.'

Gabe grumbled about it, but Nathaniel took his stalking off to mean agreement.

'You think we can't protect ourselves?' Vaera sniffed.

'Do you two *really* want to go there with just each other for company?'

The girls shared a look and grimaced almost simultaneously. At least the matter looked to be settled.

'Are we going now?' Samir's voice rumbled from the cavern wall.

Nathaniel glanced at the tunnels reluctantly. His bag seemed to weigh twice as much all of the sudden. 'We'll rest first, for a moment,' Nathaniel decided. 'Get some sleep, I'll take first watch.'

Aside from Gabe, giving himself away with his rockslide of a snore, Nathaniel doubted any of the others managed to catch any sleep. When Samir came to relieve him about an hour later, Nathaniel could only manage to shuffle about in his cloak, though he teetered on the edge of fatigue. Bleary eyes stared back at him, when they stood at the tunnel entrances later on.

'If it turns out to be a dead end, double-back and take our tunnel,' Nathaniel told Gabe.

The Lycan gave a sour grunt in reply.

Brey mouthed *good luck* to Kaira and Samir, and offered Nathaniel a less than convincing smile before the tunnel mouth swallowed her and Gabe whole. Vaera paused outside and looked at Nathaniel strangely. It wasn't quite as hostile as he was used to from his fellow Regal but nor was it entirely friendly. If anything, it almost felt like an appraisal. As if this might be the last time they would see one another. Vaera sniffed once and then she too was gone.

'Right,' Nathaniel slapped his hands against his thighs and peered uncertainly into the second tunnel. He thought he could hear a faint dripping noise coming from within, which he quickly convinced himself was just more water.

What if there are more of those whispering shadows inside?
Nathaniel buried that unpleasant thought before it got the chance to fester inside his stomach. Gripping the torch tightly,

Nathaniel strode forward, as confidently as he could manage, into the tunnel's frighteningly dark maw.

Chapter 36

Drip. Drip. Drip.

Illumina was not sure how much longer she could last. Her body was screaming for release, be it by blade or slip of the tongue. She had thus far managed to avoid revealing the location of the Lycan hideout, but she could not say for how much longer she'd be able to hold out.

A moan escaped Illumina's lips at the scarred man who entered her chamber. Her brother had a grim, determined look to his face, which usually meant bad news for her.

She hung her head and concentrated on clouding the amber-rimmed grey eyes that hung, tantalisingly, before Illumina in her mind. She had to protect Nathaniel... and Thorne, even if the fool didn't think he needed her.

'Oh, sister,' Kusk sighed. 'Look at you.'

Illumina spat onto the floor in response. Even that trifling effort seemed to take a lot out of her.

'Look... upon your work, *Emperor*,' Illumina wheezed.

Kusk glanced back outside of the chamber. Two Royal Guards, draped in black and gold, marched inside, having to tip their lances as they crossed the threshold. The ice had returned to Kusk's blue eyes by the time he had turned back.

'Clean up her wounds and get her something to wear,' Kusk instructed the guards. 'There's something I want my sister to see.'

Chapter 37

The path was a little less claustrophobic than the last, though just as unsettling to walk through. The dark seemed to almost overwhelm their solitary torch, encasing its light in a narrow circle around their feet.

Nathaniel couldn't help thinking about Gabe and the two girls he'd sent in the other tunnel, hoping he'd not further endangered their lives by separating. He kept reminding himself of the mission, of what Zaine might say were he with them now, bearing down upon the darkness with his stone-faced assuredness.

The Hunter couldn't be gone, he just couldn't. Hadn't Pegs mentioned that some of his kin had made it back home from Dün Moine's mine?

But they were mad, Nathaniel remembered with a shiver.

'Nathaniel,' Kaira said tentatively. 'What are we going to do when we reach Obsidia? Didn't the Dwarf mention that these mines will only take us as far as the mountains? How are we going to get past Obsidia's walls?'

It was a genuine question. Also one Nathaniel hadn't really given as much thought to as he probably should have.

'How does a Regal return home?' Samir chipped in curiously. 'Can one only seek safe passage, if they bring with them a bounty? Must you prove your valour against the gate's guards in a battle to first blood? Solve a riddle?'

'Um... we usually just gain entrance through the gates,' Nathaniel replied.

'Oh,' said Samir, looking perplexed.

Nathaniel gripped the hilt of the sword Zaine had gifted him. Truth be told, if any of the Regal guards spotted him outside Obsidia's white walls, it would be impossible to avoid a conflict.

Nathaniel stopped suddenly in his tracks.

'Nathaniel... are you okay?' Kaira asked.

'I... It's nothing.'

They continued on for a moment before Nathaniel whipped round, peering down the back of the tunnel.

He thought he'd felt something... a familiar twinge.

'Nathaniel?' Samir said.

Nathaniel turned back the right way and quickened his pace.

The further they went the more prominent that exalted feeling became. Nathaniel felt a smile touch his lips as he remembered that time in Sanctuary's library, the tingling sensation at his fingertips.

'Nathaniel, what's going on?' Kaira said worriedly.

'Here,' Nathaniel replied.

The torchlight revealed another break with the tunnel splitting into two diverging paths.

'Not again,' Samir murmured.

Nathaniel led them through the path to the right, into what appeared to be another cavern, though slightly smaller than the first they'd encountered.

'This is a dead end,' Kaira noted. 'We should head back the other way.'

Nathaniel held up a hand, 'just a moment. I can feel...
something.'

Samir looked about the cavern nervously. 'We shouldn't stay
here. What if–'

THUNK

'What was that?' Nathaniel spun round to find Samir crouched
over something by his feet. The Scorched boy was peeling
away clumps of earth from a bump jutting out of the ground.
Something glinted under the torchlight, after Samir removed
another layer of dirt. It looked metallic and, unless Nathaniel's
eyes were deceiving him, golden. Samir dipped his hands into
the ground either side of the object and, with an almighty tug,
managed to wrench the thing free of the earth. A square
helmet, with a hilt-shaped slit for the eyes and nose, looked
back at Nathaniel.

This was it. This was the object that had been touched by
Majik.

'What is it?' Samir's brows knitted together as he twisted the
golden helmet about in his hands.

'Is that what I think it is?' Kaira gasped.

'That's a Kingsguard's helmet,' Nathaniel said, looking on in
awe.

Just standing near the helmet gave Nathaniel such a warm
feeling inside. It was incredible how, after all these years, it
still retained even a trace of Majik. Yet it was unmistakably
there. Nathaniel could feel it.

'Let's take it with us,' Nathaniel said.

He only took one step back towards the tunnel, before recoiling suddenly away from the approaching shadows. The whispering shadows had found them.

'Sun above!' Samir gasped, almost tripping over himself as he stumbled back.

The shadows spilled into the cavern, spreading around its walls and over its jagged ceiling. Within seconds they would be completely and utterly surrounded.

Nathaniel hurriedly fumbled about his bag and drew out the inscribed rod. *We're in a lot of trouble!* Nathaniel tried to focus his frantic thoughts at the rod. It remained cold in his hands.

You stopped the assassins! Help us now! PLEASE! The rod's runes ran green with life and Nathaniel heard a yawn.

'You Greys have a knack for getting into trouble,' the rod spoke in his mind.

The shadows were beginning to sink down the walls towards them. *We're going to die!*

The rod sighed.

'Open the door, Nathaniel Grey. Open it and I will do what I can.'

Nathaniel shut his eyes and tried to drown out the cries of his companions. He pictured himself running to the brass-knobbed door, the shadows at his heels. He tugged and tugged on the handle, but the door refused to open for him.

'...three shall rise... three shall rise...'

Like a plague, the shadows began to infest the corners of his mind, draining his will, and swamping his dreams. Nathaniel hammered his hands against the door and screamed.

YOU PROMISED!

The shadows closed in.

Chapter 38

Black and gold carpets blurred by Illumina's eyes. The toes of her now slippered feet trailed over the carpet. Illumina almost fooled herself into thinking she was floating. At least, that was until she looked down at the gauntleted hands either side of her, keeping her upright.

Black and gold... So, she was still in the Emperor's Palace. But where was her brother taking her?

Illumina felt her chin slide down to her chest, as if drawn suddenly by a great weight, and drifted off into darkness. Someone was patting her gently on the cheek a moment later, rousing her from slumber.

'Come now, Sister. You won't want to miss this.'

Illumina peeled her eyes open slowly, amidst the glare of the rising sun. Kusk stood beside her, a thin smile crossing his scarred face. He extended a finger beyond the brazier-lined balcony that overlooked the entire city of Obsidia. One by one, Regals began to spill out from white brick houses, below the mountain. Peddlers tugged their wares in carts along the paved stone path, which split the city in two, hurrying to get to the prime spots. Children skipped to the gardens lining the concentric circles of the markets, their laughter carrying even as far up to the mountain as where Illumina stood.

'What... am I supposed... to be seeing exactly?' Illumina muttered.

'Look closer at the markets, Sister.'

The markets were largely bare at this time of the day, save for some of the more eager peddlers, who had already set up their stalls, in anticipation of early customers.

326

'Closer,' Kusk whispered in her ear.

A platoon of Royal Guardsmen, distinguishable by their black and gold armour, marched two apiece behind the Guard Captain. His black cloak billowing about in the wind.

'Intimidating our people with the Armada... brother?' Illumina said accusingly.

'You're not looking at *who* the guards are escorting,' Kusk replied.

A cold dread filled Illumina's stomach. She knew with absolute certainty then that she didn't want to look. But Illumina did anyway.

The Royal Guard escort was too far away to make out individual faces. Though, with horror, she could just about spot the shock of blood red hair amidst the sea of black helmets.

Chapter 39

As if struck suddenly with a battering ram, the door burst open, swatting Nathaniel to the ground. Nathaniel reached up and basked in the warmth of the Majik flowing through his veins. The power to split the Southern Seas and break the Black Mountains danced gloriously across his fingertips.

Surrounded by the coiling flames that had sprung up around the cavern, the whispers ceased, and the shadows shrieked.

*

The Majik had fled Nathaniel's body just as quickly, leaving him fatigued on the cavern floor. That is, until Samir had thrown him over one of his broad shoulders. Nathaniel didn't have the energy in him to object. Kaira spurring them on, they left the horrible grating cries of the whispering shadows behind and set off back down the tunnel.

'How did you do that?' Nathaniel heard Kaira ask him.

'Mmf,' Nathaniel mumbled into Samir's back. Truth be told – he wasn't sure either. The *door* had refused him entry then changed its mind a second later. Perhaps the rod had helped them after all.

'You're welcome.'

And about time, Nathaniel thought. *Those shadows were getting awfully close. What did you do?*

'I... did very little,' the rod admitted, sounding a little abashed.

Wait... so that had been all him? No wonder he could barely stand. The warning from the book he found in the Lycan library came back to him.

To use Majik, even when chained, is to wrestle a mountain. Unchained... the mountain would collapse upon you.

Nathaniel wondered how much more Majik he could get away with, until this warning came true. His Grandfather would probably be furious, were he ever to find out about what happened in the cavern. But it wasn't like Nathaniel had any choice.

'Is that... light?' Samir said.

'What? What is it?' Nathaniel said, struggling and failing to peek over the Scorched boy's shoulder.

'The end of the tunnel!' Kaira exclaimed, 'we've made it!'

Nathaniel breathed a sigh of relief at the daylight streaking down by Samir's feet.

'HALT!'

Nathaniel felt Samir's shoulders tense under his stomach.

'Drop the Kinslayer, boy!' a voice edged with authority ordered Samir.

'He can barely stand,' the Scorched boy replied, moving a hand to keep Nathaniel firmly stapled to his shoulder.

'It's alright, Samir,' Nathaniel patted the boy's back. 'I can manage... I think.'

Samir sighed but relented, gently lifting Nathaniel off his shoulder and onto the ground. Nathaniel stumbled slightly, before the Scorched boy caught him.

329

A platoon of Royal Guardsmen surrounded them, swords extended towards Nathaniel and his party in a half circle of steel. The Guard Captain, looking extremely pleased with himself, paced across his men. One hand on his helmet, which he held clutched to his side, and the other atop the pommel of his sword. A waterfall of black hair gushed down the Regal's breastplate.

Gabe, a still hooded Vaera, and Brey stood nearby behind their dropped bags and weapons. Nathaniel was glad to see them.

'Right on time, ginge,' Gabe said sarcastically.

'Shut up, Lycan,' the Guard Captain roared.

'Captain...' Nathaniel croaked.

'What's wrong with you, Kinslayer,' the Guard Captain rounded on Nathaniel. 'Is the guilt weighing you down?'

'Captain... we need to see the Elders...' Nathaniel said.

The Guard Captain withdrew a long, thin blade – the length of which would have put Zaine's to shame – from his scabbard. He ran a gauntleted finger down the blade's edge then narrowed his chestnut eyes at Nathaniel.

'My Lord Emperor gave me instruction to bring you to him... alive,' the Guard Captain said regretfully. He stabbed the sword into the mud and advanced towards Nathaniel. 'But he said nothing about the condition I might bring you in.'

Vaera swooped in and stood between Nathaniel and the Captain. 'You will do no such thing. Stand down, Aviendel,' she commanded him.

Captain Aviendel threw back his head and let out a barking laugh. 'Who are you, girl, to stand in my way?'

The Regal raised a hand, as if to bat Vaera aside. Then she pulled down her hood.

Aviendel's face warped into a mask of horror, the Regal recoiling so suddenly he almost slipped on the mud. The Captain shot down to one knee almost as fast as his guardsmen, bending his head down to Vaera.

'Princess Illiara!' he cried. 'I didn't–'

What? Nathaniel thought.

'What in the blazes…' Gabe's brow furrowed.

Samir and Brey shared a confused look.

Kaira had a rare grin plastered across her face. Nathaniel could almost hear the Féynian chuckling.

'Are you generally this insufferable to my people, Captain?' Vaera inquired. Her voice had taken a certain proud loftiness and the Regal seemed to stand a foot taller.

'My Princess, I–'

'Do you know penalty for striking your Empress-In-Waiting?' She took a step closer to the Captain.

'I–'

'I can assure you, Aviendel, you would have far more to fear than the loss of your Captaincy.'

Captain Aviendel winced at that.

'Forgive me, Princess… but the Kinslayer–'

'At this moment in time, Aviendel, my authority supersedes that of Kusk. You will escort us immediately to the Elders. I am sure the Szar will find the time to join us.'

Chapter 40

Princess Illiara.

The Empress-In-Waiting.

Nathaniel was struggling to wrap his head around it. How had he not figured it out sooner?

He watched her ahead with Captain Aviendel, as they wound their way up the paved road spiralling up the mountain to the Emperor's Palace, leading rather than following. The girl who had once hidden herself in the shadows of her cloak embraced the morning sun, as if she were its equal. The Regal guardsmen who escorted them kept glancing in her direction, perhaps contemplating whether to hold up the cape trailing behind her like the train of a queenly dress.

No wonder Vaera – no, Illiara – had tracked him down to Dalmarra. She thought he'd murdered her father; she probably still did. Yet, she had spared him from the Szar's clutches, if only temporarily.

The Hall of the Elders was guarded by two white-armoured Regals, with gold lances and closed visor helmets. They crossed their lances as Captain Aviendel approached, denying entry past the heavy iron doors between them. Aviendel glanced nervously back at Illiara, before clearing his throat.

'Captain Aviendel of the Emperor's Royal Guard, escorting the Empress-In-Waiting, Princess Illiara Tolken; the accused Kinslayer, Nathaniel Grey; and his... companions.'

The lances hung over the door momentarily, then the white guardsmen cracked their lances against the marble floor. Spinning on the spot, they turned to lead the group through the in-swinging doors.

Sunlight streamed inside the Hall through its glass, domed ceiling. Hexagonal patterns of light striking the cream floor. Their footsteps echoed sharply, as they strode across the seemingly endless length of marble towards the Elders.

Chalk white thrones, simple in their design, seated the three Elders at the end of the Hall. Their seats were so high up that they had to be accessed by three sets of steps.

The Elder in the middle looked very old. Long, white, somewhat bedraggled, locks plumed beyond the shoulders of his grey robes. He sported a magnificent beard of the same snowy white that fell between his legs. He was also fast asleep and snoring loudly.

The Elder to his right was his opposite. Bald and clean shaven, the man scowled contemptuously as they neared the steps.

The third Elder, bearing a nest of wild, dark hair and a mischievous grin, leant over to the bearded Elder and gave him a nudge. The middle Elder gave such a loud snort that it made Nathaniel jump.

'Eh? What?' the Elder shot up in his seat, twisting his head to-and-fro as if searching for a pestering fly.

'We have guests, Elder Morlen,' the bald Elder rolled his eyes.

'Oh, yes, of course,' the bearded Elder waved at Aviendel invitingly, before promptly falling back to sleep.

'To what do we owe the pleasure, Captain Aviendel?' the grinning Elder spread his hands inquisitively.

'Elder Calaem… Elders,' Aviendel bowed deeply in turn to all three, 'I bring with me–'

Aviendel was caught mid-speech as the iron doors creaked open behind them, followed immediately by heavy footfalls and the *swish swish* of a cloak.

'AVIENDEL! WHAT DID I TELL YOU? BRING THE BOY TO ME! I SAID—'

The Szar stopped dead in his tracks at the sight of Illiara.

'Princess Illiara! What are you doing here—'

'Forgetting something, Draeden?' she spoke bluntly.

The Obsidian Crown trembled atop the Szar's head. Kusk narrowed his eyes at the girl but eventually submitted himself, with apparent reluctance, on one knee, holding his head up defiantly.

'As I said, Aviendel, the Szar will make time,' Illiara told the abashed Guard Captain.

Aviendel winced at Illiara's words. He gave an apologetic look to Kusk, which was returned with an icy stare.

'That's the guy?' Gabe grunted behind Nathaniel.

'Yes,' Nathaniel replied through gritted teeth.

'The one who wants to kill us all?'

'The one and only.'

The crack of Gabe's knuckles echoed across the Hall.

'So, Captain Aviendel. I presume your visit concerns the return of this—' the bald Elder paused to grimace at Nathaniel, '—Kinslayer?'

'By Athrana's grace, Elder Ailas, it is indeed the truth,' Aviendel nodded.

335

'Then our Empress-In-Waiting has left her grieving to deliver her sentence?' Elder Ailas turned expectantly to Illiara.

Nathaniel dared not look at Illiara, as they awaited her verdict. He did not remember whether it was he who had reached for Brey's hand but there they stood, gripping each other tightly in anticipation.

'It's going to be okay,' she spoke in a hushed tone beside his ear.

He truly hoped she was right. How fitting it was the girl who had hoped to kill him, the one girl with enough cause to deliver the execution herself, who should hold his life in her hands.

Elder Morlen's snores rumbled loudly throughout the Hall, then fell silent as the Princess took an intake of breath.

'I would hear the accused speak,' she said.

Nathaniel let out the breath he hadn't realised he'd been holding. Had he heard her right?

'WHAT?'

The Szar stomped up to Illiara in a red-faced fury that seemed to make the puckered scars splitting his face pulse.

'You can't be serious, Princess! This boy murdered your father! Say the word now and I'll have him put to the Stone!'

'I am quite serious, Draeden,' Illiara replied coolly.

The Szar flapped his arms against his sides and spun to face the Elders. 'This is ridiculous! Why are we wasting time with words when we should be consigning Tolken's murderer to the Stone?'

'I had a similar thought,' Nathaniel growled. Aviendel's sword was already against his throat, preventing him from taking another step forward.

'I agree, your Grace,' Elder Ailas said. 'But... the Empress-In-Waiting is entitled to hear the Kinsalyer's plea.' The Elder looked as disappointed as Kusk on the matter.

'Regardless of either of their intentions, we've yet to hear the boy's initial testimony,' Elder Calaem said.

'Let him speak!' Elder Morlen woke suddenly, slapping a hand against an armrest enthusiastically, before swiftly nestling back in his seat and snoring once more.

Elder Calaem gave his fellow Elder a bemused look then beckoned Nathaniel to come closer. Aviendel sheathed his blade and backed away to allow Nathaniel entry into the space between Illiara and Kusk. Nathaniel gave an appreciative smile to Illiara, which was met with an uncertain look in response. Gabe gave a brief encouraging nod; Brey a trembling smile; Samir dry washed his hands, clearly eager to get his hands on whatever book he could find; Kaira bent her head slightly and gave him a narrow look, as if assessing his chances of survival. He hoped things looked better than they felt.

The Szar's chest heaved angrily beside him but he refused to give Nathaniel so much as a glance.

Nathaniel's eyes flickered to the Obsidian Crown. He had to resist the urge to snatch it from the Szar's head and hit him with it.

'Don't do anything stupid, boy,' the rod's voice intervened in his thoughts.

'Nathaniel Grey, you stand accused of the murder of Emperor Jael Tolken, before the triumvirate of Elders, Emperor, and Szar. How do you plea?' Elder Ailas said.

'Innocent, Elder Ailas, I have come to clear my name,' Nathaniel replied.

'Preposterous!' the Szar spat.

Elder Calaem held up his hand. 'We are listening to Nathaniel's testimony, we have already heard yours in considerable detail, your Grace.'

The Szar folded his hands behind his back and pushed out his chin but thankfully held his silence. So, Nathaniel began his tale, starting with the abduction by Crow from the palace cells. Calaem's ears pricked up at the mention of the Crow's apparent collusion with the Szar, as Nathaniel had overhead in the warehouse in Morne, and he leaned forward in his chair.

'I do seem to recall one of the guardsmen reporting of this 'shadow-wielder,' Calaem turned to his fellow Elders.

'One guardsman,' Elder Ailas scoffed, 'it's hardly sufficient evidence!'

Elder Morlen jolted awake. 'Necromancers,' he whispered ominously then slumped back.

A sharp silence fell over the Hall and the other two Elders shivered.

'One guardsman,' Elder Ailas repeated quietly.

Elder Calaem coughed loudly into his arm. He then waved to Nathaniel, urging him to continue with his account.

Kusk was impressively nonchalant whilst Nathaniel spoke of the Sisters' attempt on his life, during the journey from

Dalmarra to Obsidia. Though, the Regal's lip curled, nastily, after Nathaniel mentioned the mines of Dün Moine and the loss of Zaine in its lower tunnels.

'Troubling indeed…' Calaem ran a hand through his upturned hair, as if in a futile attempt at smoothing it down.

'Troubling as it may be, Elder Calaem, I hardly see how this exonerates the Kinslayer!' Elder Ailas threw his hand dismissively in Nathaniel's direction.

'I also have this, Elders.'

Nathaniel dug a hand into his pockets and withdrew a handful of crumpled envelopes, each bearing broken Regal seals. He turned to give Kusk a triumphant glare of his own. The Szar's eyes seemed to have turned an even icier shade of blue.

'What are those?' Elder Ailas squinted down at Nathaniel.

'Correspondence,' Nathaniel waved the letters in the air. 'Between Emperor Jael Tolken and Thorne Grey of the Brotherhood of Lycans.'

There was an audible gasp from the gathered Regals. There was also a look of longing in Illiara's eyes that made Nathaniel feel awfully guilty. Suddenly he realised that he'd been withholding Tolken's words from his own daughter, without knowing otherwise.

'Forgeries!' Ailas pointed an accusing finger at Nathaniel.

'That looks awfully like the Emperor's seal,' Calaem contested. The Elder did look slightly uncomfortable with that point. 'Captain Aviendel, if you would be so kind as to bring the letters over?'

Aviendel snatched the letters from Nathaniel's hand, before Calaem had so much as completed his sentence and passed them over to the Elder. Elder Calaem turned the envelopes delicately in each hand before pulling out the letters folded within. His eyes ran over the contents once and then he placed the letter back within the envelope without touching the others.

'It's his. It's Tolken's handwriting and seal.'

'Impossible!' Ailas palmed the armrest of his throne fiercely.

'Have a look if you wish, Ailas,' Calaem sighed, 'in fact, take as many as you need. It won't change their authenticity.'

Ailas didn't bother to consider his fellow Elder's words. His eyes were fixed on the envelopes back in Aviendel's hands.

When they reached Elder Ailas' groping fingers, the Regal took less than half the care Calaem had, ripping the parchment out of the envelopes in a mild frenzy. He seemed to go over Tolken's scrawl a dozen times, each time closely scrutinising the envelope's broken seal, eyes bulging increasingly after every read.

'It cannot be…' Nathaniel thought he heard the Regal murmur to himself.

Eventually, the Elder slapped the letters against his thigh and slumped into his seat.

'Elder Calaem… is not wrong,' Ailas muttered regretfully.

The Szar, the veins in his neck practically throbbing, took a step closer to the Elders' thrones. He looked angry.

'This proves nothing!' Kusk insisted. 'A few foolish words from Tolken won't exonerate the boy! The matter of…

relations… is a separate thing entirely. The Kinslayer wastes your time with irrelevancies!'

'Irrelevancies?' Nathaniel said quietly.

The Regals turned to him.

'Those were the last written words of Emperor Jael Tolken. Words looking to forge a peaceful relationship between Lycan and Regal,' Nathaniel could feel himself shaking as he spoke.

'Foolish words,' the Szar repeated himself. 'A pity you killed him before he could discuss his plans with the Elders.'

'Stop it! Both of you!' Illiara cried, 'your childish bickering gets us nowhere!'

Ailas bit his lip thoughtfully as he drummed his fingers against the armrest of his throne. He pointed at Illiara with the letters still clutched in one hand.

'You've travelled with the accused, Princess Illiara,' Elder Ailas said. 'What do you make of his evidence?'

Nathaniel felt his stomach leap to his chest in anticipation.

'I… I don't quite know anymore, Elders,' Illiara bowed her head.

'Then the Stone awaits,' Kusk said. He thrust a finger out at Nathaniel, 'Aviendel! Seize the Kinslayer!'

Aviendel moved initially, with the instinctive step of one used to following orders without question. However, he hesitated at the second step, and turned to Illiara with his sword halfway out of its scabbard.

'Enough!' Elder Calaem barked, 'there will be no sentencing whilst the accused's guilt remains in question!'

341

'Remains in question?' Kusk looked stupendous, 'the boy's own father saw him murder Tolken in cold blood! Before he was eventually turned on by the accused in question!'

'LIAR!'

Two Regal guards seized Nathaniel's arms, before he could launch himself at Kusk.

The Szar leaned towards Nathaniel, close enough that he could see the whites of Kusk's eyes. 'Just can't get enough of killing, can you, Kinslayer?' he hissed.

The creak of the Hall's doors brought the Szar's attention away. The sneer that had enveloped his features was not in the least bit comforting.

'How kind of you to finally join us Laevan. I was just telling the Elders about the day of your son's wedding.'

The footsteps stopped.

Nathaniel felt a lump rising in his throat. He didn't want to turn around. He didn't want to look at his father. Curiosity, however, is a funny thing. If all else fails, curiosity will drive you. Laevan Grey's newly grown red bush of beard looked alien on his face. From the way his nose wrinkled above it, it seemed he was not particularly used to it either.

'Nathaniel…'

The beard hid much but not all. Not the way his father's eyes pinched at the corners, so subtly Nathaniel could easily have missed it.

Do you regret it father? Do you regret throwing me away like an old toy?

Nathaniel didn't care, in truth. Though he wasn't quite sure what to feel. Perhaps all the anger he'd directed at the Szar had left him too numb to spare any feeling toward his father.

'We've heard Laevan's testimony long ago, your Grace,' Calaem cut in.

The Szar's cloak whipped as he twirled to face the Elders. 'Yet you seem to have forgotten about it already, Calaem.'

Calaem's eyebrow raised. Perhaps at not being afforded the use of his title. 'We have not. And now, there is fresh evidence to consider, your Grace.'

The Szar scoffed.

'The rest of you are willing to consider the Kinslayer's lies?' Kusk inquired of Elder Ailas and the slumbering Elder Morlen.

Elder Ailas grimaced as she shifted about his seat. 'We must consider all evidence, your Grace.'

'I see...'

The Szar moved his hands to grasp the crown on his head.

'If you will not permit the boy to Stone, then I will be forced to permit him death instead!' the Szar tossed the Obsidian Crown away. The other Regals gave out a combined cry and, half-heartedly, made to reach towards it. The crown bounced once over the marble floor with a metallic *dink*, rollicked side to side, before finally settling below the Elders' feet.

'What is the meaning of this, your Grace?' Elder Calaem demanded.

'Come now, Calaem, let's not play games here. But for your sake, I will be official.' Kusk bent on one knee and placed a palm against the floor. 'I, Draeden Kusk, do wilfully, in the presence of the Elders of Obsidia and her Empress-In-Waiting, abdicate the Obsidian Crown and return to protecting Obsidia and her borders.'

'You can't do this, Draeden!' Calaem looked infuriated.

Even Elder Morlen had awoken from his slumber, holding a grave look as he observed the proceedings.

Kusk's eyes glinted madly as he continued undeterred. 'In my first act as Szar, I proclaim a state emergency and demand the trial of the Kinslayer, by blood!'

'This is unacceptable–'

A touch from Elder Morlen was enough to silence Calaem, who immediately lowered his head shamefully.

'You freely forsake the Obsidian Crown?' Morlen inquired of the Szar. The Elder looked a few decades younger, all of the sudden. He gripped the arms of his seat, no longer with the desperation of one close to slipping from their chair, but with the assuredness of a King.

'I do, Elder Morlen,' Kusk replied.

Elder Morlen sighed. 'Then we release you from your bonds and accept your... request.' Morlen turned his wrinkled eyes to Nathaniel. 'Take the day to ready yourself, Nathaniel Grey. Tonight, the arena will test your innocence.'

Chapter 41

Nathaniel paced back and forth across the red velvet carpet, muttering to himself furiously. The white guardsmen that had been assigned to Nathaniel watched him quietly beside the door, motionless as statues.

How could he have been so stupid as to think he would just arrive at Obsidia and clear his name? Of course, the Szar had a plan up his sleeve, just in case he couldn't execute Nathaniel on the spot. And now he was faced with a more terrifying prospect – fighting in the arena. No one had fought in the arena for centuries, as far as he was aware. To make matters worse, the Szar would have near full control over what he would face there.

Eventually, he got bored of all the pacing around and slumped into the plush armchair in the corner of the room, next to the ornate wooden desk and chair. The room was bordered, on both sides, by tall bookcases that touched the ceiling. Nathaniel had been tempted to pass the time by grabbing one of the books, but it seemed stupid, when he was mere hours away from fighting in the arena. He couldn't practice either, having been stripped of his sword and dagger.

The Elders had arranged for a rudimentary pallet to be brought into the study. Though, he hardly felt like sleeping, especially not with the guards watching him. Nathaniel almost wished that he'd been whisked off to the arena immediately.

He wondered how the others were doing. Despite the severity of the situation, Gabe's eyes had lit up like fireworks when the Szar mentioned the arena. He was probably fuming that he couldn't take part. Kaira was likely admonishing the Lycan with a roll of her eyes, whilst Samir sat a world apart in his book. And Brey…

A knock at the door quickly dissipated the thought. One of the guards drew back and slapped the haft of his pike horizontally against his side, the tip pointing at the door.

'Begone!' the second shouted, 'the Elders have declared this room sealed.'

'I know Nathaniel's in there, guardsman, I've come to speak. I'm unarmed.'

Nathaniel frowned. *It couldn't be...*

'My name is Solas Grey, I'm the Kinslayer's brother.'

Nathaniel jumped out of his chair immediately. 'Let him through,' he pleaded with the guard nearest him.

The white guard with the raised lance considered this for a moment then nodded his helmet at the second, who unlocked the door, allowing the younger sibling inside. The door closed quickly again with a click and the boy raised his arms to be searched.

Solas looked better rested than when Nathaniel had last laid eyes on him. Yet his brother's cheeks seemed strapped more tightly to the bone than Nathaniel remembered, as if he'd aged in years rather than a few paltry months. His blonde hair, once wild and unkempt, had been trimmed to half the length atop the crown of his head and shorn bare around the sides.

A black and gold breastplate, burnished heavily it seemed to hide the nicks and scores that marked the surface, held him in a stiffly straight pose. Nathaniel felt his heart sink in his chest at the realisation – the Szar had claimed his brother, body and soul.

'Brother,' Solas spoke first. His smile was tight, controlled, almost mechanical. His face quivered, as if it longed to break out one of his mischievous grins.

'Solas, you look–'

'–like I can't breathe? I think I might have strapped my armour too tightly this morning. I almost fainted climbing up those stairs!' Solas chuckled at the thought. That was more like his brother. He pointed at the unused pallet, 'can't sleep?'

'Would you be able to?' Nathaniel asked.

'Probably not,' Solas shrugged in reply. 'Though Pegs' wine seemed to help last time. Speaking of which – how is he doing? I heard you went through the mines.'

'Same old jovial Pegs,' Nathaniel said.

'Hm.'

Solas's face became pensive as he moved towards one of the bookcases. 'You're probably wondering why I'm here,' he said, running a finger absent-mindedly over the ridges of book spines.

'That has crossed my mind,' Nathaniel admitted, joining his brother at the bookcase. 'I assume you're not here to admire Elder Calaem's collection?'

'Not quite. I've come with a proposition.'

'I'm listening.'

Solas glanced casually back at the white guardsmen then leant in ever so slightly towards his brother. Speaking quietly, he said, 'I want to free you.'

Nathaniel was careful to hide his laugh. 'You seemed happy to let me rot in the cells, Solas,' Nathaniel snorted. 'Why the sudden change of heart?'

Solas chewed his lower lip. 'I was angry,' he said after a moment. 'I don't want to see you die, Nathaniel, even after all you've done.'

'After all I've done?' Nathaniel scoffed. 'You still think I killed the Emperor, don't you?'

Solas wrung his hands together pleadingly, as he drew his voice to an even barer whisper. 'I can get you out of here, Nathaniel, I... don't really know how yet but I swear I'll do it.'

'And what about Samir, Gabe, Kaira, and Brey? Can you get them out too?' Nathaniel asked.

Solas blinked. 'The Lycans? Who cares?'

'Then I guess I'm staying, thanks,' Nathaniel replied coolly, throwing himself back into the chair to underpin the point.

Solas looked at his brother with a stunned expression, his jaw almost dropping to the floor. 'You would rather die with those... with those *dogs*?' Solas spat the last word out with pure venom. 'Why else did you murder the Emperor, if not to stop his insane plan?'

'Better the dogs than the murderers, brother,' Nathaniel retorted.

SMACK!

Solas' fist had cracked across Nathaniel's face so quickly he barely had time to register it. He fell out of the chair, clutching his profusely bleeding nose.

'You damned– you bloody damned idiot!' Solas yelled. He was struggling against the grip of one of the white guardsmen, who had burst forward and seized the Regal, not a second after the punch had been thrown.

'Do you have any idea what the Szar has planned for you? You're going to die in that arena, brother! All that will remain of you is a patch of blood in the sand before you fade into nothingness!'

The look of pure malice on Solas' face, just before the white guardsmen slammed the door shut, hurt even more than when he had left him in the palace cells. Nathaniel sank to the floor, half-wishing the carpet would swallow him up, fighting hard against the tears that threatened to well up in his eyes.

Chapter 42

The arena was an intimidatingly large amphitheatre, buried beyond the Emperor's Palace and into the adjoining mountain. With its cavernous, craggy roof and hundreds of torches working to keep the place alight, it reminded Nathaniel a little of Dün Moine. A circle of sand covered paving stone, roughly two hundred metres in diameter, waited for Nathaniel beyond the portcullis. Beyond the sand, Nathaniel could make out one of several, red-bricked tiers of seating, rising up into the mountain wall. Each tier, no doubt, filled to the brim with his kin.

Nathaniel stole a look at the white-armoured Elder guard, who had accompanied him to the portcullis. The guard had kept his helmet on, holding himself stiffly beside Nathaniel, lance in hand. He was quietly thankful it hadn't been one of the Szar's Royal Guard who had escorted him to the arena. The sneers and whispered threats that Nathaniel had received... well, they had made it very clear that the white guardsman was all that stopped them from inflicting harm upon him.

A gong, diminished by the din inside the arena, sounded off from above somewhere. This was followed by the screeching tremble of gears as the portcullis slowly began to rise.

'It is time.' The white guardsman's voice rasped through his visor like a bell toll.

Nathaniel felt butterflies fluttering in his stomach but ignored how suddenly uncomfortable his armour felt across his shoulders. He took back his longsword and dagger and secured them at the belt. With a closed fist to his forehead, Nathaniel mouthed a quick and silent appeal to the Gods, then stepped through the open portcullis into the arena.

*

From the Royal Box, the Szar, Princess Illiara, and Nathaniel's father watched the lone figure emerge onto the sand with mixed emotions. Kusk thought he heard Laevan gasp softly, but he made no comment. It was his son after all. The Princess had been glaring at the Szar ever since they had first sat down. Shaking her head intermittently, out of a mixture of anger, disappointment... and mounting fear for what horrors he had planned for Nathaniel.

'Shall I order one of the Royal Guard down, your grace?' Captain Aviendel inquired of the Szar.

'No,' Kusk replied, simply. His lips began to curl unpleasantly after a moment's thought. 'This is no ordinary criminal before us, Aviendel. I think our Kinslayer deserves something a little more... *special*... for his first round, don't you think?'

Aviendel's face dropped at first. Though, knowing his station, the Guard Captain quickly composed himself and slapped his arms against his sides.

'As my lord commands,' the Regal bowed, before whisking out of sight down the tunnel behind them.

'What have you planned, Draeden?' Illiara demanded.

'Something I think the crowd will enjoy, Princess,' Kusk said. 'Such a pity the Hunter Lord won't be here to witness one of his little pets.' Kusk's lip curled at the mention of Zaine. A pity it most certainly was not.

Illiara tensed in her seat.

351

'You wouldn't...' she breathed.

The Szar's smile was paper thin.

'Draeden. It will tear him apart.'

The crowd within the arena fell silent as Kusk rose and held aloft his arms to embrace them. 'What the crowd wants...' the Szar called back over his shoulder.

'But he's just a boy.'

'The boy who murdered your father in cold blood.'

Illiara had been about to refute that statement, before she bit down sharply on her tongue. She didn't know what to think of Nathaniel's supposed innocence but she knew she strongly disliked this method of determining the truth. What good would it do to exonerate a liar well versed in swordplay or, indeed, murder an innocent with fumbling hands?

'Don't do this, Draeden.'

'Is that an order, Princess? Sadly, I'm afraid, until your crowning ceremony, it counts for naught at this moment in time.'

'You! Guard-Captain!' Illumina fixed her eyes on Laevan Grey. 'You're Nathaniel's father, aren't you? You can't surely think this is true justice? Convince the Szar of his foolishness!'

Laevan swallowed guiltily but refused to meet Illiara's penetrating gaze. Staring straight ahead, over the expanse of sand, he replied limply, 'the Szar has the right, your highness.'

'Athrana's grace... are all the Royal Guard this lacking in backbone?' Illiara demanded.

Laevan Grey didn't have an answer to that, but continued to stare blankly ahead, lost in his own thoughts.

'REGALS OF OBSIDIA!' Kusk's voice boomed suddenly across the arena. 'YOU HAVE BEEN PATIENT FOR LONGER THAN YOU NEEDED! BUT NOW THE MOMENT HAS COME AND THE KINSLAYER STANDS BEFORE YOU ALL, AWAITING JUDGEMENT FOR HIS HEINOUS CRIME!'

A wave of pumping fists cascaded around the arena, as thousands of Regals roared and booed at the red-haired boy standing in the sand.

'LET ATHRANA'S JUSTICE BE SWIFT!'

With that announcement, the Szar dropped, smugly, back in his seat and awaited what would come out of the arena pen. That fool boy was well and truly doomed.

*

A pungent smell, like that of a wet dog, scoured Nathaniel's nostrils as another, considerably larger, portcullis rose before him. Noticeably, scraping off years of rust as it did so.

A pair of ghostly white eyes blinked curiously at him, eyes too large for any humanoid opponent. Nathaniel would have appreciated the manticore as a truly magnificent beast, were it not the case that the thing was about a hundred metres away from eating him alive. He had almost dropped his sword when its grizzled mane emerged out of the shadows, snout raised appraisingly. It ruffled its wings and wafted its tail lazily across the sand. The spines on the club-end of the tail, making

353

deep furrows in the sand, were as long as Nathaniel's forearm and as sharp as daggers. No wonder Solas had tried to spare him from the arena.

Nathaniel calmed his breathing, as much as he could, and focused on remembering the lessons Zaine had taught him. Trying not to focus on the fact he hadn't been trained to fight monsters. It seemed ironic that the Hunter hadn't considered he might one day need to fight a creature such as this. Or maybe he hadn't expected it to be so soon.

He crouched, holding his sword parallel to the ground at shoulder height, as the manticore approached him tentatively. Keeping his knees bent, ready to spring at any given moment. The manticore didn't roar or give any other warning of its opening attack. It unfurled its black wings and leapt, covering the distance separating the two in the blink of an eye. Heavy paws slamming into the sand where Nathaniel had been standing, as he dived and rolled out of the way. The creature did not follow him immediately, as he sought refuge closer to the arena wall, perhaps surprised by his agility.

The baying crowd cheered, urging the beast to end the contest. The manticore uttered a derisive snort, dust pluming up around its legs, as it pawed against the arena floor.

CRACK

One of the spines shot off from the beast's arched tail. Nathaniel ducked just in time, feeling the spine brush past the tips of his hair before sinking deeply into the wall.

Then, with a savage growl, the beast charged.

Nathaniel's eyes widened but he, again, just managed to dive out of the way, slashing his sword across the beast's leading leg, before the manticore's jaw snapped shut around the space his upper body had formerly occupied. But his escape had not been without cost. Nathaniel cried out as the tips of the creature's claws caught his thigh, sending him rolling in the sand.

Once again, the arena roared its approval, as Nathaniel crawled away with his bloodied leg. A relatively minor graze from this creature but it felt like someone had stabbed a dagger into his thigh. Nathaniel's eyes fell on the sizeable gash he'd inflicted upon the creature's thigh, spilling a steady stream of turquoise down its leg. Though, out of the two of them, he imagined he was far worse for wear.

The manticore padded slowly towards him, apparently in no rush to finish off its prey, despite the crowd's desperate pleas. How in the world was the Szar allowed to get away with this? How was this a fair contest?

Growling through gritted teeth, he clambered back to his feet. Nathaniel backed away from the manticore, as quickly as he could manage, his right leg burning all the while.

How am I going to get out of this?

No one answered his thoughts. Nathaniel suddenly remembered that he'd left the rod back in his saddlebag. Truly, he was alone in his plight.

The manticore seemed to sense his desperation and increased the pace of its hunt, eyes glistening hungrily. Nathaniel half considered proffering his head forward, in the vain hope the beast would grant him a quick death. The thought of the Szar lapping up the crowd's praise afterwards vanquished the idea, as quickly as it had come, and Nathaniel held his sword more tightly before him.

355

Perhaps, now bored of playing with its food, the manticore had settled into a gallop towards the Regal, clouds of sand dancing in its wake. Its roar made the ground tremble.

Though his heart pounded fiercely against his chest, Nathaniel's grip remained steady on his sword. Defiantly, he yelled a hoarse battle cry at the onrushing creature. To his great surprise, the manticore suddenly slid to a halt, as if stunned by Nathaniel's cry. When Nathaniel followed the creature's gaze down to its side, however, and to the golden lance buried in its flank, it was clear that the beast's hesitation was not his doing. The white guardsman holding the lance swiftly pulled the bloodied tip out, jumped over the manticore's sweeping tail, and then clambered up its leg and onto its back.

Nathaniel glanced up. The Szar had risen up in the Royal Box, gesticulating wildly at the battle unfolding beneath him. Though it was impossible to hear what he was saying, over the clamour of the arena crowd, Nathaniel was pleased to see his obvious anger.

Staggering side to side, the manticore struggled to shake the guardsman off its back. The guardsman twirled the lance about in the air, batting away and dodging the flurry of spines that burst from the manticore's tail, whilst somehow maintaining his balance. The man's movements were so quick, so fluid, he may as well have been a shadow dancing on the beast's back. When the last spine had been flung, the guardsman snapped up his lance in the air with both hands and drove the blade into the beast's neck. The manticore's white eyes widened and then it slumped to the floor, with such force that Nathaniel almost lost his footing where he stood.

The Regals in the arena were speechless and, in the silence, the Szar took the opportunity to express his rage. 'HOW DARE YOU! YOU HAD NO RIGHT TO INTEREFERE!'

Kusk pointed accusingly at the grey robed Elders sat in the Eastern box.

'WE HAD NOTHING TO DO WITH THIS, YOU WARMONGERING FOOL!' The reply sounded like it came from Elder Calaem.

'REVEAL YOURSELF! IMPOSTER!' Elder Ailas cried, shaking his fist at the white guardsman below.

The white guardsman left the lance impaled in the creature's neck, as he hopped down onto the sand and placed his hands either side of his helmet.

The man looked too tall to be Gabe... maybe it was Samir? No. The boy hated fighting...

The helmet made a dull thud as it hit the sand. Nathaniel gasped as the guardsman's silver eyes met his. 'Zaine!'

The crowd suddenly found its voice. Though, while the majority were clearly hostile, Nathaniel was sure he heard some cheer.

A dozen guardsmen, half bearing the royal black, half the Elder white, spilled into the arena. The white guardsmen held their lances with the poise of statues but some of the Royal Guard looked uneasy, underneath their open-faced helmets at the sight of the Hunter.

'Stand aside, stand aside!'

Black cloak whipping about behind him, Captain Aviendel pushed aside two of his guard on his way over. Another, garbed in a cloak and armed with a sword, followed after him, patting the shoulders of the guardsmen Aviendel had barged past.

Of all the things he had hoped to say to Laevan Grey, 'father,' was simply not it. A hundred times Nathaniel had ran over the accusations he'd lay at his father's feet. Face-to-face, however, Nathaniel felt his resolve melt.

'Nathaniel,' his father whispered back solemnly, his eyes remaining downcast. 'You did well.'

'As touching as this is, Laevan, we've the next round to get on with,' Aviendel butted in. His eyes ran over the dead manticore with a grimace. 'You lot!' he pointed at his guardsmen, 'get the beast out of here! And you!' Aviendel's sword blurred into his hand, which he used to point at the Hunter, 'don't make me put you down.'

Zaine raised a brow, bemusedly. 'I'd advise you call back your guard, if that is truly your intention, Captain.'

Aviendel glanced at his men surrounding the manticore. He looked unsure about his chances alone.

'However, I have no wish to harm you Aviendel, I'll come willingly,' Zaine said.

'Zaine…'

The Hunter laid a hand on Nathaniel's shoulder as he passed and leant in briefly. 'Remember what I taught you, Nathaniel. Whatever comes into this arena, you must survive it. What-or who-ever comes.'

To Nathaniel's puzzlement, the Hunter looked pointedly at Nathaniel's father. Laevan's chin seemed to sink deeper into his chest, a mournful expression painted across his face.

The Szar wasted no time, as both the Hunter and the manticore's corpse were escorted out of the arena. 'REGALS OF OBSIDIA! THE KINSLAYER MAY HAVE SURVIVED THIS ROUND BUT KNOW THIS – ATHRANA'S JUSTICE IS PATIENT. NO ONE MAY ESCAPE IT!'

The portcullis rumbled and began to rise once more, with the *clack clack clack* of gears. 'WELCOME ATHRANA'S CHAMPION! READY TO DELIVER JUSTICE IN HER NAME!'

Nathaniel squinted into the darkness, beyond the portcullis, hoping that the Szar didn't have a spare manticore to throw at him. What walked out into the arena, however, was a thousand times worse than any number of manticores.

Oh no. How could you?

The blonde boy strode towards Nathaniel, grimly. The Regal's hand gripped the lance shaft, so tightly, his knuckles were white. Nathaniel glanced up at the Royal Box, at the Szar leering down.

Not even you could be so cruel.

'You should have ran while you could... brother,' Solas said.

Chapter 43

No, no, no, no, this couldn't be happening.

Once he was a few paces away from Nathaniel, Solas spun on his heels. He planted his lance into the sand and dropped to one knee, in acknowledgment to the Szar.

Kusk replied with a half-bow before returning to his seat beside Illiara. Nathaniel squinted his eyes at the Princess but from the distance between them her face was unreadable.

Solas jumped back to his feet and held his lance out before him.

'Pick up your sword, Kinslayer,' Solas said.

Nathaniel's hand clenched against nothing but thin air. He hadn't even realised that he'd dropped it.

Please don't make do this.

He scoured the Royal Box for their father. Aviendel had just appeared next to the Szar but Laevan Grey was out of sight. Had he known? Could he not bear to watch?

'Pick. Up. Your. Sword,' Solas said.

'Solas... don't allow the Szar to get away with this.'

His brother lunged forward suddenly, the lance ripping through Nathaniel's tunic but fortunately only grazing skin.

Nathaniel gasped and jumped away, clutching his wet side.

Did he just... No... Please... No...

'Think about what you are doing!' Nathaniel pleaded.

Solas launched a boot at Nathaniel's sword, kicking it towards him.

'I won't ask you again, brother.'

Nathaniel glared at the Royal Box, as he bent down to the sand. *How dare you?* He thought. Framing him for murder was one thing but this... this couldn't be happening. It had to be some terrible dream he was about to–

The moment the Regal had grasped the handle of his sword, Solas had launched another attack with his lance. Nathaniel managed to parry the lance tip, as it flashed a few inches from his face.

In almost perfect sync, they two brothers jumped back and began to circle each other in the sand.

The addition of the cut in his side, to the wound he'd received from the manticore, made moving awfully painful. Though Nathaniel made every effort to move as if it wasn't really bothering him.

'I gave you a chance, Nathaniel, and you threw it back in my face!' Solas barked at him.

'Athrana's grace, Solas!' Nathaniel protested, 'I'm innocent!'

'Then prove it, Kinslayer!'

Nathaniel batted away the stab of the Solas's lance. He considered launching an attack of his own but decided to draw back. If he were to win this battle, he couldn't make the first move. He'd have to draw him into close-quarters and...

Nathaniel felt a pang of horror at the way his thoughts were shaping. He wouldn't fight Solas, he couldn't.

Solas was unrelenting in his attacks, throwing jab after slash, after jab. Sometimes catching Nathaniel's arms or legs with the end of the lance. Nathaniel could already feel the bruises forming on his flesh as he wheeled away. The curl of Solas's lips suggested his brother thought he had the beating of his opponent. The Regal had been trained well but he was leaving himself increasingly open to ripostes with each attack.

Stop it! Nathaniel scolded himself. *I will not hurt him!*

The lance jutted forward again, though stopped, strangely, a foot in front of Nathaniel, whose sword was already travelling to meet the expected blow. So, it came as a surprise when Solas spun around, twisting the lance under his armpit, cracking the staff end against Nathaniel's wrist.

Nathaniel cried out in surprise and fell to his knees, cradling his broken wrist against his stomach. Clouds of dust parted for the boots that approached Nathaniel's hunched form. The round end of Solas's lance smacked into the sand in front of Nathaniel, so the staff was mere inches from his nose.

'It appears Athrana does not favour you, Kinslayer,' Solas spoke softly.

Nathaniel barked a bitter laugh. Given all he'd been through, he sincerely doubted that any of the Gods ever had.

A flick of Solas's boot heel brought Nathaniel's back against the sand, the lance point hovering over his eyes. Rivulets of sweat were streaming down his brother's face and he panted heavily. Still, he refrained from stabbing the lance into Nathaniel.

'You don't... don't want to do this,' Nathaniel grunted.

Solas ran his tongue over his lips, as if to consider Nathaniel's words, then shook his head profusely.

'For the Empire... I have to,' he replied.

Nathaniel snorted. 'You sound just like the Szar.'

It sickened Nathaniel to his core to see how much Solas liked the sound of that.

Kusk can't have taken him body and soul.

Nathaniel had to know if there was something of his brother left. Some small trace of compassion.

'Whatever you do... save the Lycans, Solas... please.'

'Save them?' Solas's lance lowered. The Regal's jaw almost swung to his chest. Then he laughed. Cruelly. That scared Nathaniel, far more than the sight of his brother's open admiration for the Szar. His next few words practically dripped with malice and his eyes had set into a hawk-like stare, as if Nathaniel were a juicy worm fumbling in the dirt.

'You still don't get it do you, brother?' Solas sneered. 'The Szar is going to purify Horizon once and for all of those dogs, starting off with your hairy little friends.'

'Solas...'

'SHUT UP!'

The lance tip tickled Nathaniel's throat, drawing the smallest trickle of blood.

Solas's eyes softened at that. 'I can promise you they will be killed quickly,' he said quietly.

The lance began to rise slowly. Nathaniel became aware of a steady drumbeat, marking each passing second. The cries of the arena were only a dull hum, less perceivable than a fly in his ear. Each fraction of second brought a new face, flashing across the forefront of Nathaniel's mind.

Gabe and his easy grin.

Samir's dark, hooded eyes, peering over the top of a book.

Kaira with a wryly raised brow.

And Brey... with her freckles, her crooked smile, and bright green eyes...

He couldn't just let them die. He couldn't!

The lance was driven down.

Nathaniel twisted and, in a fluid motion, reached for his boot. The lance cracked against the paving stone, missing Nathaniel's neck by fractions, then fell from his brother's grasp.

Solas frowned, then the realisation hit him, as he collapsed to his knees. He titled his head down towards his armoured chest and gasped at the dagger embedded underneath his armpit above the chink of his breastplate.

His hand flew to the handle.

'No!' Nathaniel yelled. 'Don't take it out–'

The bloodied blade was out before Nathaniel could stop Solas. His brother uttered an oath and then collapsed into Nathaniel's arms.

Nathaniel had already stripped off his tunic and bundled it against the wound. Still, the material was becoming quickly sodden.

'So... Athrana favours you after all... brother...' Solas muttered. He coughed hoarsely, as though an apple core was lodged in his throat, grimacing as the little colour he had began to drain from his face.

'You bloody idiot,' Nathaniel shook as he spoke. 'Why did it have to be you?'

'The Empire demanded it,' Solas said. He eyed his burnished black and gold breastplate and sighed. 'I could have... served at your side... had everything not gone wrong.'

'Just stay still, Solas. HELP! OZIN'S THRONE SOMEONE HELP MY BROTHER!' Nathaniel shouted up at the arena's occupants.

'You don't remember do you brother?' Solas gurgled. 'The girl at the wedding? You still don't know who she is?'

'Forget about that,' Nathaniel shook his head, 'you can tell me later.'

Solas grinned.

No one moved, no guard burst through the portcullis with bandages and needles.

A dark voice cackled in the corner of Nathaniel's mind.

Kinslayer, it whispered tauntingly.

'I'm so sorry, Solas, so sorry,' Nathaniel sobbed into his brother's neck.

Solas's lips parted, releasing a gurgled breath, then his body went limp in Nathaniel's arms.

'Not Solas,' Nathaniel shook his head violently. 'Not Solas.'

Nathaniel wanted to howl up to the roof of the arena but all he could do was stare down at Solas' lifeless eyes.

'REGALS OF OBSIDIA!' the Szar began once more. 'THE KINSLAYER–'

'NO!'

Anger bubbled up inside Nathaniel, a deep fury that he was scared to admit even existed. It rested in a place deep beyond the darkest pit of his soul, in a place where not even nightmares would dare tread.

'NO MORE.'

Only the tears streaming down Nathaniel's face belied the thunder in his voice. He thought he saw Aviendel shrink back into the shadows of the Royal Box but the Szar, though his arms had fallen, remained resolutely where he stood.

'YOU THINK ALL THIS IS A GAME. HIDING BEHIND THE SACRIFICE OF YOUR OWN PEOPLE?

At that moment, Nathaniel suddenly noticed the Regals in the arena falling to their knees, bowing their heads, as if in prayer.

'HAIL!' cried a lone voice.

'HAIL!' cried a handful in response.

Others joined, hesitantly at first before Nathaniel was met with a wave of 'HAIL.'

What are they–

The sight of his own outstretched arms ablaze, brought a moment of shocked pause.

Desperately, Nathaniel tried palming out the flames but if anything he seemed to be helping encourage them. Nathaniel couldn't understand this. He should have been screaming in pain, begging for an execution, yet he felt... blissful. Perversely so, with Solas lying, not even cold, on his lap.

'ALL HAIL!'

'Stop,' Nathaniel whispered. Had he the strength, he would have lifted his brother's body for all the arena to see, to remind them what the Szar's deception had cost. But he just sat there, as the flames spread to his torso.

'ALL HAIL!'

'STOP!' Nathaniel bent his head back as the flames began creeping up his neck.

'ALL HAIL THE PHOENIX!'

Epilogue

Shadows, black as tar, sprouted from Crow's palm, rippling in the air around his hands, like flames licking a log.

Two men garbed in white ceremonial robes stood guard, as he approached. They both died quickly, if not entirely painlessly.

The first was impaled by shadows the size of stakes, pinning his lifeless corpse to the wall. The other was quicker than Crow had expected, throwing himself forward, the man's ring beginning to unfurl over his hand. A whip of shadows, flicked from Crow's fingers, sent the assassin sprawling, before he too suffered the same stake-ridden fate. He had neither the patience, nor the desire, to grant them anything better.

Crow passed under the stone archway and into the faintly lit room beyond. What he sought sat perched on an altar, in between two gently flickering candles, half consumed, standing in their solidified remains.

A hairless head, without an accompanying body attached, bobbed back and forth atop the alter as it snored. Its ashen skin was shrivelled and deeply shadowed around its drooping eyelids and sunken cheeks.

Crow paused before the altar for a moment. So, this was the pathetic little thing these fools worshipped. The source of their *balance*.

'Can you feel the darkness, thing?' Crow spoke sharply.

The head stopped snoring immediately and peeled open a glazed eye. The head trembled, as if shivering.

'I cannot touch it, I cannot see it. Yet, I feel it, this... corruption. I cannot smell it, I cannot taste it. Yet, there it lies, this... living death. Like the rot that consumes the apple from within. It slithers, it crawls. It... It–'

'What you sense, creature, is the coming of a new dawn,' Crow interrupted, 'and before all dawns there must be darkness.'

Crow went into a deep lunge, holding both palms flat to the ground. Black tendrils began to flick out from his shadow, dragging themselves into the mortal world. Whispers followed the shadows' emergence, promises of darkness, suffering, and exultance. They slithered across the floor to the altar, slowly creeping upwards.

The head uttered a low hiss. 'The balance turns... the balance turns!'

With a snap of Crow's fingers, the whispering shadows leapt at the head, slipping past wrinkled lips.

'The balance turns...'

A film of black inked across the grey of the head's open eyes. It uttered a soft moan and then pinched its eyes shut.

'There's something I want, creature. A name I need you to pass unto your followers.'

When the head opened its eyes again, they had returned to their ghostly grey.

'Never...' it vowed. The head's cheeks pinched against its brows. 'I will... not... submit,' it spoke in a strained voice.

Crow smiled and, with a flourish of his red-trimmed cloak, stepped into the shadows bubbling up at his feet.

'Oh, you will,' he promised, before slipping away into the darkness.

TO BE CONTINUED…

A thousand thanks for getting through to the end of the second instalment of the Phoenix Saga! It being my second novel, it would mean the world if you would recommend the book to your friends, family, the village goat... heck... everyone. (That way my overbearing captors may finally deign to release me from my typewriter cell... ha ha ha... send help).

When I'm not writing, you can find me spilling nonsense on the Facebook group:
https://www.facebook.com/farrellkeelingofficial/?ref=bookmarks